Dollhouse

A ROCK STAR ROMANCE

THE REVOLVER DUET
BOOK TWO

THEA LAWRENCE

EDITED BY
BEN BROWNING

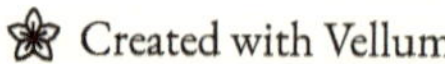 Created with Vellum

For the girls who have always wanted to peg a rockstar.
This one's for you, babes.

"Rock 'n' Roll might not solve your problems, but it does let you dance all over them."

— PETE TOWNSHEND

Playlist

The Beach Boys - *Don't Worry, Baby*
Elton John - *Goodbye Yellow Brick Road*
Taylor Swift - *Mastermind*
Jordy Searcy - *Love and War in Your Twenties*
David Bowie - *Oh! You Pretty Things*
Kings of Leon - *Slow Night, So Long*
Noah Kahan - *Growing Sideways*
David Bowie - *Lady Stardust*
Hozier - *Moment's Silence (Common Tongue)*
Meg Myers - *Desire*
Soft Cell - *Tainted Love/Where Did Our Love Go?*
Nine Inch Nails - *The Perfect Drug*
Kate Bush - *Running Up That Hill*
Florence + The Machine - *Bedroom Hymns*
Hozier - *Like Real People Do*
Taylor Swift - *You're on Your Own, Kid*

INXS - *Never Tear Us Apart*
The Cranberries - *Dreams*
The Temptations - *My Girl*
Bill Medley and Jennifer Warnes - *(I've Had) The Time of My Life*

Dicktionary 🍆

For those who want to dive right into the spice, or avoid it completely, please consult this handy (pun intended) dandy guide:

Chapter Three
Chapter Four
Chapter Nine
Chapter Ten
Chapter Twelve
Chapter Fourteen
Chapter Eighteen
Chapter Twenty-Four
Chapter Twenty-Five
Chapter Twenty-Six
Chapter Twenty-Nine
Chapter Thirty-Five
Chapter Thirty-Seven
Chapter Thirty-Nine
Chapter Forty
Chapter Forty-One

Chapter Forty-Two
Chapter Forty-Six

Contents

Author's Notes

Dollhouse is **book two** in an interconnected duet. If you've picked this up without reading, *Babydoll*, you're going to be very confused by the plot, relationships, and characters, as this book picks up right where *Babydoll* left off.

This book contains content and scenes meant for an 18+ audience and contains the following triggers: Mentions of alcoholism and PTSD, body shaming, recreational drug use (ecstasy), toxic family dynamics, emotional and psychological abuse by a parent, an on-page interaction with a police officer, dom/sub relationship, bondage, impact play, fetish/kink clubs, public sex and voyeurism, very light (and I mean *light*) pet play, choking/hand necklaces, sex toys, spit kink, degradation kink, unprotected sex, pegging, overstimulation, orgasm denial, anxiety attacks, stalking and harassment by paparazzi.

Don't Worry, Baby

DAMIEN

The roar of the crowd carries him off the stage, but his chest is already hollow the moment he hits the wings. It's strange not feeling her arms around him; even stranger not being able to weave his fingers in hers as they head for the dressing room.

Troy weaves his way to the front of them, his face beaming as Damien fights through those empty feelings.

"You kids fucking killed it. That new song's going on the album, right?"

"You know it, Sullivan."

Damien forces a smile despite the weight in his chest. She should be right here with them, staring up at him with those warm brown eyes.

"I can see that gold record now." Troy tips his head back and throws his arms in the air. "You hooligans are gonna make me rich!"

"I thought it wasn't just about the money!"

Not even two minutes offstage, and Ophelia's already getting her jabs in.

"Powell, I've got a kid to put through college, and if Bell is gonna send me to an early grave, I want to make sure she's got more than enough to live off."

"Hey, Troy!"

Damien follows his manager's gaze back the way they came, one of the roadies standing halfway up the stairs.

"Phone call, up front!"

Troy sighs, pausing for a moment before pointing aggressively at the four of them.

"Alright, you're gonna sit in the dressing room and behave yourselves for a few minutes unsupervised. I gotta take this."

"What if we don't?" Johnny asks with a smirk.

"Then I'll lay you out with Slater's guitar."

Damien snorts, the old man didn't even miss a beat.

"Hey! You leave Lucille out of this!" Shaun snaps.

The band piles into the dressing room and Shaun immediately gets to divvying out their stash of beer. Damien flops onto a couch in the corner, ripping the cap right off of the bottle with his teeth. He and Johnny used to do it all the time at parties. They thought they were impressing girls, but most just winced and asked how much it hurt. He's chipped two teeth over the years, and still can't seem to shake the habit.

Thank God for dentists.

He scans the room, watching his friends' rockstar personas melt off of them as they sink into their seats and enjoy the fading high they got from the crowd. Theoretically, Damien should be on top of the fucking world right now. He has a brand new song that a packed house just went wild for, and all of this shit with him and Phoebe is about to go public. No more secret dates, no more having to stay away from her in elevators or restaurants. No more hiding.

Damien rubs his face, grabbing his bag and pulling out a pack of cigarettes, popping one quickly into his mouth. He'd give anything for her to be here, with her little camera and her dorky laugh, cracking up at any of their assorted jokes.

He exhales, smoke winding around his head in tiny ribbons as he feels someone ease into the seat beside him.

"You good?"

Johnny ruffles his hair, recoiling slightly at the sweaty mess.

"Never better."

Damien takes another drag of his cigarette before Johnny plucks it out of his hand.

"Really? Because Troy said not to eat the sandwiches the crew left out because the mayo smelled weird, and you look like someone beat the shit out of you." Johnny flashes him a comforting smile. "You sure you didn't take a bite?"

Damien shrugs.

Usually Johnny can get anyone to talk to him, he's just got that kind of sparkling personality. Damien remembers watching his first interview with Phoebe, and the way her guard dropped as Johnny poured out his heart and soul to her. His natural sincerity just puts people at ease. Damien wishes he could be like that, but more often than not he's all sharp edges and snark.

"You miss her, huh?"

"Yeah," Damien sighs. "Is that sad?"

"I mean, a little. What's it been, like an hour?"

"Fuck off, man."

Damien lifts his beer to his lips and takes a long drink.

"Nah, it's normal, dude." Johnny takes a sip of his own drink, pacing himself. "You're in love. It's fast and intense, and it's natural to want her around all the time."

"Is that what it's like with Erin?"

"From time to time, yeah. But we've been together for so long that the kind of urgency you and Pheebs have is long gone. Sometimes things are a little less intense, but it's not a bad thing. I'm not climbing the walls every time she leaves."

"But you still get bummed out, like all the time."

"Yeah." He smiles, his eyes shining and sweat still kissing his tanned skin. "You're right, I miss her so damn much every time. But I know we'll be back together again before long."

He reaches out and squeezes Damien's shoulder.

"And so will you."

Damien peels away at the label on his beer bottle, shrugging his shoulders.

"But what about the press? How's she gonna handle that?"

"One crisis at a time. Has she even told her boss about you two yet?"

Damien checks the old ratty clock on the wall.

"I think she's still on the flight to New York."

"Call her," Johnny urges.

"Dude, she's on a plane!"

"No, idiot, in a couple of hours when you get back to the hotel. I don't think she'll be sleeping much tonight."

"Yeah," Damien murmurs. "Neither will I."

"So give her a call, maybe tell her you love her," he pauses. "If you think that's where you two are at."

Damien's cheeks warm at the mention of the word.

"Oh yeah, for a while now."

Johnny chuckles.

"For real? When?"

"God, Phoenix I think? It's been forever."

"Damn, that was fast."

"You told Erin you loved her on your first date, you can't say shit to me."

"We were fifteen!"

"Still," Damien mutters. "You two are crazy."

He envies the stability that Johnny and Erin have.

"How do you deal with it?" Damien asks. "Being away from her for so long?"

He's heard them arguing about it a couple of times on the way back to his hotel room. Part of him has always felt guilty for adding that stress to their lives, the band was his idea after all.

"Phone sex helps."

Damien almost chokes on his drink, struggling as Johnny chuckles.

"Nah, but really, it's knowing that whenever we come home she's the first person I'm gonna see. It's kind of like we get the chance to get to know each other all over again. I think if she were on every tour with me, things would be better, but even like this it's enough."

"I just hate not being there for Phoebe, you know? For the shit that matters."

Johnny grabs him by the shoulder, shaking him gently.

"You gotta be positive, dude! That song you wrote for her, did she even get the chance to hear it?"

"Not yet," his voice is soft and unsure. "That was the plan tonight, but she had to catch that flight."

"You know what you should do? Call her answering machine and sing it to her."

Damien's shoulders slump as he's hit with a brutal realization. He might throw up.

"Fuck, I don't even have her number."

"You don't have her *fucking what*?!" Ophelia looks flabbergasted, shouting from across the room as she cups her hand over the mouthpiece of a phone.

"Everything happened so fast! She was supposed to be here for another couple weeks."

Ophelia lifts the receiver and cackles.

"Babe, listen to this shit, he doesn't even have her number."

"Who the fuck are you talking to?" Damien snaps.

Ophelia rolls her eyes, covering the phone up again.

"I'm about to save your ass, dude, so shut the fuck up." She shakes her head, returning to her call. "God, he's so embarrassing. Hey, Jan? What's Phoebe's number? Yeah, in New York. She's going back to tell Brian–"

She holds the phone away from her ear while the sound of Janis's incoherent screaming blares on the other line.

"Babe, focus. I'm sure she'll call you when she gets in, but right now we need her number."

As Ophelia is scribbling in Damien's notebook, the door swings open, Troy's booming voice filling the room.

"Bad news, kiddos!"

"The retirement home denied your application?" Johnny snickers.

Shaun raises his beer.

"Don't worry man, you always have a place on our couch."

"Wow, I never get tired of these jokes," Troy grumbles. "The bad news is that our venue in Oklahoma has asbestos, which could *apparently* kill us." He rolls his eyes. "The label is trying to find you a new city to terrorize. So, we're stuck in Denver for another couple of days. Same hotel, just find something to do that doesn't involve annoying me, or breaking the law, and we'll get along great."

The hotel room looks so empty without her suitcase, her typewriter and her notes scattered all over the desk. Damien sighs as the door shuts behind him, trudging toward the bed, exhausted, but unable to sleep. It's 2:00am, which means it would be about 4:00am in New York. She's gotta be home by now.

He eases himself onto the bed, flipping his notebook open and tracing her phone number with a fingertip as his stomach flutters. Slowly, he reaches for the receiver and double checks each number as he dials. He feels like he's a kid again, calling a girl for the first time as he anxiously twirls the cord around his finger.

And it rings and rings.

And rings.

"Come on, Pheebs."

What if she doesn't even have an answering–

"Hey, this is Phoebe. Leave a message after the beep." There's an awkward pause and the sound of rustling. *"Is there even a bee–"*

Beep!

"Can't even work the answering machine, Miller!" He laughs before taking a breath. "I'm just calling to check in. I hope the flight was okay. You wouldn't even let me pay for first class, but you're getting it on the way back. No arguing– listen, uh... I hate saying it to the machine but I called to tell you that I love you."

His throat clenches.

"You're it for me, Pheebs, and however this shakes out, I'm not giving you up, and I'm not giving up on us. That song I wrote for you? The crowd went *wild* for it. It's going on the next album for sure. First track."

He stares at the curtains billowing in the breeze.

"It's... weird without you here."

Damien runs a hand through his hair. He doesn't know what else to say.

"Oh hey, do you know what asbestos is? My dad always talked about it, but it sounds like a bad rash or something." He laughs again. "Uh... yeah, sorry. Anyway we're gonna be in Denver for a couple more days so just... call me, okay? I love you. A lot. A lot, a lot, a lot. Okay. Bye. I love you." He pauses, struggling for something to say and failing completely. "Okay, yep."

Damien hangs up the phone and stares at it, the impression of her handwriting still present on the hotel notepad from the previous night.

He rubs his face, grabs the remote, and turns on the TV before picking up his pen from the bedside table. As the high from the show swirls with his anxiety, he begins to write. About her, about them, about all of it, in the midst of this quiet chaos.

The whole time he keeps his focus on Phoebe, finding her warm smile in his mind's eye as his pen glides along the paper, holding onto it long into the night.

Big Yellow Taxi

PHOEBE

She always used to look forward to coming home after an assignment. Her apartment, as shitty as it is, is her little sanctuary. Sure, there are clothes strewn all over the floor, papers piled up in random places, and she's got a couple of cockroaches as roommates, but that's your standard New York apartment.

And it's home.

Her key sticks in the lock and Phoebe growls, slamming against the door with her shoulder until it pops open with a loud click. The second she's inside she drops her suitcase, heading straight to the kitchen to get a glass of water, and spotting the little red light on her machine blinking as she guzzles it down.

Probably her mom.

Abandoning the empty glass on the counter, Phoebe trudges toward the answering machine and flops down onto the couch next to it. Out of the corner of her eye, she catches the Revolver tour poster sitting above her desk and smiles. A month ago she thought this was just going to be a standard assignment, and now she's sitting in her living room wearing Damien Bell's jacket. She grabbed it in a frenzy to pack her things, only realizing her mistake when she was in the taxi on the way to the airport.

How quickly things change.

She presses a button on the machine, the sound of rain beating against her window providing a calming accompaniment to the whirs and clicks as it preps itself to play. Staring out the window, all she can see are rivulets of water and the moonlight cutting through them.

"Phoebe, it's your mother–" She doesn't like the sound of her clipped tone right off the bat. *"I'm just a little worried about you. All this hanging out with those... rock... people. I know it's your job, but I just want to make sure you're okay, darling. Call me, please."*

"Jesus, mom, they're not an alien species," she sighs.

She'll call her back tomorrow. Or maybe when she gets back on the tour and has the chance to get some rest. Rest is a hot commodity in her life right now, each day somehow feels more exhausting than the last.

The machine beeps and the next message plays.

"Phoebe, what the fuck?!" She's slightly taken aback as Janis's voice rings out so forcefully from the machine. *"Ophelia just told me you're going to tell Brian about you and Damien?! Have you even finished the article?! Okay, okay. Sorry. I probably sound like your mom. Gross. But call me, for fuck's sake! Iloveyoubye."*

Phoebe smiles, happy to hear a friendlier voice, but when the little red light just keeps blinking, she groans.

If she's this popular, she might be up all night, starting to pace toward the kitchen as the machine beeps for the third time, intent on at least getting herself some coffee.

"Can't even work the answering machine, Miller!"

She stops cold in her tracks.

Hearing his gorgeous voice filtered through that terrible tiny speaker is surreal after spending so many days together. After being so close. She lingers in the doorway of the kitchen, staring at the machine intently like he might crawl right out of it and appear in her living room.

She definitely needs some sleep.

"I'm just calling to check in. I hope the flight was okay. You wouldn't even let me pay for first class, but you're getting it on the way back. No arguing– listen, uh... I hate saying it to the machine but I called to tell you that I love you."

Her body tingles as she rushes back into the living room, jamming the rewind button to hear him say it one more time. The tape grinds as she presses play, the machine's version of Damien's smoky voice filling the room.

"I called to tell you that I love you."

Again.

"I love you."

She could listen to him say it all night, but there's clearly more to the message.

"You're it for me, Pheebs, and however this shakes out, I'm not giving you up, and I'm not giving up on us. That song I wrote for you? The crowd went wild for it. It's going on the next album for sure. First track."

He pauses for a moment, and in the silence loneliness unfurls around her. Maybe she could have asked him to come with her, she's certain he would have agreed, but she couldn't tear him away from the rest of the band like that.

"It... weird without you here."

"It's weird here without you too," she whispers.

"Oh hey, do you know what asbestos is? My dad always talked about it, but it sounds like a bad rash or something."

His laughter gives her goosebumps, and she pulls his jacket tighter around her. They've only been away from each other for a handful of hours, and already it feels like weeks.

"I love you. A lot. A lot, a lot, a lot. Okay. Bye. I love you." He pauses, clearly struggling. *"Okay, yep."*

The whir of the small tape inside the machine grinds to a stop, silence finally filling the living room.

As much as she wants to call him, she can't bring herself to pick up the phone. It's the middle of the night for him, even with the time difference, but he's got a packed day ahead. Unfortunately after listening to all those messages she's wired, her body and her brain still coming down from all the adrenaline. She needs to relax, and she's pretty sure she still has that bag of pot stuffed underneath her favorite reading chair.

Phoebe grabs her favorite pair of pajamas, an oversized sweater that she stole from an NYU open house and a pair of fuzzy pants, and heads back out into the living room, crouching down in front of her records. She smiles. When she was a kid, her record collection was her most prized possession. She kept them all meticulously placed on the shelf in her bedroom, organized by genre.

Her fingers dance along the spine of each record and she instinctively pulls out Revolver's album, staring at the cover: a car in the middle of a misty night, the window lit up and a hand pressed against it. Phoebe slides the vinyl out, holding it up to the light and checking for scratches. She's meticulous about her records. Janis has always said she's a little anal, but even though she gets a lot of these albums for free, she tries her best to keep them in mint condition.

Phoebe carefully places the record onto the turntable and drops the needle. The crash of Ophelia's drums and the whine of Shaun's guitar fill the room. She's back on stage with them, snapping pictures and watching from the wings. She can feel the warmth of the lights, hear the roar of the crowd, all while Damien's strutting around onstage. She smiles reflexively as she pictures that little nose scrunch he does when he's really enjoying himself.

Perching in her favorite chair, she digs underneath the cushion and pulls out the bag of pot she's had stashed there for far too long. Phoebe pours the bag out on her little table, busting up the buds and making her fingers sticky. She seals the joint and sparks it, inhaling deeply as she sinks into her chair.

She loves this spot.

She's devoured books here, written stories here, all while listening to the albums that changed her life. Tonight, she sings along with Damien's lyrics like she used to, except now she knows all the spots where he adds little whoops and howls when they're live, absentmindedly filling them in on her own.

Smoke swirls around her, drifting out of the open window while little drops of rain spatter against her skin. Exhaustion washes over her and she loses herself to the gentle buzz, letting her mind wander.

Her career and her life are in her hands. A little bit of that self-assuredness is from spending all of her time with Damien, but Phoebe walked off the plane tonight feeling like a brand new woman. She's a rockstar's girlfriend, and she's going to walk into that building with his brand of confidence. She'll be unwavering with Brian, pitch him the article she's writing, even if it's not what he asked for. He'll see that it's better, so much stronger than some bullshit puff-piece that any paper could toss out on a slow news week. And if he doesn't, she'll find someone who does.

Pretty soon the band is going to be back in New York, back in the studio working on their new album. They'll have some downtime for a few months. She'll get to see Damien when he's settled down, no longer ruled by the adrenaline that seems to propel him on the road. She'll get to see him create.

As her mind wanders into that future, she tries to picture what he's like at home from day to day. What kind of routine does he have? What is he like when there's nobody else around? He definitely sings in the shower, but does he cook? Is his house at least relatively clean, or does he leave his dirty socks lying around like he does in every hotel room?

On top of that, they can *actually* date. She can have a real boyfriend, and she won't be someone's secret anymore. The thought of that freedom makes her grin like an idiot as she takes another drag of her joint. Fancy dinners, concerts, private getaways, breakfast dates, walks in the park... all of that cute stuff she sees couples doing and not so secretly aches to be a part of. He'll do it all with her.

Damien was right back in Portland, when he told her that being in love is the best feeling in the world. Phoebe would describe it as terrifyingly beautiful, like sprinting into an abyss not knowing what's on the other side. Despite how many times she's been burned by guys who told her that she was special, only to turn around and say the same shit to five other girls, Phoebe's taking another running leap into the dark.

You're it for me, Pheebs.

She flicks away a happy tear.

Until Damien Bell came careening into her life, she'd never heard a man say that to her. He wanted to love her. He didn't treat her like she was disposable– not like Alex. He was the one who made her feel afraid to open her heart again. When she started to feel something for Damien that was more than just pure physical attraction, it scared her. He made all of these big promises, promises that Alex made too.

But Damien kept his word. About everything.

And he called, just like he said he would.

Take On Me

It's strange not being loaded onto a bus in the morning, heading to the next venue with the band. She misses that specific kind of chaos. It somehow felt lighter, less compact, and certainly less stressful than this.

When the elevator doors open, she heads straight for Brian's office. A few of her colleagues glance up from their typewriters, clearly a little surprised to see her, but she ignores them. She's pumping herself up, everything she wants to say perched on the tip of her tongue. She's got her notes jammed in her pocket in case she gets off topic, and Damien's dog tags around her neck for good luck. She's ready.

But the door's wide open, and his office is empty.

Phoebe checks her watch, chewing at the inside of her cheek. It's almost 8:00. He should be here by now. He's the first person in the office and the last person to leave. Maybe he wanted an early coffee? She huffs, pacing off to check the break room.

But again, no Brian.

She curses under her breath.

Glancing around, she catches one of the interns at the fax machine.

"Hey, is Brian here?" He glances up at her, his face completely blank, and she pauses, frowning. "You know, Brian Gordon? Runs this whole place, probably signs your paycheck?"

"Oh, right. He's out sick today," the man replies, looking back down at the machine. "Apparently he was doing shots with Eddie Van Halen last night. Called and said he'd be in tomorrow."

She runs a hand through her hair and lets out a shaky breath. She had all of this nervous energy and now there's nowhere to put it.

"Great, thanks."

The intern gives her a little nod and saunters back to his desk in the bullpen as Phoebe heads into her office. It's filled with posters, concert tickets stuck on a big billboard next to her desk, and a shitload of sticky notes, a good chunk of which are now littering the ground.

She flops into her chair and grabs the phone, dialing Janis's office. It takes a few rings, but eventually the line clicks.

"Yeah?" She groans.

"Jan! It's me!"

"Well well well, if it isn't Phoebe Miller. You waited this long to call, after I left such a heartfelt message? I thought we were friends."

Phoebe rolls her eyes.

"You really wanted me to call you at 5:00am?"

"No, obviously I would have kicked your ass. Are you seriously in New York right now?"

"Yeah, I'm at the office, but Brian's not here."

"Bummer. Hey, why don't we have breakfast tomorrow?" Janis clicks her tongue. *"Also, I uh... I was talking to Ophelia and Shaun about joining the rest of the tour."*

Phoebe grins.

"You're gonna leave your job for another month?"

"Who cares? I fuck rock stars now," Janis scoffs. *"And I've got vacation time banked. So, how about breakfast, huh?"*

"Well, I've got money for *me*."

"Okay, cheapskate. Let's go to the fancy place across from my work. Meet me there tomorrow at 10:00."

"Sure, love you Jan."

Phoebe pulls her notebook out of her bag and flips it open, finding the number for the hotel in Denver. She dials and the concierge puts her on hold.

For a little too long.

"Come on, Bell..."

He's probably still asleep. He rarely wakes up before 11:00. Phoebe contemplates hanging up and trying again a little later just as the line clicks.

"*Yeah?*" His voice is rough, and a little confused.

"Damien?"

"*Pheebs?! How'd it go? Are you coming back? I'll book you a flight when we're–*"

She laughs, relieved just to hear his voice again, but sad to be the bearer of bad news.

"Brian's not in today, *apparently* he partied a little too hard with Eddie Van Halen last night."

She leans forward, grabbing a pen just to have something to fiddle with. The silence on the other end of the line is crushing.

"*You're serious?*"

The disappointment in his voice floods her with guilt. Maybe she shouldn't have come back here. She could have waited until the article was published. Ask for forgiveness, not for permission.

"I'm sorry, I–"

"*No, no, no!*" Damien's tone shifts into a light panic, desperate to comfort her. "*Pheebs, I'm not mad at you at all, okay? I just...*" his laugh shifts into a groan. "*Of course this would fuckin' happen to us, right?*"

"I was just thinking the same thing." She leans back in her chair, nervously bouncing her leg. A whole 'nother day of waiting.

"*Fuck, this sucks.*"

"It really is just one more day."

"*But I miss you now!*" He whines, his somewhat playful tone taking the edge off.

"I miss you too."

Just knowing he's there, even if it's just his voice, is enough to calm her anxieties for a moment. Damien feels like home.

"How was the show?" She asks, trying to lighten the mood.

"Not as good as if you were here, but still good. People went nuts for the new song."

The sleepiness in his voice has almost faded, replaced with bubbling excitement.

"Yeah, you mentioned that in your message."

She smiles. She can't wait to hear it in its entirety, not just the notes that spilled outside after her as she left the venue.

"Talked to Johnny after the show, too. Gave me some tips on how to handle being away from you."

She grins, staring up at the ceiling.

"Right, you wouldn't want to wallow too much."

"No, exactly. That's humiliating for a guy like me." He pauses. *"You know Pheebs, Johnny was telling me that he and Erin sometimes have... phone sex."*

"Phone sex? *Johnny?*" Phoebe chuckles. "But he's such a pristine, pure young man."

Damien cackles on the other end of the line.

"I've heard the shit he says to Erin when they're doing the nasty."

She would never have guessed. The guy's full of surprises.

"So, how did this particular topic of conversation come up?"

Phoebe shrugs off his jacket and tosses it onto her desk. She knows exactly where this is going.

"Well, I was talking about how much I miss you, how sad I was, and he said phone sex kinda helps when they can't see each other in person." His voice becomes a little huskier. *"You wanna try?"*

She grins.

"Now?"

"I'm ready if you are."

"Damien, I'm at work," she purrs. "*Anyone* could walk in."

"That's what makes this so fun," he replies. *"We could make it a little game. Remember how quiet you were for me in that little supply closet in Vegas?"*

Her eyes land on the door, her body brimming with tension. Technically, she's not even scheduled to be here today, and her office is tucked away at the end of the hall.

Nobody would know.

"I remember," she whispers.

"You were such a good girl, so quiet for me while you soaked my fucking cock, made all those adorable little noises."

"I'm... gonna lock the door."

"Mm, so easy to convince, Miller."

"Better watch that mouth, Bell."

"Oh, babydoll, you know I love it when you're mean to me."

Phoebe rests the receiver down on the desk before heading to the door. She pokes her head into the hallway and glances around to make sure the coast is clear, locking it before flopping back into her chair.

"Okay, I'm back. But we have to be quiet."

"Sounds like you want to be in charge of this thing, Miller. You ever done this before?"

She winds the cord around her finger, starting to feel a little parched.

"Once. I wasn't very good at it."

"Oh yeah, how come?"

The one time she tried she was seventeen. It was embarrassing and awkward, fumbling even. Neither of them had any idea what they were doing, but her boyfriend didn't make her feel any better about it.

"Didn't feel confident."

The line crackles as Damien hums.

"I can change that."

Phoebe holds the phone tighter to her ear, desperate to catch every single exhale, every movement. She can almost picture him right next to her. His smile, the gleam in his eyes, the way he licks his lips when he's really turned on.

"You know, you left a pair of panties here. Got 'em wrapped around my cock. I woke up thinking about you in that little blue dress I bought in Port-land." There's a moment of silence, and she can imagine what he's doing. *"You know what I love the most about that dress?"*

"What?"

His voice is weighted and he lets out a little groan that almost gets swallowed up by his breath. She squeezes her thighs together and pops the button on her jeans, her cheeks burning as she begins to tease herself. Her fingers dance along her warm skin and she closes her eyes, conjuring an image of him in her mind. She can smell him: smoke, leather, and spice.

"How easy it would be to push it up, bend you over, and fuck you nice and slow."

Phoebe spreads her legs, her fingertips gliding up and down her inner thigh, teasing herself through her jeans.

"Tell me more."

"Thought about being on the bus with you. Playing with you until you're begging me to let you come."

Her fingers slip beneath the waistband of her panties, greeted with a surprising amount of wetness.

"I've been teasing myself for a while now." His voice is caught somewhere in between a laugh and a moan. *"Fuck, I'm so hard. Get your fingers nice and wet for me, but no touching your clit. Just a bit of teasing. I want you fucking aching. Can you do that for me?"*

She nods, closing her eyes and imagining his head between her legs. The pressure of his tongue, the way his stubble scratches against her skin...

"Yes, sir. It feels so good."

"Atta girl. Nice and slow, just for me."

Phoebe listens to his whimpers through the gentle crackle of the phone, all the while making slow circles around her clit.

"Tell me what you want, babydoll."

Her skin is on fire and her stomach is filled with butterflies as she keeps her voice barely above a whisper.

"I want you to fuck me." She giggles. "And do that thing you do with your tongue."

The words tumble out without a second thought. Damien's low growl on the other end of the line makes her even more excited.

"More. Keep talking."

Even from 1600 miles away, it still feels so intimate. Phoebe teases herself, wishing it was him; missing the way his rings bump up against her when she rides his fingers. Her eyelids flutter and she licks her lips as she sinks further into the fantasy. She's got a rolodex of images to run through: the tour bus, the supply closet, the first time he spanked her with a paddle while she was on all fours on their hotel bed.

The first time she said I love you, and the look on his face when he found the courage to say it back.

Her senses cloud as she loses herself in the moment.

"I want you to tie me to the bed and keep me there all day. Spank me. Choke me with your cock until I can't fucking breathe. Make me come until I barely even remember my name."

"Holy shit." Even through the crackling phone line, she can hear him stroking himself. *"You've got quite the mouth on you, babydoll."*

"Yes, sir." A tingle rushes down her spine. "I learned from the best."

"Mm, good girl." The words come out between heavy breaths. *"Put your fingers in your mouth. Suck on them like you're sucking my cock. I wanna hear you moan for me."*

"Damien, I have to be quiet, I'm at wo–"

"Do as you're told."

She Drives Me Crazy

DAMIEN

amien spits on his palm and wraps his hand around his cock, gliding his thumb over the tip, just the way Phoebe does it. His grip remains soft, mimicking her hand as he closes his eyes, anchoring the phone between his shoulder and his ear. Her moans are the only thing he's going to be thinking about until she gets back here.

"That's it," he growls. "Good girl."

Damien's hips buck, his cock throbbing in his hand.

"Tell me what you're thinking," she moans.

He wants every part of her, the gentle curve of her ass, the softness of her lips around his cock, and the little gasps she makes as he buries his face in her cunt. Right now, he'd give anything just to feel her sweat on his skin.

"I'm thinking about how beautiful you look when you come for me, how sweet you sound when you moan my name." He swallows. "And how badly I wish you were here right now."

He tightens his grip as he speeds up his strokes. The lace in his hand provides a delicate friction that only makes him crave her more. He can smell her perfume on his pillow. Lavender and fresh soap.

They're both so focused on their own pleasure that the conversation between them lulls for a moment. Damien listens to her delicate mewls as she tries to keep her voice down. The thought of her getting caught makes it so much hotter. He closes his eyes, picturing her bent over her desk, his hand covering her mouth as she comes over and over.

And over and over again.

"You're too quiet. Tell me what you're doing."

She whines, the line crackling again. Heavy breaths fill his ear and he can hear her trying to swallow her moans. Damien doesn't know how much longer he's going to last.

"I'm teasing myself, picturing your mouth on me, doing- oh fuck- that thing you do with your tongue."

She lets out a soft sigh, almost frustrated. He's frustrated, too. But that's all part of the fun.

"I want you to get up and walk to your office window, and don't forget to keep teasing yourself."

Damien doesn't hear anything on the other end of the line, and he grins, sitting up a little on the bed. This could be something new for them both; something really fucking fun.

"Are you doing it? Or are you being a bad girl? Bad girls don't get to come." He licks his lips. "Fuck, maybe I should make you edge yourself until you get back."

"You fucking asshole," she moans. *"You wouldn't dare."*

"Tell me when you're up at that window."

He can hear the phone scrape against the desk as she picks it up and carries it along with her.

"I'm here."

Damien loosens his grip and starts to tease himself again, dragging his finger up and down his shaft, circling the head. He can feel it growing tight, precum dripping onto his stomach.

"When you get back here, we're not leaving the hotel room for a whole goddamn week."

Her laughter is the sweetest sound in the world.

"That sounds like heaven."

Damien can't stand it anymore, he needs to come hard. His hand wraps around his cock again, working it slowly from base to tip. Every time he reaches the top and glides his thumb over the slit his back arches, a moan escaping his lips. Phoebe's newly confident voice cuts through the static.

"Is that me you're moaning for, Bell?"

"Maybe," he rumbles. "Can you see people out the window?"

"Yes." Her breath catches and a moan fills his ear. *"A lot of them."*

"Good. I want them to see what a filthy fuckin' girl you are."

Damien can't stroke himself fast enough, his hips bucking desperately. He only pauses to spit on his palm again, trying to recreate the feeling of burying himself inside her, but he can't quite get the pressure right. The ache in his chest deepens, and he loses himself in her whimpers and moans on the other end of the line.

"Keep touching yourself, I want those fingers soaking."

He misses the way he pins her to the mattress; the way she likes to be fucked so deep that her eyes roll back. He craves the taste of her, the deep raspy moans that sound like hymns as her body rolls like a wave.

"When you get back here, I've got a whole lot of new things for us to try."

She cries out, but the sound is quickly stifled and she curses on the other end of the line. Damien laughs, heat pooling in his belly as he pictures her pushed up against the window, one hand down her pants while the other playfully teases a nipple. In his mind, her lips are parted, mouthing his name as someone looks up and spots her. But she doesn't give a shit. She's swept up in the moment, begging for release.

"Damien, I'm gonna come!"

Her strangled whimper is all it takes for the knot in his stomach to unravel, exploding as he cries out. Cum spurts all over his chest, more running down his knuckles as he listens to Phoebe, still keeping herself right on the edge.

"Come for me," he commands. "Like a good girl."

A deep lustful moan fills his ears as she comes, repeating his name over and over. He slows his strokes down, trying to pull every last bit of pleasure from his body as his cock softens. Damien cleans himself off with her panties while she breathes heavily on the other line.

"So, was that better than your first try?" He asks.

She chuckles.

"Can you record yourself talking dirty to me so I can play it on my Walkman?"

He cackles. His face is warm and he leans back against the headboard, twirling the phone cord between his fingers.

"I'll make you a special LP, how about that? The Sultry Stylings of Damien Bell."

"Mmm. I like that."

Exhaustion is working its way into her voice. Damien feels it too, his sleep was fitful and interrupted. He's tired right down to his bones.

"Damien?"

"Yeah."

"When you said you had new things for us to try, what did you mean?"

He grins. If she were here right now, she'd be peering up at him with those big brown eyes he gets lost in every time he looks at her.

"Like, have you ever thought about riding my face?"

"Wouldn't I smother you?"

"Hey, if that's the way I go out, I want you to tell every single fucking newspaper I died doing what I loved. I don't care if my parents are embarrassed."

She cackles.

"Okay, well, I'll try not to–"

"Oh, no no no. I want your full weight. Crush the shit out of me."

Phoebe scoffs.

"You're crazy."

"Crazy for you."

He bites his lip, that little bit of dread creeping back into the pit of his stomach and making itself at home.

"So, you'll call me tomorrow after it's all over?"

"Are you gonna wait by the phone?" She giggles.

"It sounds a little desperate when you put it like that, but I could do it for you."

It's not the fact that she's telling her boss, it's the scrutiny, the way people have talked about his ex-girlfriends, the looks, the press, the invasive fucking questions. Damien also doesn't want anyone to question Phoebe's integrity, or her talent as a writer. She didn't get this gig because of him, she got it because she's smart as a fucking whip, but that's not what they'll say.

"Damien, there's nothing to be nervous about. We're not going anywhere, and nothing is happening to us." Her voice is so calming that he can feel his eyes sliding shut. *"Please, tell me you understand that."*

For someone who's normally the anxious one in the relationship, Phoebe is holding her own pretty damn well.

"I understand," he breathes.

"Good. Now, I've gotta go, but I'll call you the second I'm out of my meeting with Brian tomorrow, okay? I promise."

He smiles, feeling a hell of a lot better than when he left her that rambling message last night. Sometimes, just hearing her voice is all it takes to turn his whole day around.

"Love you, babydoll. I'll see you soon."

Walking on Broken Glass

⤳

PHOEBE

P hoebe and Janis wound up having breakfast at a shitty diner near the Titanium office. Fluffy pancakes, burnt coffee, and Janis's office gossip kept Phoebe's mind from swirling around the inevitable confrontation with Brian. But now, the walk to the office is agonizing, even with her friend here for moral support.

People keep staring at her, like they know her little secret. She's been checking as they walk past each and every newsstand. No photographs, no glaring headlines... nothing.

It's been pure paranoia since her phone call with Chris back in Denver. He was drunk and desperate for a scoop, so certain he'd figured out their little secret and ready to tell the world. Honestly, he was so wasted he might not even remember the conversation, but that hasn't stopped the feeling of unease from slowly choking her over the last few days.

"You've gotta be cool, Pheebs." Janis grabs the door and holds it open, ushering her inside.

"I can't help it! I'm a sweaty, anxious person!"

They make their way through the lobby both going for the button at the same time, but Janis playfully swats Phoebe's hand away with a warm smile. Phoebe's body feels like it's made out of lead as the doors close and she hits the number for the Titanium offices.

As the elevator doors ding, Phoebe is assaulted all at once by the smell of burned coffee, ink, and bad cologne. She leans over and gags, all of her nervousness creeping up the back of her throat.

"Whooooaaa! What's up, Miller!" It's one of the guys who works in advertising. He's always in a suit with greasy, slicked back hair, and his high school football ring always jammed on his pinky. She barely remembers his name, maybe Josh?

Janis snarls, forcing him to take a step back as she grabs Phoebe and they head for Brian's office. Unfortunately it doesn't take long for the shock to wear off, and Josh's stupid fucking voice cuts through the sound of clacking typewriters.

"Hey, Kaneko, I never got your number the other night at that thing–"

"It's 1-800-Get-Fucked!" Janis calls, turning back to Phoebe with an only slightly lowered voice. "Why does he dress like a two-bit Italian mobster?"

"He really likes Scarface," Phoebe mutters as they approach Brian's office. "Because of course he does."

They reach the door and Janis gives Phoebe a small, reassuring hand squeeze before taking a step back.

"I'll be right here."

Phoebe doesn't even bother to knock, she just grabs the handle and pushes it open in one quick movement. Brian is sitting at his desk, dressed in a soft purple sweater with his dark, curly hair in disarray. She can see streaks of gray running through it. He hasn't shaven, and his glasses are pushed down his nose as he reads over an article.

"Josh, I'm busy. Can you knock?" He grumbles, without even looking up.

Phoebe's heart is in her throat, pulsing wildly as the sweat gathers on her forehead. She swallows the anxious lump that's forming, wiggling her fingers to make sure that she can still feel them.

"Brian."

He looks up at the sound of her voice, his brows knitting together.

"Pheebs?"

She does her best impression of a sincere smile.

"That's me."

He pushes the papers aside and takes off his reading glasses.

"What the hell are you doing back here? What happened?"

"I have to talk to you."

Brian pinches the bridge of his nose, pushing out his chair and rounding the desk.

"Jesus, what did Bell do? I had a feeling this was going to go south—"

"It's not about Bell–" She stops herself, struggling to find the right way to begin. "At least not like that."

"You look like you're going to pass out, come here."

He walks her to the chair in front of his desk, making sure that she gets into it in spite of her trembling legs.

Phoebe leans over and takes a breath as Brian pats her on the shoulder and crouches down to catch her eye.

"Phoebe, you've gotta tell me what's going on. If there's something I can do to help–"

"I— we— uh..." She stammers, wringing her hands, wanting to laugh and not even sure why. "Um..."

"You can tell me, you know."

Can she? She can't even get the words out. She stares at Brian, who only manages to stare right back. Is there even a lead-in? The mounting pressure is overwhelming as she opens her mouth again and again, unable to come up with the right words; everything she wanted to say to him yesterday has flown out of her mind, so maybe she should stall for time, or come back later, maybe she–

"I'm in love with Damien!"

She blinks, mortified as the fear shoots ice-cold through her veins, both of them waiting in stunned silence as her words settle around them. It just came out like that, sudden and completely unbidden.

Her one and only shot.

Brian steps back, a bemused expression taking over his face as he chuckles nervously.

"What?"

"I'm–" She slows herself down, taking a couple deep breaths. "I'm in love. With Damien Bell."

Brian's eyes dance around her face as he tries to process what's happening, trying to figure out if it's a joke.

"I won't take you off of this assignment for a crush, Phoebe. That's kid's stuff."

She pulls Damien's dog tags out from beneath her sweater and shows them to him, her hand quaking.

"What are these? I don't get it," Brian laughs.

"He gave them to me. We're together."

Phoebe's heart beats so hard against her ribs it feels like they're going to crack. She managed to say it, but that was the easy part. Her vision is hazy at the edges and all she can hear is the sound of Brian's chair creaking. When she looks up, he's back in his seat, his gaze hardened.

"So, you're fucking Damien Bell."

Fucking. That's what he sees this as?

"No, I told you, I'm in love with him," she whispers.

Brian's lips are pressed into a thin line, like he's on the verge of exploding. She shrinks backward in her chair as he scratches his stubble.

"You did the one thing I told you not to do."

"I'm sorry–"

"Don't give me that bullshit, Phoebe! You compromised your work because some fucking rock star gave you a keepsake?!"

Fear gets pushed back like a tide, making way for a brutal wave of anger that she can't stop. She grabs her bag and slams it onto the table, rooting through it for her notes. She's not backing down. This is *her* story.

"Your objectivity bullshit might work for you, but it doesn't work with this band. Believe me, I fucking tried. Do you know what works, Brian? Immersing yourself in the experience. *That's* the shit people want to read about."

"You're done. You're off the assignment."

"The hell I am," she growls.

She'll fight tooth and nail for this, because she knows she's right. She thrusts her notes out toward him.

He shakes his head.

"Sleeping with the lead singer is not immersing yourself in the experience! You're suspended until I figure out what the hell I'm gonna do with you."

"No."

Brian raises his eyebrows, a flash of irate amusement flickering across his face like lightning.

"No?"

"I'm the only one with this kind of access to the band." She steels herself, ready to appeal to his more reasonable side. "I've got a story, and they trust me to write it. You suspend me? I quit and take the pitch straight to Rolling Stone."

He can threaten her all he wants, but her stubbornness is kicking in. Phoebe started writing to carve out *her* voice, and she'll be damned if anyone is going to take that from her.

"It's not even your pitch!" Brian exclaims. His face is red, fist resting clenched on his desk. "I'm putting Chris on this. He's already in Denver."

Phoebe scoffs, shaking her head.

"Everyone wants a piece of that band, and Troy wouldn't let Chris within ten feet of that tour bus. Imagine being the editor who screwed it all up—"

"That's *enough*," Brian snarls. "I'm putting him on this thing, and that's the end of it."

There's no way Chris fucking Meyers is taking this from her.

"Chris was trying to blackmail me!" Phoebe shouts.

"What?" Brian leans forward, brows pinched together.

"He called me, drunk off his ass, saying he'd heard rumors. Rumors about Damien and me. And he told me that if I didn't give him the exclusive he wanted, he'd go right to you with shit he just made up. You know how embarrassing that would be to fact check?" She gestures toward the legal pad. "I know you don't run a gossip rag, so wouldn't you rather hear the truth? From me?"

Brian's jaw ticks as his eyes lock with hers. Despite his earlier threat, he doesn't want to lose her.

"I heard you at the last writer's meeting. We need something that'll bring in more readers. Revolver is at the top of the charts, and what I've pitched in that outline would draw a hell of a lot more eyes to the magazine."

He stares at her legal pad, a little crumpled and ragged from her extended adventure. Her anxiety starts to ebb away, replaced by her newfound confidence. The pitch is solid and she knows it, and it looks like he's starting to realize it too.

"This isn't just going to be some fluff piece, it's a real look at them, as artists and as human beings. I'd be the narrator, we follow my relationship with Damien and the band, how it develops and grows as they all open up. I have more than enough information on each band member to write a tell-all book, let alone an a story like this, and it's all on the table."

She lets out a breath, studying Brian's body language. She's gotten past his initial anger, now she just has to hook him.

"And sure, Chris could knock out some trash on the band even without direct access, but then what's the point? If you put him in my place, you lose all the draw, everything that makes the story unique."

Her eyes land on the pad, but Brian is already staring it down like it's a fucking bomb waiting to go off. She flicks her head.

"Go on, read it. See for yourself"

They stare each other down, and for a moment, Phoebe's convinced this was all for nothing. Finally, without breaking eye contact, Brian reaches for his reading glasses, cleaning them off on his sweater before reaching for her outline. She lets her body relax, exhaling as the iciness in his eyes slowly melts away into intrigue.

Time for one last push.

"I'm good at my job. Fuck, Brian, my article on Delirium was good too, but you shoved that to the back of the magazine."

He sighs, his eyes on the page.

"Phoebe, this thing with Damien is a whole different ball game. You're opening yourself up to major scrutiny here. There'll be questions: did you sell out? Is this real journalism? Hell, ignoring all that, there'll be photographers on your asses all the time, following you everywhere."

Phoebe leans forward, her whole body tingling.

"Brian, what are you saying?"

"I'm saying that this pitch and these notes you've given me are good, but–"

"Tell me you're going with my story."

He frowns, looking conflicted. Good.

"I have to think about it, just give me a couple days to–"

"No, you don't." She leans further in, refusing to break eye contact.

The Phoebe Miller who let people walk over her in this industry is fucking dead. She's got rockstar confidence now. "I want your answer today. Now."

He bites into his thumb nail, chewing at it nervously.

"You're really going to take this thing to Rolling Stone?"

"Brian, it's your call. If you really don't want the best story of the year, I'll clean out my office in half an hour. I go back to finish the tour, you get a shitty puff piece with Chris's name on it, and all the regret that comes along with it."

He sighs, sliding her notes back across the desk, a little gleam in his eye.

"You know I fucking hate Rolling Stone."

Running Up That Hill

DAMIEN

She said she would call.

They'll be leaving for soundcheck soon, and every time the phone rings, he jumps out of his skin. But it's never her.

Damien lights another cigarette, something like half the pack already gone, his notebook splayed open on the desk where Phoebe's typewriter would normally sit. He needed to fill the space with something.

She seemed fine during their call the other day. More than fine. So, did something happen? Did she decide to back out of all of this? Did *her boss* tell her to back out?

"Dude, you need to calm down," Shaun mutters.

He's not even looking at Damien, too busy fiddling with his guitar. He doesn't get it.

"I'm calm."

"You're freaking out."

"I'm not freaking out," Damien snaps. "You're freaking out."

Shaun chuckles, leaning his guitar against the wall and turning to Damien with a warm smile.

"Look at me, man. Tell me I'm anything but chill, I dare you." He gestures at the large hotel mirror with a quick flick of his head. "Now look at yourself for a second, and tell me you don't look like the exact opposite."

"She always calls, man." Damien shakes his head. "She said she would call."

Phoebe Miller and taxes are the two things you can count on in life. She says she'll do something? She does it. Her follow-through is amazing — inspiring, really.

"That girl loves you, Damien. She left so that you two could be together, there's no chance in hell she's not coming back."

"I know," Damien mutters.

Shaun slaps him on the back with an obnoxiously goofy grin on his face.

"Good! I know it and you know it, so that's over and done with, yeah? I just wanted to make sure you're good, we need you to be on your game tonight."

"I know, man. I just–"

"We gotta go!" Ophelia shouts, pounding on the door.

Damien curses under his breath, changing into a black t-shirt and grabbing his notebook and pen. By the time he's done, Shaun's already waiting at the door with Ophelia, both looking fantastic in their whirl-wind-mix of leather, ripped jeans, and strategically applied eyeliner.

"You look great."

Ophelia glances back at him with a quick tilt of her head.

"Thanks dude, but you sure don't. Where's your razzle dazzle at?!"

"My what?" He asks, his voice laced with irritation as he digs out yet another cigarette.

"Your jacket, your eyeliner, fuck, even your attitude... you know, the razzle dazzle!"

"I'll do it in the dressing room," Damien growls as he grabs his bullet belt from the closet. "And Pheebs has my jacket."

"Damien, come on, she'll be back before you know it." Ophelia lets out a quick sigh, the kind you usually save for children who just can't quite get things right. "Look, Phoebe wanted to surprise you, but Jan called me from the airport. They're on a plane right now, and apparently she's got news."

Shaun's face is a mixture of scandalized and bemused.

"You weren't supposed to *tell him* the surprise!" He exclaims. "You always do this!"

"I do not!" She yelps. "Look how sad he is! I can't let him live like this."

Damien opens his mouth to defend himself, but she's kind of right. He's been absolutely pathetic since Phoebe left.

"So, she kept her job?"

His voice is pinched with worry, despite his best efforts.

"Look, Janis just said they had news, but I'm assuming, unless the two of them have been sadistic freaks under our noses this whole time, it's good news." She slaps him on the arm, hard enough to make him grimace. "So no more sadness! Turn that frown upside down, all that good shit!"

He swats her away, laughing as a wave of relief crashes against him. She's coming back. Tonight.

Ophelia moves back toward him, readying another big slap with a raised brow.

"Hey, listen up! You have to act surprised. I want some Meryl Streep level shit when you see Phoebe tonight. I'm not going down for revealing this super secret info."

Damien gives her a solemn salute, his face quickly slipping back into a giddy smile.

"You got it, boss."

The promoter removed all the temporary seating so they could sell more floor tickets; standing room only. The atmosphere is heavy, and while the crowd outside is coursing with tension, Damien's only focus is trying to not stab himself with Ophelia's eyeliner.

"It feels weird out there, doesn't it?" Johnny asks, fluffing up his shaggy hair in the mirror. "Like, tense?"

"I feel it," Shaun agrees. "Not too sure if I like it."

"It's gonna be fine!" Ophelia sighs. "They're just a little riled up. You guys are freaking out over nothing."

"Ten minutes, kids!" Troy calls as he struts into the room, flopping down right next to Damien. Ophelia tries to ruffle his hair, but he swats her away. "Hey! Cut it out! I paid good money for this!"

"Yeah? To who? Freddy Krueger?" She asks, lunging back in one more time.

"I'll have you know this was an 80 dollar haircut!" Troy barks. "The finest shears in the state formed this masterpiece, so hands off, Powell!"

"I'd ask for my money back," Johnny replies offhandedly.

Troy turns on a dime and snaps his fingers.

"Hey! You're supposed to be the least mouthy one out of the whole group, you can't go turning on me now!"

Ophelia giggles, scurrying off to join Shaun on the couch, while Troy turns his attention back to Damien.

"So, big shot, how'd it go with Phoebe in New York? That was today, right?"

"She hasn't called yet," he sighs, "but the good news is Ophelia said she caught her flight a few hours ago."

"Woah, woah, why would she call them and not you?" Troy elbows him, leaning in close with a big grin. "You in the doghouse, Bell?"

"Hardly," Damien scoffs. "I think she just wanted to surprise me."

Troy nods, clearly annoyed that his bait went ignored, and Damien's eyes follow along as he returns to surveying the room. The rest of the band is a mix of excited and jittery. Johnny's pacing back and forth and mouthing lyrics to himself as Ophelia drums on Shaun's thighs, smiling in between kisses. Meanwhile, Damien keeps hoping that the door is going to swing open with Phoebe right there. He can't wait to see her smile.

He leans back in the makeup chair, staring at himself in the mirror. His mess of hair engulfs his head, so long now that it almost hits his shoulders. Sometimes, he barely recognizes himself. The braces he had until he was 18, the boyish features, the chubby cheeks... it's all fallen away. That's the stuff the magazines don't show people. At least one part of his life is still kept private.

He grabs a can of hairspray to give his unruly waves one last spritz while Troy checks his watch.

"I'm gonna go out there and make sure all of your equipment's set up properly." He ratchets up the volume of his voice, intent to have at least a little impact on the group before the show. "Five minutes, no loitering!"

Ophelia and Shaun each throw up a rigid salute, but Johnny walks right past him and grabs a burger from the small table, shoving it into his mouth. A giant blob of ketchup splatters on the floor, and Troy just stares at it for a moment before letting out a long sigh and finally exiting the room.

"Nice one, Reed," Ophelia teases. "You're the pinnacle of class."

"What did I do?!" Johnny grumbles through a mouthful of burger. "Is eating a crime now?"

Damien gets up and heads for the door. He's itching to get onstage. His whole body is lit up, filled with the same kind of electricity he always feels before a show. He needs to crush it, to blow the crowd away, but behind all that is that lingering little thought:

The sooner it's all over, the sooner she's back in his arms.

The four bandmates head down the long corridor toward the stage, a swell of noise coming from just beyond it— excited murmuring already being overwhelmed by the rising volume of shrieks and cheers. He used to get so high off of this shit, a single show fueling him and his ego for days. Now, it's all he can do just to shake off his jitters and focus on the performance.

As they make it to the wings Damien spots Troy giving aggressive instructions to a roadie.

"When *isn't* that dude chewing someone out?" Johnny asks, shoving the rest of his burger into his mouth.

Damien sighs.

"Today I'm just glad it's not me."

Ophelia claps him on the shoulder, a big grin on her face.

"Give it time, Bell, I think he's going easy on you until your girlfriend gets back. The second you see those big beautiful eyes it's over for you. It'll be old man Sullivan nagging all the way to the end of the tour."

The roadie nods to Troy, scurrying away as their manager jogs down the stairs toward them.

"Okay, they're all ready for you." He frowns, glancing down at Ophelia. "There's a second set of sticks beside your kit. Those ones look like they came out of a woodchipper!"

"Hey, they're fine," Ophelia scoffs. "These are my lucky sticks!"

"Lucky?" Troy asks with a raised brow. "It looks like the Wolfman's been using them as toothpicks for months. They're probably gonna snap the second you go in for your solo!"

Ophelia rolls her eyes.

"I like my drumsticks a little weathered. Gives 'em personality. You should understand the concept more than most."

Damien can see the tiniest smile tug on Troy's face before he quickly pushes it back. The man really knows how to change the energy in a room, and all it takes is playing the fool from time to time.

"Look, whatever makes you happy, kid. Anyway, you guys are on in..." He checks his watch, cringing a little. "Well, pretty much now. We'll wait for the lights to drop and then you run on in and do your thing."

As if on cue, the lights dim and the crowd lets out a deafening roar. Somehow, even after all this time, it's still a little surprising.

"Go!" Troy hisses. "What part of 'do your thing' did you not understand?!"

The audience's energy is intense, people screaming and cheering so loud that it makes his stomach flip as they take the stage. Damien smiles through it, raising both hands and striding forward like he owns the place.

When he first started doing this, his stage fright was so bad that he invented this persona, this cocksure asshole without a care in the world. It got him through all his nerves and jitters, and more importantly people loved it. Now it's second nature, a second him.

"Kansas!" He bellows, arms outstretched as he drinks in the applause like wine. "How the fuck are ya tonight?!"

Another roar and Damien chuckles, catching Shaun amping up the crowd out of the corner of his eye.

"Alright, alright, I get it. I was thinking about drawing this out, making you all wait for it. Build up the tension to make it all the sweeter, you know?"

He doesn't know how it's possible, but it gets even louder, the mass of bodies already crushing against each other back and forth just past his feet. Damien grins.

If the crowd was at a 10 before, this is 11.

"But you know what? You've all been such good little boys and girls I figure we can skip all that and give you what you came for. We're Revolver, and we're here to blow your fuckin' minds tonight!"

Ophelia's sticks are already clacking together before the final word leaves his lips, bringing them down hard on the cymbals. Shaun's guitar howls as he steps into the spotlight and guides them through the opening bars of Automatic. He walks up to join Damien on the edge of the stage, leaning over the crowd as his fingers effortlessly glide along the fretboard.

In an instant, all of Damien's doubts and anxieties are swallowed up by the tidal wave of competing sounds. The band is in perfect rhythm, Johnny and Shaun play off of each other as Ophelia's drumming lifts them all up to new heights. He glances into the wings and even Troy is bobbing his head.

It's like clockwork.

Halfway through the song he drops to his knees, reaching for the audience and feeling his heart swell as they reach back. He's on cloud nine, effortlessly belting out lyrics like he was born for this. The only thing that could make it better is if Phoebe was there with him.

But she will be.

The crowd moves, flowing along with the music, splitting and parting here and there until, like fate, someone catches his attention. His heart nearly stops as his eyes flick over to them, landing on a head of mousy-brown hair sat on top of a round face, half obscured by a pair of coke bottle glasses.

There was no fucking way Chris Meyers chose today to be the day he was going to show his face.

Damien had seen Chris before, mostly at industry parties, although each time he'd been rescued by Troy or another bandmate before he had the chance to actually interact. But he didn't need to meet him. He knew all he needed to, long before Phoebe ever brought him up.

Damien had never been the best at taking criticism, but there was something particularly cruel and heinous about Chris's review of their first album. It was like he had a personal grudge against them, that they were somehow not worthy of actually making it on their first real try, like they hadn't really earned it. Even back then Chris was intent to make it personal, and to his credit it had worked.

Damien's pulse races as he looks over at Shaun, who's already staring right back at him. His eyes are wide in a panic as he shouts over the the sound of his wailing guitar.

"What the hell are you doing, man?!"

Damien looks around, bewildered as he sees his bandmates all look equally distressed. He's missed half of a verse, maybe even more, but luckily the audience is filling it in for him. He chuckles nervously, sweat clinging to his brow as he tries to shake off the newly intruding feelings.

He screams the chorus into the microphone, channeling all of his rage and frustration into the song until his voice begins to break. He can feel his vocal cords shredding as Chris glances up at him with a smug smile, scribbling casually in a notebook as the crowd gently shoves him back and forth.

Motherfucker.

Damien gathers himself, toning down the vocals as not to fuck his voice up any further, and gets back in tune and tempo with the rest of the band. Just another few songs and they'll be done, and he can write this all off as just a little slip up. Sure Chris'll publish some bullshit, but no one will take it seriously. He's Damien Fucking Bell, and Revolver's top of the world.

He glances back down at Chris, ready to shoot him a confident grin just as he stumbles over the mic cord mid-chorus. He kicks it away, swearing a little before trying to center himself again as the song nears its conclusion. That anxiety which had melted away with the crowd's warm reception returns with a vengeance, clinging to his skin like tar as Ophelia counts them in for their next number.

Damien shakes himself off and gets back to singing, but he realizes all too soon that he's jumped in early. To his own fucking song, one he wrote all on his own. He grimaces, faltering as he feels the audience begin to turn on him. Some of the screams turn to heckles that he tries to shut out, but reality quickly becomes impossible to ignore. The show was already delayed, the venue is too fucking full, and now he's bombing up on stage.

And it's then, in the midst of stumbling through their last song before intermission, that he sees her. She's standing in the wings, confusion marking her face as she stares on. And then all of a sudden he's got tunnel vision, needles pricking at his throat; he's unable to see anything else but her.

It's hard to breathe,
to swallow,
to think.

Everything else shifts into the background as the final chords of the night are consumed by the overwhelmingly brutal sound of the crowd.

And all he can feel is her disappointment.

Love is a Battlefield

PHOEBE

Phoebe and Janis practically fall out of the cab, almost forgetting to pay and rapidly stuffing the money through the driver's side window as they race toward the venue. Her head spins as she desperately scans the building, chomping at the bit to get in front of Damien and tell him the news. She can almost see that big, beaming smile, feeling his arms as they wrap around her.

Janis pounds on the door, snapping Phoebe out of her reverie in time to join in on the assault.

"Hey!" She barks. "Hey, open up, motherfuckers! I've got a woman in love out here and she's driving me nuts!"

"Yeah!" Phoebe bellows, slamming the door even harder as the anticipation begins to overflow. "But, uh, not in a dangerous way!"

Janis kicks the door, rattling the handle again.

"Can we go around the front?"

Phoebe groans, frustration cracking in her voice.

"We don't have tickets. Damien wasn't exactly sure what day I'd be back, so..."

Janis's eyes light up in a moment of brilliance.

"Ah, but we *do* have press passes!" She slams her fist against the cold steel door again.

With little warning the door swings inward, and Phoebe almost clocks a big, burly security guard right in the gut, stopping herself just in time. He's got lightly tanned skin and long blonde hair that's cut into the worst mullet she's ever seen, tattoos stretching down his trunk-like forearms. Any other day she'd probably be terrified, but today she's managed to keep herself at 'really scared.'

"No groupies."

He starts to head back inside, but Janis yanks on the back of his t-shirt and pulls him toward her as Phoebe puts her foot against the door.

"Not so fast, Hulk Hogan! We're journalists."

Phoebe bounces on the balls of her feet and tries to get a glimpse of the hallway as they dig their press passes out of their bags and shove them into his hands. If she can catch a glimpse of Troy it would make this whole thing a lot easier.

As the bouncer looks over their passes she cranes her neck past him. She can't see anyone in the long hallway, but she can hear the music pouring out from the stage, echoing all the way outside. From the sound of it, the crowd is rowdier than usual.

The security guard takes a long skeptical look at their press passes before letting out a long sigh and taking a step aside. Phoebe books it for the stage, Janis trailing behind her with their suitcases. After a minute or two of following the music, she finally spots Troy standing in the wings and bolts up the stairs. He barely gives her a side-glance when she makes it up next to him, but one look out at the audience tells her exactly why.

The crowd is starting to turn on the band; Damien is forgetting lyrics, and he's off-tempo, half destroying his voice as he blows out his microphone. He seems to almost recover, shaking each moment off before another mistake cascades over the last.

"Damien..."

All of that excitement that was sitting in Phoebe's chest fades away, replaced by a feeling of complete helplessness. Her body deflates as she watches the carnage unfold in front of her. He's covered in sweat and stumbling over lyrics he knows all too well as he keeps looking out at the audience in frustration. The rest of the band is trying their best to hold things together, each member a range of baffled to upset.

Phoebe turns to Troy, his face twisted up with the same helplessness she can feel churning inside her.

"I'm pulling them off after this one. No more songs, and no encore, obviously." He doesn't even turn his head to acknowledge her. "There's no need to extend this humiliation any further."

''What's going on?" Phoebe asks.

Troy lets out an incredulous laugh.

"Sweetheart, if I knew that I'd be doing whatever it took to squeeze the life out of whoever made this happen."

In the final moments of the song, Damien turns helplessly toward the wings, and his eyes lock with hers. He sways a little as a strange half smile flickers across his face for a moment, his shoulders slumping with defeat as he hangs his head.

Finally the song is over, and Damien drops the mic onto the stage. The feedback is so loud that Phoebe has to cover her ears. The crowd jeers at the band, full cups of beer splashing out at their feet.

"Get off the stage!" Troy bellows. "Now!"

Shaun, Johnny, and Ophelia rush off first, blowing right past Phoebe just as Janis catches back up. Damien gives a quick, mocking bow, maybe an attempt to save face, before he flips the crowd off and turns to head backstage.

Phoebe takes a step forward, but Damien is already there, moving so forcefully that he might have knocked her over if he hadn't wrapped her in such a tight hug, but Troy only gives them a moment before prying them apart.

"Bell. What the fuck. Happened. Out there?!"

Damien shakes his head, shame overtaking any rebelliousness that might have normally filled his eyes.

"If you can't pull yourself together enough for one show without your girlfriend, then we need to sit down as a band, and–"

"Troy?" Phoebe places her hand on his arm. "Can Damien and I have a couple of minutes first? You can have him after that for as long as you need, I just..."

Troy's chest heaves and he straightens out his suit, tugging at the fabric with nervous energy. She can tell his brain is already working over-time to figure out how to salvage this.

"I'm calling the opening act back for the last half hour, so you can have your few minutes. Then we're gonna regroup. We gotta get this all sorted before the next show." He points at Damien, gritting his teeth. "You need to get your fucking head in the game, you hear me?"

"Troy, we can finish the set, I can–"

"No, you can't!" Troy barks. "Not tonight. Maybe we should've just canceled this altogether after the fucking asbestos thing. It's like a curse! A mold and a curse!"

Janis takes a step forward.

"It's actually a fibrous–"

"Kaneko, you know I love you, but I swear to god–"

She picks up her suitcase and scurries to the dressing room before he has a chance to finish. He gives it a few seconds before he follows, grumbling under his breath and leaving Phoebe to pick up Damien's pieces.

The moment Troy is gone Damien buries his head in the crook of her shoulder. Phoebe wraps her arms around him as the house lights begin to switch back on. All she can do is hold him, running her fingers through his hair as she guides him down the small set of stairs and into the shadows. It's a couple of minutes before he raises his head, and she gets to stare into those beautiful blue-gray eyes she's missed so much.

"I missed you."

He laughs shakily, sounding half relieved and half ashamed. She doesn't want to push him, but Troy was right. They need to figure this out as soon as possible.

"So... what happened out there?"

"I fucked up, Pheebs. I let him get in my head, man. What the fuck is wrong with me?"

His chest looks hollowed out, like someone's carved straight into it and took his heart. His mouth is dry and his lips are cracked, rust-red from his own gnawing anxiety and anger. She glides her thumb softly along them before cradling his face in her hands. The only thing she wants to do right now is make this all better, but to do that she has to figure out the why.

"Who?" She frowns. "Who got in your head, Damien?"

"He threw my whole fucking game off. I was nervous, you know? But

Ophelia told me you were coming back, and I was over the fuckin' moon. I kept looking for you in the wings."

"Damien, *who* is here?"

"Chris."

White hot rage cracks through the walls of her chest, seeping all over her. Phoebe clenches her teeth.

"Why?"

Damien throws his hands up and gives her the most helpless look she's ever seen from him.

"I don't fuckin' know, Pheebs! Maybe he's here for a review. Maybe he just wanted to see the fucking show. But all I could think about is him seeing something, finding something that he could spread before we have the chance."

She feels trapped, her mind spinning too fast to pin down a single thought. He crossed the line she warned him about, and now It's more than a work rivalry. He made this really fucking personal.

"Bell!" Troy calls from the dressing room. "Debriefing. Now. Miller, no offense, but no journalists on this one."

She can only imagine what waits for Damien in that room. This is all because of her. And them. Guilt gnaws at the back of her neck and she pinches her skin. The last thing she wants is for the band to resent her because of all of this.

"I gotta go," he whispers. "You'll be here when I get back?"

"Can't get rid of me that easy Bell. You're stuck with me."

Her joke rings hollow, but in the moment it's all she's got.

Damien gives her one last kiss before heading to the dressing room, Janis passing him halfway after Troy shoos her out.

"So, what did they say?" Phoebe asks.

"He just fucking bombed," Janis replies, folding her arms over her chest. "Shaun's annoyed, Johnny's pissed, Ophelia is just trying to keep the peace in there. What happened? Did he tell you anything?"

"Chris fucking happened."

Janis presses her mouth into a thin line.

"You're kidding."

"Nope. He was here. Still is, probably."

Just as Janis is about to reply, Phoebe spots someone skittering for the back door. Mousey hair and a bit of a slouch, the man shifts his bag on his shoulder as he makes his way out. Her fists clench as she storms toward him without a second thought.

"Hey!"

He doesn't say anything, and Phoebe speeds up, certain that he heard her.

"Chris!" She barks. "You take another step, and I swear to god..."

He freezes in place for a moment before he slowly turns, the fear on his face present for only a moment before it's replaced by a much more confidently cruel smile.

"Oh, hey Pheebs! You managed to catch the show?"

Phoebe grinds her teeth, barely holding herself back from grabbing him by the collar and slamming him up against the wall as Janis makes her way up beside her.

"Clearly." There's enough venom in her voice to kill a grown man twice over. "I heard that you might be the reason they're not still up there."

Chris snickers, giving a quick shrug.

"Oh, I don't know about that. I figure it just might have been a bad day. Everyone has them, after all."

Phoebe's jaw clenches, and she can feel the back of her neck grow hotter by the second. The anger only makes her more desperate for answers, but she keeps it cool.

"Why are you here, Chris?"

"Aw, you know, I was in Kansas, saw that tickets were–"

"Chris."

That same fear flickers back into his eyes for only a moment, before it's once again replaced by a wicked smugness.

"I promise you, I don't know what you're talking about."

Chris is jealous. He always has been, and now he's looking for a way to break her. To break them. His arrogance makes her want to put her fist through the wall, but she needs to hear him say it. He's never been one to let anyone take too many jabs at his pride.

Her tone shifts to painfully pleasant.

"I have to say Chris, this new more confident you is a sight to behold. I'd have a hard time saying you're the same person who called me drunk off his ass and begged me to give him an exclusive. Things must be looking up for ol' Chris Meyers, huh?"

All he can give her is another shake of his head, shrugging his shoulders again, but this time she can see his cheeks beginning to flush.

"That doesn't sound like me at all. Maybe the road's making your memory a little fuzzy, Miller." He feigns a look of concern, raising his eyebrows. "All that partying, the late nights... It's clearly taking one hell of a toll. You look like you could use some rest."

Phoebe lets out a long sigh.

"No, you know what? I don't think that's it. I guess I shouldn't have expected you'd even have the balls to come clean. I get it though, things are tough when you're stuck being a second-rate writer for any rag that'll take you. Gotta protect yourself from the *real* competition, any way you can I suppose."

"Real competition? That's fucking rich coming from you. I know how you're getting these stories, and soon everyone else will too."

"You'd better watch your fuckin' mouth," Janis growls.

"Or what, Kaneko?" Chris sneers. "What are you gonna do? You gonna fuckin' hit me? You'd lose that cushy New Yorker gig in a second. You think they're not *itching* to replace a useless hack like you?"

"Motherfucker, I–"

Phoebe holds out an arm to stop Janis.

"Why do you even care if I'm sleeping with Damien?"

Chris's eye twitches as he clicks his jaw back and forth.

"You know what, fine. It's because Brian handed you the story of a lifetime, straight over my head. That pissed me off, sure, but I can handle shit like that." Chris leans forward, the words almost spitting from his mouth. "But then I find out you can't even do the job without fucking around. This shit could have changed my entire career, and there you are too useless at your job to get it done without lifting up your fucking skirt for a B-tier wannabe rockstar!"

"Chris, why do you even want this assignment? You've always fucking hated Revolver! It's like you think they owe something just for showing up, like some kind of exposé of their private lives just to prove they deserve to be where they are. You think you could do this better than me? When you can't even treat them like people?"

"Oh, so sitting on the frontman's dick for a scoop is treating him like a person? I don't think you got that story on account of your literary prowess, Phoebe. All of your sappy, masturbatory think pieces–"

All of a sudden Phoebe's removed from the scene, watching as her fist collides with Chris's nose. There's an audible *crunch* and he screams, stumbling back until he hits the wall. He tries to cover his face as blood pours out through his cupped fingers. His eyes are wide as he quivers, clearly unsure exactly what to do.

In the middle of her trance, Phoebe hears the clack of heels against the floor. Janis is already around the corner, heading toward the dressing room for help. Fuck. She has to calm down. This isn't her. It's not how she solves things. She takes some deep breaths, trying to center herself, the pain starting to shoot through her fingers. Chris might be a sack of shit, but he doesn't deserve–

"You fucking bitch, if it wasn't for that cheap shot I'd kick the shit out of–"

She lunges forward, grabbing him by the shoulders and using all her momentum to ram her knee straight into his crotch. Chris drops to the floor and Phoebe doesn't even let him sit there for a moment before giving him another hard kick in the ribs.

"I have more talent in my little fucking *finger* than you have in your entire body!"

Another string of kicks land in his gut and ribs.

"You insufferable– Useless– Fucking– Asshole!"

Chris groans, blood dripping from his nose. Her ears are ringing, and her body sings with pure adrenaline-fueled hatred. As she's about to go in for more, a pair of strong hands pull her backward and she stumbles, flailing desperately to get back to him. To do anything to hurt him even more.

Even more than he hurt her.

I'm Still Standing

DAMIEN

"What the hell happened out there?!" Troy is snapping at him the moment the door to the dressing room shuts behind them. "What were you trying to do, bring back the nostalgia of the first time you ever stepped on a goddamn stage?!"

Damien is picking at his fingernails, feeling like a kid getting shit from his dad, keeping his gaze trained on the floor.

"I fucked up. It won't happen again."

"So tell the class what happened," Troy replies. "Come on, Bell. Don't be shy. We deserve an explanation."

"Fuck you, Troy!" Damien shouts. "You always treat me like this!"

"Like what?"

"Like I'm a child!"

"Because you act like one!"

Damien's jaw clenches and he looks to his band mates for support. Shaun's brows are knit together, completely stoic as he takes everything in. Ophelia shoots him a sympathetic look, but it's Johnny's eyes that make Damien's spine straighten.

"It's embarrassing, Damien. We looked like fucking amateurs out there."

"I know!" Damien snarls.

"So why the fuck did you fall apart?!"

Damien swallows, struggling to find the right words. There's no way they're going to understand his sorry ass excuse for fucking up this bad. It was so petty. Childish. Is he going to be like this every time someone challenges his relationship with Phoebe? Or when there's even the slightest hint of a threat? It's beyond humiliating. Damien Bell doesn't let anyone get to him.

Except when he does.

"Something shook you out there, man," Shaun murmurs. "And I never see that happen anymore."

Damien sighs, staring up at the ceiling.

"I know, it's just..."

Silence invades the room; he's never felt smaller in his life. The weight of his band mates' eyes on him just adds to the embarrassment. He wishes he could march back onto the stage, call the crowd back in like it was all some big joke.

"Is it Phoebe?" Shaun asks. "Did something happen with her job or something?"

"No, it's– well, it's sort of..." He sighs as Shaun passes him a beer. "You know that guy who trashed our album in Titanium last year? He called Pheebs, back in Denver. He was trying to get something out of her; he's been bitter since she got this job over him, and he has this *hunch* about the two of us. I think he showed up to catch us in the act, maybe see if I'd slip up. He probably didn't even know she was back in New York."

"Why would he care about any of that shit?" Troy asks.

"So that he can be the first one to break it," Ophelia mutters. "Suddenly he's got a front page story that's going to get him a shitload of attention. Remember what almost happened to Shaun and I in Athens?"

Shaun clicks his tongue and nods, a hint of bitterness on his face as Damien groans. Some photographers followed them to a bar after a show; kept asking questions about the two of them and their relationship. Damien got involved, as he always does, and nearly tore the guy's head off for being a nosy little prick. Johnny had to pry Damien off of the guy. They ended up bribing him with more liquor to keep him quiet, damn near bought out half the bar.

"Look, I get it," Johnny grumbles, the anger in his eyes beginning to simmer down into small embers. "But you could have told us this might be coming, instead of letting us all get blindsided."

Somehow, even as everything starts to settle, it feels worse. Johnny's the most positive guy he knows, letting almost everything slide right off his back. If something concerns the health of the band, though, it's a different story. Damien put them at risk, and for what?

"I know, Johnny, I just..."

His heart aches. Keeping this secret had become so normal. For a month, it'd been Damien and Phoebe against the world.

"Alright, I've heard enough of this mopey shit."

Troy gets to his feet, pointing at Damien with his cigarette dangling from his lips.

"The next time he shows up, you say something or give me some kind of signal. Even if we can't ban him from venues, we can damn well be prepared but that's only gonna work if we know what's coming, so you gotta be open and honest with us."

Johnny pats him on the shoulder, punctuating Troy's point.

"We're a family. The whole point is that none of us have to go it alone. That's why I was pissed off, man. You should have told us what was going down. We've got your back as long as you've got ours."

All of this attention and support... He almost wishes they were still yelling at him. Luckily, it's only a moment before Troy jumps back into motivation-mode.

"Exactly Reed! It's impossible to plan for a play we can't see coming, that's why they call it a blindside! So, as long as we scout out the competition, make sure we know everything about them, there's no way they'll be able to break our defensive line!"

"Oh god," Ophelia groans. "I thought it was gonna get awkward with the boys wrestling with their feelings, but now we're on to old-man sports metaphors. Just fucking kill me."

A pounding at the door interrupts what would surely have been a passionate response from Troy, but he channels all that energy into stomping straight over to it and flinging it open.

"I said no journalists, Kaneko–"

Janis shoves past him and stumbles into the room, panic painting her face.

"You guys gotta get out here, *now*. Phoebe's gonna kill Chris."

Damien's jaw drops and he lets out an incredulous laugh.

"*My* Phoebe?"

There's no way.

"I think she broke his nose– no, she *definitely* broke his nose, and maybe some ribs," Janis says with a grimace. "There's a lot of blood, but she's not stopping."

"Goddammit, Bell!" Troy growls as he storms out of the room.

"I didn't do anything this time!" Damien shouts, already on Troy's heels.

He just can't picture Phoebe hitting anyone, not like that, at least. A slap across the face, maybe. But a broken nose? Ribs? Damien can't see his sweet little Phoebe hauling off on someone like that.

But the evidence presents itself as they round the corner.

Chris is on his knees, hunched over in an attempt to protect himself, after what Damien imagines must have been one hell of a hit. Phoebe's towering over him, her fists clenched so tight they're bone-white. She's shaking, sweat glistening on her face.

For a split second Damien thinks they're catching the end of it, but then she lunges, her leg smashing into Chris's crumpling body.

"I have more talent in my little fucking *finger* than you have in your entire body!" She kicks him over and over again. "You insufferable– Useless– Fucking– Asshole!"

"Holy shit, Miller's gone off the deep end," Ophelia laughs nervously.

"Honestly, it's... kind of impressive," Troy replies, a look of disbelief flickering in his eyes.

Damien takes a deep breath.

With a heavy heart and a hell of a lot of regret, he rushes for Phoebe and grabs her underneath her arms, yanking her backward. She flails and kicks her legs in a desperate attempt to get away. He's never seen her like this, and it's a little shocking.

All of a sudden he has a flash of her standing over him, red marks covering his body as she pulls at the collar on *his* neck. The one he bought for her. He can feel that all-too familiar rush of excitement before quickly snapping back to the moment.

What the fuck was that?

He doesn't have too much time to think about it as her arm crashes against his head in her struggle to get free.

"Let me go!"

She fights harder to get out of the hold, tears in her eyes and sweat clinging to her brow. Damien tries to drag her backward, at least far enough away from Chris that her flailing legs won't be able to reach him, but she almost slips out of his grip. This time, he catches her by the waist, turning her around to face him before wrapping her in a bear hug. Tiny fists crash against his biceps as she struggles.

"That's enough, Pheebs."

"Fuck you!"

He can't even tell if she knows it's him.

She tries to push herself away but he grabs her forearms and holds on tight. Her right hand is red and swollen; there's already a bruise forming. She's going to need ice, maybe X-rays.

"Hey, it's okay."

Finally their eyes meet, and for a moment the anger is all he can see.

"It's just me, babydoll."

Her eyes soften, all the rage seemingly melting into exhaustion as he lets her free, her arms wrapping around him as she trembles. He can feel her heartbeat begin to slow, her breathing returning to normal as he holds her. It's strangely peaceful, and for a moment Damien's able to forget the awful situation they'd found themselves in.

But only for a moment.

"Isn't anyone gonna help me up?!" Chris shouts, his sneakers slipping on the floor as he struggles to brace himself against the wall.

"Nah, I think you've got it, dude," Janis replies.

"He looks like a baby deer," Johnny chuckles.

"They're called foals, you idiot," Troy snaps back.

"That's a horse."

"*No*, it's a deer."

"Guys! Priorities, please!" Shaun groans.

Chris is a mess, blood still pouring from his nose and staining the once-olive fabric of his shirt a dark rust color.

For a fraction of a second, Damien feels sorry for him. And then he remembers why Chris is here, why he's been following Phoebe and the band since they were in Denver.

"You're done, Miller, you're fucking done. Where's the phone, I'm calling the cops right now. Pressing charges."

"What do you mean?" Shaun asks. "Nothing happened."

Chris frowns, not quite cluing in.

"I'm not really sure if I caught anything," Troy replies, rocking back and forth on his heels. "Thank god we were here though, because everyone else in the whole place was out front. How about you, Bell? You see what happened?"

Damien shrugs.

"Hard to say. I do think I remember someone trying to make his way into the dressing room uninvited. That's a real safety risk you know, just by itself, but maybe he was angry, tried to attack someone he had a beef with..."

"For all we know, Phoebe was defending herself," Ophelia chimes in. "Right, Pheebs?"

Damien watches as the realization sets in on Chris's face. The veins in his neck and forehead pop and his nostrils flare as he steps toward her.

"You lying bitch–"

Damien steps between them, Chris almost stumbling straight into him before barely stopping himself in time. They stare into each other's eyes, each man daring the other to blink, but while Chris is a bloody mess of nerves and rage, Damien is surprisingly calm.

"You were gonna hit her."

Chris spits blood right in his face.

"She deserves it. Just look at me."

Damien smiles, wiping it away with his sleeve as he blocks Chris's path.

"You come after my girl and you're gonna be leaving on a fuckin' stretcher, you understand?" He gestures absently at Chris's bloody face. "This is you getting off easy."

The reporter's eyes flick over to Phoebe and Damien takes the moment to step in even closer, gripping his chin hard and forcing him to look right at him.

"Eyes on me, Meyers. Tell me you understand what I just said to you. Or did she kick your fuckin' brains out of your head, too?"

He doesn't know what Chris said to Phoebe, but it must have been pretty goddamn terrible for her to go after him the way she did. She wouldn't throw punches without reason. She's not like him. He knows it.

"I– I understand."

Damien smiles, a big wolfish grin.

"Good. Now, you're gonna walk out that door, get back in your car and drive the fuck away. And if you so much as *breathe* in the same room she's in, I'm coming after you. Is that clear?" Chris nods and Damien taps him on the cheek. "Glad we're on the same page."

He lets the man go and takes a couple steps back, his hands in the air. Chris pulls himself together and heads straight toward the door, but he pauses for a moment, hand perched on the knob, seemingly hoping to get the last word.

Damien beats him to the punch.

"Oh, and Meyers? That was all off the record. I'm sure you can respect that, you're a real champion of journalistic integrity after all."

With some curses under his breath Chris slips out, slamming the door and only leaving the sound of the empty venue behind. Damien hugs Phoebe tight, the silence lingering for a few moments before Troy cuts back in.

"Alright children, it's time for you to head back to the hotel. No need to wear out our welcome. Grab your shit and hit the bus."

As most of them start to walk back to the dressing room, Troy leans in toward Damien.

"Bell, Miller, I'm gonna talk to the management here, clear some things up about Chris. You don't have to worry about what happened today, it's covered."

Damien lets himself relax for the first time all night.

"Thanks Troy, you're the man."

"Don't mention it, kid. You know how it goes, you idiots fuck around, I fix everything back up, and we all live happily ever after." He grins, turning to walk away. "Just never write a song about me, and we're even."

Damien lets out an exhausted sigh, turning to Phoebe and taking her swollen hand in his. He looks it over carefully, running his fingers over her bloodied knuckles as she winces.

"We'll get you some ice." He wipes her tears away, giving her hand a quick kiss. "You've got a hell of a right hook, Miller, I'll give you that."

"I'm sorry," she whispers, shame flooding her eyes. "I'm so embarrassed."

Her features soften as tears drip down her face. There's fear in her eyes; she knows she went too far. This was supposed to be a happy reunion for the two of them, but Damien is determined to fix it, no matter what it takes.

"Tell me what happened."

"I... I just saw him back here. He was already on his way out, and it's so stupid but... He's been fucking with us this whole time, ready to ruin our lives for a cheap headline, and I– I needed to hear him say it. I needed him to admit it to my face."

He can tell the memories are already starting to stoke that fire inside her again.

"Everything was fine at first. He kept trying to rile me up but I wasn't gonna let him under my skin, and then... I don't even remember what he said. Whatever it was, a switch just flipped and I lost control. He fucking deserved it!"

All that fire that had been building up melts away in a second as her shoulders slump, her words tinged with regret.

"Fuck, Damien, I shouldn't have hit him."

She's distraught, and all he wants to do is make it better, but he just can't get that image of her out of his head.

"Let's not go that far, babydoll. To your credit, it was pretty fucking hot."

Here Comes the Rain Again

PHOEBE

"I just got my job back and now I'm gonna have to beg for it all over again."

Damien is stuffing ice cubes into a little Ziploc bag just out of sight as she paces back and forth through the hotel room.

"Stupid. I was *stupid*!"

They were only alone in their room a few minutes before Phoebe noticed herself spiraling. Damien had clearly noticed too, flipping on the TV to some movie for background noise. They've barely been together a couple months but he already knows she hates that pregnant silence.

As shitty as she feels about the whole Chris situation, there's something about Damien's tenderness that almost makes things okay.

Almost.

"I still think we should get you checked out," he says, glancing over his shoulder. "You hit him *hard*, Pheebs. I don't even think I've drawn that much blood from a couple punches."

"No hospitals," she insists, barely registering any of the other words.

"Not a fan?"

"The only times I've been to a hospital were when I got my tonsils out when I was 10, and then again when my grandma was dying."

He drops down onto the bed, shifting over to snuggle up next to her as he gingerly places the makeshift ice pack against her swollen knuckles.

"Fair enough, but you need to keep this on your hand for at least an hour or two, okay, Rocky?"

She chuckles, Damien's words and the background chatter of the TV slowly bringing her back to herself.

"Don't give me so much credit. That punch was amateur."

"None of what I saw looked amateur. You almost KO'd that dumbass. Flat on the canvas, one two three!"

Pain pulses up her arm along with the memory, and she winces as a sharp corner of the ice pack digs into her skin. It almost feels like a punishment.

"I'm so embarrassed."

She presses a little harder.

"What? Why?"

"Because I hit him, Damien! That's not me. I don't know what the hell came over me!"

Damien shrugs.

"From what I can tell you didn't just hit him, you kicked the shit out of him. It was kinda sexy, honestly."

She scoffs.

"Can you be serious for two seconds?"

"Okay, okay." He climbs on top of her, straddling her thighs, and pressing a tender kiss onto her lips. "Phoebe, you have nothing to be embarrassed about. If anyone should be embarrassed, it's me. It was my fault."

Phoebe's face twists in confusion as she stares at the man in front of her.

"What? No, that's not true."

"Yeah. Yeah it is. He didn't even have to say anything and I let him get to me. Once it got down to it, the shit he said to you? *About* you? Sure, that definitely warranted a punch in the fuckin' face. He's just lucky I didn't decide to clean his clock, too. But it never should have gotten to that point. I should have been a goddamn professional up on that stage, treated him like any other random asshole in the audience."

That's the part that she hasn't been able to reconcile since the car ride back. How the hell did someone like Chris get under his skin? As far as anyone could tell he was just standing near the stage, just another face in the crowd.

"So then... how did he get to you like that?"

Damien sighs.

"I just... I got angry at first, and then I got real nervous, you know? You weren't back yet–"

"But you knew I was coming back, right? We promised."

"That's why I feel so stupid. The last thing I want is for someone else to break the news about the two of us. I knew, I *knew* in my gut he was there to see how I'd react. He wanted to catch me slipping up, and he did."

She sighs.

"He really is a master of pushing buttons. I think it's how he's gotten over half of his stories, honestly. He just gets people pissed off enough to say what they're really thinking."

She thought everything would be back to normal, that the moment her plane touched down they'd be right back to the way they were. Instead, there are dozens of questions, and she doesn't have any answers. Is their relationship going to change once they decide to go public? How the fuck are they going to navigate all of this? Will they even get to decide how and when it happens, or will Chris just publish a big fucking exposé before they can get things sorted?

It's eating away at her.

"I'm worried," she confesses.

Damien gnaws at his lip.

"About Chris?"

"About everything," Phoebe whispers. "When I finally left Brian's office it felt like I had it all under control, like it was all starting to go so fucking well. Now all I can think about is how I can't control what anyone says about us, about why we're together, about what we are, and I hate it. I hate that Chris gets to say whatever he wants, and people will probably believe it."

He flashes her a mournful smile, trying and failing to look strong in the face of everything.

"Look, Pheebs, if this is too much pressure we can always shift gears, focus on a no-nonsense version of your article. All about the band and the music, no extra frills. Then there's no issue, nothing for anyone to point to."

Phoebe shakes her head. She promised Brian an intimate look at the band, their dynamics, and how they all fit together, her included. That's the whole pitch now, and it's probably why she still has a job.

"Damien, this whole time you've said you want to hold my hand when we walk down the street, go dancing, kiss in a crowd without a care in the world. You wanted everyone to know who you were singing about, right? Well, you want to sing about me, and I want to write about you." She smirks. "It's only fair, right?"

Damien's eyes well up with tears as she continues.

"I want to write about the little family I found. I don't know, it sounds stupid when I say it out loud, but it's like with your songs... I want to tell the world exactly how I love you."

Her chin quivers as she tries to keep herself calm, and Damien adjusts the bag of ice on her knuckles, making sure it's covering the bruise that's starting to form.

"God, this is so fucking humiliating," she mutters. "If he didn't have one already, I handed him a brand new fucking story."

"We both did," Damien confesses. "And I know you're embarrassed about that hit, but that was... insanely hot."

He keeps bringing it up, and she can't keep herself from smiling at how enamored he is with the idea.

"Is that all you've been thinking about all night?" Phoebe giggles.

"Hey, it's a momentous occasion. I remembered something about myself today."

Phoebe arches a brow.

"Is this your way of asking me to beat you up, Bell? Slap you around a little?" His eyes tell her everything she needs to know and she leans in toward him, gripping his chin. "Speak up."

Damien's demeanor changes in the blink of an eye, quivering a little as his mouth ghosts along her jaw, all the way up to her ear to nip at the lobe. His stubble sends a rush of tingles down her spine. This is what she's missed the most, being near him, smelling his cologne, and listening to the sound of his voice as it rumbles in her ear. Even for a few days, the separation was torture.

As he moves to kiss her again, a sharp knock at the door pulls him back.

"Hold that thought, we're definitely coming back to it." He climbs off of the bed, spinning back and pointing at her dramatically. "Remember to keep that ice pack on, missy!"

She grabs the remote and flips through the channels, trying to take her mind off of the dull throbbing in her hand. When she hears Shaun's voice from the doorway, she turns the volume down a little.

"Hey, Bell, you got condoms?"

"Yeah, hang on. I think they're in my suitcase. You wanna come in?"

"I'm not interrupting anything, am I?"

"Not at all, man."

Damien heads for his suitcase and rifles through it, pulling out notebooks and clothes while Shaun steps inside and gives Phoebe a quick wave. She catches a smear of neon pink lipstick on his neck that stands out against his dark brown skin.

Janis's lipstick. Good for her.

"How's the hand, Rocky?" He chirps.

She groans. Back at the venue Johnny kept screaming '*Adrieeeennn*' while one of the security guards was checking to make sure she hadn't split her hand open. Once Ophelia and Janis joined in, it was all over.

"Are you all gonna call me that forever? Am I cursed?"

He winks at her.

"The curse of a great nickname! You want a worse one? Troy could come up with a dozen in less than a minute. You'd have your pick of the trash."

Phoebe chuckles.

"I guess Rocky's fine, then. So, how are you guys doing?"

"Recovering," he replies.

Shaun clears his throat, and Phoebe can see Damien's head turn slightly in recognition as he continues to root through the bag.

"It was, uh... kind of a shit show out there tonight. I don't know how much of the carnage you caught, but..."

Damien's jaw ticks.

"Yeah, just a bit," Phoebe murmurs as silence worms its way in between the three of them.

Her hand starts to throb, but it's nothing compared to the guilt that sits like a rock in her gut. Even though she wasn't out there tonight, she's the reason Chris showed up. Sure, he would have continued to hate Revolver without her involvement, but it would have been from a distance if Phoebe hadn't gotten this story. It's her fault that it got so personal.

"I'm... really sorry about Chris," she offers after a few seconds. Damien's eyes volley between them, the box of condoms clutched in his hand. "That was shitty of him to show up on purpose like that. I didn't mean–"

"You can't control that bullshit," Shaun offers with a gentle smile. "I know you wouldn't haul off on a guy for no reason– actually, I *don't* know that, but I just assumed–" His smile turns into a mischievous grin. "Miller, is it going to turn out you've got a dark side? You part of some street gang? An underground fight club? Are you holding out on us?"

"God, if only I was so cool," she laughs. "No, I've never even really hit anyone before. I feel so terrible."

"Nah, it's all water under the bridge. We get some rest, regroup, and play the next city like nothing happened. If something comes up, we'll deal with it."

"You're seriously not mad?"

Shaun brushes it off, waving his hand in the air.

"You're part of the family now, Pheebs. Sometimes we fight, but we always make up." He glances over at Damien, who's been conspicuously standing stock-still for the entire conversation. "Ain't that right, Bell?"

Damien looks a little embarrassed, but more than a little relieved.

"Always." He holds up the box. "But, back to the important issue at hand: how many?"

Shaun rubs the back of his neck, a sheepish smile on his face.

"Uh, as many as you can spare. I'll pay you back."

Damien nonchalantly tosses him the box, sitting back down and putting his arm around Phoebe.

"Don't worry about it. I got like three more boxes."

She bites her lip, her face flushing. When she was packing, she felt like a magician pulling scarves out of a hat. She put all the ones she found into a little bag and sealed it up so that airport security didn't ask her questions.

"Don't use 'em all at once, hotshot."

"Thank you, fearless leader." He pauses, halfway out the door. "And, hey, uh... don't worry about the show tonight, okay? We've all got your back no matter what that Chris asshole writes."

Neither man seems to really know what to say, and they both just stare at each other for a moment as Phoebe tries not to crack up.

"Okay, cool. Well, I'm gonna go get laid. I'll see you guys later."

She giggles, waving at him as he heads out the door.

"That's the spirit."

By the time the door clicks shut, Damien is already halfway toward it, locking the deadbolt as quickly as he can before slipping his shirt off over his head. She can feel herself heating up underneath the weight of his gaze and his eyes rake up and down her body.

"Is it warm in here, babydoll? Or is it just you?"

He walks to the fridge and grabs the ice bucket, popping one of the cubes between his lips as he saunters back toward her.

"Warm?" She whispers.

She finds her throat completely dry as Damien climbs onto the mattress, playfully pushing her down before crawling on top of her.

He slips the ice cube out of his mouth and nods, sliding it around in his hand.

"You're flushed."

"That might not be something entirely in my control."

"Hmm. Well, if I'm the one to blame, It's only fair that I help fix the problem."

Her whole body is on fire.

"That– Yeah, that sounds fair."

"We *were* interrupted, after all."

She leans in toward him, right up next to his ear with a whisper.

"And you finally learned how to lock the door."

She gasps the second the ice makes contact with her skin, her back arching as she lets out a little squeak.

"Let me show you what else I've learned," he purrs.

All Through the Night

DAMIEN

She's beautiful, even with her tear-stained face and the swollen knuckles. This looks like a brand new Phoebe. Despite the setbacks, there's a confidence in her eyes that sparks something in him. He sits back on his haunches as she puts the ice pack down and pulls off her sweater.

The thought of being buried between her thighs makes his mouth water.

Damien trails an ice cube along her skin until he reaches her sternum. She's trembling beneath his touch and he's fucking insatiable, aching to feel her fingernails rake down his back.

Every inch of her is gorgeous, from her breasts, adorned with little bone-white stretch marks, to the way her tummy protrudes just a bit over the top of her jeans. The second she walked into that first hotel room in LA, he knew he had to have her, but at the time he had no idea what that would mean for either of them.

Damien traces the ice cube over her nipples, grinning as she gasps, and taking the opportunity to pop it between her lips. She crunches down on it, pretending to snarl at him as she chews.

He bites down gently on her nipple, her back arching. The room fills with soft grunts and groans as he reaches up, wrapping his hand around her throat and squeezing the sides. He can barely control himself as her fingers dance through his hair.

He feels like he could pin her to the mattress and fuck her as hard as he can, but he wants to savor this. His tongue swirls around each nipple until she's squirming beneath him. Damien puts a little more pressure on her neck and drags out a raspy moan from deep inside of her, right as he slips his lips off her nipple with a soft pop.

"You make such pretty sounds, babydoll."

She shivers, her face flushed pink as she looks at him with a sultry smirk. Damien releases her throat and turns back to her little ice pack, popping out another cube and tracing it over her pebbled nipples. She groans and shudders at the sharp temperature change, and he can see the goosebumps rush all the way up her skin as he leans down and cleans up the small rivulets left behind with his tongue. Quickly he shifts back to his mild brand of torment, clamping down on her nipple with his teeth once more, and tugging at it to draw another whine from her lips. He can feel her fingers continue winding themselves in his hair, twisting and pulling to the point of pain.

He loves it.

All he can hear is the buzzing of the television in the background and the sound of Phoebe's labored breaths as he slips the ice cube between his lips, holding it there as he trails down her belly as slowly as he can. When he reaches the waistband of her jeans, the two of them move for her zipper at the same time, fingers bumping into each other. Laughter fills the space between them as Damien takes the ice cube out of his mouth, resting it on her belly button.

"This is supposed to be sexy, Miller."

"It is!" She squeals, covering her mouth with one hand. "It's just cold!"

Damien tugs her jeans down her hips and pulls them off of her before shedding his own. She's exquisite, her dark, silky hair strewn across the snow white pillows and those warm honey-colored eyes that made him weak the second he saw her.

He takes his time gliding his hands along her skin, feeling how smooth she is before he dips his head and drags the tip of his nose up and down each thigh. Her smell invades his senses: mint and lavender. He bites down on her inner thigh until she cries out and he picks the ice cube up again, trailing it just below her waist. Her giggles quickly fade, turning to a quiet whimper as Damien laps up the water left behind.

"Are you marking me up, Bell?"

Her eyes are focused only on him, her pupils so dilated the color is lost in complete blackness; he feels like a single star being consumed in an expansive sky. Damien glides the ice cube along her clit, and she sucks in a sharp breath. He takes that as a sign to change things up and pull back the intensity. Instead, he sucks on the ice cube until he feels his tongue go slightly numb.

Damien softly exhales, his breath fanning her cunt. Just as her moans start to fill the room, he wraps his still-cool lips around her clit, sucking in little pulses while she squeals and squirms around. He loves that sound; he could listen to it for the rest of his life.

With one hand he pins her hip to the bed, still teasing her with his tongue before he pulls away to suck on the ice all over again. His fingers are getting numb, but he doesn't give a shit. They've both needed this. One phone sex session wasn't enough to satiate their hunger.

He pops the ice out of his mouth and flicks her swollen bud, playing with pace and pressure. When he flattens his tongue and licks a long, delicate stripe up her cunt, she responds with a carnal groan that's music to his ears. He tosses the ice somewhere onto the floor before wrapping his lips around her clit once more. Damien runs his still cold fingertips down her waist, inching agonizingly closer and closer. The feeling of her shivers and twitches makes him ache for her even more.

He hears Phoebe inhale sharply as he slides two fingers inside her, followed by another lewd whine as he pushes further, pressing them up against her G-spot. He looks back at her face, his eyes fixed on her rapturous expression. Her head is tipped up toward the ceiling, eyelids fluttering as she moans his name between sweet little words of affirmation.

Yes.

More.

Need you.

Something greedy burns inside of him and his mind rushes back to that image of him on his knees for her.

"Call me a good boy," he whispers before he laps at her again.

Phoebe makes an unintelligible noise and lifts her head, her fingers swimming through his hair and a devilish smile creeping across her face.

"You'd like that, would you?"

"Only when it comes from those sweet little lips."

She practically breathes the words into him.

"Good boy."

Damien groans, burying his face in her pussy and devouring her like she's the best meal he's ever had. He grabs her hip with his free hand, fingers digging in hard as he pulls her toward him, his other still busy thrusting at a purposefully agonizing pace. He wants to be as close to her as possible; the desire to feel her quiver beneath him is insatiable. She grips his hair even tighter, hips rocking back and forth as cracked and ragged moans fill his ears.

"Fuck!"

It might be his new favorite song.

He can feel her body go into overdrive as he wraps his lips around her clit. She holds him tight against her, writhing and rolling her hips as another and another and another cry fills the room.

"Damien, please!"

He doesn't know what he wants more at this point, to feel her come apart in his mouth, or to listen to her beg for mercy. He grinds his hips against the mattress, matching her manic pace as he plays her like an instrument.

He slides his fingers out of her pussy, replacing them with his tongue as he reaches up to play with her nipples. Her body is an endless landscape of goosebumps, all thanks to him.

"Oh, fuck! Right there!" She keens.

The more desperate her moans, the more he wants to be inside of her, but he hasn't been able to stop thinking about the fantasy he concocted back when he saw her standing over Chris. He needs to see what she looks like when she's really in charge, not just pretending to pin him down like she did in Vegas, but actually in full control.

Phoebe Miller isn't as sweet or as meek as she thinks she is, and someday soon he's going to bring it out of her. For now, however, he's happy to be the one making her scream.

Just as her cunt begins to flutter around his tongue, he lifts his head and she lets out a frustrated wail.

"What the fuck, Damien?! I was so–"

He shoves his briefs down past his hips, his mouth colliding with hers to shut her up. Her legs wind around his waist and he's greeted by her warm, wet pussy. He glides his cock up and down her folds, brushing up against her stiff, swollen clit before breaking the kiss, wrapping one hand around her throat as she whimpers, the other pressed against the bed to keep suspended up above her.

"I need you," he rumbles.

Her eyes are glossy and full, with only a thin line of amber stretched around black pupils. Those soft lips that he loves to kiss so much stretch into a confident smile as she nods her head.

Damien releases her throat, snatches a condom off of the nightstand, and sits back on his haunches. He tears the packet open and makes a little show of rolling it onto his cock while Phoebe watches on. Her chest heaves, little beads of sweat all over her flushed skin as her fingers circle her clit seductively.

Silver-moonlight drips through the little gap in the gauzy curtains, carving her out like a statue. Every curve, every freckle, every mark on her body is uniquely her, exactly the way they're supposed to be. He climbs on top of her, her hand immediately wrapped around the base of his cock as she guides him inside.

"I've been needing this for three fuckin' days."

"Don't sound so desperate, Bell," she teases, just before her voice breaks as he bottoms out.

"I thought you liked desperate." He nips at her earlobe, starting to roll his hips to meet hers. "You can't lie to me, Babydoll. Your pussy always gives you away."

She clenches around him, pulling him deeper as her fingernails sink into his back like tiny knives. Their kiss is breathless and messy as he picks up the pace, thrusting ferociously, just like he's been aching to since she left.

Damien slams down into her, grabbing both of her wrists and pinning them above her head, careful not to hurt her bruised knuckles.

Phoebe lets out a needy whine, and he grins.

"Tell me how you want it, babydoll."

"Harder," she whimpers.

Her pussy is like a vice grip as her thighs squeeze tighter and tighter around his waist, her back arching, exposing her throat. He can't help himself; his mouth latches onto it in an instant, sucking what will surely be a deeply mottled bruise into her skin. He'll make sure she wears it as a mark of pride. No makeup, no scarves, no fucking turtlenecks. No hiding, never again.

The idea of someone seeing his teeth marks on her makes him feral, and he snarls as they begin to slam the headboard against the wall. Phoebe's moans quickly become rapturous and pleading, and he drinks them down like communion wine.

He can feel her struggle beneath him as she begins to shudder; she's close. There's a deep ache in the pit of his stomach, like an elastic band being pulled too tight. Heat spreads through his belly, creeping all the way into his lower back. He moans with her, louder and louder as the head-board provides a chaotic drumbeat for their duet.

Damien's toes dig into the mattress, desperate to find just the tiniest bit more leverage to carry them through those final few steps. Phoebe takes every thrust, begging for more as the two of them teeter on a knife's edge.

With one final crash of his hips, his climax erupts. This one has teeth, ripping and shredding through him as his body comes to a complete stop, every muscle clenched so tightly that it fucking aches.

His cock throbs, filling up the condom as his hips rut against hers like his body has a mind of its own. He finally feels the marks her nails made down his back again as the adrenaline fades, for the first time in what feels like an eternity. Her fingers play with his long hair, twirling it gently as he buries his head in her shoulder.

Damien peppers kisses along her collarbone biting down gently next to her brand new hickey. She shivers, laughter bubbling up from her chest. That fucking sound, it's like a button in the back of his brain that turns up the dopamine.

"You're an animal," she whispers.

"Mmm. You like 'em wild."

"I do."

He rolls off her and grabs his cigarettes off of the nightstand, pulling two from the pack and lighting them one at a time before passing one over. After a minute Damien leans over, grabbing the now mostly-melted ice pack as their long-abandoned Johnny Carson show plays in the background.

"Put that back on your hand for now. I'll make you a fresh one in a bit."

"Yes, sir, Dr. Bell," she replies with a serious expression. "Was the examination a success?"

He grins.

"Everything's in prime working order, ma'am, but be sure to come back for frequent checkups just in case."

And then it's quiet between them for a while, smoking in silence as they let their minds wander. It's clear they both know there's still something to discuss, but neither wants to be the one to do it. In the end, it's Phoebe who breaks first, but this time it's not out of fear or anxious worry.

Her voice is solid, confident in spite of the unknown.

"What do you think is gonna happen when everyone finds out?"

Damien sits with the question for a moment, choosing his words carefully.

"I'm not really sure. Some people will call your credibility into question, that's a guarantee, but that was always going to happen. Honestly Pheebs, as long as we do it right, I think most people aren't gonna give a shit."

She nods, more to herself than anything.

"Didn't Jim Morrison marry a rock journalist? The woman from Jazz & Pop Magazine?"

Damien blows a smoke ring.

"Yeah, I've heard that, but the dude is more myth than human being at this point, so who knows if it's really true. Everyone has a story about him – you know, Troy says he saw Morrison at the Tropicana Hotel in '67? Dude was high as a fuckin' kite on acid, naked in the hallway and barking like a dog."

"Troy, or Morrison?"

Damien cackles.

"You know, now that you mention it, it's hard to say. But if I was a betting man, I'd think it was Morrison. Troy strikes me as the kind of guy that'd have a much more chill narcotic of choice."

"Well, that's definitely not the weirdest story I've heard about that guy."

"Absolutely, dude was wild. I'm a boy scout compared to him," Damien snorts.

"You are," she gives him a little pinch on the arm. "And I'd like to keep it that way."

"Don't worry, Sweets, I think Troy would kill me if I started down that path."

"He wouldn't get the chance."

Damien grins, laying a kiss on her cheek. He can tell her anxiety has been creeping back in, and he's been feeling the pull of his own as well, but there's no going back now.

It's all only a matter of time.

Blue Monday

DAMIEN

The hotel restaurant is abuzz with servers rushing back and forth, trying to make sure everyone gets their orders on time, all while maintaining the façade of a calm and collected operation. Damien is sat next to Phoebe, his arm draped over the back of her chair as he plays with her hair. Ophelia snagged two tables near the back, out of the way of everyone's view, giving them that little extra bit of privacy.

"Tour's over," Troy announces as he slams the newspaper down on the table. "Two more weeks, and we're going home."

Johnny laughs, clearly thinking it's some sort of joke.

"Who says?"

Troy plants his finger on the headline, flopping down into his seat as the group leans in.

REVOLVER FALLS APART IN KANSAS: A SIGN OF THINGS TO COME?

Damien catches little snippets as he quickly scans the page:
Disastrous blunder caps off tour.
Is it drugs, or something more serious?
He rolls his eyes.

"Stupid fucks." Beside him he can feel Phoebe shift as she pours over the article. He forces a smile. "It's fine. This is what they do after all, right?"

She glances over at him, her face neutral as Johnny cuts in.

"Wait, does this mean we're cutting the New York gig too?!"

Damien can't bring himself to look at his bandmates. He knew there was a chance something like this was coming, since all the way back with that bouncer he took a swing at in California.

"I called up the label, told 'em it was one bad show, that it'd be stupid not to let us finish things out, but..." Troy's eyes dance around the table before he forces a smile. "Ah, well you know those bastards. Never ones to take a risk."

"But he's cleaned that up," Janis chimes in. "He's a golden boy now, been on his best behavior."

"Telling Meyers he'd be leaving on a stretcher? That's what counts as good behavior with you, Kaneko?" Troy asks, his eyebrow lifted incredulously.

Damien sips his coffee in silence as Troy sighs, patting the table.

"Look, we had a good run, right? If we cut things off now, we can end this somewhat triumphantly. You kids played your hearts out this whole tour, and you got one stinker in the batch. Nothing to be ashamed of."

Damien rubs his face. Troy's in dad mode now, trying to smooth things over and cheer them all up, so of course it feels twice as bad.

"New York's our homecoming, dude!" Johnny whines. "Come on! They can least give us that!"

"Yeah, no offense Troy but you're talking total bullshit. Going out on a bad show is gonna look way worse for us," Ophelia pipes up. "We need to end on something big."

"It could taint the album, too," Shaun adds, watching Troy out of the corner of his eye. "We're heading back into the studio for album number two, right? Well guess what might not do as well if it's coming off a tainted tour!"

Troy glares at Shaun, before glancing back down at the paper. They all know he'd do anything for the band.

"Okay, look, we might be able to use that as leverage with the suits, maybe for a cute little surprise show, but they want you guys back in the studio ASAP. You're nothing more than a liability if you're burning out, and that's how it seems." Shaun and Johnny each look like they're about to jump in, but Troy silences them with a quick gesture. "We had a bad day, you get that and I get that. It's not the end of the world, but there are consequences here kids, and this is one of 'em."

"All those fuckin' suits see is the product," Johnny grumbles, violently stabbing his pancake and shoving a piece into his mouth.

Damien studies Johnny, who seems torn between relief and indignation. The label can control nearly everything about them, right down to their image and sound if they had the mind to. Right now Revolver's popular, which gives them a certain amount of freedom, but eventually that tide will turn, and as much as he hates to admit it, Troy's right. They *are* burning out.

"Well, maybe this could be a good thing then," Ophelia chimes in. "I don't know about you guys, but I miss home, and I even miss the studio. So what if we lose a bit of time on tour if we balance it out by making some real magic in there."

"I agree." Shaun clears his throat, looking a little surprised to see everyone's attention quickly fall on him. "I know this is all part of what we signed up for when we started this band, but we've been touring for five months straight now. Maybe taking some extra time to work on the album, really dig into it... maybe that'll do us all some good. We don't have to be going 100 miles an hour *all* the time."

He chuckles, shaking his head.

"And you know what? I miss my fuckin' dog, man. You know my mom had him *say hi* to me over the phone the other night?"

Damien can already feel the mood around the table lightening up. Maybe the tour really had been grinding them harder than he'd thought.

"The saddest part? I *cried* listening to him sniffing the receiver on the other end. And then Phi cried because I was crying."

"Woah, woah, this is character assassination. I was watching Sixteen Candles, it's a tear-jerker!"

"Keep telling yourself that, babe." Shaun leaves a little kiss on her cheek before leaning *way* back in his seat. "Anyway, that's my two cents... if it makes a difference."

"It does, man." Damien looks around the table. "Okay guys, I know this whole thing is my fault–"

"Damien," Johnny sighs. "That's not what we said. Things just got heated last night, that's all."

Damien holds up a hand.

"Just let me say this, and then we can drop it: I shouldn't have let that weasel get into my head, and I want to take full responsibility for that. We're losing out on the grand finale of our tour, and that's on me. I'm gonna do whatever I can to make that right going forward, but for right now, you know what? It's true, we *are* tired; never know if we're gonna wake up jazzed or feeling like we're running near-on empty. So maybe we get an early start in the studio, and if we're lucky we can play some little gig in New York on the side, you know? Make it up to the hometown crowd."

He turns, looking to the only bandmate who's remained mostly silent.

"Johnny, bud, I know you hate the idea of going out on a rough one, I get it, but just think... Hey, you'll get to see Erin two weeks early!"

Johnny blinks, looking like the thought was just hitting him for the first time as he perks up.

"She wants to go house hunting. We've been talking about it a lot because, uh..."

He flushes, stammering a little as Troy nearly chokes on his coffee.

"Wait, I'd know that tone anywhere. You're planning for kids?!"

Johnny and Erin had been together since high school, and had been starting to get pressure from their families to start one of their own, so Damien had been a little worried when Johnny first told him the situation. As he listened to his friend muse about moving to a little place upstate however, it all quickly melted away. This was something Johnny wanted, maybe even something he'd wanted for a long time, and that conviction gave Damien a lot of joy, along with just a little pinch of envy.

"Maybe focus on getting married first, pal. Don't put the cart before the horse." Johnny chuckles nervously as Troy looks him up and down. "Any other secrets you been keeping from us, lover-boy?"

"We're just talking, Troy. It's nothing serious yet. Trust me."

"Good," Troy sighs. "Just trust me when I say you wanna be absolutely prepared. A kid you're not ready for is a *big* adjustment. We had

Madison right when I took you hooligans on and I barely survived that year."

"I don't think that had anything to do with you having a kid," Ophelia fires back. "Pretty sure Bell spiked your blood pressure the second he shook your hand."

"Alright, everyone shut up!" Troy claps his hands. "Talk of Erin and Johnny's potential demon spawn aside, we're all on the same page that this album has to blow everyone away, yes?"

He points at everyone around the table, finally falling on Damien.

"Bell?" Troy asks. "I need your word on this one, kid. The best damn work of your life."

Damien grins.

"You know it, boss."

Ophelia raises her drink.

"To the best damn album of all time, or at least going out with a bang!"

Damien follows suit, glancing around at all the smiling faces.

"Literally *and* figuratively!"

Regardless of how awful it had all felt just minutes ago, they'd managed to rally, to pull back together as if it was all nothing more than a minor inconvenience. And it was true, none of this was anything but a speed bump on the way to their real destination.

For the first time in a long while, Damien Bell is excited to go home.

The bus is parked outside of an old church behind the hotel, and Damien's in nothing but a t-shirt and a pair of ripped up jeans, leaning against the wall and smoking a cigarette while their equipment gets loaded up. It's not exactly the most appropriate attire for the setting, but he didn't think they'd be out here this long.

He's fucking freezing.

He can hear Troy 'directing' the roadies on how to properly store their gear from around the side of the bus. The old man knows damn well they've done this song and dance a thousand times by now, but little moments of control are just how he deals with the stress. It's always been like that, but it's never stopped Johnny from getting on his case about it.

"Stop trying to orchestrate everything, man! You've gotta *relax*!"

Troy gives Johnny a quick shove.

"I'm your goddamn *manager*, what do you think I'm supposed to do?!"

"Maybe you can *manage* the pain in my ass instead, got anything for that?"

"That's my line, you think you can just throw my material back at me?!"

Damien chuckles as he pushes himself off the wall, dropping the cigarette and snuffing it out with his boot and heads toward the church. On the way back up to the hotel room the energy between them all felt lighter than it had in months, and in the face of how dour things had gotten the other night, he wants to ride that high as long as they can.

They were planning on hitting St. Louis tomorrow, and then over the next couple weeks Chicago, Indianapolis, Detroit, Cincinnati and finally Philadelphia. It's a truncated schedule, and everything after Philly had to be cut, but he's spent the day trying to avoid thinking about how wrong it felt. He's been bouncing between wired and nervous the whole time since the disaster that was Kansas City, but now he's trying to focus on the good things: Phoebe's back, and that means things are on track again.

Damien pushes open the heavy doors with both hands as a loud creak reverberates through the old wood of the building.

"Hello?"

He glances around, surprised to find the lights are already on with no one in sight. Carefully, he steps inside, shutting the door behind him.

There's an altar at the front, decorated with flowers and adorned with a large statue of the Virgin Mary. An oversized golden cross hangs at the front, and a stained glass window brings it all together with a beautiful kaleidoscope of ambient light as the sun filters through it. He takes a seat near the back and stares up at the altar, breathing in a familiar scent of must, incense, and beeswax.

Damien grew up Catholic. He was a loyal altar boy all the way up until he was fourteen, then his priorities changed: suddenly he had girls to chase, and big ideas of starting a rock band kicking around in his head. His parents didn't think he was serious about it at first, but to be fair, they didn't really ever think he was serious about much of anything. He liked to talk and fuck around more than he liked to actually hunker down and work, and they knew it. He got shitty grades in math, and science, and history, but then there was English class.

It's where he found and fell in love with poetry.

He never missed a day.

It became a sort of replacement for him, something to devote his time and energy to, in the wake of his mild falling out with faith. By then, Damien hadn't believed in God for quite some time, and now he sometimes wonders if he ever did. What he is sure of, though, is that everything changed after he saw the shape his father was in when he returned from the war.

For years George Bell drank and drank and drank, hiding himself away in his office, never really opening up to his children. The man who came back from the war haunted their house, lingering in doorways and taking his anger out on any wall he could find. Never in front of the kids, not if he could help it, but they always heard it.

It was always like that, infinitely on repeat, until one night Damien and Ava woke up to an explosion of voices coming from their parents' bedroom. He grabbed his sister and the two of them left, hopped right in his Trans Am and headed for the beach. They sat there in the dark for hours listening to music, neither of them saying a word. When they got back to the house they found his father dumping his liquor down the sink.

Damien didn't blame him for any of it, not really. How could you be anything other than what he was, after you'd seen what he must have seen? But understanding isn't always enough, and even after Rosaline Bell put the fear of God and divorce into that man, Damien never really got to know him, as a father or otherwise.

To his credit, though, he hasn't touched a drop since.

Damien digs into his pocket and pulls out his little floppy notebook, his other hand running across the wooden pew. He's been trying to grab ahold of some inspiration again, and Phoebe's return sparked a flood of the stuff. He eyes over some hastily scribbled lyrics from the previous night, smiling to himself. He came up with a vague melody as well, one that he just might be able to shape into something real.

A sudden creak of wood shocks him out of his musing, the door behind him ajar as he turns to find Phoebe backlit in soft greys and some gentle fading sunlight.

"There you are."

He gives her a toothy grin as he tucks his notebook back into his pocket.

"Hiya, babydoll."

Sure it might be the sun, but she's fucking glowing, decked out in the blue dress she picked out back in Portland with his leather jacket on top. Her hair is up in a bit of a bun, held in place with nothing more than a couple of pencils, her notebook in hand as she shuts the door and saunters toward him.

Phoebe Miller has got to be the hottest nerd he's ever seen.

"So, what are you doing here?" She whispers, sliding into the seat next to him. "I mean, it seems wrong. Shouldn't you be burning up or something?"

"Miller! Sliding in with the sick burns!" He laughs. "But no, the big man hasn't decided to cast me into the pit yet. I just come to these places sometimes. Good for thinking."

"About?"

"Well, if you keep looking this cute, all I'll be thinking about is writing more songs about you."

She bumps her shoulder up against his, a little snort escaping as she does.

"Wow, look at you! All it took for you to lose your edge is falling madly in love."

He looks her right in the eyes, placing the notebook in her hand as he presses his lips softly against hers.

"Maybe you softened that edge a little." Damien grins, pulling back and tapping the notebook. "Read it. I wrote it for you after all."

Phoebe glances down at the words scrawled across the page, her eyes flicking quickly back and forth as she reads. He's written songs about women he's loved before, sure, most of the first album is about that, but those songs were all endings. Shockingly, he had never penned one about new beginnings.

Really, he always thought that the beginning wasn't worth writing about. It was all hormones and fireworks anyway, a big show his brain and body were putting on to hook him straight into another person. It was always the crushing finales that he managed to squeeze the most heartfelt angst and anger out of. But it was time for something new.

"You wrote this for me?"

"Along with a few more." He cups her face in his hands. "Believe it or not, half the album is for you."

She giggles and presses her forehead to his; this quiet little moment more exciting than any of his one-night stands.

"I love you."

"I love you too."

He never gets tired of hearing that.

"Just don't tell the rest of the band about all the songs being for you, I promised them they'd get more of a say this time and I'm trying to–"

She cuts him off, her laughter making the first few moments of the kiss a little awkward as their mouths collide, and it's only a few brief moments before the passion's built enough that she's nearly climbing onto his lap.

"They're all waiting for you outside, you know," she whispers, her lips brushing against his. "I promised I'd come and find you."

His hand slides between her legs as he glides his mouth up her neck, the little moan that escapes her making him shiver.

"Well, looks like you found me."

Phoebe's thighs slam shut on his hand before he can get a good grasp, and he's forced to follow her gaze as she slowly turns her head toward the confessional booths. Already, he can see the gears spinning as her tongue slides across her lips.

"There has to be someone here, right?" Her voice is soft, barely above a whisper. "Like a priest, or a janitor, or...?"

"A janitor?" He laughs.

"Well, I don't know. We never went to church when I was a kid. Who cleans these places?"

"Volunteers sometimes, sometimes the priest. Either way, I haven't seen anyone yet, and I've been sitting in here for twenty minutes." Damien runs his fingers along her cheek and down her neck, lightly caressing her skin just above her neckline.

He can feel her chest heaving, and even see her pulse thrumming in the side of her throat, calling to him like a drumbeat. She smells like the most intoxicating combination of leather and cinnamon, with the tiniest hint of tobacco just for him.

"You up for some more experimentation, babydoll?"

Her eyes light up like fireworks in the sky.

"If we get caught, I'm blaming you."

She shivers as he reaches down past her leg, lifting up her dress just the tiniest bit.

"Wouldn't have it any other way, but just so you know, the place was unlocked and open when I got here."

He can feel her straighten at the thought, her body tensing as he runs his hand slowly up her thigh.

"So let's put on a real good show."

Faith

DAMIEN

Damien slides the door to the confessional closed as quietly as he can, taking one last look to make sure there's nobody around. There's a small bench at the back, with just enough space for one person to kneel. It might be the tightest spot they've ever tried anything in, but he's never been a quitter.

Phoebe gazes up at him, those soft pink lips parted as she waits for a command.

"On your knees."

She obeys without question, gazing up at him as a strand of dark hair falls in her eyes. Damien brushes it aside, gliding his hand down her cheek, and resting it just beneath her chin. She looks like a Renaissance painting, fitting enough for the setting, but he's going to reveal the truth of the canvas that sits hidden only a layer or two deeper.

He braces himself on the back wall with both hands as Phoebe slides his pants down past his waist, playfully tugging his cock out from behind his waistband. She starts slowly, swirling her tongue around the tip and keeping her eyes locked on him the entire time. Damien sighs, his stomach swirling with an even mix of anticipation, pleasure, and trepidation, the risk of getting caught top of mind.

Honestly, he'd probably just ask the priest for five more minutes.

"Wrap your lips around it, babydoll."

She bats her eyelashes, taking him in only an inch or so, putting just enough pressure down to make him inadvertently push his hips out ever so slightly. He can feel her reverberating around his cock as she takes him a little further, the light humming sound she's making acting as a little bit of extra stimulation, all while one of her free hands begins to stroke the base.

He rolls his hips, purposefully this time, and forces himself deeper down her throat a little faster than she might have expected, but Phoebe takes it all. Tears start to form in her eyes as she looks up at him, that pitiful expression sending pleasure shooting up his spine. He begins to find his rhythm, pumping his hips slowly, careful not to choke her.

Yet.

"You were made for me, weren't you? You filthy fucking girl."

Her sinful moans begin to fill the space between them and Damien grins, sliding one hand down to grip her hair tight as he starts to move faster. He can feel the tip of his cock hit the back of her throat with each thrust, again and again and again. He can feel that delicious tension building at the base of his spine, and suddenly he wants to test some of her limits. He only gives her the slightest warning, giving her a light little tug on her hair before pushing her head straight down on him. She chokes and grunts, sucking in a sharp breath through her nose as his cock slides all the way down her throat. He only holds it there for a couple seconds before he pulls out, but the brief moment of gagging struggle riles him up even further. He lets her rest, watching with glee as she coughs and gasps for breath, before he grabs his cock and rubs it against her mouth, smearing her lipstick.

"I knew you could take it, what a good girl."

She sticks out her tongue, her mouth open wide and her eyes are glazed over like she's already drunk on him. There's a soft rustle of clothing and she shifts her body until she's straddling his boot, her legs wrapping around him.

"What are you doing?" He asks.

She giggles, both hands on his thighs as she begins to grind her pussy against his boot. Her mouth wraps around him again and he groans, looking down at her. She's a chaotic mess of smeared lipstick and wild hair.

A pleasurable buzz gathers in the back of his head as she picks up the pace. Her warm mouth glides up and down his shaft as his fingernails dig into the wall behind her, but he can't keep himself from smirking as the moans start to leak out of her.

"That's my girl. I want that boot soaked."

His abs tighten and he shivers, trying to stave off his climax for as long as he can. He can feel her body moving faster, rutting against the boot like an animal as she claws at his jeans. The confessional is filled with a chorus of slightly muffled moans and whimpers that neither of them have the strength to hold back.

Phoebe taps on his thigh, the signal he gave her to tell him to ease up the first time they took things a little rougher, and he pulls out of her mouth, his cock dripping with saliva as she presses her forehead into his leg. She tips her head up at him, lips parted and her eyes rolling back as she comes. Even if she was completely silent he could tell by how her face is twisted up in ecstasy.

"I'm gonna fuck you now."

There's only the briefest of pauses before she's on her feet, with Damien not far behind, slipping off his belt before quickly looping it around her wrists.

"Just like Vegas," she whispers.

"Well, I said we'd put on a show, didn't I? Can't keep the big man waiting."

"You really are a man of your word."

He presses his lips to hers, pulling her into a tight embrace she'd have no hope of escaping, biting down just enough to almost break skin before grasping her arms and turning her around.

"Climb on the bench, arms above your head."

Damien digs into his pocket, fumbling around for a moment but finding nothing. He frowns and tries the other pocket.

Empty.

"Shit."

Phoebe glances back at him.

"What's wrong?"

"No condoms."

As she stares back at him, he can feel a shiver run down his spine. There's a fire behind her eyes, the kind he's sure he's seen before, and he's certain he knows exactly what she's thinking.

"No?" Damien asks.

"I want to feel all of you."

"Yeah?" He chuckles. "Maybe an awkward fuckin' time to ask, but you're still on birth control?"

"Uh-huh, and I've been tested." She doesn't seem to find this awkward, in fact it seems to be turning her on. His heart beat picks up a little and he quirks a brow.

"Me too. You wanna do this?"

Damien hasn't been this nervous to have sex in a while; he's had sex without a condom before, but the last time was at least a year ago. Something about the idea makes him want her even more.

Phoebe arches her back, her supple ass sticking straight out at him.

"Fuck me already, Bell."

He exhales and takes a step forward, the floorboards straining beneath his weight as he grasps her hips. Phoebe lets out a little hum of anticipation, her arms still above her head. Damien slides his hands between her legs, caressing her warm thighs. She shivers, goosebumps running up her arms as the hairs stand on end. If there is a God, he's on Damien's side today.

He pulls down her panties and lowers himself to his knees, sliding his tongue inside her. He begins licking her slowly, flicking his tongue upward, aiming for the spot that always makes her scream.

The more she writhes against him, the harder he gets. He wants her pussy to feel like a reward; when he finally slams his cock inside her, he wants to be aching.

He slides two fingers into her dripping cunt, teasing her as he savors every sound that drips from her lips. Only a minute in and he's already shaking with anticipation, his mouth dry and his heart pounding like a drum.

Little beads of condensation drip down the wall of the confessional as Phoebe holds her hands in front of her, the belt binding them together as if in prayer. Damien grins, watching her struggle a little to keep her balance as she looks back at him.

"Are you gonna fuck me, or not?"

"I just wanna make sure you're ready for this."

"I can take it."

Damien gets to his feet, spitting on his palm in preparation. He wraps his hand around his cock, savoring the last few moments of that ache he's been craving before pushing the tip inside her.

"Please," she begs.

She's bent over on her knees, her forehead pressed down onto her bound wrists. The sight of her like this is making his heart race.

"Again," he growls.

"Please, sir."

Her voice is quaking, she sounds like she could shatter at any moment.

Finally, he allows himself the thrill of pushing all the way inside of her, with no barriers between them. He can feel *everything*, each and every muscle twitch, the sensation that much more intense as she clenches around him.

Damien can't help but groan as Phoebe rocks her hips back and forth, her breath coming out in a shudder as he smacks her ass in response. The two of them take it slow at first, the languid rhythm between them growing more desperate as sinful sounds fill up the confessional. Her pussy flutters, another quivering moan spilling from her lips, and he can tell she's right on the fucking edge.

Damien reaches out and grabs her hair, tugging her close and brushing his lips against her ear.

"I won't come until you do, babydoll."

His words turn her into an animal as he ratchets up the intensity, her moans becoming more and more desperate by the second. The buzzing sensation in his spine returns, quickly turning to a heavy warmth that engulfs him like a wildfire as skin slaps against skin.

"Good girl." He smacks her ass again, the sharp sound turning him on even more. "You're close, aren't you?"

She laughs, craning her neck and listening for a sign someone had heard them.

"I thought we were supposed to be quiet."

"All I said was someone might catch us, you were the one who assumed that's not something I want."

She shudders and moans beneath him as Damien takes full control, setting a brutal and relentless pace. He fucks her right through her first climax, shivering as she pulses around him, but already he can feel her clenching again. He wants to drink everything in, the way she smells, the texture of her skin… all of it. His hands map every curve of her body. She's his constant. His home.

His own orgasm comes quickly, too overwhelming to subdue, washing over him as he clenches his jaw. His head rocks back and he lets out gentle grunts as he fills her up, legs wobbling like jelly, threatening to collapse as his hips rut against hers. Everything feels drawn out into eternity, the warmth radiating through him over and over and over again, until he finally collapses on top of her, nothing left for him to give.

The aftershocks of his climax linger in the tips of his fingers and toes, their moans fading away as all that's left between them is breath rushing like water. He pulls his cock out of her and tucks it back into his jeans, propping himself up against the wall as he stares down at his girl.

"Let's get this belt off of you before my sense of shame comes back."

"When have you ever had any shame?"

Damien snickers as he gently pulls the belt off of her wrists, and she's on him in a second, her arms winding around the back of his neck and her eyes locked right on to his.

"There's nobody else I'd rather commit heresy with."

"Well, that's real hot, sweets, but we should probably get the fuck outta here."

He takes her hand and slowly slides open the door to the confession booth, poking his head out.

"Coast's clear."

They stifle giggles as they run for the exit and push the church doors open to breathe in fresh air. The relief is short-lived when Damien spots someone he doesn't recognize chatting with the rest of the band near the back of the bus. Janis is smoking a cigarette nearby while Troy is pacing around with his big cellular phone, occasionally staring at it like it owes him money.

"You two!" He barks, storming straight over the second they catch his eye. "Where have you been?!"

"Uh…" Damien's eyes volley back and forth between Troy and the stranger, whose attention veers away from the rest of the band, right onto them.

Damien squeezes Phoebe's hand, but Troy intercepts any potential questions, cutting the man off before he can speak.

"Sorry kid, gotta get moving. No more questions."

The man's eyes land on their linked fingers.

"I just want to ask—"

"We'll be sure to send a fruit basket to the Kansas City Times in lieu of a comment, alright?"

Troy ushers them quickly past the journalist toward the bus, doing his best to avoid a scene.

"I think it's happening, Pheebs." Damien kisses her temple. "You ready?"

"Ready if you are."

"Hurry up, you two! Before that big vein in Troy's forehead finally pops!" Janis calls from the door to the bus.

"I heard that, Kaneko!" Troy bellows.

Three more men with cameras are lingering nearby, just far enough to be considered a nuisance to Troy and the roadies. For a moment, Damien contemplates dropping Phoebe's hand. But they've come too far to chicken out now.

"Hey, Damien!" One of the men shouts. "Is this the mystery woman we've been hearing about?"

"What's your name, sweetheart?" Another one calls, snapping off a picture of the two of them.

"Are you two dating?"

A small, mischievous smile sneaks across Phoebe's face.

Damien ignores the questions being lobbed at them, pulling her in for a kiss instead. It reminds him of back in Portland, when they kissed for the first time in public, full of electricity and nerves. Phoebe falls into his arms, camera shutters going off rapidly as the men shout things he can barely make out. He doesn't care. He's more in love than he's ever been, and the entire fucking world is going to know it.

He breaks the kiss and brushes her lower lip with his thumb, only faintly aware of Troy cursing in the background.

"That wasn't so bad, huh?"

"I think *someone's* gonna need a refill on his blood pressure medication," Phoebe giggles.

"He'll get over it."

What a Feeling

PHOEBE

SOHO, NYC, TWO WEEKS LATER

"Damien, is the blindfold necessary?"

He had insisted she wear it, even back when they first got in the car, and it probably caused some raised eyebrows. Now, after a bit of a drive, he was leading her up a set of stairs, holding both of her hands.

The first couple days back in the city had been a little tense, everyone waiting to see exactly how quickly the news took off. The Kansas City Times was the first to announce their relationship - just a small line underneath a picture.

DAMIEN BELL AND HIS MYSTERY WOMAN: WHAT WE KNOW SO FAR.

After that, it spread like wildfire.

The bubble had burst. The photographer probably made a shitload of money selling the photo to other papers, because it accompanied each and every new headline. Surprisingly, so far there'd been no word about the incident with Chris.

Her sneaker catches on one of the steps and her stomach lurches, like someone's pulling the rug out from under her.

"Jesus! Careful, babydoll."

His arms are around her in a heartbeat, her panic bubbling into a relieved giggle.

"You're supposed to be guiding me!"

"I am! You just suck at this, *Miller.*"

"Well, it's hard when I can't fucking see, *Bell.*"

Damien grips her tight, helping her up each step.

"Look, it's a big surprise. I'm pulling out all the stops."

"Ooh, expensive wine?"

"I've got plenty of that," Damien replies, pulling her close as she hears a door creak open. "This is something better."

She snorts.

"A *massive* bottle of *really* expensive wine?"

This time he manages to stay silent.

"Just tell me!"

"Fuck no, this is so much more fun. I made a couple of calls while we were on the road."

Her stomach is all butterflies as he ushers her inside.

She can hear the door shut behind her, the smell of fresh paint immediately heavy in the air. A pair of strong hands turn her to the left, each step forward adding more and more excitement to the moment. There are a few twists and turns, little creaks of the floorboards and minor bumps against a wall here and there.

She chuckles as Damien keeps a firm hold on her.

"This isn't a surprise party, is it?"

"I know you hate them, so no, but it is birthday-adjacent. You have to promise not to freak out."

"What am I freaking out about?" Phoebe asks. "Are you taking me to your secret sex dungeon?"

"You'll just have to find out, sweets."

Phoebe giggles, warmth creeping up cheeks as anticipation builds. She can feel one of Damien's arms wrap around her waist while the other begins to tug at the knot of her blindfold.

"You're gonna love this. I built it just for you."

The blindfold tumbles to the ground as her eyes adjust to the light.

The room is *gorgeous* with a big floral mural painted on the wall. The colors are bright and vibrant, making the space feel modern yet cozy.

She looks around the room, her eyes quickly falling on a small desk tucked into a corner with a brand new typewriter.

Damien kisses her temple and proceeds to give her a little guided tour, gesturing at everything she's already seen.

"There's a bookshelf, a record player, some plants..."

But the best part is the framed articles hanging above the desk, her favorite album reviews she wrote for Titanium.

He really did keep every copy.

Phoebe knew Damien was prone to dramatic gestures, but this is the sweetest thing anyone's ever done for her. She can already see herself perched at that desk, writing while she sips her coffee.

"It's quiet, you've got a great view of the yard." He gestures out to a beautiful little overgrown garden with trees and a little cobblestone path. Excitement sparks up in his eyes as he rushes for the desk, pulling out a brand new Walkman from the drawer. "I got Ava to put the new Queen tape in there for you."

She laughs, one hand covering her mouth as Damien continues, growing more and more excited by the second. It's almost as much fun to watch him as it is to take in the room.

"The door even locks— hell, you can lock *me* out if I bug you! Or whatever, nevermind that." He wrings his hands, exhaling. "What else... uh... the books were all in my room taking up space, so if you don't want them in here, I can take 'em back. But I tried to pick stuff I thought you'd like."

The shelves are filled with poetry, philosophy, and rock 'n' roll. She recognizes some of the books– Chaucer, Nietzsche, Camus– he's got good taste.

Phoebe shakes her head.

"They're perfect here."

"Okay," he sighs happily. "Okay, great. Well, we've got a rehearsal space right below you, but don't worry, Shaun and I soundproofed it so you won't be able to hear anything while you're working."

"Damien, this is *so* much."

"Too much?"

He looks panicked, and she shakes her head, a tear spilling down her cheek. He wipes it away with the pad of his thumb.

"When did you find the time to do this?"

"I made a couple of calls while we were on the road. It wasn't hard. Ava's been itching to paint something on this wall. Said it looked hideous and wanted to spruce it up. This is an old office that I never use, and I remembered you said your apartment was really small and noisy."

"I did, and... It really is."

"And so I thought, well, you deserve somewhere you can do your thing without any distractions."

"This is so sweet," she flings her arms around him for a kiss, her lips brushing against his lightly stubbled cheek.

"Happy birthday, Pheebs."

A small jingling sound causes both of them to look toward the door. It takes her a moment, but before long Phoebe spots a beautiful white cat with bright blue eyes and a little pink nose peeking past the door frame.

"Maverick!" Damien crouches down and drums his hands on the floor, glancing back up at Phoebe. "She's deaf, so if you wanna call her, you have to do this. C'mere, sweetheart."

Maverick lets out a little trill before she trots toward him, her tail held high in the air. Damien scoops her up and peppers her face with kisses. There's nothing sweeter than seeing a grown man cuddling a tiny cat.

"You have to be nice to Phoebe." He gives her another kiss. "No peeing on her stuff— oh, uh... Maverick likes to sleep in this office, so if she's passed out and you want her to move, you just blow real gentle on her face and she'll wake up. She'll be pissed and swat at you, but she's only ever a dick for like ten seconds."

"I'm sure she'll be great."

Phoebe smiles, scratching beneath Maverick's chin.

"You wanna see the rest of the place?"

"Yeah, that'd be great."

"Cool, well next stop's the kitchen. I was thinking I'd make steak for dinner," he leads Phoebe out of the office and down the hall, Maverick still cradled in his arms.

"You cook?"

"My mom taught me. She does these elaborate spreads at Thanksgiving and Christmas— shit's crazy. There's a lot of yelling in the kitchen. It's my dad's fault, really. Every year, we tell him not to help, and every year, he's got his fuckin' nose in my ma's business."

Phoebe chuckles. She can practically feel the pure chaos of the Bell household.

"Sounds like you guys have fun."

He shrugs as he leads her down the hall.

"Sometimes."

Damien sets Maverick down on the floor as they reach the kitchen, giving Phoebe a moment to take in her new surroundings. She struggles not to let out an audible gasp. This room is the size of her entire apartment.

Teal walls make up a perfect backdrop to the dark granite countertops, brand new chrome appliances, and copper pots and pans hanging from a rack above the kitchen island. There are even more plants perched on the windowsill, adding some extra life to the surroundings.

"Holy shit..." She spins around, not knowing where to look. "You know, my kitchen is about half the size of a closet. Fuck, I barely have a hotplate."

"Well, if you like to cook, you can use any of this whenever you want." He pauses, pointing to something tucked below the counter. "There's even a wine fridge! You're welcome to anything in there."

Phoebe bites her lip.

"Mister Bell, it seems like you're trying to entice me."

"Oh? How's that?"

"An office with a view, this gorgeous kitchen... who knows what else could be hiding around the next corner?"

Damien wraps his arms around her waist.

"Babydoll, you can stay here any time you want for as long as you like." He pauses, clearly feeling a little self-conscious for a moment. "And I can stay at your place too, of course. If you want."

She grins.

"Yeah? You wanna hang out in a broom closet?"

"I'd hang out anywhere with you." He brushes his nose softly against hers. "C'mon, I'll show you the rest of the place."

She slips her hand in his and Damien takes her on a whirlwind tour around the apartment, from the rehearsal space that's full of Revolver posters, merchandise, and nostalgia, back through the living room, and finally ending up at a hallway, a door on either side.

"That's the guest bedroom down there," he gestures to the further one before heading to the other. He pauses dramatically, his hand on the doorknob. "But *this*... is the main attraction."

Phoebe sighs, placing her hand on her hip.

"Is that what you tell all the girls?"

He leans forward, a big grin on his face.

"Well, when I do, I'm usually talking about my dick."

She smacks him in the gut and Damien feigns doubling over, groaning loudly as she rolls her eyes.

"You're such an ass."

He cackles, scooping her up and carrying her into his bedroom in a single motion. Phoebe's jaw drops as she looks around. She didn't know what to expect, but whatever it was, it wasn't anything like this.

Her attention is immediately drawn to a big four poster bed with black silk pillows and a plush navy duvet. The surrounding walls are a soft cream color adorned with Revolver's gold record and flanked by framed photographs of the city. At the back of the room is an oak dresser littered with bottles of cologne and two jewelry boxes, along with polaroids of the band and other various people taped to the edge of an oval mirror.

He turns to her with a big smile on his face.

"I wanna show you the best part."

Damien leads her to a walk-in closet and opens it up. On the back wall are paddles, blindfolds, floggers, leather cuffs, and the same soft silk rope that he used on her during the tour. A while ago she'd be shocked, but she's come to expect things like this from him.

"These are for me?"

He smiles.

"Well, I've had 'em for a while, but they *can* be part of your second birthday present." He turns to her. "There's a BDSM club in the Meat-packing District–"

Phoebe holds back a snicker. It's a little on the nose.

"Yeah, I know, hilarious. Anyway, it's called The Vault because it's...

well, a vault that existed before the Civil War— at least, that's what I've been told. It's got cool people, it's a little grungy, but I kinda like it."

"You've been there with someone?"

"By myself," Damien confesses with a chuckle, rubbing the back of his neck. "Remember that dominatrix I met in Paris? She told me about it. Said I should go and experience the scene for myself. I was too chickenshit to try anything, but I was curious. I mostly just watched, talked to a few people, got a handjob... but I've always wanted to take someone there."

He stops suddenly, and she can tell he's worried that he's gone too far too quickly.

"You don't have to, it's just an idea—"

"I want to." She places a soft kiss on the tip of his nose. "I'd love to."

Damien sighs, wrapping his arms around her.

"I was thinking maybe dinner with the gang first, and then we can head over."

She can't even picture the club, having no context for anything like it, her mind only conjuring an empty room; being tied up inside, with Damien in total control.

"So, what exactly do people do there?"

He bites his lip. He's getting off on this.

"You know how you like the idea of getting caught?"

She nods, her cheeks burning as her thoughts wander back to the confession booth, the supply closet, and the bus. Anyone could have caught them.

"There's a place for people with an exhibitionist streak." His fingertips play with the button on her jeans. "Do you think you'd like that?"

The idea of everyone watching him devour her, fuck her, make her scream out his name... she shivers at the thought, sliding her hands underneath his shirt.

"Yes I–" She smiles to herself, meeting his eyes with her own mischievous gaze. "Yes, I think I would sir."

She can feel his cock against her thigh as she presses up against him.

"Good girl," Damien whispers. "You won't have to keep those pretty moans to yourself when we're there."

She smiles, closing her eyes as he sucks a hickey onto her neck, goosebumps prickling down her spine.

"Can I show you what I wanna use on you?"
Her breath is heavy as she presses her hand against his chest.
"Oh, is this the end of the tour?"
Damien pops the button on her jeans.
"Babydoll, we just got to the best part."

PHOEBE

"Strip down to your panties."

She shivers under the weight of his words as Damien disappears into the closet, grabbing a pair of thick leather handcuffs off the back wall. She slowly peels off her t-shirt, tossing it onto the ground, along with her bra.

Damien saunters toward her, a big smile on his face as he playfully twirls the cuffs around his finger. Phoebe can't get her jeans off fast enough. She lunges for him, grabbing his face with both hands as their mouths collide.

His kiss hits her like a car crash and she moans as he nips at her bottom lip before sucking on it gently. Phoebe fumbles with the buttons on his jeans, whimpering in frustration when they won't give. Damien chuckles against her mouth, quickly taking over and shedding them within seconds.

They only break the kiss so that he can strip off his t-shirt. The gentle jingling sound of his bangles makes her smile reflexively. She loves that sound.

"I'm gonna fuck you from behind while you wear these." He leans in and presses a kiss to her cheek. "But first you're gonna ride my face like a good girl. Couldn't stop thinking about it after our little phone session."

He's staring her down like a starved animal. A warm tingle cascades down her spine like a waterfall, starting all the way at the top of her head and ending at the tips of her toes.

"With my panties on?"

Damien grabs her ass, squeezing tightly before he smacks it.

"Yep."

Within seconds, he's leading her toward the bed, getting on first and helping her up. She nearly falls and they both giggle as Damien kisses her.

"It's the front steps all over again," he murmurs.

"Your fault both times."

He pulls her toward him and she straddles his hips.

"I'll make it up to you," he rumbles, tapping her thigh. "C'mere. I'm gonna make you scream for me."

His words light up her body, her nipples so hard they ache as Damien grasps her waist, helping her shimmy upward until she's hovering over his face.

His lips ghost along her skin.

"Hands on the headboard."

Heart in her throat, she does as she's told, gripping the wood tightly. His hands are strong, holding her in place.

"I told you to *sit*," he growls as he yanks her right down on top of his mouth.

Phoebe doesn't even care that he's talking to her like she's a fucking pet. That's exactly what she wants to be.

He teases her with his tongue, flicking her clit through the lace of her panties while forcing her to grind down harder. Tiny beads of sweat pop up on her forehead as Damien growls like a fucking beast below her. His fingernails sink into her ass as he guides her hips, his tongue circling her aching bud.

Phoebe throws her head back, releasing one hand from the headboard as she cups one of her breasts, trying to recreate the feeling of Damien biting down. Her voice is hoarse and ragged as grunts and moans spill out. Her eyes roll back, her pussy getting wetter by the second. This friction is fucking everything right now, and she's aching for him.

"Damien!" She cries. "More! Fuck, please!"

She hears and feels fabric ripping. How many pairs of underwear has this man destroyed at this point? She was keeping a tally in her notebook, but that stopped a few weeks ago. It doesn't matter anymore. The sound of that sharp rip just means something really fucking delicious is coming.

His tongue slides inside of her cunt, fucking her slowly while his nose provides the perfect amount of friction for her clit. Phoebe gasps at the new angle and sensation, but soon, the pleasure overwhelms her and she's back to gripping the headboard for dear life. Damien's sultry moans fill the room and spurn her on, her whole body consumed with desire. She can hear him stroking himself; feeling his tongue deep inside of her as her hips rock back and forth with ferocity.

He wanted to be smothered? He might just get it today.

"Just like that." Damien Bell likes to be worshiped onstage, she's seen the spark in his eyes when she looks at him like he's a god, but it's a different reaction entirely when she takes charge. "You're being such a good boy."

Damien lets out a groan, slapping her ass hard with one hand.

"You like that?" She purrs. "You want me to come for you?"

She makes sure there's a little mocking edge to her tone, mimicking the way he taunts her. The hand that struck her ass is now gripping hard enough to leave a bruise. Phoebe smiles to herself and picks up the pace, her moans filling the room like a symphony as the pressure on her clit gets more intense. Her fingers and toes tingle, the muscles in her legs ache from rocking back and forth, but all she's focused on is how good his tongue feels.

And then there's an explosion that starts deep inside of her, consuming her. She sees fireworks behind her eyes and her head drops, moving through the pleasure that's filling her veins with the most exquisite warmth, like being pleasantly drunk on a sunny beach. She can feel the sweat gathering on her skin, a small bead trickling down her spine despite the chill in the room.

When she closes her eyes, all she sees is him.

All she feels is him.

All she needs is him.

He guides her through her climax until the world comes back into focus, panting as he lifts her off of him. He's covered in her slick with a big smile on his face. Phoebe's breath is ragged, but she can't stop herself from smiling back.

"You wanna keep going?" He asks.

"You didn't get those handcuffs for nothing, right?"

"You have no idea how much I love you," he whispers.

His eyes soften as the words tumble from his lips. It still feels so new to hear those three little words, ones that Phoebe had only ever received from a handful of people in her entire life.

"I have a bit of an idea," she whispers warmly, scooping up the cuffs and handing them over. "Now, how do you wanna tie me up this time?"

He slips behind her and she feels his lips on the back of her neck.

"On your stomach, hands behind your back."

Without saying another word, Phoebe slides onto her belly and hears the soft jingle of the handcuffs as Damien gently pins her hands behind her back, securing the cuffs. Her cheek is pressed against the soft cotton sheets and he leans over.

"What do you say if you want me to stop?"

"Daisy," she whispers.

Damien presses a kiss against her cheek.

"That's my girl."

She's practically melting into the mattress as she waits, Damien leaning over to the nightstand and grabbing a small bottle of lube.

He grins as Phoebe arches a brow.

"Don't worry, I'll talk you through it."

She feels the bed shift as his weight sinks into it. Rough palms glide up and down the backs of her thighs before he pushes her legs further apart, dragging the tip of his cock through the wet lips of her cunt. Phoebe shudders and her toes dig into the mattress, her back arching a little in response. He smacks her ass hard, his bangles gently clinking together.

"Eager, aren't you?"

"I need you," she begs.

She's shivering in anticipation as Damien lets out a low growl.

"You're so wet. I could slide right in and fuck you nice and slow. Until you're begging for more." He slides the tip of his cock inside of her and Phoebe gasps.

"Fuck," he groans, pushing her further into the mattress.

Her mouth curls into a smile, but cruelly, he pulls out and she's rewarded only with another harsh smack against her ass.

"I said I *could* slide right in. I didn't say I would. I wanna take my time with you. Now, are you going to be a good girl?"

There's something a little more primal about him today, the texture of his voice is rough with a slightly more degrading edge than usual, like he's just barely trying to keep himself under control. She wants to see just how far he can take it.

"I like when you talk to me like that," she whispers.

"Yeah?" He asks. "What else do you like, babydoll?"

Phoebe swallows, desperately thinking of a way to coax it out of him.

"What am I?"

"What?"

She grits her teeth, her cheeks burning. She doesn't know where the desire comes from, but she's following it; he taught her that. Damien hums as he gently runs his hand over her ass, soothing the red welt he just made.

"What do you think of me?"

"I think you're beau–"

"No. Degrade me," she demands.

She feels dirty even asking for it, but when his hand slides up her lower back, Phoebe feels cared for, like she could break a thousand times over and he'd be right here to pick up the pieces.

"Call me a slut."

"Is that what you want?"

"Only from you."

He pushes himself upright and Phoebe hears a soft snapping sound, like someone opening a bottle cap. And then there's a small pool of lubricant in the palm of her hand, Damien smearing it around. She wiggles her body and he slaps her ass again. Phoebe groans and huffs as he laughs, the sound sending a trail of goosebumps rushing down her spine.

"Greedy little thing," He purrs.

"Please, sir."

"I want you to indulge me for a second. Been thinking about doing this to you since the first day I saw you."

His cock slides through her hands and she instantly wraps her fingers around it, listening to his sinful moan that coats her body like honey. Phoebe can't see him, still pressed into the mattress, but she can feel him pulsing, every vein and ridge gliding against her skin, and she wants more. His hands grip her hips, and she's completely at his mercy.

"You thought about this the day we met?" She rasps.

"Uh-huh. Thought about a lotta things," he grunts. "What you'd look like tied to my bed, what my hand would look like around your throat, what you sounded like when you begged me to fuck you. And after you called me a condescending piece of shit, I couldn't stop thinking about what you'd look like with my cock down your throat."

She whimpers, skin ablaze, as he chuckles.

"The harder you pushed back, the more I wanted to discipline you."

Her pussy is aching to be filled, and the desire spreads through her body like wildfire. Damien's a little different on his own turf. Still gentle, but there's more of an edge to him; a comfort that this is his space.

Then he pulls away, leaving her hands empty for a moment before she feels his cock pressed up against her wet pussy. She expects teasing, but instead, he pushes it inside of her at an agonizingly slow pace. He's torturing her on purpose, going inch by inch as her pussy tries to clench around him.

"This is what you wanted, right? Isn't this what you *begged* me for?"

The sharp sting of him filling her quickly turns to pleasure and she cries out.

"You can take it. Be a good little slut for me, babydoll."

Hearing the degradation as he bottoms out causes her brain to short circuit, and she lets out another strangled moan. Damien grasps her bound wrists and thrusts slowly, rocking her body like she's being pushed by a wave.

"You feel so good," he rasps. "Never fucked a pussy this wet."

He grabs her hair with one hand, forcing her back to bow. She's completely at his mercy, each stroke deeper and more intense than the last. He slips the hand that's holding her wrists down so that their fingers can interlock in a brief moment of tenderness.

Her nerves are frayed wires, crackling and bursting with pleasure as he hits *that* spot every single fucking time. The new angle already had her feeling like her muscles are made of jelly, but Damien's thrusts continue to speed up, driving himself harder and faster inside of her until she's quaking around him.

Her stomach tightens as she tries to prolong the pleasure; to stay right on the razor's edge of her climax. The sound of the headboard beating against the wall in a rough and manic rhythm makes her smile, her eyelids fluttering.

"Oh fuck," he moans. "Fuckfuckfuck— I can't—"

He cuts himself off, fully giving in to his desires and slamming into her so hard that she can almost feel his cock in her guts.

It's perfect.

Damien gives her hair one last yank, and she's coming so hard that her fists clench, holding onto his hand for dear life.

With a few more rough thrusts, he's coming, practically singing her name like a hymn. Phoebe's mouth drops open as his final push against her G-spot sends her toppling over the edge a second time. This climax is softer, like being wrapped in a warm blanket, but it doesn't stop her toes from curling as Damien fills her to the brim.

The sound of panting breath replaces their wanton moans and pleas for pleasure as the bed stops moving. Damien releases her hair, running his fingers through it as he continues to move his hips. The aftershocks of their climax ripple through the two of them, making them giddy. They stay like that for a while before he finally pulls out of her and unlocks the cuffs.

Phoebe rolls onto her back and he's already right there, crawling on top of her and peppering her face with kisses before he wraps her in a warm hug. She feels so safe with him.

"Fuck, that was amazing."

"Is that what you want to do to me at that club?" She asks, nuzzling into his chest.

"That and so much more." He looks down at her. "If you're into it."

"Anywhere you lead, I'm right behind you."

Two of Hearts

DAMIEN

TWO DAYS LATER

"I didn't know you could wake up before 11:00am."

Damien hands Phoebe a steaming cup of bodega coffee in a little blue and white Anthora cup.

"I'll have you know, I've gotten up before 11:00 in the past. On two occasions, in fact."

"The Portland Morning Show?"

"Good memory!" Damien nods, sipping his coffee as he leads her out of the shop. "But let's not forget the far more important example: that time Johnny ran into our hotel room naked."

Her face scrunches up in confusion for a moment before smoothing out into a smile.

"No revisionism, Bell. You had a wrestling match, remember? *You* were naked, he had clothes on."

"Right, right. See, this is why I need that beauty sleep, I'm useless without it! It helps get the creative juices flowing, helps with recall... Really, I'm never any good first thing in the morning," he leans in and gives her a quick peck on the cheek. "Except at sex, of course."

"I'll be sure to include that in the article."

"Put it right at the top. Bold font."

She snorts as Damien slips his hand into the back pocket of her jeans, gently squeezing her ass. He's been starved for real public displays of affection since they started dating. It's been hell not being able to reach for her hand, to kiss her in public; even holding her gaze for a little too long felt like it was off the table.

But not anymore.

"So, are you ready for today?" She asks, pulling him out of his little daydream.

"I think so," Damien murmurs.

They've got a full day in the studio lined up, their first since the tour started, and that's not to mention the show tonight. Troy used every connection he could to secure the venue, sliding them in as a secret act. The place was already set to be packed, and they all agreed it'd be a great spot to debut a few of their new songs, generate some buzz for the album, and most of all to offset the negative press. More than that, though, Damien knew it'd be a great place to show off some of the songs he wrote just for her.

"Hey," Phoebe's voice snaps him back to the present. "What are you thinking about all the way up there?"

He inhales deeply, taking in the crisp fall air that's quickly turning to winter.

"Nothing really," he grins. "Just how much I love you."

Her cheeks dust pink, but she doesn't shy away from it at all. It's such a change from just a month or two ago when they could barely talk to each other, and that's not the only difference. Phoebe's look might shock anyone who hadn't seen her since her time away from the city, decked out in an old Revolver t-shirt she found tucked in the back of his closet, a pair of ripped up black jeans, with her long dark hair completely loose and free, flowing down her back.

"You're such a sap, Bell."

Everyday she seems more and more like a rockstar's girlfriend.

"I try."

As they turn the corner the recording studio emerges from the surrounding buildings, taking up a good chunk of the block. Damien's heart beats a little faster at the sight, the anticipation beginning to gnaw at the back of his neck the moment it comes into view. The risk of being a one-hit-wonder looms over Revolver like a bloated cloud, and with the blunder back in Kansas they can't just settle for good. They need whatever comes next to be a revelation.

Damien remembers *wanting* the first album to be a hit, but he didn't really expect it. None of them did, save maybe for Shaun with his ear for the craft. Years in this industry, playing shows and selling records for a buck a piece at dingy bars, all of it taught them that building a loyal fan base was the most important thing, even more than catching lightning in a bottle. Miraculously, they managed to do both. But it would be a lie to say it was all them, or even that it was luck. When he thinks about it, Damien can't help but be a little annoyed by how much of what they have is thanks to their producer.

"Hey, so I feel like I need to prep you for Liam," he announces as they close in on the entrance. "He can be a little..."

"Intense?"

"Something like that, yeah. He's very dramatic, theatrical, knows what he likes and *really* knows what he doesn't."

Phoebe drains her coffee before tossing the empty cup into a nearby trash can.

"Are you saying I'm going to be meeting an older, wiser version of you? Oh god, how much do the two of you butt heads when you're in the studio?"

Damien snorts.

"Butt heads? That's one way of putting it."

Yelling and wild gesturing had basically been their sole form of communication, but it was primarily well intentioned enough. There were a couple times when they were recording the first album, though, that the two got into some real screaming matches.

Liam made it clear from moment-one that he required a level of discipline in the studio that Damien simply didn't have when he started out. It was all early mornings, late nights, and take after take after take. It was exhausting, and there were times when each and every member of the band wanted to quit, but Liam provided what he promised: results. There's a reason why he got six chart-topping albums under his belt in less than ten years.

Damien slips his hand out of her pocket and holds the door for Phoebe, who flashes him a flirtatious little smile as she brushes past.

Revolver's gold record hangs on the wall, along with dozens of other artists who record at the label. As he walks in behind her, he's surprised how much like home the place feels.

Erin sits up at the front desk, chatting on the phone and popping her gum from time to time. She's the first line of defense against people who wander in looking to crash a recording session, for some signatures, or just the latest gossip on one of the artists. Lately though, she's been doing double-duty as Liam's assistant, a job which she's made *extremely* clear she prefers. Her face lights up as the two of them catch her eye, and she quickly raises her hand, nodding furiously to no one in particular and scribbling on a Post-It before slamming the phone down.

"You're heeeere!" She squeals, running up and practically slamming into Damien before reaching and pulling Phoebe in for a big group-hug.

"Well hello to you too, Erin." He smirks. "Are the others here yet?"

"Yep, beat you to it. Early birds, the lot of them. Shaun said he wanted to get started on laying down some guitar tracks, Ophelia needed to check on her equipment, and Johnny..." She blushes. "Well, everyone's just really excited."

Suddenly, a look of realization creeps across her face and she steps back, glancing between the two of them for a moment.

"Oh! But I've seen the papers, the news about you two– congratulations! How does it feel to finally be in everyone's face?"

"A little different," Phoebe admits. "We have to thank you and Johnny for paving the way for us. Otherwise, I don't think we'd have the guts."

"Hey, I heard what you did. Flying back to New York for a big confrontation? That's what takes guts! I have to assume it paid off too, because..." She gestures broadly in their general direction. "Well, because of all this! I'm just so happy for you!"

Damien links his pinky finger with Phoebe's just to watch her cheeks dust pink for a second time.

"So, can we give you a tour? We've got a little bit of time before you have to be in the studio, although Liam wants to talk to you at some point, D."

He's already steeling himself. Damien knows having her here will be a good thing, for productivity, inspiration, all of it, but he still has to convince Liam. It's his house, after all.

"There's not much to tour," Damien mumbles, running a hand through his hair.

Erin rolls her eyes at him.

"Just because you've been here a million times doesn't mean there isn't anything worth seeing! There's the studios, the offices…" She taps her chin and looks up at the ceiling. "Uhhh…"

"Can't forget the bathrooms," Damien chimes in sarcastically.

"Hey, watch your mouth, I helped decorate those. Let me tell you, Pheebs, things were dire before I showed up."

"How dire?" She asks.

"No decoration, no color… Liam gave me full reign. Except for his office. That's his space."

Damien watches with amusement as Phoebe stops briefly at some of the framed photos on the wall, grabbing her camera and snapping a few shots here and there, all the while Erin rattles off some history.

"So, Liam opened this place about four years ago. He intended it to be an inexpensive space for local artists to record, comparatively at least. That's always been really important to him, so even after getting pretty big he still tries to keep things from getting out of control. Obviously as such a young business there isn't too much of a backstory–" She pauses. "Well, actually Liam doesn't like to talk about it, but this place used to be a warehouse during prohibition. I'll give you three guesses what they used it for."

Phoebe perks up, raising her eyebrows and leaning over to give Damien a playful shove.

"A history of crime? I thought it looked a bit stuffy, but it seems like this might be the perfect place for you after all."

Lately she's been taking any chance to be cheeky, and he's not sure if she's just gotten more confident with their whole dynamic, or if she's just trying to push his buttons, see if she can get him to react. It feels like a game, and there's not much he enjoys more than a little bit of play.

Damien puts on a somber expression, shaking his head as he slips his arm around her waist, squeezing her ass tight.

"Tsk tsk tsk, not taking our history seriously? I thought better of you, Miller."

She jumps a little, a wild look flashing across her face for just a moment before she regains her composure, giving him a coy little glance before catching back up with Erin.

Fuck, maybe it'll be harder to focus than he thought.

"Anyway, It's got 10 rooms that people can book at any time; it's not nearly as big as some of the other studios, but we're real flexible. Apparently it was more than enough at the start, but when a few of Liam's acts blew up all of the sudden this place got super popular, and now it's packed. We have to turn down a surprising number of groups these days, I guess it's about the notoriety?"

Phoebe nods, taking notes as she walks. Damien loves to watch her work. She's so confident without being cocky, and she shows genuine interest. You just know when she asks a question she genuinely wants the answer. None of that useless filler bullshit.

"So, how long has Revolver been recording here, since you started?"

"Fuck no," Damien laughs, cutting in before Erin can answer. "Pheebs, we used to record out of Shaun's parents' garage. Probably still would be if his dad didn't decide he wanted to make room for a brand new hot rod. Never been kicked out of somewhere so fast."

"Must have been a bummer," Phoebe replies.

Damien shrugs.

"Well, the space was cool at the time, but looking back, the sound wasn't the best, as much as Shaun and I tried to soundproof it. In the beginning we actually did everything at my place, but Johnny always said I got distracted at home."

Phoebe doesn't say anything, only smiling as she lets him take a step or two ahead of her before slipping up beside him. He can feel her fingers brush across the back of his neck, sliding around and down his chest as she passes him again.

Yep. This is going to be the best sort of problem.

The rest of the tour is pretty standard, and before long they find themselves standing in front of Liam's office, waiting. Damien can hear his sharp English accent through the slight crack in the door, his nerves starting to get the best of him again as Erin pipes up.

"I'm gonna go and grab some donuts from across the street, for the recording session. Do you two want anything?"

Damien digs a ratty five dollar bill out of his pocket.

"Pack of smokes."

Erin nods.

"You got it. Phoebe?"

"I'm okay," she replies. "There's coffee in the studio, right?"

"Tons of it. Feel free to make a fresh pot whenever you need. There's a little mini fridge, too. But be careful not to touch Shaun's cookies. He'll take your hand off."

"Noted," Phoebe laughs.

"Thanks, Erin," Damien mutters.

She pats him on the shoulder as she walks past.

"Good luck in there, you two."

"Wait, why do we need luck?" Phoebe asks him. "Did we do something?"

"It's nothing," Damien sighs. "Liam's just... very particular. Don't worry, you'll see what I mean in a minute."

He knocks at the door, waiting a couple seconds before pushing the door open and beckoning Phoebe to follow. No matter how many times Damien sees the office he can't quite shake the feeling he doesn't quite belong, despite the fact that it looks more like a goth kid's wet dream than a serious place of business. Massive shelves stacked with Grammys flank them, old books and records filling most of the rest of the space.

Liam sits at an ostentatious oak desk with a black typewriter at the far end of the room, dark red curtains covering the windows all around it. He's lounging back in his seat, resting both feet on his desk, his emerald green boots aimed at the ceiling. He rolls his eyes at the phone call, beckoning them forward. As they make their way over, Damien follows Phoebe's gaze to the three mounted swords on the wall, and he smiles to himself. A couple years back he and Ophelia tried to fight with them. It was all over pretty quickly when Liam pulled the third one down, threatening to send them both to the hospital.

The way he held it, it was hard not to believe him.

Liam has short, curly dark hair, and a soft, round jawline topped off with deep brown eyes, a slightly crooked nose, and full lips. Interestingly, stubble dusts his chin today, a feature Damien's not quite used to seeing. Liam's usually much more cleanly shaven, taking pride in how put-together he is. In fact, as he looks a little closer, Damien thinks he can spot just the tiniest bit of gray in his hair, making him look slightly older than his 38 years.

Liam usually sports a black turtleneck and a matching pair of dress pants, it's his signature look, but today he's opted for a tight t-shirt that shows off his notably toned biceps, along with the tattoos that adorn his dark brown skin.

"I told you, it's $500 an hour to record here— well, I own the bloody place and I make the rules. Listen, I don't care how much the band is going to *change music forever*. Do you have any idea how many times I hear that, only to be chronically underwhelmed by the material?" He rolls his eyes again, sliding his legs back off the table and sitting up straight as he abruptly ends the call.

"Third call like that today. Everyone's offering me the next big thing, but not a one of them can tell me what the fuck they think that even means. It's depressing, man."

Liam's eyes only linger on Damien for a moment before sliding to Phoebe, the corner of his mouth curling into a smile. She shifts nervously on her feet, and Damien feels a sudden little pang of guilt. In his waves of anxiety, he may have set some less than positive expectations.

"You're not meeting the queen," he chuckles. "You can chill, Pheebs."

The morning sun seeps through the curtains and makes Liam's hazel eyes shine brighter as he grins at the two of them.

"It's barely 10:00 and I already need a drink, is that sad?"

"I don't know about sad, but I'm pretty sure that's called alcoholism," Damien chuckles.

Liam clicks his tongue.

"Not in England it's not."

"Rough morning is it, old chap?"

Damien leads Phoebe to one of the big leather chairs in front of Liam's desk, pulling it out for her before he takes his own seat.

"More than you know, Bell, and you seem content to add to it. You've still not learned my little rule, it seems? I know waiting after knocking is a complex and difficult task, but you've had years of practice."

It always amazes him how Liam can bounce between warmth and venom at a moment's notice. It makes any conversation with him a tightrope walk, you never know quite how safe you are, and that's what makes it so exhilarating, not to mention fun.

"Erin said you wanted to see us, said it was urgent. I couldn't *bear* to keep you waiting any longer than necessary, but I do *beg* your pardon."

There's a moment where Damien thinks he may have gone a step too far, Liam's ice-cold stare freezing him in place just long enough for it to be awkward, but a moment later it's melted away and he's all smiles once again.

"First, if it's quite alright with you, I'd like to introduce myself to this lovely little lady." He sticks out his hand. "Liam Lewis, producer."

"Phoebe Miller, smiling politely."

"Troy told me you're smart as a whip, and that you even manage to keep this one in line from time to time."

"All true," Damien interjects.

Liam gives her a little wink before turning back to him.

"Then we all agree she's way out of your league! So I have to ask, is it blackmail, trickery, or both?"

Damien straightens, used to the goading but still a little sensitive on the subject of Phoebe, but Liam only laughs.

"I'm fucking with you, of course— isn't that what you Americans say?"

"You act like you haven't lived here for fifteen years."

Liam smirks, leaning back in his chair, obviously resisting the urge to put his feet back up.

"Anyway, Miss Miller, it truly is fantastic to meet you. I've heard great things, and even read some decent album reviews. No mention of me, though, no matter how many times I've been involved."

Phoebe smiles back at him, looking much less tense.

"I'll be sure to rectify that in the next one. We can't have any unsung heroes after all this time."

Liam chuckles, reaching for a metallic cigarette case painted black, popping out a long thin menthol and striking a match.

Damien shakes his head.

"You know, we have lighters now. They work pretty good, too."

Liam sucks on his cigarette, ignoring Damien as he snuffs out the match, tossing it down to smolder in the ashtray.

"So, Miss Miller," he exhales. "I don't mean to be indelicate, but I feel we should get right to the point. I understand that you and Damien are in..."

Liam dramatically swirls his hand in the air, as if he can't quite grasp the right word.

"Love," Phoebe finishes for him.

It shouldn't be a surprise, but no matter how many times Damien hears her say it, it still makes him shiver. Hopefully Liam doesn't notice.

"And that's all very lovely," he smiles. "Regardless, these sessions are usually private. I've already granted your friend from the New Yorker permission to sit in, Miss Kaneko I believe, but distractions tend to make for short attention spans, and even shorter tempers. All of that combined makes for a bad product," he rocks his chair backward and gestures to the Grammys sitting on his shelf. "And I don't *do* bad product. So, while I have no problem extending my hospitality to the two of you, that will only remain the case as long as your presence does not affect our work. Do we have an understanding?"

"I wouldn't want it any other way," Phoebe replies. Damien can't even sense an ounce of her usual anxiety in her words. In fact, all she's exuding is pure confidence. "You won't even know I'm here, if that's the way you'd prefer it, but I was hoping to get a short interview with you, to put in my story, at your convenience of course."

Liam sucks on his cigarette, blowing the smoke out the side of his mouth.

"We can chat today, I'll make some time around the recording."

"I look forward to it," Phoebe replies, extending her hand.

Damien grins. That meek girl he met in LA is nowhere to be found. He's so proud of how far she's come, and where she's going to go.

Under Pressure

PHOEBE

The recording studio is small, but charming. The control room looks more like a little cabin than a studio space, and it's very clear that even after one album, the band has made it their own. There's a big leather couch, pictures of them from throughout the recording process taped up on the wall, a coffee machine, and a mini-fridge tucked into the corner. There's even a string of tiny Christmas lights hanging up on one of the walls. Ophelia told her they're for ambience.

The live room is just as cozy, with Ophelia's drum kit taking up a good chunk of space off in its own little isolated area. Shaun has a spot carved out in one of the corners with four guitars lined up, a big cup of coffee resting on the floor next to a box of chocolate chip cookies.

Johnny's spot is directly across from him, his sneakers just barely peeking out of his black gym bag as he paces. He'd briefly mentioned he likes to play barefoot in an old interview; says it helps to ground him when they're in the studio.

The vocal booth itself is relatively sparse. All Phoebe can see from her vantage point is Damien's notebook sitting on a solitary music stand, and his headphones hanging across the overhead mic. He blows her a kiss, his eyes twinkling with excitement when he notices her.

Phoebe sits down behind the mixing board, taking the spot next to Erin as Liam leans into his microphone with the press of a button.

"Alright, playtime is over children. It's time to get to work."

Damien salutes him while Ophelia breaks up a mini-fight between Johnny and Shaun and they both stumble back to their instruments.

"God, they're insufferable sometimes. Did they get worse on tour?"

"You made 'em what they are, Liam. You have responsibility in this, too," Erin laughs.

Liam grumbles to himself, but Phoebe catches a hint of pride on his face. Without him, Revolver would probably still be playing dive bars. Each individual member's gone on record stating that Liam was the person who really figured Revolver out, molded their unique sound into just the right shape.

He knows how to get results.

"Well, my little hooligans, I'm sure you've had a lovely little vacation away from the dungeon, but now that we've all returned to this quaintly charming little slice of hell, I have to ask: are you ready to record some fucking hits for me today?"

Shaun plays a riff on his guitar as Damien gives another one of his overly-theatrical salutes. Johnny and Ophelia simply snicker as they make their way to their own little corners of the room.

"So what are we doing first?" Liam asks.

Damien slips into his booth and puts his headphones on, his husky voice filling the room as he leans into the mic.

"Babydoll. Pheebs still hasn't heard it yet."

"That's the title?" Liam asks, wincing a little.

"You got a problem with it?" Damien fires back.

Liam shakes his head.

"It could stand to be a little less pedestrian, is all." He waves his hand as if dismissing his own train of thought. "It's fine, it's fine. We'll work on it!"

"Jesus, just press record already!" Ophelia shouts, impatiently hitting her snare a couple times.

"Hey, don't rush me!" Erin laughs.

"The four of you just play the bloody song, we'll see what we have to tweak to get it right." He turns to Phoebe, flipping off his mic. "I like to record rehearsals, even the early ones, especially if I haven't heard the tracks before."

"He takes them home and listens to them," Erin says accusingly.

Phoebe grabs her notebook and scribbles down the quote as the band begins to warm up.

"How many takes do they usually do?"

"As many as it takes to get it right," Liam replies, Erin mouthing the phrase along with him from behind. She and Phoebe exchange a smile as Liam settles into his seat. "I want to see how things have shifted since they started touring. Maybe they've evolved, and maybe they've regressed, you never really know. I do find that some of the new work that springs up on tour is often of a type; they write more of the same songs they're already singing. Stuck in a loop."

He taps at the console in front of him.

"We'll see how much of this ends up being usable. I've got somewhat of a vision for this album already."

Liam is surprisingly invested, especially considering how many ongoing groups he has personally under his wing. He's also clearly more interested in planning and preparation than even the most practical members of the band.

"What's your vision based on? An evolution from their first album, or a reaction to the current market?"

"It's sort of both," Liam replies, flicking a switch and pressing a couple buttons. "Sometimes what the market wants is *terribly* fucking boring. Just rehashing the same rubbish we've heard a thousand times. I like to mix things up where I can, push things in the right direction."

In his booth, Damien's all smiles, and Phoebe can feel the energy in the room, like a champagne bottle being shaken up. Erin checks the tape a final time, making sure that everything's in place to record while Liam slides his chair back, chewing his thumb nail and taking in the view.

Erin leans forward, tapping the mic to get their attention.

"Are we ready, team?"

Johnny steps up, his lips bumping up against his microphone a bit before he sheepishly responds.

"Ready, sugar."

Phoebe hears the door click behind her, turning to see Janis slip carefully into the room, pulling up a chair beside her just in time to catch the rest of the band signal one by one that they're ready. Erin glances over at Liam, her finger hovering over the record button. He nods and she leans into the mic.

"Let's make some magic."

The rich sound of Shaun's guitar is the first thing to hit Phoebe's ears, watching as his fingers dance along the fretboard. He's already sunk six feet deep into the rhythm by the time the rest of the band starts to hit their cues. Ophelia comes in first, then Johnny, with not a missed note between them. The blend of weighty percussion and soulful guitar is compelling, but it isn't until Damien's voice comes vibrating through the speakers that Phoebe's truly hooked. It feels intimate, holding her firmly like it's just the two of them in the room, so much softer than anything they've done before. He's just as magnetic here as he is in front of thousands of screaming fans.

But it's the lyrics that catch her off guard. Tiny details of their time together: the first time he saw her in that hotel room, the first time they kissed, the time they spent together at Red Rock Canyon, his tags that still hang around her neck.

"This might be their best song," Janis murmurs.

Liam is focused, leaning back in his chair and watching with a hardened expression. His jaw is tense and his eyes are cloudy. She can't tell if he looks confused, compelled, or if he flat-out hates it. As his eyes dart between each band member, Phoebe finds herself feeling a bit worried. If this isn't good enough, what possibly could be? Shaun's guitar is just the right accompaniment to Damien's more delicate lyrics, Johnny's bassline fills the space between them perfectly, and Ophelia drives the song forward, underlining everything and giving it all an extra weight. While it's a style change, it fits them well, more mature than the howling and screeching any fan of the group would be used to.

As the song fades out, Erin applauds, Janis and Phoebe joining in while the band waits for the final verdict from Liam. He grabs his cigarettes off of the counter and lights one, gently moving Erin's chair aside so that he can talk into the mic.

"Okay, let's go again. Shaun, I want the guitar tighter toward the first bridge, and a more melodic solo. It's too stiff right now, so improvise;

make it work for you, not the other way around. Johnny, I want you to follow Shaun's lead, fill in those gaps and make it all mesh. Ophelia, lighter on the cymbals, alright? Make sure to keep up, you got a little lost after the chorus– and Bell?"

"Yeah."

Damien's voice sounds tight, maybe even a little choked.

"That was good. Looser vocals though. If you're going for Springsteen, you're *almost* there, but I want it warmer. You've got a rich timbre, and I want to be drowning in all that gold."

Damien nods, and Phoebe can see his body relax just a little as Liam takes his finger off of the button. First test passed.

Liam takes another drag of his long cigarette, thinking to himself for a few seconds before slumping back down in his chair, and sliding over toward Phoebe.

"Miss Miller, it frustrates me to no end, but your boyfriend may, in fact, be some sort of genius."

Janis snickers.

"Don't tell him that, his head'll get bigger than it already is."

Erin snorts, nearly spilling her coffee as Liam raises a brow.

"I like you, Janis. You can stay."

Erin sets up the second tape as the band takes a few minutes to regroup, going over the notes they were given before they get back into the groove.

"Babydoll, studio take 2."

Phoebe waits a few seconds into the take, ensuring everything is going smoothly before turning to Liam, her recorder ready.

"Are you good to talk in here, or should we wait?"

Liam puffs on his cigarette and nods.

"The equipment won't pick up our conversation, and I'm an excellent multitasker."

She doesn't have any questions prepared, giving up on that sort of thing only a few weeks into the tour. Listening back on her tapes feels more like a conversation between friends than anything formal, and ideally she wants to keep it that way.

"Alright, so, Liam– Er, Mr. Lewis? How did you get into producing?"

"Starting me off with a softball question," Liam laughs. "Alright...

well, I always loved to take things apart and reconstruct them as a kid, toys, electronics, all that, and music is no different. There's something beautiful about knowing what pieces fit where, right down to the layers and the volume on a track. It can make or break even the catchiest song, and there's a different kind of artistry to it." He smiles. "And Liam is fine, by the way."

She chuckles.

"Great. So, did you always want to be a producer, or was there another ambition there?"

"Ooh, good question, Pheebs," Janis chimes in.

Liam's eyes bounce between them, amused, but still a little guarded.

"Do you two come as a set?"

Janis grins, leaning back in her chair.

"Trust me, pal, you couldn't handle my questions."

"Try me," Liam retorts. "You get one for free."

"How come you wear such tight pants?"

"Because I'm proud of what's between my legs," Liam snaps. "It's a shame I can't legally show it off."

Janis waves her hands in defeat.

"Damn, no fear. You've got my respect, bossman."

"*Anyway*, to answer the more pertinent question: When I was a child, I tried to start a band myself. We were rubbish. Didn't have the discipline or the focus to sit down and do the work, no stomach for anything that it took to actually make it. I had an uncle who had connections to a record label, though, and somehow, years later, he managed to remember that oh-so-cursed aspiration from my youth. So, he got my foot in the door. Not as a performer, obviously, and thank god for that."

Phoebe leans forward in rapt attention, scribbling in her notebook while keeping her focus on him. She's shocked he's being this open, especially considering all of Damien's warnings.

"I worked at a few different studios, all through college to pay rent—real shit gigs, you know? But we do anything we can when we're working toward a dream. Sure, I was just sort of messing about at first, but then it became... I don't know, an obsession? Maybe that's not the right word."

He taps away at the console a couple times, glancing quickly between the members of the band. It seems like he takes impressively detailed mental notes, and Phoebe wishes she had that level of recall. It'd mean she wasn't constantly glued to her notepads.

"I think it's probably an appropriate term when it comes to music," Phoebe replies. "That's why I write about it, at least. I've never been able to shake it."

From the look in his eye, she can tell she's found some common ground.

"Back then I just wanted to make things sound good. It takes a certain level of patience, care, and attention to make a record, and double or triple that to make a good one. A lot of people think it's just about laying down the track, but there's so much more to be done behind the scenes."

"Do you feel like you don't get your dues as a producer?"

He pauses, obviously weighing his words carefully.

"It's not really about me, is it? It's about them."

He gestures toward the band, all playing their hearts out. Phoebe tunes it all back in, the final chorus almost finished. Everything sounds smooth, like they've been working on this one song for years.

"The trick is I'm nothing without a great band. I can't make garbage sound good, and mediocrity is even worse. There has to be something to work with, and these ones give me more than enough."

He takes a long drag, blowing a smoke ring up into the ceiling.

"Off the record?"

She nods.

"Sometimes I give that boy a hard time, but he's an incredible lyricist, a real poet. He knows just how to fit things together, and the few times he hasn't, Shaun fills in those gaps. They're a great team."

Phoebe grins.

"How did you get involved with the band? Was it through Troy, or…"

"I know Shaun's dad. He used to record out of a small studio in Manhattan and Shaun would come in to jam with him sometimes. We hit it off right away and so when they were looking for a producer, he rang me immediately. I was working out of this studio, about a year in at the time, and one of our records had just taken off, so we were just getting ready to start taking on more work. Anyway it all worked out, even if it was sort of a favor for a friend at first."

The band lucked out with Liam. His talent is evident in the album.

The way each song perfectly flows into the next, almost like a story is what really drew her to Revolver's music. But despite his talent, she doesn't know much about him. Maybe that's on purpose, but she'd like to high-light him a little in her article.

"What did you grow up listening to?"

"Well, I'm from Manchester, so as you can imagine I was obsessed with the Beatles as a kid. At some point something shifted and I moved on, first to Chuck Berry, then Muddy Waters, Bowie, Zeppelin, Black Sabbath, Pantera— oh! And a lot of Coltrane. That one's completely thanks to Shaun."

"So you have an eclectic taste."

"Of course," Liam laughs, his face lighting up. "I pity anyone who doesn't. It keeps things interesting and– hang on, sorry, we'll have to pick this up later."

Phoebe presses stop on her tape recorder as Damien's final notes rever-berate through the speakers; Liam motions to Erin to keep recording as he leans over and addresses the band.

"That was better."

"I dunno man," Damien replies. "It feels a bit off, too rough."

Liam shakes his head and kills his cigarette, crushing it in the ashtray next to him. His brow is furrowed in concentration.

"It's strong is what it is. You've written a power ballad, and we're getting closer to what that's supposed to sound like."

Damien's jaw clenches, and he shakes his head. Shaun's fingers tap out a nervous rhythm on the body of his guitar as Johnny deflates a little. It's pretty clear that this time, the band is on a different wavelength than their producer. They were so confident when they walked in. She casts Damien a sympathetic look. She liked the track, but Liam's got an ear for this stuff.

"I want something acoustic," Damien says. "Shaun and I agreed we want something more mature for this album."

"Nothing about this track is acoustic, Bell. It's a ballad, and it's a power ballad at that– and remember, you might want a particular sound, but I'm the one who makes it all happen."

He's not wrong. He's won Grammys for a reason. Phoebe shifts in her seat, catching Janis's eye. She flicks her head toward the door, a little silent signal that they should get out of here and let the band work. It might be a good idea.

"Look, the song is... fine. More than fine, the lyrics are beautiful and it has a lovely hook, but it needs that extra kick." He glances between the bandmates. "You want this album to be great, right?"

"Liam, we don't even have a concept yet. We just have a bunch of songs, and they're killer," Ophelia replies.

"I'll be the judge of that."

All of Liam's words are polite enough, but curt. He doesn't seem like the sort of person to budge when he thinks he's right. Phoebe slumps down deep into her seat as the rising tension makes her want to disappear.

"Bell, I'm telling you, your soft version of it isn't going to put you at the top of the charts."

"Fine, whatever," Damien mutters.

Even from here, Phoebe can see the frustration written all over his face. He had to have been expecting some kind of feedback from Liam, right?

"I'm not trying to be a hardass here, okay? It's your first day back and I'm working on getting the four of you in top shape as quickly as possible. You're still in tour mode, riding the high from all the applause and creative buzz, but we need to start sitting down and re-working some of these tracks."

He sighs, rubbing his eyes.

"How about you show me what else you've come up with, we can come back to this one later. Erin, make sure you're recording this."

The entire studio is silent.

Damien looks like a kid who just got yelled at, shoving his headphones back on and trying to make the scowl on his face look like concentration. But Phoebe knows better. She doubts he's fooling any one of them.

When Erin hits the hits record, it feels like all of the joy and high energy has been sucked out of the room. Now they're all just... working. When Damien's vocals come in with half the passion she's used to, Liam clearly notices. He motions for Erin to cut the tape.

"Alright. We're going to take a break and come back to this. It'll give you time to get back in the right headspace. Relax, take some time for yourselves, but be back here in an hour, alright?"

Everyone's a little shaken, but they seem content enough to take a bit of time to bounce back, each member nodding as they put down their instruments. All except Damien, stuck staring at the ground. He looks completely defeated, even worse than he did that night with Chris.

Liam taps his microphone.

"Bell? You heard me, right?"

Damien raises his head, his expression muted and dull.

"Loud and clear."

Everybody Wants to Rule the World

DAMIEN

Goddammit.

Damien could hear it in Liam's voice– that *I'm not mad, I'm just disappointed* bullshit tone that parents use. It's fucking humiliating, just as bad now than it was back then. Worse. It sends him into a fucking spiral every goddamn time.

Damien removes his headphones as Shaun steps into the vocal booth and shuts the mic off.

"You good, dude?" There's concern in his eyes. Damien nods, but Shaun shakes his head. "Don't bullshit me."

Damien turns his back to the studio, Shaun quickly following suit so that nobody can tell what they're saying. They did this a lot when they were recording the first album, first because they just thought it was pretty funny, but later on because Damien became convinced Liam could read lips.

"I'm just pissed, man." Damien lights his cigarette, hoping it'll do something to calm his nerves. "It's just embarrassing. I'm not a fucking child. None of us are."

"I know, man, I know, but this is how he works."

"Well, I forgot how much I hate it," Damien grumbles, the sense of helplessness beginning to overwhelm him. "I get it, I really do. It's his job, he's making us better, just like he did last time. I just thought these songs were solid. They came out so smooth, it all felt so right, and then in a few minutes he's reconstructing our entire vibe."

There's that other part, too, the part he's not quite willing to say out loud. He wrote that song for Phoebe. About how he feels for her. It's like Liam's saying his love is too soft. Not enough. He knows it's pure projection, but knowing something doesn't actually do as much good as you'd think. Brains are great like that.

"The songs *are* good. What we wrote this tour? It's fucking incredible." Shaun pats him on the back. "Look man, I'm a little mad too, who wouldn't be?"

Damien lifts his head. Shaun's gone to bat for Liam a bunch of times in the past, and it's led to some tension in the studio, so he's always surprised when the two of them butt heads.

"You are?"

"Yeah. I think the song's meant to be softer, and it should stay that way. You've got, like, a Purple Rain thing going on with that refrain, and the guitar really carries the lyrics gently. That's how it should be. If it sounds heavier, I think... I don't know, I think it takes away from how personal it all feels. So, I'm right there with you, bud."

"Thanks, man. It's nice to know someone's got my back."

"Maybe we can come to some kind of compromise with Liam."

"Or maybe find a new studio," Damien mutters.

Shaun chuckles.

"He's right about one thing, though. We don't have a concept that ties everything together. Our last album was wall-to-wall heartbreak, all that shit people can put on and scream their lungs out to." He takes a breath, tapping out a little rhythm on the mic stand for a couple seconds. "So maybe we should flip it, just like with Babydoll we go a little softer with this one. I mean, everyone's into Metallica and Slayer and shit–"

Damien snorts. Even *he* likes those bands, but Revolver isn't metal.

"We could never pull that off."

"Exactly! And hell, I wouldn't want to. Love and heartbreak is our bread and butter."

"Not if Liam fucking hates it."

Shaun rolls his eyes.

"He doesn't hate it. If he hated it, he'd tell us to cut it from the record after we played the first four bars. You've gotta get that out of your head."

Damien lets out a pained sigh, offering Shaun his cigarette. He doesn't just want to shovel out easy hits, he wants to put out work that he's actually proud of, that they built up together from scratch. But that really is just a piece of it. You have to sell records to get your shit out there, to get it played. More often than not, what the market wants and what Damien wants are two very different beasts. The trick is learning to tame them both.

Shaun takes a long drag on the cigarette. The smile on his face is only the tiniest bit annoying; he knows how Damien thinks, how easy it is for him to fall into a pit of self-doubt over the stupidest little things.

"Alright, fearless leader, all that in mind, what are we pitching to Liam?"

Damien nods absently as he taps out his own little rhythm on his music stand.

"The whole vibe has to be sweet, but heavy. Melodic. Like..."

"Oh! you know those caramel shortbread cookies Ophelia makes?"

Damien's stomach growls.

"Caramel in the middle and the sea salt on top?"

"Yeah!" Shaun laughs. "The ones that make you feel like you're gonna throw the fuck up 15 cookies in, but you keep eating them."

"Last time I did throw up," Damien reminds him. "So did Johnny."

"You're not supposed to eat 40 of them, D–" Shaun shakes his head. "But that's besides the point. *That* is the sound we want."

"Throwing up?"

"No, you clown." Shaun shoulder-checks him playfully. "Heavy, but sweet. Songs about falling in love, about being afraid of falling in love... all the shit you write about with Pheebs– we weave all of that in there along with a new sound. We get fucking violins, cellos, maybe even a harp."

"Kind of like the horns in The Soft Parade."

Shaun grins.

"Your favorite Doors album."

It's genius. No thanks to Morrison, he was drunk for most of it, but the rest of them knew exactly what they were doing. Damien played that record until it was a crackling warped mess.

"It's just so different. The second they brought in those trumpets and trombones it was like…"

"Magic."

Shaun's eyes gleam. He can feel that old spark between them, a kind of creative lightning that's like a rush of blood to the head. Damien snatches the cigarette out of his hand, whirling around in time to see Janis crack open the door to the recording booth, with Phoebe right behind her.

"We're going to go shopping and–"

He doesn't even let her finish, stuffing the cigarette between his lips and leaning past her to thrust his wallet into Phoebe's hand.

"Take my credit card. There's no spending limit. Both of you."

"Hey, hey, hey!" Shaun laughs, pushing Damien aside. "Listen man, I appreciate the generosity, but you can let *your* girlfriend spend *your* money." He puts on his best Damien impression, over-exaggerating every movement as he daintily pulls out his wallet. "Janis, *darling*, you take my card. And just so you know, there are *absolutely* no limits."

Janis gives an approving nod, turning the card over in her hands.

"Alright, cool. Thanks, babe."

Phoebe takes the opportunity to pull Damien out of the booth, her brows pinched together with concern.

"Are you okay?"

Her tone is hopeful, but still a little worried. He probably gave her a bit of a scare, but he's not going to fall apart anymore, not for shit he has control over.

"Yeah, I talked with Shaun and I'm– Yeah, I'm good, Pheebs."

He was hoping he'd be able to skate through this with a cocky grin and a joke, but he can tell by her expression she doesn't quite buy it. Phoebe wraps her arms around his waist. Her kiss is sugary sweet, her cherry lip gloss lingering in the air as she pulls back just the tiniest bit. He can feel himself begin to melt, groaning as she runs her fingers up and down his spine.

"You're lying to me."

There's something about the way she says it that's impossible to deny. It's not that she's disappointed, she's simply stating an irrefutable fact, and he's compelled to agree.

"Yeah," he sighs, looking down at her. "Liam made me feel like shit."

"You don't hide it well."

Damien chuckles as she strokes his cheek. Again, there's a certain playfulness in her voice. The moment she sussed out that he wasn't spiraling, it became a new little game.

"Liam wasn't chewing you out for nothing, he's got his own ideas on what'll make it work, but *I* loved the song, and so will everyone else. They'll all love it, in whatever form it takes, you know why? Because you wrote it."

"You sound like my mom when she'd put my homework up on the fridge."

Her little smile doesn't falter, her voice controlled but a bit breathy as her fingers play on the back of his neck.

"I think that's the last time I want to hear you comparing me to your mother."

"Got it. So no mommy in the bedroom then?"

"Not unless you want to get spanked."

"Now *there's* an idea."

Damien presses his forehead against hers and takes a deep breath. This is why he wanted her in the studio. And it's not just here, with this. Even in all of their secrecy, having to keep things under wraps, Phoebe makes him feel more open than he ever has before. It's the rarest possible feeling, love that comes freely, but that's molded by the balance of their honest compromise. It's impossible, imperfectly perfect, yet it's theirs.

And he's going to hold on to it as long as he possibly can.

Phoebe's fingers run through his hair, playfully tugging every now and then as she keeps staring into his eyes. He can feel her chest heaving against him, her breath notably heavier than it was just a few moments ago.

"If I'd known you'd be this pent up I would have set aside some alone time before the show. Take the edge off."

Her eyes flash, a devilish smile on her face.

"Well, I've never been one to turn down one of your *excellen*t ideas, Miss Miller. As luck would have it, there are more than a few.... Less used bathrooms that don't show up on Erin's tours."

She steps back, playing with the wire hanging off the ceiling mic.

"*Very* Interesting."

Delicately, she wraps it around her wrist, a soft little sound barely escaping her lips as she tightens it on her own. Damien can feel his heart pounding in his throat.

"Don't start something you can't finish, Miller."

"Oh, I can finish it." She licks her lips, holding his gaze for a moment that feels like an eternity, before uncoiling the cord with a cute little smile. "Well, I'm sure you have work to do, I'll be back later."

If he could fuck her right here in this booth, he would.

"You're gonna leave me hanging like this?"

It's wild how quickly she makes him forget how to play it cool.

"Well, like Liam said, you've all got work to do." Her tone is sultry, her voice thick with desire. She's definitely working to control herself, but she's doing a damn sight better than he is. Damien takes a step toward her but she slips into the doorway. "You're gonna be great, Damien."

He grasps her waist before she can quite make it out, pulling her into him. He leans down, his lips brushing against her ear.

"You're playing a dangerous game, babydoll."

"Oh, I know," she purrs. "That's part of the fun, right?"

He growls and nips at her neck.

"Get outta here before I do something that's gonna get us blacklisted."

She giggles and slips out of the room, blowing him a kiss before joining up with Janis. Damien watches as the two leave the studio, Phoebe's neck still a little flushed as they giggle and laugh about who knows what. He runs his hand through his hair, a sense of certainty overwhelming the thousand other things that might easily claw at him any other day, and leaving him with only a single thought.

"I'm gonna marry that fucking woman."

"Shaun, baby, that's the weirdest way anyone's ever described a sound," Ophelia chuckles as she twirls her drumstick in her hand. "You want our record to sound like my cookies? Because you love them, *and* they make you throw up?"

They've been sitting in a circle on the floor for the better part of the hour. Shaun and Johnny have their instruments close at hand, while Damien's lyric book is splayed wide open between them.

"No, our fearless leader added that last part."

Damien smiles, remembering this was the exact formation they were in when they came up with the band's name, way back in Shaun's garage. It feels like the old days when they were still experimenting and finding out who they were as artists.

"I want our record to sound melodic, with fucking violins and shit. Liam said he wants an extra kick to round out the track, but what he was giving us was an example, because we didn't have anything prepped. No plans of our own. So I'm saying we pitch him this. Sure, some of it we can't do ourselves, but I know Liam can wrangle up a bit of classical talent. There's no shame in getting some folks to sit in if it helps our sound."

Johnny looks a little nervous, or maybe he's just unsure. Either way, Damien can tell there's something he wants to say.

"What's going on up there, Reed? You got tumbleweeds again?"

"Nah," Johnny murmurs. "Just thinking."

There's a brief silence as everyone waits for Johnny to speak up, but Ophelia quickly cuts in, never a fan of awkward pauses.

"Would you... like to share these thoughts with the class?"

Johnny sighs.

"I just... you wanna bring in more musicians? We've got a pretty good thing going on, don't we?"

Damien tries not to laugh, the poor guy looks like he's about to be dumped the night before prom. The band is the only thing Johnny really knows, never really working with musicians outside of the three of them. It started as Revolver against the world, the lot of them playing dive bars and selling records for a buck a piece with Erin as their sole merch girl. In those early days there were a lot of late nights, and a lot of thinking they would never make it, but the tide turned.

Fast.

"Hey man, it's just an idea for now. I think it would help round things out and give the songs a little more meat, and this way it's us and not Liam who gets to decide how it all gets seasoned."

Shaun's tone is soothing, he knows how to deal with pretty much all of their neuroses by now.

"Remember The Soft Parade?" Johnny's eyes immediately light up the moment Damien mentions the album. "We listened to that for an entire summer, tried to come up with songs that sounded similar because we loved that record so much, right?"

"Yes! Touch Me! It was…" His jaw drops. "The horns. It was those damn horns! Okay. Alright, yeah, if that's what we're going for, I can get on board with this."

"I think it's a good plan," Erin chimes in. "It fits your theme, and it helps you tie some different tracks together that might not quite fit otherwise. It'll make the mix pretty interesting too."

They exchange a look between the four of them. Ophelia chuckles.

"Hey man, I'm always down to experiment with sound. I loved the first record, for sure, but I get really fucking tired of playing the same shit over and over again."

They'd never talked about it this honestly before, but it's impossible to deny Damien does get tired of singing about the same old heartbreak. It's why he's been pushing these new songs out, and why he was a little surprised by how easily they caught on.

Fuck, maybe Liam's right.

Maybe it did sound like their old stuff just slowed down.

"So, is that how we're gonna handle it?" Ophelia asks. "We can do a test with Babydoll, then figure out how we want the album to sound based on that."

"Yep. We take Liam's notes, but make it sweet and heavy. It's still a ballad."

Damien defaults to Shaun in these instances. He knows the mechanics of music better than any of them. He can pick out the weakest points in a song and tell them exactly why they aren't working and what they can do to fix things. Damien flies by the seat of his pants while Shaun understands a song's bones in a way that makes him wish he'd gone to school for this shit, too.

"Knock knock!" Liam calls, pushing the door open.

He looks a little more relaxed than he did in the studio, he and Damien locking eyes for a moment. Liam raises a brow and Damien nods his head, a silent signal to tell him that everything's cool.

"You had a chance to chat and go over some of the notes?" He asks.

"Yep," Johnny replies as he hauls his guitar over his shoulder, everyone returning to their places. "We think you're really gonna dig this."

The first day usually sets the tone for how the rest of the recording process is going to go, and Damien doesn't want to spend it bickering with Liam about how things should work. He knows Liam's job is to make them sound good and the guy's a fucking genius when it comes to putting together a cohesive record. A little bit of guilt starts to gnaw at him, but he pushes it down.

"It's good, man," he assures Liam.

"You feel happy with it?" Liam asks.

Both of them are trying not to step on each other's toes. Damien nods as he closes his notebook and flashes Liam a warm smile.

"I think so." He looks around to his band mates. "How about you guys?"

"No complaints," Ophelia replies.

"Good," Liam sighs. "Let's do this again. Clean slate, yeah? Show me what you've got, Revolver."

He winks and heads out the door with Erin trailing behind him.

"Sweet and heavy," Shaun reminds them. "You fuckers ready?"

The anticipation makes the hairs on Damien's arms stand straight up as he slips back into his booth, excitement crackling between the four of them while they prep their equipment. He can see Liam through the glass, nestled in his usual spot, his eyes completely impassive. He can't help but think back to all the times they'd clashed in the past. Some he'd regretted pushing, others he'd regretted backing down from. Liam was usually right, and he may have been this time too, but they needed to take the reins.

The click as Erin leans into her mic shoots him back into the moment, just in time to give a quick glance to his bandmates, each one of them ready to go.

"Babydoll. Take three."

Immediately he can tell it all feels different; something clicked and it just feels right. Liam's watches with narrowed eyes, his lower lip pressed between his teeth as Damien starts to sing. This time, the texture of his voice matches the weight of Shaun's chords, tumbles over Ophelia's drumline and Johnny's bass. He closes his eyes, not thinking about Liam, about the notes, about any of it. He's singing to her, just her, on a beach, in bed, in his apartment, in the shower. And she's right there, clinging to him, laughing with him, crying beside him. Damien can feel her fingernails on the back of his neck, the sting of the tiniest bit of blood. He can see those warm amber eyes peering up at him as she mouths the words along with him.

It's not until Johnny plays Shaun into the outro and Ophelia gives one final crash on her drums that Damien opens his eyes. Liam is standing, fully engrossed. He's saying something to Erin, fiddling with switches on his own. This is it.

They've got something.

The reverberations fade out, and Damien basks in the silence for a couple moments, cut off too soon by a quick click and Liam's voice.

"Better. Not perfect, but much better."

Damien's shoulders sag.

"Come on, man–"

"I said it was better. This is what, your third go at it? And you want perfect? We're getting there, but it needs more work."

Shaun flips on his own microphone, sounding excited, but obviously jumping in to keep Damien from getting them into more trouble on their first day back.

"Yeah, we were talking about violins, maybe some other classical stuff as backup. You know, fill things out and carry a bit of the mood."

"Might be good," Liam replies. "I can make some calls. But it's not just that. I need more from those vocals."

Irritation digs into him like a splinter. It's never enough. He can never give enough in this booth.

"I don't have any more," Damien replies, surprising even himself with the bluntness.

Liam scoffs, one hand on his hip as he blows a smoke ring.

"Of course you do. This is good, Damien, and I like it, but it's not your best. I've heard your best, we all have." He takes another drag, turning back to Erin. "We'll need some backup vocals too, make some notes for the mix. We need to really round out that sound."

Damien grabs his water bottle off of the stool beside him, pacing with a nervous energy. There's a world where he takes the extra moment, calms himself down and resets, just gets right back to work. But it's not this one.

"What's your deal, man? I get that it's your job, but I know my own work and this is the best shit I've ever done. Why're you so intent on tearing everything down all the time?"

Shaun and Johnny glance over at him, both of them shaking their heads, silently begging him not to start a fight. But obviously it's too late. He knew it the second he didn't flip off his microphone.

Liam crushes his cigarette in the ashtray and leans over the mic, his eyes dark and locked with Damien's as his jaw ticks, silent for an extra moment before the telltale click spikes through their headphones.

"My *deal*, sweetheart, is that I just spent the last hour on the phone with Allan Harris. Yes, *that* Allan Harris. He asked about you lot, wanted to know how all of this was going. But really, Damien, he was asking about you. From what I can tell, parsing corporate bullshit, the label's concerned; they want to make sure they're not wasting their money on a bad bet. The one thing he told me straight is that he wants a solid record that's going to sell, something marketable. No risks."

The atmosphere in the room immediately feels twice as heavy, and as Damien glances around he can tell the others are feeling it too.

"Now, luckily for you I don't give a shit about what Allan wants. He's been out of the game so long that he wouldn't be able to make the right call in a primary school talent show. What you lot have is *good*, it's got soul and it stands out, but my job is to make it *great*. You've got some ideas, and so do I. We're going to put it all together and we're going to blow your first album out of the fucking water."

Damien stands completely still, embarrassment and anger swirling around inside him. Liam's right. He's almost always right, and he definitely is here. He even went to bat for them with the suits, and he's willing to invest in their vision for the album. But it doesn't make any of it easier to swallow when he's still talking to Damien like he's a fucking kid.

"So, now that we've got that out of the way, are you all ready to get back to work, or are we just going to fuck around in that booth all day?"

"Ready," Damien mutters.

He's going to need a hell of a distraction when Phoebe gets back.

Need You Tonight

DAMIEN

"D!" Johnny calls out as the band is packing up for the night. "We're heading to a place near The Roxy, getting some food before the show, you guys in?"

Despite a grueling day, they made good progress. But Damien wants to keep working on his own, at least for another hour. He's almost got a handle on Liam's notes.

Damien spots Phoebe crouching down to take a picture of Shaun's guitars lined up against the wall. She's had her camera out since she and Janis got back from their little shopping trip, snapping pictures of the band in between takes.

"In a bit! I'm gonna hang out and record some of those backup vocals Liam wanted. It'll let us get a head start on things tomorrow." Phoebe glances up from Shaun's guitars, sliding her camera into her bag. "You wanna help, Pheebs? All you gotta do is press a button."

"Yeah, I'm sure that's *all* she's gotta do," Janis snickers.

Phoebe looks over her shoulder and shoots her a dirty look as she sets her bag down. Everyone else is lingering by the door, itching to get out of here for the night. Normally, he'd be the first out, but Phoebe's been making eyes at him all afternoon. She was extra handsy at lunch, sitting in his lap and running her fingers through his hair. And now she's looking at him like he's a four course meal.

"Come on, man. We can lay down that track tomorrow. We've got a show to prep and beer to drink," Shaun calls as he hoists his bag onto his shoulder. "It's not like you to work this hard."

"I know, I know!" Damien laughs, his eyes still lingering on Phoebe's curves and the way her sweater exposes just a sliver of her belly. "I just wanna lay these vocals down. It won't take long."

The plan really is to record those vocals, and he will, but they've got a few hours before they have to be at the show. As much as he loves his friends, he likes the idea of fucking Phoebe on every surface of the studio even more. It would be a shame if they didn't get to use the space to their full advantage.

"We'll save you a spot if you change your mind!" Johnny calls as Erin tugs him out the door, mumbling something about burgers. Damien's stomach growls, but food can wait. "Don't be too late!"

The door closes and Phoebe takes a confident step toward him. There's a part of him that wants to play this cool and act like she doesn't have this effect on him, but she got her hooks in deep and he doesn't mind it one bit.

"Are you really going to record something, or did you just say that to get me alone?"

Her voice is like a warm summer breeze as she closes the gap between them and slides one hand underneath his shirt, smirking as he feels a shiver run over his skin.

"I would say anything to get you alone." Damien swallows, his heart thumping faster. "But I do want to record those vocals."

"And you need me as inspiration, right?" She purrs.

His cock is straining against his zipper as she delicately trails her fingers along the waistband of his jeans. She's so different from the woman he met in LA, so much more confident now, it bleeds into everything she does. Even the way she looks at him.

"I do," Damien whispers. "You wanna give it to me, babydoll?"

"Remember your little game of focus?" Phoebe bites his lip and tugs until he moans. "You must remember it, you invented it. You, under the desk with your head between my legs. Do you remember how hard I came?"

Her voice is like silk, and his skin sparks, the hairs on his arms raising as she teases him, slipping her fingers beneath the waistband of his briefs. All he wants to do is grab her and kiss her, but he needs to see what she's going to do next. She's in the driver's seat right now, but he'd love to see what she's like when she *really* takes control. Towering over him, dressed in nothing but a pair of heels, while he's on his knees, begging to touch her. He can picture it so vividly that it takes his brain a few seconds to catch up to what she's asked him.

"I— I remember."

He'd never forget something like that. He wasn't sure she'd go for it, had no idea just how open Phoebe was when they first started their relationship, but so far she's rolled with every single one of his kinks. He's a lucky, lucky man.

"Then teach me how this stuff works, and we can play."

Damien grasps hold of her hands; if he lets them wander any further, neither of them will get anything done. The two of them stumble out of the recording booth, and into the editing suite, stopping at the mixing board. Damien points at a big red button.

"That's to record." He lays his finger on a switch and flicks it up and down. "This is for playback, so that I can hear it in my headphones."

"You're sure I won't record over all your work?"

Damien shakes his head.

"Liam's got the masters, and we'll put this one in his office when we're done, label and all."

If they make any progress.

He points at the tape that's still in the reel.

"Nothing gets recorded on the playback track."

This little show-and-tell session is going better than he expected, and he's surprised by how much he managed to recall from Liam and Erin's instructions. There was always a chance the band would have to record something without either one of them around, he just didn't think it would be a situation like this.

"Alright, good to know." She pushes the button, her eyes brazen with a big smile on her face. "Get in the booth, Bell."

"Well, I might need some convincing," he murmurs. "What're you gonna do for me?"

Phoebe reaches down and caresses his cock through his jeans. His eyelids flutter as she squeezes it gently, leaning into him.

"Anything you want, pretty boy."

Pretty boy. That's a new one. The praise goes right to his head.

"What's gotten into you tonight, Miller?"

"I think all that rockstar confidence is rubbing off on me," she whispers, giving his cock another gentle squeeze. "Do you like it?"

"Yes," he rasps.

She hits the record button and grins.

"Then get in there and show me how much."

Phoebe takes his arm, tugging him back into the vocal booth. She shuts the door and leans against the wall, one hand gliding up past her waist to cup her breast.

"You think you can handle this, Bell?"

Damien slides his headphones on, music blaring in his ears. He has a few beats of grace until his own vocals come in. His finger hovers over the button on his mic, smirking back at her.

"Try me, babydoll."

Phoebe doesn't waste time, unbuttoning her jeans and licking her lips.

There's no way he's going to be able to focus on this fucking song. He watches as she teases herself underneath the rough denim, her free hand wandering under her sweater.

Feels so good, she mouths as she pushes her sweater up just the tiniest bit, exposing a dainty lace bra. He's certain it's a new pair of underwear, something she must have picked out today.

This was all part of her plan.

His mouth is dry, blood roaring in his ears as the sound of Shaun's guitar swells into the clash of Ophelia's drums. He's already losing this game, his cock so hard it aches without a single stroke. He could watch her do this forever, but he's got work to do as well.

He belts out a few bars with ease, showing off a little as he does. He can win this, it's his home turf and he knows the song by heart.

But Phoebe has other plans, taking her time tormenting him; her body rocks against her hand as she lets out a string of quiet moans, finally removing her fingers just in time for his next cue, holding them up so that he can see just how wet she is.

Jesus fucking Christ.

She pushes off of the wall and strips off her sweater, tossing it aside as she walks confidently toward him. Anyone could walk in and she doesn't seem to give a shit.

Phoebe grabs his arm with one hand and takes up the mic cord with the other, her cheeks burning bright pink as she uses it to bind his wrists together. Damien's focus is split between the music and Phoebe, but admittedly it's barely a competition. She slides his belt out of its loops, unzipping his jeans and pulling them down past his thighs as she releases his aching cock.

She gazes up at him with those big doe-eyes as she flicks the tip of his cock with her tongue. He'll be shocked he has any self control left by the end of this, but he's got to hold it together. So far, the sound of his heavy breathing into the microphone would be enough to make anyone suspicious as to what's going on, but they're not quite into 'getting fined for misuse of equipment' territory yet. Even so, there's no way they can use this track.

But maybe *he* can.

He lets his head fall back as she begins to stroke him, a confident smile lingering on her lips.

"Focus, Bell. Wouldn't wanna have to do a second take."

Her breathy whisper is only audible through a small pause in the music.

"Pheebs—"

She presses a finger to her lips.

Focus, she mouths.

He's not sure if he's loving or loathing this taste of his own medicine, but he can decide that later. Right now, it's all about the experience.

Her tongue is like silk, swirling around the tip of his cock as one of her hands cups his balls. Damien swallows a whimper, taking a deep breath to calm himself. He wants her, her pussy, her mouth, whatever he can get, he wants it.

He knows the chorus is coming up, the one part in this little game he can't just keep his mouth shut for, but he simply can't hold himself back when she finally takes him all the way down her throat. He does manage a little bit, shifting his more guttural sounds into an extended note that a charitable person might call passable, grasping her hair tight as he forces her to take every inch. He just needs to find a rhythm, and then maybe he'll be able to keep singing, but clearly she's determined to make that really fucking difficult.

Damien's mind is fuzzy, static building in the back of his head as his cock throbs in her mouth, but he keeps singing all the same. She taps his thigh and chokes a little before tearing herself away and sucking in some heavy breaths, a line of spittle dribbling down her chin. She's all smeared makeup and hazy eyes, looking ready to be fucked. He doesn't even bother to finish the song, untangling the cord from his wrists and ripping off his headphones, letting them fall to the floor with a light clatter. This part of the game is over. It's time to move on to round two.

"It's still recording, you know."

Damien backs her against the wall the moment she makes it to her feet, caging her in with both arms. Her voice may sound a little labored, but it's still confident, even cocky.

"Of course it is. We're gonna take it home and I'm gonna make it into a little cassette. Maybe I'll listen to it on the road if I'm ever feeling lonely."

Damien slips her jeans down, dropping to his knees. The tops of her thighs are dotted with tiny freckles that he traces with his mouth, kissing each one. Her body is a map that he's been craving to commit to memory. More than anything he wants to know every spot that lights her up; he wants to be able to turn her whole body into a sky full of fireworks.

"Well, you better start talking dirty to me, Bell. And make sure to send me a copy when we're done."

"Anything my girl wants, my girl gets," he breathes, helping her step out of her panties before slipping them into his back pocket.

Phoebe gasps and wriggles against him as he teases her entrance. He hums, sliding two fingers inside of her, crooking them in just the right way to make her hand slam against the wall. He knows he's hit that spot, continuing to torment her with his slow, deep thrusts.

"Gotta make sure you're ready for me."

She laughs at his cockiness, the sound rippling through him. She lifts one leg, draping it over his shoulder as Damien torments her swollen clit, frantically grabbing his hair as she tries to pull him closer. He chuckles, her desperation is intoxicating.

"I want an appetizer."

Damien torments her the same way she did to him only a couple minutes ago, his gentle licks light but quick enough to get a big reaction. Her hips buck with need, trying to force him to devour her, but Damien holds steady. He can tell how much she's aching for him; she's quivering along with every move he makes.

He rises to his feet, pinning her wrists above her head as he leans in for a brutish kiss. Phoebe moans, smashing against his lips while she struggles to hook her leg around his waist. He holds her close to him and bites her earlobe, just to rile her up even more before reaching down and lining himself up with her entrance. He waits for a moment, teasing her with inevitability before slowly sliding into her, a satisfied groan escaping his lips.

"Look at how well you take me," he purrs, moving his hips nice and slow as he savors each stroke. "You feel that? How good it feels when I fill you up?"

Just watching her being pushed toward her peak is almost enough for him, and he can feel his cock twitch deep inside her as she grinds her clit against him. Intensifying pleasure gathers at the base of his spine and he dips his head to suck on her neck, his teeth just barely grazing her skin.

"Tell me how good it feels when I fuck you."

"So good–" She starts, but the sound is whisked away with a sharp gasp as her body shudders against him.

"Louder," he demands. "We need to be able to hear this when I play it back, otherwise it'll all be a big waste, won't it?"

Damien fights to stay in control as her body begins to roll against his, more and more blush cascading across her collarbone by the minute, spreading out in delicate pink splotches.

"It's so good, Damien! God, fuck me harder!"

His thrusts get faster until he hits the perfect pace to make her tits bounce along with the rhythm. He cups her breast with his free hand, sliding his thumb across her pebbled nipple, and Phoebe arches her back with an agonized groan.

"You're all mine, aren't you? Completely."

"Yes, sir," she mewls. "Oh god, please, just keep fucking me like that!"

A man can only have so much self control, especially around her. Damien closes his eyes and lets himself get lost in the sensation, breathing in the scent of cinnamon and bergamot. He can feel her heel digging into the back of his thigh as he pounds into her, giving into his most primal urges. Her arms wrap around him as he releases her wrists, her fingernails raking over his biceps and across his back as she cries out.

"I want you to let go for me."

Damien thrusts harder, seeing just how much she can take in the state she's in, right on the edge and moaning incoherently until she finally comes.

Damien loses all sense of control, their bodies crashing into each other like waves against the shore as their moans get louder, creating a lust-filled harmony. Then his own climax hits, sending jolts radiating through his body as he lets out a deep and broken moan. Panting breaths fill the room as they come down from their collective high.

He presses his forehead against hers, completely silent as she hugs him tight. She runs her fingers through his hair, speaking so softly he can barely hear.

"You okay?"

Saying *I love you* never feels like enough when it comes to her.

"I don't know when you became my whole world," he whispers. "But I can't imagine my life without you."

Don't Dream it's Over

PHOEBE

There are no paparazzi, no fans waiting outside as they step out of the taxi and head for the back entrance of The Roxy. It should be a good night. A hometown show for the first time in a year; a chance for them to debut some brand new songs for a crowd that has no idea what's in store. Damien's been in a much better mood since their little recording booth session, the tapes stashed in Phoebe's bag, safely hidden away only for the two of them. She can feel a little prickle of heat on her neck just thinking about it.

But all that positive buzz takes a dive the moment she spots Liam and Troy outside having a cigarette, feeling Damien tense up as he squeezes her hand a little too tightly. He pushes his shoulders back and lifts his head up higher as Troy marches straight for him.

"And where the hell have you two been?" He barks, his tone sharp.

Damien laughs, which only makes Troy angrier.

"At the studio, Troy. Chill out. I'm here on time, so what's the problem?"

Phoebe bites back a smile, catching Liam's eye as he silently tosses her a knowing glance.

"The problem, smart guy, is that you are, in fact, late," Troy snipes back.

Damien frowns.

"What do you mean, the show doesn't start for at least another 10!"

"You know what, you're right!" Troy taps his watch. "You've just barely got ten minutes, and Allan fucking Harris is here."

Allan Harris, head of Phantom Records, Phoebe recognized the name immediately.

"Why didn't anyone tell me?" Damien growls.

"That one's on me," Liam shrugs. "I didn't want to spook you in the studio. I figured it would just throw things off."

Damien sighs.

"Look, Liam, I appreciate—"

"We're wasting time!" Troy grabs Damien by the sleeve of his jacket. "Let's go!"

Helpless, Phoebe follows them inside and into a small makeshift dressing room that feels like it might have been an old closet at some point. Allan Harris is seated, decked out in his infamous white suit. He's smoking a cigarette, casually exhaling as they enter the room; he's relaxed, but it doesn't serve to make him look any less intimidating. Everyone else is already seated, waiting nervously, but the tone shifts the second he rests his eyes on Damien.

"There he is." Just like outside, Phoebe can feel Damien stiffen as Allan approaches. "Thought you were going to be late."

"No, sir,"

Phoebe's never heard him call anyone sir before unless he was being a smartass.

"Just polishing up some stuff in the studio."

Allan looks him up and down for a moment before his eyes flip over to Phoebe.

"Are you the one who's been keeping him on his best behavior?"

She smiles politely. There's something about the way he looks at her, coupled with the implication, that immediately puts her on edge. Damien's a grown man, he knows he screwed up. The frustrating part is there's no way they can explain it was all just Chris trying to shake them.

Especially because it worked.

"I've been pretty tied up with writing about this lovely group, and babysitting isn't really part of the job description, but Damien's been wonderful."

"What happened in Kansas isn't going to happen again," Damien cuts in.

Allan huffs and sucks on his cigarette, blowing the smoke out of the side of his mouth, all while staring Damien down.

But Damien holds his gaze.

"There was a reason why we signed you, and I'm hoping tonight you can remind me what it was."

Phoebe feels like all the air in the room gets sucked out in a split second, and she glances around at the band, almost desperate for a confident face in the crowd. All she finds is anxiety and panic. Ophelia glances down at her shoes, and one of her drumsticks clatters onto the floor. Shaun scoops it up and hands it to her, almost shielding her from Allan with his body, but he needn't bother. The man hasn't looked away from Damien since they walked through the door.

"It was one bad night," Damien assures him. "It won't happen again."

"I'm sure it won't!" he grunts, slowly standing up from his seat with a brand new grin on his face. "You're a good group of kids, and I know you'll make us proud."

Allan pats Damien on the shoulder and somehow Damien stiffens even more; luckily Troy grabs the executive's attention fast enough that he misses the clenched fists shaking at Damien's sides.

"Allan, let's give them a few minutes to regroup. Still drink whiskey? My treat."

"I'm on to scotch now, MacAllan Adami."

Troy chuckles nervously.

"Well, I don't make *that* much money, and I don't think this place does either. But we'll see what they've got."

Troy escorts Allan out into the hall, the sound of the two of them bantering back and forth like nothing's happened fading into the distance as Liam shuts the door behind them.

"I really am sorry I didn't tell you he was going to be here, but trust me, you're going to be fine. Just play like you did in the studio, and everything will go great."

Damien stuffs his hands in his pockets.

"You said we were good, but not great."

"And I meant that. I'm not going to bullshit you guys, but all Allan's looking for stability. All you need to do is put on a solid show, and he'll be satisfied. And then, well, we can work on getting you back to great."

Shaun shoots up out of his seat, standing to attention.

"Aye aye, Captain."

Liam smiles, probably the warmest one Phoebe's seen from him so far. He really is looking out for them.

"Break a leg, you lot. I'll see you out there."

He disappears, shutting the door behind him, and Ophelia puts her head in her hands with a groan.

"God, why the fuck did he have to be here?! He's such a buzzkill!"

"Hey, Liam's just trying to help us out, you don't have to-"

She lifts her head and swats at Johnny.

"I was talking about *Allan,* dipshit."

"Oh, yeah, right. That dude is..." Johnny exhales and shakes his head before looking over at Damien. "You gonna be okay tonight?"

Phoebe's hand finds his, and she gives it a reassuring squeeze. She knows Johnny means well, but if they don't stop babying him none of them will be able to get over any of this.

Damien nods.

"Yeah. We're solid, man." He turns to Phoebe, only half whispering so everyone can still hear. "Hey, Pheebs, If we bomb again, promise you won't write about it."

She chuckles.

"Sorry Bell, but my job is to report the truth."

"Damn," Damien murmurs. "I really thought the incredible sex would get me out of that objectivity clause."

"Hey, just put on the best performance of your career and we'll be fine."

He's still smiling, but his eyes are unsure. She can see the echoes of Kansas rippling through him. Normally, he'd probably shrug it off, but it's the reason the rest of the tour got canceled, and Phoebe knows Damien is still taking that hard despite what he says.

"You're going to go out there and do what you do best: you're going to work that crowd and sing your ass off. Believe in yourself, believe in your talent—" She whips around and flashes the rest of the band her most encouraging smile, "and that goes for all of you, but unfortunately that's all I've got. I was a shitty cheerleader in high school."

"Hey, we're not complaining," Ophelia chuckles. "You want Troy's job?"

"Not a chance in hell. I've seen what you guys put him through."

"You're right though, Pheebs," Shaun sighs as he grabs his guitar. "We can't let Allan get to us. We have to put on a real show tonight or the label's gonna want to tack on more restrictions, and that's the best-case scenario."

Phoebe watches as his expression shifts, and she turns to follow his gaze.

"You good Phi? Look like you might throw up."

Ophelia exhales dramatically and gets to her feet, opening her arms wide in time for Shaun to wrap his own around her. Phoebe can feel her heart break a little. Usually she's all smiles and jokes, and It's strange to see her down like this.

"I just want us to kill it tonight," she murmurs. "I want the album to be good, I want… I don't know, man, I just want things to go back to the way they were a week ago. I want to play some fucking good music and make people smile. And Allan? Like what, the label can't forgive one fucking mistake?"

Phoebe sees the guilt splash across Damien's face all over again; he knows it's not just the one bad show, it's a pattern of behavior. Things were getting better right up until they weren't, and the *reason* shit goes wrong is never something that matters to someone like Allan.

"That dude stresses everyone out," Shaun reminds her gently. "You saw Troy, he can barely hold his own when they're face to face."

"I know," she sighs. "I just hope…"

"We will," Shaun reassures her with a little kiss. "We'll be great."

Johnny steps in, squeezing Ophelia's shoulder and glancing over at Damien.

"Get the fuck in here, D. Group hug."

Phoebe kisses Damien on the cheek.

"I'll leave you to rally the troops."

While a part of her still feels the urge to get every little scrap of information she can, she knows better.

She gives his ass a gentle pinch before sauntering out the door. They're going to be great tonight, even with that prick watching from the wings. Especially with him there. Revolver's never been a group to shy away from a tough crowd, and Damien's always been one to take a challenge head on.

Phoebe immediately heads to get a drink as she takes in the place. It's a packed house, and she has to squeeze through a crush of people to even make it to the overcrowded bar. There's a real electricity in the air; none of these people have any idea who they're about to see tonight, just that it's gotta be something big. As she finishes scanning the room she catches a glimpse of Allan, Liam, and Troy heading her way from the edge of the stage, and quickly grabs her double G&T and melts into the crowd. None of the men have anything against her at the moment, at least as far as she knows, but it's always better safe than sorry.

As she pushes through the crush of people toward the edge of the venue, she suddenly feels a tug on her arm, mortified for a moment that Troy or Liam had caught up with her, but when she turns around she's more than a little pleased to see Janis leaning out from a booth.

"Where the hell have you been all night, girl?"

Phoebe grins, immediately feeling more at ease.

"You got room?"

"Of course, how much of a booth d'you think my ass takes up?" She cackles. "But, just to be sure, let's take a poll! We letting Miller sit with us in the cool kids booth?"

Phoebe glances past Janis, happy to see Erin's warm smile for the first time that night, and beside her...

"Why are you here?"

Brian chuckles, caught in the midst of cleaning his glasses on his shirt.

"Well, I could leave."

"No, no, that's not what I meant, I'm just—"

"Troy invited me. Said I should spend less time in front of my typewriter and more time outside." he glances around with a grimace. "I gotta say, so far I'm not such a big fan of this rendition of outside. That said, you're more than welcome to join us."

"Of course you are!" Erin's eyes have been bouncing between Phoebe and the stage the whole time. "So, how are they?"

"Nervous," she replies. "Last I checked they were rallying, maybe moving on to some secret band-only stuff. Actually, I'm surprised you weren't backstage."

Erin snorts and shakes her head.

"I was in there for a bit with Jan. We left because she was gonna take a swing at Allan."

"*I* actually suggested we get a drink," Janis corrects her. "Erin was the one ready to fight. Anything for her man, isn't that right?"

Erin giggles as the two clink their glasses together.

"Wait, what did he do?" Phoebe asks.

Brian perks up at the mention.

"Nothing," Erin mutters into her drink. "That's the problem. He was just standing in the corner talking to Liam, but the whole time he would just... looking at everyone. I dunno, it just felt like he was planning something. He does this kind of stuff in the studio whenever he comes to visit, and it makes whoever he's there to see really nervous. Anyway, after the tour got canceled and after everything in the studio today, I don't know. They don't need to be dealing with all of this."

"We're talking about Allan Harris, right? He's made some of the biggest artists in the industry." Brian leans forward on the table, shaking his head. "It's probably not too complicated. If Revolver's popularity tanks before the album, he loses a lot of money. He might just be trying to figure out if they're still worth the risk."

"That's part of my problem with him," Erin replies. "He's all about money. And I know that's his job, but when he looks at them it's clear he doesn't really *see* them. They're just dollar signs with big hair."

"Great hair, though," Janis chimes in.

Erin takes another sip of her drink as Janis slides closer toward Phoebe.

"So, Pheebs, you thinking of putting Allan into your article then?"

She frowns. It's actually the first time she's really had the chance to think about it. Obviously it'd be a good angle to use, everyone likes a little twist on the good vs evil story, but...

"I don't know. It might actually put them at risk, maybe make things worse." She glances over to Brian, his brow already raised in interest. "What do you think?"

"Well, It's a bit tricky," he says candidly. "Include him and you get a nice and easy little villain for your piece, but you're right, there's a real risk there. You also have to worry about seeming objective or you lose a bit of credibility." He scratches at his chin, mulling it over for a moment or two. "More important than that though, I think focusing on him makes you lose hold of your thread. Allan is too macro, too big. You want your story to be small, completely focused on you and them. He doesn't really mean a whole lot in the grand scheme of things, not with your new angle at least."

He grabs his glass and takes a big swig.

"Oh, and speaking of, I expect to start seeing drafts."

Phoebe grins.

"So, after all that helpful advice it turns out you really did swing by just to give me shit."

"I came because I was *invited*." His smile is wide. "And if giving you shit is the push you need to get this thing done, then that's just a bonus for me. So far all I have is half a page, plus whatever I can remember from all those crumpled notes."

She can feel Janis gently nudge her foot under the table, checking to see if she's okay in those little ways she always does, but Phoebe gives them both a reassuring smile.

"I know I've been distracted. I promise I'm still on top of this."

Brian's eyes twinkle in the dim light.

"I know you've got a lot going on now, and I want you to do what you have to to take care of yourself, but just don't lose focus, okay? We've still got deadlines to meet, and I want to make Rolling Stone seethe with envy as soon as humanly possible."

"You got it boss."

Phoebe *has* been writing— sort of. She spends most of her days in her new office transcribing, making notes and analyzing interview clips, piecing together photos, but when it comes to actually sitting down at the typewriter and putting down anything new, she gets stuck. It feels like she's too close to the finish line, and that inevitability is starting to get to her. It'll get done either way, but what if she's bitten off more than she can chew with all of this? What if she can't provide what she promised?

Luckily, before she can truly begin to spiral, the lights dim, and the accompanying rush of feedback pulses through the bar. There's a moment of hushed silence before the entire place erupts in a cacophony of applause and screams as the curtain parts and they see *him* at the microphone. He's shed his t-shirt, wearing nothing but a leather jacket and a pair of shredded blue jeans, his long dark hair obscuring his face. But even behind it all Phoebe can see those icy eyes taking in the crowd. If ever there was a moment he was doubting himself it was over; the smile spreading across his face is pure confidence. The other members walk onto stage one by one, drinking in the adoration flooding in from the crowd.

Ophelia twirls her drum sticks over her head as Damien waits at the mic, raising his hand to signal everyone to be quiet, only cutting down the noise by a tiny bit.

"Surprise, New York," he purrs. "Did you miss us?"

Whatever they all did backstage, whoever stood up and took charge, it worked. The crowd is frenzied, by now the realization hitting anyone who didn't recognize Revolver right away. Even more people push toward the dancefloor, some already clamoring for the stage. Damien reaches down to grab hands, with a bigger grin than she's ever seen.

As he straightens up and returns to the middle of the stage, Phoebe catches a glimpse of Allan just off in the wings. He looks completely neutral, neither impressed or underwhelmed, simply taking in every moment and studying them as he sips at his drink. Troy, in stark contrast, is already bouncing on the balls of his feet, and even Liam looks caught somewhere between anxiety and hope as he cranes his neck.

But Damien doesn't seem to notice, or if he does he simply doesn't care, slipping so easily into his rockstar persona, albeit a little different. It feels softer this time: there's no sneering, no pouring whiskey down his bare chest, no flirting with every girl he sees. It really is strange to see how much he's changed in such a short time. How much of it was him, and how much of it was her? How much of it was both?

"Well hey, New York, you might not know this but we're Revolver, and we want to play you some brand new tunes tonight, just because we love you *that* much."

A chorus of sound rings out from their booth as all three women scream as loud as they possibly can, all while Brian covers his ears.

"Come on, old man! You're a rock journalist!" Janis cackles.

"A rock *editor!*" He bellows over the noise. "I'm too old for fieldwork!"

Damien catches Phoebe's eye, giving her a little wink before pointing right at her.

"This first one's for the loudest table in the club!"

The melodic howl of Shaun's guitar fills the room as the band launches into Babydoll. They're in perfect sync, and this time it's clear Damien's sole focus is on the music. Right from the first note he's pitch perfect, strutting around onstage like he owns it before they've even hit the bridge. In all his confident swagger it seems like he's completely forgotten about Allan, or maybe he's simply realized it's hard to put on a great show while worrying about some asshole the whole time. Either way, she can't really afford herself that same luxury.

Phoebe's eyes volley between the two men, watching with rapt attention as Damien gets right down on his knees to sing straight at the girls crammed up against the front of the stage, then quickly glancing over at the wings to try and catch any reaction she can from Allan.

She can feel her nerves getting the best of her after a while, wondering if there's a chance Damien could crack under the pressure, to tilt out of control with a single glance from this new antagonist, but he just keeps on belting out that perfect tune. And soon enough, even as the crease between Allan's eyebrows refuses to budge, and he continues to stand almost completely stoic and still, Phoebe spots it: his right foot tapping ever so slightly as the song comes to a close.

And it's then, for a single moment in the afterglow of that first song of the night, when she catches Damien finally turning to the wings to catch Allan's eye, microphone in hand.

"How'd that feel, New York? I hope you fuckers are ready for a show, because we're not going anywhere!"

Wild Child

DAMIEN

The entire set, he felt like he was on the brink of collapse. The pressure from Allan right before the show had almost been too much, and it took all the willpower in the world to keep himself from staring the man down.

Sure, they all want Allan to like the tracks, if only to get him off their backs, but these songs aren't for him. They're not even for the label.

Every note, every word, is for Phoebe.

The crowd pulses along with the music, reaching for him every time he gets anywhere near the edge of the stage. He returns the gesture, kneeling and leaning out, brushing his fingers against as many outstretched hands as he can. This feeling, these people, this is what music is about. All of the shit about his image and the business? It's all tacked on bullshit to push their popularity and drive sales. Art is supposed to make people feel something, and judging by the reaction the audience is feeling a whole lot right about now.

Shaun howls into the mic along with Damien as he hits his final chord, Ophelia crashing down on her drums one last time. The entire place erupts in a sea of screams and applause. They take all of it in, each member abandoning their instruments and heading right up to the edge of the stage with Damien to bask in the adoration as he jumps to his feet and leans on his mic stand.

Their last show before they truly head back into the studio for a while. There's a small pang of sadness that ricochets through his body, but judging by the response, these new songs are gonna be a smash-hit, exactly what they need to get back in the saddle again.

"New York, we've been Revolver, and you've been fucking beautiful tonight! Please remember to tip your waitress like the absolute legends I know you are! Goodnight!"

With that, he makes his way backstage, skipping steps on the rickety little staircase and landing right in front of Troy. He's waiting with a big grin on his face as Allan stands opposite, his own expression just as inscrutable as usual. The other three catch up to them, all stopping right in front of the two men, almost challenging Allan to say something first. He looks them over, taking in a big breath before the smallest smile graces his otherwise concrete face. He raises his eyebrows, placing a firm hand on Damien's shoulder as he stares directly at him.

"You had us running scared there for a second, kid. Glad to see it was a false alarm."

He knows how badly Allan wanted an apology for Kansas, which makes this all the sweeter. Even the greats screw up from time to time. What really matters is exactly how you bounce back.

"Everyone has bad nights," Johnny quips. "We try to keep them few and far between. This though? This is the standard you can expect from a night out with Revolver."

Allan nods at Johnny with a wry smile, his dismissive look enough to put Damien dangerously close to some very ill-advised behavior. Thankfully, he just turns back to Troy, clapping him on the back.

"Let's talk, Sullivan. You can buy me another drink and we'll discuss the best way to get these kids back on the fast-track."

Troy lets the man step ahead of him, rolling his eyes the moment his back is turned before giving the band a warm smile, and heading off behind him.

Damien chuckles and whirls around, motioning for the team to bring it in for a group hug. He's relieved, as much as he's exhausted. Hell, they probably all are, but they needed this. To prove they still had it. Even if it was to some asshole who hadn't ever seen them live.

"You were a fucking star out there," Ophelia whispers in his ear.

"*We,*" he murmurs, ruffling her hair. "You good?"

Ophelia beams, any of the confidence she'd lacked in that meeting before the show long since flooding back.

"Better than ever."

A powerfully giddy shriek slices through the air, and they all turn as one to see Janis running right for them at full speed. Ophelia's beams even more as she leaps forward, the two of them colliding and locking lips instantly. Erin has already glommed on to Johnny, peppering his face with kisses and congratulating him by the time Damien catches sight of Phoebe, heading toward them with a warm smile on her face. Walking beside her is an older guy with pallid skin and a thick mustache, his confident stride complimented by his well-fit brown leather jacket. Damien jogs down the stairs, heading right for Phoebe, who's prepped for the occasion, already holding a whisky for him.

"Hiya, babydoll," he purrs, kissing her.

She giggles, waiting until he takes his drink to introduce the newcomer.

"Damien Bell, this is Brian Gordon. Brian, this is Damien."

The newly christened Brian sticks out his hand. Phoebe's boss doesn't quite look how Damien expected. He seems less like a hard-nosed journalist and more like that reasonably cool uncle everyone hopes to have. The one you just know has a whole lot of fucked up stories they're waiting to tell you when you're old enough.

"Nice to meet you Mr. Bell. That was a hell of a set."

Still in the buzzing warmth of the afterglow, the compliment hits him much harder than he expected. He nods to himself, trying to keep from breaking down.

"Thanks, man. Yeah, I thought we were really tight tonight."

"Yeah, those new songs are something else. Obviously I didn't catch the rest of your tour, but it feels like a real departure from your old sound." Brian pauses for a moment, taking a sip of his drink. "In a good way, of course. A bit of an evolution."

The walk back to the dressing room is a blur, his conversation with

Brian, Phoebe's grinning face, and the chatter from the band all blending together into a wave of sound. When they arrive, however, the big table of food immediately grabs his attention.

"I'm gonna grab something to eat," Phoebe whispers. "You hungry?"

Hungry? It all hits him at once. With all that anxiety and stress from Allan's visit he was running on fumes, but as it fades away... he feels hungrier than he's been in years.

"I could eat that whole spread. Grab us some good seats and we'll get to work!"

"You got it, gorgeous."

Phoebe hunts down some chairs, an extra stolen from Janis who's just a bit too busy with Shaun and Ophelia to care, and sets them up in front of a mountain of fresh looking fries. As he sits between Phoebe and Brian, the three of them wordlessly devouring their food, Damien finds himself at a loss for words for what may just be the first time in his life. This was the guy the two of them were terrified of, since pretty much the moment started their relationship. He was the guy that could, with a word, completely torpedo everything. But together at the table, with everything now out in the open? He didn't seem so scary.

"Hey, man, I want you to know that... you know, Pheebs and I... it just sort of happened. I wasn't trying to fuck everything up for you guys."

"Well, that's how a lot of great love stories start," Brian lights a cigarette and passes the pack to Damien. "They just sort of happen. I'm glad everything worked out."

Brian sucks on his cigarette as Phoebe stands, Erin calling her over to chat. She looks so free, no more tucking herself in the back of the room where she can observe unseen. It's like sometime over the past couple months she shed her skin and a new woman emerged. The confidence, the ease with which she made friends with them all, how skillfully she navigated everything...

"Have you guys talked to her parents about this whole thing yet, or are you waiting for the papers to do it for you?"

"So far it's the second one," he laughs. "Why?"

Brian shakes his head.

"Phoebe's mom is... kind of like a helicopter. I'm surprised she hasn't forced her way into your lives yet."

Jesus, how bad is this woman? Phoebe didn't mention this stuff, just that her parents didn't really get her.

"Is it just her mom who's a pain in the ass, or is it both parents?" Damien lights his cigarette and exhales. "Because for me, it's my dad who was always on my case. Wanted me to join the Army, be a real man... you know, that kind of shit."

"My dad too," Brian mutters, clearly a little uncomfortable, but quickly coming around. "As for Phoebe, I'm not exactly in the know, but her mom's the one who always calls the office. If Phoebe's not around she tries to get through to me, leaves a lot of messages with my secretary. Phoebe knows. She's always extremely apologetic, but family's complicated, right? Of course it is. Hell, no matter how hard I've tried I often end up feeling a little more like a dad than a boss when Phoebe's concerned, but..." He glances over at her, ensuring she's still out of earshot. "All I can say is more than a couple times I've come to her office and found her in tears at the end of one of those calls."

Damien can't imagine how this situation with her mother came to be, but he does know he's liking Ma Miller less and less by the minute.

"Has she talked to you about this stuff?" Damien asks. "You know, like how it makes her feel?"

"No," Brian snorts. "She'd rather die than come to me about something personal like that. Fuck, Bell, her coming to talk to me about *you* two was probably absolute torture for her. She never wants to feel like she's getting babied, getting special treatment, anything like that. No, she's dealing with her family stuff all on her lonesome. Seems to be how she wants it to stay."

"Sounds like my idea of hell," Damien sighs.

Brian chuckles and pats him on the shoulder.

"You'll be okay, champ. It's not like it's the Wicked Witch of the West you're dealing with."

"Ladies, germs, and esteemed guests!" Troy booms, bursting through the door with as much fervor as he can muster.

"Oooh! Esteemed?" Janis asks.

"Not you, Kaneko. You're old news at this point."

Janis flips him off, but Troy ignores her, clapping his hands together with glee. It's rare to see him this... happy? The creases from his permanent scowl are still pressed into his face, but he looks like he just won the lottery.

"I have *incredible* news. The label is hosting a big event in Paris over Christmas, and–"

"France?!" Johnny yelps.

"No, Tennessee," Troy replies, rolling his eyes. "Jackass."

"Well, you weren't specific," Johnny mutters. "And there is a Paris in Tennessee, so…"

Troy sighs.

"Alright, look, before Reed spikes my blood pressure any further: Allan was telling me that if you kids can get your shit together and get that album down quick enough, they'd throw you a big release party out there. In Paris. You'd play live, get to meet a bunch of—"

"I'm not doing another Christmas away from my mom," Shaun announces. The room gets quiet in an instant as he clears his throat. "Guys, look, I'm not trying to be ungrateful, but I don't wanna spend another Christmas on the phone with my parents just telling them how much I miss them. I wanna be home. You promised me that we'd get to rest after this tour for a while."

"So go home early," Troy replies with a shrug. "You're not on tour, nobody's keeping you there. Besides, you never let me finish my sentence."

A big smile spreads across Shaun's face.

"What else you got?"

"You'd get to spend Christmas in Paris *if you want to*. All expenses paid by the label. They're putting you up at– Damien, you're a huge fucking nerd. Where did Oscar Wilde die?"

Damien rolls his eyes.

"L'Hôtel in Paris."

"Yeah, that place. And yeah, it's a big fucking deal. Anyway, as long as you lock in your travel time in the next couple weeks, you can be back whenever you want." Troy holds up his hands. "It's only October, you've got a lot of time to think about it, so just keep it in the back of your minds."

"Okay, but when do we need to finish the record by?"

Johnny looks excited. In fact, everyone does. They'd done a bit of traveling on tour before, but that's just another form of work. They'd never been flown out somewhere for a celebration.

"November, let's say the 20th. And hey, I know it's a bit of a rush considering everything that's gone on, but Liam says you guys can handle it. He's talking with Allan— actually, last I checked he was anxiety-drinking while Allan yammered in his ear. I should probably go and rescue him, no one should be trapped with Allan Harris for more than a few minutes. I think it's considered a war crime."

Brian stands up, tapping his jacket pockets.

"Well, maybe I'll come along with you. I need a refill and I gotta buy some more cigarettes. There a machine around here?"

"Yeah, I'll show you." Troy points at the band. "And you lot, if Allan somehow sneaks past me and comes back in here, behave yourselves. We've gotten this far, and I do *not* want to find out one of you said something smart and fucked it all up!"

"Yes, dad!" Damien calls out, Troy flipping him off as he leaves with Brian in tow.

Phoebe slides into his lap, wrapping her arms around his neck.

"So, you wanna come along to Paris?"

"Definitely." She beams. "Are you kidding me? Christmas in the most romantic city in the world?"

"There are a lot of pickpockets there!" Johnny shouts from across the room. "Kinda takes the romance out of things!"

Erin swats at him.

"Nobody's talking to you, Debbie Downer!"

Phoebe chuckles, coiling Damien's hair around her finger.

"Christmas in Paris would be lovely..." She stops. It seems like she's struggling with exactly how to broach the topic. "It's just... I was kind of hoping that we could be back for New Year's?"

She's fiddling with the dog tags around her neck, blush creeping up to her earlobes.

"You don't want to do New Year's in Paris? Just think of what it'd be like to fuck on the Eiffel Tower during the fireworks," Damien teases, rubbing his nose against her cheek. "What's so important about being back in New York for New Years anyway?"

She takes a deep breath.

"I, uh... my mom does this New Year's day brunch thing, and..." She doesn't look at him, the flush in her face deepening. "I don't know, I don't even really know if I want to..."

She's winding the chain of his dog tags around her finger.

"Brian said your mom's kind of..."

"You were talking about my mom?" There's a touch of venom in her voice, but it's the way it mixes in with her laugh that makes Damien nervous. He should have just kept his mouth shut. "Why?"

Damien's heart pounds, his skin prickling with anxiety. He has to be delicate about this. He softens his tone, putting a bit of pressure on her shoulders before he lets his hands slip down her back. To his surprise, she leans into the touch, her eyes still piercing his.

"Brian mentioned he's protective of you, and he's, you know... seen you... upset after you talk to her."

"Families have conflict. It's totally normal," she replies. "My mom's just... you know– she, uh..."

Sometimes we don't see things for what they really are when we're too close to them. Back when he was a kid, hearing his parents fight over his dad's drinking was just one of the sounds of the house, and he didn't realize how fucked up it all really was until it became too overwhelming.

Phoebe swallows and shakes her head.

"She can be difficult, and she just doesn't get me all the time, you know? Just normal stuff."

Way back on the bus, she said her brother was the golden child, and that she sometimes felt like a disappointment. It seems like when it comes to her mom, maybe there's a part of her that *needs* approval. *Any* kind of approval– but he resists the urge to say any of that. Still, sitting through sneers and glares at the dining room table isn't his idea of a good time.

Her eyes search his face for a moment, and he immediately regrets not being able to hide his feelings.

"Sorry, I didn't mean to dump this on you, it's–"

He pulls her tighter toward him, planting kisses on her neck.

"You're not dumping anything on me, okay? We've all got shit, Pheebs."

"Yeah?"

"God yeah. My dad used to drink a lot when I was a kid, and things between us have never been great. He doesn't get me either, not really, and the bad press doesn't make things better. Thing is, I think he's trying." He clears his throat. "So, I was thinking maybe you could come and meet them for Thanksgiving. We could go for the weekend, maybe even the week? Unless your parents have a thing for that too."

"I love my mom, but a week with her?" Phoebe laughs.

"Well, *my* family would love to meet you. We can head straight to Paris after the weekend if you like. Get away from all of this shit. The studio, the press, all of it. We can even do your mom's thing when we get back, if you really want to." He grins. "Oh, and heads up, my mom makes fucking *amazing* stuffing."

He wants his parents to see how much he's settled down, how much she's changed him in such a short period of time. There's no way they'd believe he'd found such an amazing person, and Damien wants to show her off. Ava's going to love her, his mom's going to love her, and his dad will, at the very least, be shocked he's actually planning to settle down. Hoping to, at least, if she is too.

Phoebe sighs, letting him hold all her weight.

"You always know exactly what to say, don't you?"

Bette Davis Eyes

DAMIEN

Tonight is Phoebe's birthday, and with everything Damien has planned she's in for a hell of a ride.

Horns blare in the distance, people rush past him and Shaun, probably on their way to fill up the bars and nightclubs. Everything in Manhattan is glowing tonight. His nerves feel electrified, like he has to keep moving no matter what. It's been this way for the better part of a week. The record is actually turning into something incredible; It feels like they're finally making real art and he's never been happier, but he also knows that this is the calm before the storm.

They haven't heard anything from Chris. He hopes there's nothing left *to* hear, but in his heart he also knows there's no way that weasel would give up so easily. But tonight? It's time to forget about that asshole, the work, even the trip to Paris. Tonight, he's not a rock star. He's just a man in love, showing his girlfriend the time of her life.

Tonight is all about Phoebe.

It's 7:15, and Damien's ordered a car to pick all of them up from Ophelia's just before the hour. Dinner's at 8:10, and The Vault opens at 11:00, and everything has to be perfect.

"Damn man, how much stuff did you buy her?" Shaun asks, eyeing the bags Damien's carrying as they make their way toward the jewelry store.

"I mean, it's not that much." Damien lifts his arm, shaking the bags full of gifts that he'd been picking up over the last couple weeks. "I don't think it's enough, actually, that's why we're making this last stop. She's turning 24, that's a big deal."

"I thought 25 was the big deal. Or is that 30?"

Damien shrugs.

"Whatever man, I'm more than happy to do something nice for my girlfriend. Maybe you should step up your game, you ever think about that?"

"Like build her an office in my house?" Shaun chuckles. "Take her out for dinner and follow it up with a BDSM club?"

Damien runs a hand through his hair as they pause to make way for a couple and their little boy. He grins as the kid waves at him.

"And a nice pen," Damien adds, holding up one of the bags.

There's a hell of a lot more than just a pen in here, but he's pretty sure she's going to love all of it.

"A *nice pen*?"

"Yeah, I mean, she has that typewriter already, but when she's on the go she writes with these chewed up Bic ones all the time. She needs a nice pen."

Shaun bends over laughing, leaning heavily on his knees as Damien gives him a playful shove.

"She needs a pen, dude! Get off my dick."

"It's not about the pen, *dude*. It's just fucking hilarious how hard you're going in on this. You've known her for what, two months?"

Damien scoffs.

"It's not that much, just a few little things. You're just judging based on your own–"

"Based on facts, my man!" Shaun pats him on the shoulder. "When you go big, you don't just go big, you go olympic-sized."

"Yeah, well, I love her, okay?" He grumbles. "She's the best thing that ever happened to me, and she risked everything so we could be together. I owe her."

"Sure, fine I get it. It's devotional, it's love, no one's more on board with that stuff than me. But remind me again what we're going to this place for?"

Damien mumbles the words, completely inaudible.

"What was that? Sorry, you're usually so much more articulate, Bell."

He sighs.

"A collar."

Shaun shakes his finger, chastising him.

"Ah ah ah, If I remember correctly your exact words were 'a custom-made, and fitted, one of a kind collar,' right?"

Damien does his best to ignore him, pushing past Shaun to get the door as his friend's laughter fills the street. It's quiet inside, a family-run place his dad bought his mom's engagement ring from years ago. Damien's already bought a few pieces of jewelry for his sister and girl-friends here over the years. Hell, his own bangles came from here; couldn't resist when he saw them.

The owner, Leah, stands behind the counter, already waving him over only moments after the two of them are through the door. She's always reminded him of an art teacher, her colorful paisley shirt, bright pink jacket, and massive yellow hoop earrings just screaming 'I'm gonna teach your kids the best ways to make a mess.' Her short auburn hair is only partially hidden underneath a black bowler hat. On anyone else, Damien would say the outfit was ridiculous. On Leah? It just worked.

"Well hello, gentlemen. Lovely to see you this evening."

"Hey, Leah. Is it ready?"

She nods, an excited shine in her eyes.

"Right to business Mr. Bell? A man after my own heart. I'll go and grab it from the back. Just be a few minutes, so feel free to look around."

Leah's the daughter of two retired jewelers, and she's certainly inher-ited the talent. She makes the most beautiful custom stuff, and it's not the first time Damien's paid a pretty penny for her work. Luckily for him, she's almost as big a fan of his work as he is of hers, and she slashed the price when he promised to drop her off one of the first pressings of their new album, signed by the whole band no less.

Damien and Shaun linger as they wait, both of them quietly pacing around for a minute or so before congregating in front of a big glass case of rings.

"So, things with Pheebs are good, then?"

"Yeah," he mutters. "It did feel a bit touch-and-go after we all went out that night in Denver– you know, the night before Erin left and we all went to that shitty bar?"

"I remember," Shaun laughs. "Fuck, that band was awful."

"Yeah, well, Pheebs and I had a big fight that night. I thought it was over, man. I was ready to pack my shit and come to stay in your room, but... we talked it out."

"Really? You were gonna give up that easy?" Shaun asks.

Damien feels that familiar sting of embarrassment shoot through him, the kind that's only so bad because of the truth it stems from.

"Most girls don't stick around," he whispers. "Up until now... well, I was never sure if it was because of the publicity, or if I'm just a tough person to love."

Shaun looks at him for a moment, carefully weighing his words. Damien knows him well enough to know when he doesn't have an immediate comeback, he's taking things a little more seriously.

"I think a lot of people split once things get too real, or when they're faced with their first big conflict. Sometimes it's just easier that way, less painful than diving in and then having things go wrong. I know I was afraid of that with Phi, but luckily after our first big fight she made it clear she wasn't going anywhere."

Damien always thought Shaun and Ophelia were perfect for each other, and so solid– in the same way Johnny and Erin are solid. They barely fight and the way they communicate is enviable. But nobody's perfect, and he often feels a little juvenile for not realizing that earlier.

"Speaking of, when the hell are you gonna ask Ophelia to move in with you?"

Shaun shrugs.

"I don't know. We've always been pretty casual. She likes her space, I like mine. And we've got this thing with Janis now, which is great, but complicates things a bit."

Just a bit? Damien has a hard enough time with one person. He can't imagine how things work when you're three-way equal partners like that.

"Yeah, actually that's a much more interesting question. How's that whole thing going? You guys all seem really into it, as far as I can tell."

"Well, it's a test-run for Jan since she's never done this before, but I think it's going good. She's really cool, It's easy to be around her, and man Ophelia *adores* her."

Damien watches the warm smile creep over Shaun's face. Shaun and Ophelia have always been open about their relationships. With each other but also with the band. He's actually the person that Damien comes to for advice, considering he's able to juggle multiple partners and keep their needs met.

"When was the last time you guys had a third?" Damien drums on the glass with his fingertips as his eyes rake over rings. He spots one in the shape of a bat that Ava would like. "Not just a quick one, long term."

"Everett. Two years ago."

"Damn, that was two years ago? Holy shit."

"Tell me about it, man. Makes me feel old."

"He was the poet, right?"

Damien remembers his turtlenecks and his tiny circular John Lennon glasses. He always had a notebook, and the two of them talked about poetry; lyrics and structure. Everett seemed like a cool guy, and he knew a hell of a lot more than Damien did about writing.

"Yeah," Shaun chuckles. "Yeah, that was him. Had those tiny glasses, remember?"

"Yes! Loved those! So why'd you guys split up again?"

"He wanted to move to Europe. Fell in love with another poet on a retreat. He asked us to come with him, but I think he knew we couldn't. Anyway, Phi and I were happy to let him follow his heart. It was sad for a bit, always is, but you gotta let people do what's best for them, right?"

Damien nods. That's exactly what Emily said to him the day she walked out the door and out of his life. She looked so much happier the last time he saw her; It made him crave that kind of joy for himself.

"So, Janis is cool?" He twirls his skull ring around his index finger.

Shaun flashes a bashful smile, rubbing his neck instinctively.

"Very cool. We all just kind of clicked in Vegas, and kept on clicking."

"Even when she had to head home?"

"She'd call Phi and I'd listen to them talk, or she'd call me and Phi'd wait her turn. Then the two of us end up passing the phone back and forth either way. She's just so funny, and relaxed— that's the vibe we look for in partners. So it made sense to see if she was interested, if she wanted to experiment. We all agreed if it didn't work out there were no hard feelings, but since we've been back…"

"It's *really* working out?" Damien asks with a big grin.

"Obviously," Shaun chuckles. "And I mean, it's not just the sex— Don't get me wrong, it's amazing, but Janis feels like she's always been with us. I feel like we both play better, we're happier… we just feel more solid with her around. She didn't bring any jealousy in, she says exactly what she's thinking, she sets boundaries… I think the three of us hit the jackpot."

"Well, she clearly makes you glow, too. So you can add that to the list." Damien gives him a gentle punch in the shoulder as Shaun shakes his head dismissively. "I'm serious, dude! You're falling in love and shit, all three of you!"

Shaun grins.

"Maybe I should buy Phoebe a present to say thank you for bringing her along on tour," he teases.

Right on cue the door squeaks open and Leah emerges, a long rectangular box in her hand.

"Now, I know you gave *very* specific instructions, but you also said if I wanted to do anything cool I could, right?"

Damien raises a brow.

"What did you do?"

"Well, it looked like it was missing something, so I added a little flourish to tie it all together."

Damien cracks his knuckles nervously.

"Let's see what you got."

She flips open the box, revealing the silver chain link collar. The entire thing looks like it was woven together, shimmering like diamonds, and with a heart shaped hoop hanging at the front. It's discreet, but sturdy enough that he could put a rope through it. The point is for her to be able to wear this anywhere, even to work, without people fully getting what it really is. Even if she only wears it for special occasions, that's good enough for him, but the idea of her wearing it in her office… he can feel the shivers running down his spine already.

"Leah, this is gorgeous."

"You like it?"

"Yeah!"

"Well I hope she likes it just as much." Leah smirks. "Unless you're taking turns wearing it."

"We just might," Damien mutters under his breath, turning it over in his hands. "This is exactly what I pictured."

Shaun claps him on the back.

"You've got good taste. I've known for years, but somehow I'm consistently surprised by that fact."

Damien chuckles at the jab, holding the collar up to the light and smiling from ear to ear. She's going to love it.

"So? It's Damien Bell approved?" Leah asks.

"Definitely."

She puts everything in a bag and he pays for the collar. It's around $400, easily worth it for all of the detailing that was put into it.

He can't wait to see it around Phoebe's neck.

They thank Leah and head out of the store and back toward Ophelia's apartment. The whole trip back Damien bounces between checking his watch looking back into the bag to make sure that the box is still there. 7:40. Still lots of time.

"Why are you so nervous, man? It's jewelry. Girls love jewelry."

"I know, but... this all means a lot to me."

Shaun tilts his head, frowning inquisitively.

"Oh Jesus Christ, you're thinking about marrying her, aren't you?"

Damien coughs, struggling not to choke. He can't deny, the thought had taken root in the back of his mind over the last few weeks.

"Don't be fuckin' ridiculous."

"The hell you say, I can see it in your eyes! God, now that I've seen it, it's all over your face! I'm surprised you didn't buy an engagement ring, too."

He knows Shaun is just trying to get a rise out of him, but there's a part of him that considered it when they were standing in front of that display case.

"Not right now, it's obviously too soon," he grumbles, before taking on a more contented tone. "I am thinking about a future with her, though, you're right about that."

"Makes sense, you two are basically endgame."

"You think so?"

Shaun's loud snort lets Damien know his words came out a tiny bit too quickly, and definitely too eager.

"Dude, we all see the way you look at her. It's like she's the only person in every room you're in."

"Sometimes I worry that it's going to affect the band."

Shaun chuckles.

"You can love more than one thing at a time, dude. You're talking to an expert on that."

It used to be the only things Damien cared about were the band, getting laid, and having the best fucking time money could buy. Now, the band aside, it's Phoebe and his art. Even on the first day back in the studio, all he could think about at first was getting out of there and putting his arms around her. It was like the music was secondary, that he couldn't wait to put it aside, but then the lyrics started pouring out of him faster than he'd ever experienced before, his love for her intertwined with his passion for music.

It all stems from her.

She's his muse.

As they make their way back the conversation ping-pongs around a bunch, Shaun trying to get as many little barbs in on Damien before he's forced to keep his secrets again in front of the girls, until a couple blocks from Ophelia's apartment, Damien spots something.

Someone has been weaving behind the parked cars, watching them from across the street. Most people in the city don't give a shit who he is, but it doesn't mean he doesn't keep his head on a swivel. The question is how long has he been following them?

And then he spots a camera lens.

"Paps."

"Took you this long, old man? I saw him 3 blocks back," Shaun murmurs.

Damien swears they've become attuned to it over the years, hypervigilance mixed with a kind of 6th sense. Any single one of them can spot a photographer from a mile away, seeing through their shitty little routines or disguises. After a while, you start to be able to sniff them out without even really trying, like the way people can tell when it's going to rain just by smell.

They play it cool, the usual plan is to get out of these situations with as little grief as possible, and casually walk the final block. Unfortunately when the two try to duck inside, the man catches the door. Shaun whirls around and blocks the entrance while Damien tries to get a good look at him. It's hard to see his features in the dark, which just speeds up the process of Damien hitting high alert. All he can tell is the man looks worn, like he's been in this job for too long.

"No way, man," Shaun snaps, shaking his head. His shoulders are square, pulled back, and he draws himself up to his full height of 6'3". "You got your pictures, and that's fine, but now it's time for you to get outta here."

"I live here," the guy replies, not missing a beat.

Pretty fucking brazen.

"Yeah? Show me your keys," Shaun challenges.

Damien grins as the photographer sighs, rolling his eyes with a nervous chuckle.

"Look, I'm house-sitting, man. What's your problem?"

Shaun leans casually against the doorframe, unwilling to budge.

"Wow, and part of the whole house-sitting deal is taking pictures of the neighborhood, huh? I'm sure you're gonna tell me you just happened to be walking back the exact way we were, too. Such a small fucking world."

"It's a free country," the photographer replies. "A hobby's a hobby."

Damien checks his watch. 7:50. Shaun's definitely a better man than him, because he would have grabbed that camera and smashed it on the ground by now. But the night is young, and there's still a real chance he might.

"You got what you wanted, you can sell them to the Enquirer for all I care. We're done here."

Shaun steps forward suddenly, the man flinching backward just far enough for him to quickly shut the door right in his face. The photographer sneers at them, snapping picture after picture from behind the glass. They can take all the photos they want, Damien's not going to ruin his chances by decking another asshole over something like this.

"Come on," Shaun sighs. "He's not gonna give up."

"It'd be funny if he tried to climb the fire escape."

"Not so loud," Shaun chuckles as they stroll toward the elevator. "Ophelia's the kind of person who's not shy about defending her home, and I'm not super excited to have to hide a body."

We Belong

PHOEBE

Ophelia's bathroom counter is covered in loose powder, hairspray, a couple empty wine glasses, and bobby pins. Phoebe's eyes rake over her own figure in the mirror, taking in the way her brand new petal-pink dress hugs her curves. The fabric shimmers in the dim light as she turns, along with the little rhinestones adorning the spaghetti straps.

She already knows he's going to love it.

"You look incredible," Ophelia chirps, shutting off the curling iron and grabbing a brush. She glides it through Phoebe's hair, loosening the curls bit by bit. "Like a real princess."

"I can't stop staring at myself," Phoebe laughs. "Is that egotistical?"

"Nah," Ophelia scoffs. "You just have good taste. Besides, even if it is a little, I think women could use a bit more self-esteem. God knows they throw enough shit at us, on the TV, in those fucking beauty magazines... All we get told is to doll ourselves up for any and every man who walks by, and shit on everyone who doesn't."

Ophelia looks stunning herself, that fiery red hair pulled back into an elegant bun. All she's wearing on her face is some dark eyeshadow and a pop of red lipstick. The entire band is coming to Phoebe's birthday dinner, but then Shaun, Janis, and Ophelia are splitting off to hit the New

York Philharmonic. She thought it was a bit of a strange choice initially, but Shaun mentioned he wanted to see if he could poach a violinist for their recording sessions.

Ophelia finishes with Phoebe's hair, giving herself a final look up and down before the two of them head back out into the living room.

"You'll love La Saveur, by the way."

"That's good to hear. I asked around about it after Damien mentioned the name; I've never been somewhere that fancy before."

"Food's great," Ophelia replies, smoothing out her dress. "Portions are a little small. Shaun always winds up at a burger joint afterward, but that's definitely not a dig on the quality."

"Well, that might be for the best. We're going to The Vault after, so I don't want to eat too much."

Ophelia flashes her a knowing grin.

"I heard. He's really going all out, huh?"

"Yeah, he really is." Phoebe frowns, scrunching up her nose as she remembers the little curiosity she'd been stuck on all day. "Hey, Phi, do you know what he's picking up with Shaun?"

"I do," Ophelia practically sings, playfully giving her a little press on the nose. "But I can't tell yoouuuu!"

Damien said he wanted to make this night special, that she only turns 24 once. It feels like it might be a little much, but her frame of reference is a little skewed. The last time she was in a relationship during her birthday, all the guy got her was a book and the 'gift of a good time.'

"I mean, we've only been together a few months and he's already built me an office... what's even left to get me?"

"You'll see," Ophelia purrs. "When Damien sets his mind to something, he goes all-out, so don't be surprised when he showers you with adoration."

Phoebe smiles to herself.

"He said he wants me to meet his parents. I think we're going for Thanksgiving."

"That's a big step, he doesn't do that too often." She leans forward, giving Phoebe's shoulder a gentle squeeze. "That means he thinks you're a keeper."

She was already pretty certain of that part, but it's nice to hear it from one of his oldest friends. Two weeks ago, at the secret show, she was right on the verge of pushing for the same thing, for him to come and get to know her family, but she hasn't really been able to confirm the details.

It's been a while since she's been back to her apartment for more than a few minutes at a time to grab some clothes, forgetting or ignoring the blinking light on her machine each time. Every time she remembers she feels more guilty than before, but then something new comes up and pushes it further from her mind. She really has to get in contact with her mom, it's not fair to keep her out of the loop like this. Besides, the longer she puts it off the worse it'll be.

"I was thinking about asking him to this New Year's Day Brunch thing my family does; it's been a while since I brought a guy home."

The last one was her high school boyfriend, Mickey. Phoebe didn't think things went that terribly, but Mickey never wanted to come back. He said sitting at that table felt like being in a pressure cooker, which seemed like it was a bit much. It was a pretty normal dinner.

"That's so exciting!" Ophelia exclaims as she pulls out a record, slipping it out of its sleeve and onto the turntable.

"Nerve-wracking, though," Phoebe laughs.

"Yeah, well, I'm sure Damien will be on his best behavior with your folks."

"Knock knock!" Janis calls from the front, interrupting the conversation as the door slams behind her. "I brought more wine!"

"Finally!" Ophelia laughs, hurrying over to wrap her arms around her partner.

Janis is dressed in an elegant navy-blue gown with long, wavy sleeves. Her hair is curled, all swept up into a perfectly messy ponytail in the back.

"Got the good shit."

"Oooh! Cristal!" Ophelia coos, kissing her softly and plucking the bottles from her hands. "Thank you, darling."

Ophelia slips by, motioning for them to follow her into the living room.

"Come on, I'm getting the fancy glasses for this shit!"

Her apartment is spacious, yet quite cozy. She has a pastel mural on one wall, a giant shelf crammed full of romance books on another, with her favorite movie posters adorning any of the unused space: Pretty in Pink, The Goonies, Fright Night, Jaws... It's all perfectly Ophelia.

She hits the dimmer, lighting a few candles throughout the room, music tumbling out of her record player as she drops the needle. Soft blankets are draped over the leopard print chaise lounge, and the two girls plop themselves down as Ophelia heads into the kitchen to grab them all some glasses.

"You look amazing," Janis calls after her, winking over at Phoebe.

"So do you! Actually, we all clean up pretty good," Ophelia shouts, turning back around the corner and setting each of their crystal flutes down on the coffee table with a light string of clinks.

She pops one of the bottles open, pouring them each a glass before raising hers to the ceiling.

"A toast! To our beautiful birthday girl."

"Hear hear!" Janis echoes.

Phoebe takes a sip after the round of clinking glasses, the bubbles burning the back of her throat and surprising her just a bit.

Janis takes a swig herself, not seeming to have the same issue.

"So, ladies, what did I miss while I was gone?"

"Apparently Damien invited Pheebs over to his parent's house for Thanksgiving." Ophelia offers.

Phoebe laughs.

"I was going to invite him to my mom's first, but—"

"Ooh, you're not serious are you?" Janis asks.

Phoebe sighs. This is different. She's not a teenager anymore, and this might just be her first serious relationship. Damien is funny, charming, and he's quick on his feet. Her family is going to fall in love with him.

If he ends up agreeing to go.

"What's the big deal?"

"Phoebe's mom is kind of... a lot," Janis laughs. "I'm not trying to start anything, but sometimes it gets pretty tense, right?"

"I guess so," Phoebe replies.

Sure, there have been intense discussions around the dinner table, especially when she first was talking about going to journalism school, but it all worked out in the end.

"Well, every family's got shit," Ophelia replies. "Even Damien's."

"He mentioned things were tense, like his parents wanted him to join the military and shit," Phoebe replies. "Is that what you mean?"

"Kinda, yeah. Damien's parents are good people, but there's some rough history there."

"History?"

Ophelia nods, looking a bit uncomfortable, and Phoebe wishes she hadn't said anything.

"Damien and his dad have a... an awkward relationship. I don't wanna speak for him, or get too deep into it, but his dad put the family through a lot of shit. I don't think he and Damien have ever really sat down and talked about it before– you know, reconciled it. It kind of just got swept under the rug. I don't know how things are now, but I remember when he was a teenager, it was rough."

Phoebe chews at her lip. Damien's just started to open up about this kind of stuff, but she's not sure she's heard all of it yet. Hopefully, she's not walking into anything too intense. He wouldn't blindside her like that.

Janis leans over.

"All I'm saying is that if things go south with your mom, and you need somewhere to go New Year's Day, mom and pop Kaneko would be more than happy to feed you, *and* get you hammered. They don't live that far from your folks."

"Same goes for my parents," Ophelia chimes in. "Once you're in with this band, you're family."

Phoebe chuckles and shakes her head as the laughter subsides.

"My parents aren't *that* horrible."

Janis snorts.

"There's a reason why people call your mom the Stepford Wife of Upstate New York."

Phoebe shifts in her seat. She can feel her skin prickle, irritation beginning to bubble up inside her as she swirls her champagne.

"It'll be fine. I've got a great job, amazing friends... Once the story's published and I can move onto even more high-profile work she'll be relieved; she won't have to worry about me anymore. I think that's where a lot of it comes from. She just wants what's best for me."

"Pheebs, I know she's your mom, but..."

"She's just afraid for me, okay?"

Janis looks down at her glass, swirling it awkwardly.

"Did she tell you that?"

"Yes!" Phoebe finds herself staring at her friend with a lot more intensity than she intended, quickly reeling it back in. "She's worried about me being all alone here in the city, that the job's too harsh and the industry's too competitive. Once she sees I'm making it, that I can manage on my own, it'll be better."

Janis's expression softens.

This last month Phoebe's been so sure about so many areas of her life: Her relationship solidified, she saved her job, the article is going to come out exactly how *she* wants it to, no one else. For the first time in years she has the powerful sense that everything is going to be okay, and her mother will see it too. Phoebe's success, her happiness and fulfillment with Damien, it would be impossible for her mom to miss.

"You're right, Pheebs. You're killing it. There's no fucking way she won't see it."

Ophelia playfully pokes Phoebe's shin with her foot.

"You know what? If you wanna do the brunch thing with your mom, use Thanksgiving with Damien's parents as a trial run. If it sucks, you can spend New Year's in Paris as a backup. If it goes well, it'll be super easy to convince him to just do it all over again with your folks."

The sudden knock at the door pulls their attention from the conversation, Janis almost spilling her glass but recovering just in time.

"It's open!" Ophelia calls.

The door creaks as Damien and Shaun step in, and Phoebe feels her mouth fall open. They're both dressed to the nines. Suits, no ties. Gorgeous black dress shoes, not a wrinkle or tear in sight. Damien even has his hair tied back. She's never seen him this formal before, and she has to admit, it's having an *effect*.

Shaun struts forward, placing a smattering of shopping bags down in front of her as Damien saunters into the room behind him.

"These are for you, madam."

"From you?"

"Nope. Your present from me is my presence in your life," he replies with a grin.

He sits down next to Ophelia while Damien lingers in the hallway, a smile on his face.

"These are all from your prince charming back there."

Damien's eyes are locked on her.

"Hey Phi, do you mind if I talk to Pheebs in your room for a minute? Just a quick thing."

Ophelia tilts her head.

"You're not fucking on my bed, Bell."

Damien raises one hand.

"Scout's honor. No fucking, just talking."

Ophelia nods, waving them away. Damien crosses the room quickly, picking up a couple of the bags.

"Can you bring the rest of these, Pheebs?"

"Yes, sir," she giggles, scooping them up and following him down the hall.

Her friends whistle behind them as he leads her into Ophelia's darkened room. He shuts the door, leaving them in heavy darkness for a couple of deliciously tense seconds before flicking on the light. His mouth is on hers in a second and she gasps as his hand begins to slide up and down her waist.

"Careful, Bell, you're gonna smear my lipstick."

He steps back, taking a deep breath to calm himself.

"Can you blame me? You look good enough to eat, and I'm fucking starving." He gently tucks a strand of hair behind her ear. "But you know me, I'm nothing if not patient."

He clears his throat, a look of excitement flooding his eyes.

"Ophelia did lay down one very specific rule, so it's time for some distractions." He grabs the gifts from her and leads her to the bed, arranging them in front of her. "Here. Open these."

"We couldn't do this outside?"

"Call me selfish." He pats the bed and she sits, one bag quickly getting put on her lap, a second smaller one placed beside it. Damien bounces on the balls of his feet like an excited kid, a big smile on his face. "Open them."

Phoebe picks the small bag first, the pale violet tissue paper crinkling between her fingers as she slides it out, placing it carefully to the side.

Inside are at least ten pairs of underwear, each carefully separated and folded, all different colors and styles but equally delicate yet revealing.

She smirks and glances up at him as she holds up one particularly frilly pair.

"To replace all the ones I ripped off you," he says with a wink. "I told you I'd get you back."

"You did," she mutters, noticing a bright red lace bodysuit that had been sitting underneath the rest. It leaves little to the imagination, but that's exactly what's setting hers on fire. There's another beneath it, and another. He bought it in four different colors.

"Oh, and don't wear those tonight. Those are just for me to see."

The authoritative tone hits her hard, and Phoebe feels an exhilarating shiver run through her.

"Maybe I'll bring them to Paris."

"Now that's a plan," he purrs.

Phoebe picks up the second bag and looks inside. There's a long rectangular box with a lovely little bow wrapped around it. She doesn't really recognize the markings on the box, excited to find out what it could possibly be. She slips off the bow, sliding the box apart to reveal a beautiful black pen sitting in the middle of some plush fabric. Lifting it up, she immediately notes the perfect weight as she turns it around in her hand. Her initials are engraved in the metal, with a little heart right next to them.

"Damien," she laughs. "You didn't have to—"

"You chew those Bics up so quickly. I wanted to get you something nice, something practical that'll last. Ink's refillable, too, although I'm not exactly sure how that works. We can figure that all out when it comes to it."

She sighs and shakes her head, setting the pen back down in its case.

"This is too much."

"Actually, It's not enough," he insists. "Keep looking."

As she digs through the remaining bag she finds three thick leather-bound notebooks. Her old one is in complete tatters from their time on the road, the once stiff cardboard cover in shreds. These new books are completely different. The pages feel heavy and rich.

Expensive.

"I wrote something in the black one," he mutters.

She flips it open to the first page. There, in Damien's sprawling cursive, is a quote:

I would not wish any companion in the world but you.

Her eyes mist as she looks up to see him beaming at her.

"The Tempest."

"It's my favorite," he whispers, crouching down in front of her. "But here, we're not quite done."

He fishes into his jacket pocket and pulls out *another* goddamn box.

"This is the grand finale."

"Damien, this is *way* too much!"

He grins.

"Look, Pheebs. I'm gonna be spending every single one of your birthdays spoiling you. You're gonna get everything you could ever possibly want, like it or not." He sets the box down on her thigh, pulling the rest of her open gifts and empty bags aside. "Open it."

Phoebe takes the box in her hands, carefully flipping the lid open. Staring back at her, sitting on a bed of red silk, is the most beautiful choker she's ever seen. It looks like individual strands of silver have been woven together, shimmering in the dim light, with a small heart shaped hoop at the front. She grazes her fingers over it. It feels heavy, expensive. She's never seen anything like it.

She looks up at him in time to see his cheeks flush pink, making the bright blue of his eyes that much more intense. She's rarely seen him this flustered before.

"So, uh, It's a collar, but it's more... subtle than the one you usually wear for me." He swallows hard, fumbling with his words. "You can wear it out any time, every day even— if— uh, if that's what you want. Anyway I think it's really pretty. I loved the idea but couldn't find one that really fit your vibe, so I got this one made custom. I didn't know if you liked silver, or..."

"I am." She places the box down on her thigh and holds the collar up to her neck. "It's gorgeous."

The fact that he'd go to these lengths for a gift doesn't surprise her anymore, but it does make her a little teary. Nobody's done this for her, and to have something entirely unique made just for her? She can't imagine ever wanting to take it off.

Damien sits down next to her, reaching out and taking it from her hands. He pushes her hair aside and gently lays the collar against her neck, his touch feather-light, feeling sparks dance on her skin as he fastens the clasp and checks to make sure it's not too snug.

"Good?"

She nods.

"Perfect."

Phoebe turns to him and presses a kiss to his lips. Already, this is the best birthday she's ever had, and the night has barely begun. She doesn't know how to thank him for this, for the office, for his constant support.

"Happy birthday, babydoll."

Just Can't Get Enough

DAMIEN

It's only been half an hour and Damien can already sense the staff of La Saveur are pretty much over the eight of them. When they were picking the location, Damien had joked that he wanted to show Phoebe how much money he could put on his credit card, but the truth was the second he walked past it last week he knew it had to be here.

Gentle lighting, warm brick walls, racks upon racks of expensive wine, and servers who are dressed in the most pristine white outfits; it really does seem to be the ideal of the fancy restaurant. Soft music trickles from the speakers, just loud enough to be appreciated, but not so loud that it interrupts the conversation. And they have a special knife and fork for absolutely fucking everything.

An hour or so in, though, Damien feels the urge to pull them out of their chaotic revelry. It's time to put the spotlight on his girl.

"Okay, okay!" Damien laughs, getting to his feet. "Everyone shut up! I have something to say!"

"Oh, Christ, here we go," Troy sighs.

Phoebe giggles, sipping her champagne as Johnny and Shaun play at dragging him back into his seat. She's been smiling since they left Ophelia's apartment.

"Okay, everyone be quiet! It's my birthday!" Phoebe announces, her glass raised to the table.

Damien grins and grabs his whiskey, lifting it in the air.

"Tonight, we're here celebrating Phoebe, but—"

He clears his throat. Maybe he's getting a little sappy in his old age, struggling to keep it together despite his vocal distaste for sappy shit, but this is his family. As he looks around at his friends, who stare back at him with big smiles, a lump forms in his throat. Life's too short not to tell people that you love them.

"You guys are the most important people in my life, each and every one of you, and you've welcomed Phoebe with open arms." His hand finds Phoebe's shoulder and he gives it a gentle squeeze, at least partially to calm his own nerves. "Pheebs, I think I can confidently say that none of us expected this to happen when you landed in our laps to write this article, but we're so fucking glad you did. *I'm* fucking glad you did. You're the love of my life, the best thing that's happened to me... maybe ever. You've changed the way I think about the world, how I write my music..."

Damien pauses. It's starting to sound like he's reciting wedding vows, and he yanks himself back from the edge before he dives too deep into that well. He doesn't want to scare her, but he's a little surprised by how appealing the image is. A guy can fantasize, can't he?

"Anyway, I just... I love you Pheebs."

Sometimes he starts talking, expecting that something profound will come out, but when it comes to Phoebe nothing feels like it's enough. She makes him feel like anything is possible, and all of the money or gold records in the world don't even begin to touch how his whole body lights up when she looks at him. And sure, maybe the speech wasn't as poetic as he thought it would be, but it's real, and her big warm smile makes it clear that he hit the target.

"I wanna say something too," Janis chimes in.

Damien is a little relieved to have someone taking over, quickly sitting down with a brief nod. He lets out a sigh as he can feel the tension seep out of his body, Phoebe placing her hand on his thigh as Janis clears her throat.

"Pheebs, I've watched you go from a shy, almost spectator in your own life, to someone fueled by passion; passion for your work, for your friends, so much that you put your entire job on the line for it. This story is going to be the biggest thing you've ever written, and I just wanted to say how much of a fucking badass you are for sticking to your guns!"

Phoebe reaches over to hold Janis's hand, a warm smile flickering across her face, but there's something tense in her body language. It's like she doesn't quite believe what's being said about her. But she should. She's brilliant, everyone at this table knows it, and this could be the big break that shows the world how true that is.

When this all began, it was all about the publicity. He had those talks with Troy, even a letter from Allan back when they squared this whole interview thing up, all about how to put on a good show and get some free positive press. And back then, he was 100% on board. Who wouldn't want a nice puff-piece about how much they rock? Now, though? He hasn't thought about that angle in months. This article is Phoebe's baby, and however she chooses to frame it, he'll be happy.

"Alright, I guess it's my turn," Troy says, standing with a big grin. He clears his throat dramatically, gesturing with his hand as if he's about to begin a grand speech of some kind. "I guess you're alright, kiddo, so let's raise a glass to that!"

Everyone follows suit amidst chuckles, downing what's left in their respective glasses.

"So, Pheebs," Johnny chimes in, reaching for some of the appetizers. "How's the article coming?"

Damien sighs to himself. All of the bullshit with Chris, being hauled into the studio, none of it's helped her focus. Lately, when he catches her in her work, she spends more time staring at a blank page than actually writing. But she keeps pushing through, combing over her outline every morning and tweaking it a little more each time.

"It's hard to write about people I care so much about. If this were a different assignment, or if things didn't end up the way they did, it might be easier. It's just so hard to put you guys on paper–" She winces. "That's a compliment, by the way!"

She really dove into all of this head first, ready to write a very specific article that's changed form multiple times over the course of the last few months. It'd be hard for anyone to keep a grasp on that in the best of circumstances

"You'll get it, Pheebs," Johnny replies. "And if you want another interview with any of us, just ask. We're all here for you."

"He means *he'll* be there for you," Erin teases. "Johnny just wants to hear himself talk."

Johnny tickles her in the ribs and she squeals, leaning into him with a loving shove. Damien grins. They're *so* fucking in love with each other, and he only hopes the two of them will be like that 10 years on.

"So, what exactly is so difficult about it?" Ophelia asks. "I'm not trying to be an asshole, but I've read your other stuff. It feels like this'd be right up your alley."

Damien can see the gears turning in Phoebe's head as she stalls for time, setting her utensils down and carefully wiping her mouth with her napkin.

"Well, I've shifted my entire writing approach, more than once actually. I thought the changes would open up all of these new avenues, but... now I'm stuck. I want to accurately represent who you guys are as people, I want to talk about how I fell in love with Damien, and I want to show the world a view of the band that they couldn't get anywhere else. Balancing all of that while trying to not just vomit the last few months onto the page is proving to be a little difficult."

"And you're worried about revealing too much, is that part of it?" Ophelia asks.

"It is, yeah. Obviously I want to be careful about how I paint you guys, but this is going to push *me* further into the public eye too, and... well, this is all new to me and I'm not quite sure how to handle it. I have to be careful how things are framed, how everything could be viewed. If I say something wrong, if I don't catch something people end up latching onto, it could impact you, it could impact me... it's..."

"Kiddo, I don't mean to be rude here, but I'm going to give you some advice," Troy leans forward, his brow furrowed as smoke winds around his face. "We, and by we I mean you, because we're who you're lumped in with now, we *cannot* give a *fuck* about what the press is going to say. If we do that, it kills whatever drive we've got going. For you, it'll choke whatever you've got cooking in the crib before it even starts to blossom. Don't doubt yourself, and don't doubt your strengths. Whatever comes out is going to be brilliant."

"A-fucking-men," Damien murmurs, caught exactly in the middle between being inspired and perplexed by Troy's ridiculously split metaphor.

Everyone in this band gets at least two to three deranged Troy pep talks a year, usually just in time, when they're right on the verge of falling apart. As much shit as Damien gives him, Troy is the closest thing any of them has to a father figure on the road.

"Thanks, Troy." Phoebe already looks a little less in her head.

"Any time." He checks his watch. "But now, you're legally not allowed to bother me for another pep talk for six months. Always gotta check any documents you sign, there are so many obscure and outrageous loopholes."

Laughter ripples through the table, and the band descends into soft conversation as they peruse the menus. Damien finds himself distracted, watching Phoebe to ensure she's comfortable. She nibbles on her thumb nail as her eyes rake over the menu, brows knitting together every so often. He leans over.

"What are you thinking?"

"That I should get a salad," she grins, not even looking up.

"Just a salad?" Damien asks with a raised brow. "I'm buying, and I'm not sure if you know this but the French don't do salads. They do butter, pastries, and decadence— I don't know if there's anything green in that country that doesn't grow grapes."

She giggles.

"Well, I just don't know how intense everything's going to get." She lowers her voice "I don't want to throw up."

Damien snorts, the image cracking him up.

"Pheebs, if you throw up at a BDSM club, then I'm doing something very *very* wrong."

"Fair," she giggles.

Damien glances down at the menu, his nose scrunching up instinctually like when he'd sit in the back of math class trying to figure out a problem. What the hell is *pommes aligot*?

"Something wrong?" Phoebe asks.

"I forgot I can't read French."

"Neither can I. I just know *poulet* means chicken, and *vin* means wine."

"That's good to know. I'll just look for that, and make sure we're stocked up on *vin*."

Phoebe chuckles to herself, and it's another few minutes of silence with the menu before she speaks up again.

"So, how many times have you been to this place exactly?" She asks. "The Vault, I mean."

"Just once." Damien pushes the menu away and leans toward her a little, lowering his voice. "Speaking of, I was, uh... I was thinking maybe we could switch things up sometime soon. Not tonight, this is a new thing for you, but maybe a little later, maybe in Paris?"

"Switch things up?"

He smiles.

"You know, switch up who does what. You seemed pretty into the idea."

He's hooked on the thought of her standing over him, decked out in her new lingerie, all that fire in her eyes while the moonlight illuminates her curves. He's on his knees, a collar pulled tight around his throat while she praises him, calls him a good boy. He'd worship every inch of her body, let her do anything she wanted to and do whatever she asked, and in the end he'd make her come loud enough that everyone on the street below could hear it. He adjusts the napkin on his lap as he feels himself stiffen at the thought.

Phoebe licks her lips slowly.

"You think I'd be good at it?"

"You clearly didn't see what I saw in the recording booth, Miller," he chuckles. "You *are* good at it, you're a natural."

Damien's eyes flick around the table as she shifts in her seat. Everyone is engrossed in conversation, or in figuring out the menu. Perfect.

He presses his lips to her ear.

"You ever wonder what it would feel like being on the *other* end of the paddle? Or finishing the last knot of rope, ready to do anything you could possibly want to me?"

Her breath hitches and she reaches for her champagne flute, pouring herself another glass and downing it in a single gulp.

"If I wasn't before, I am now." He swears he can hear her heart hammering against her chest. "So, would you be teaching me?"

"I think we've already started those lessons."

"Excuse me, have we decided?"

The waiter cuts in out of nowhere and Phoebe nearly chokes, sitting up straight. Damien rubs his chin, brushing against the stubble and attempting to hide how red he'd become.

"Yeah," he laughs. "Yeah, uh... can I get, uh... this?"

He points to something he'd been glancing at earlier.

"Ah, Coq au vin?" The waiter asks.

"Yeah." Damien can feel the normal confidence in his own voice falter a bit as he questions his choice. "It's good, right?"

"Of course sir, It's fantastic."

Damien nods, a nervous smile forming on his face as the waiter smiles and turns to Phoebe.

"And for you?"

"I'll take the chicken chasseur."

"Ah, an excellent choice."

Damien orders them a bottle of red, something fancy sounding he can't quite pronounce, but the waiter only smiles graciously at his attempt before moving on to the rest of the table. He sighs, relieved to be done with that ordeal, looking back to Phoebe, and then past her with a frown. The sight outside the window's caught at least a couple of his bandmate's attention too, Ophelia shooting him a glance as Damien grinds his teeth. The photographer is snapping pictures rapidly, trying to get the best angles they can through the glass.

In Damien's eyes, they're just a normal couple having a birthday dinner with their friends, but this life doesn't often allow for any sense of normality.

"I think we're stuck with them for the rest of dinner," Phoebe mutters.

He was hoping to deal with this before she noticed, but he knew it was unlikely.

"Fucking scumbags," Ophelia snarls.

The waiter moves around the table and Damien twists his ring on his finger, racking his brain for some kind of solution. He can't punch the photographer; not only has it never really worked before, but he's not interested in getting blacklisted on Phoebe's birthday. Yelling at them doesn't work either, even if you're trying to appeal to their decency, they just get more aggressive when you take the bait. But then he remembers something he read about the royal family, how they had a special arrangement with the press.

Damien stands up, tossing his napkin down on his empty plate as he makes his way around the table. Troy looks like he's ready to jump out of his seat.

"Bell, what's going through your head?"

He grins, feeling the confidence swelling inside of him.

"Don't worry about it, Troy. I got this."

"Bell, no–"

It's too late, he's already heading for the entrance before Troy has a chance to struggle his way out from his own seat. As Damien steps outside, the photographer lowers his camera, clearly surprised. Damien recognizes the guy– short red hair, bright green eyes, and freckles all over his cheeks, a black sweater and matching jeans. He's been around outside the studio a couple times, in his neighborhood now and again looking for a shot. He's not one of the bad ones, not like the dude that tried to trick his way into Ophelia's apartment. Damien flicks his head, pointing at him with his chin as he digs his cigarettes out of his pocket. This could work.

"Hey, man. How's it going?"

The photographer still looks a little caught off guard, his camera firmly clutched in his hands, only half-raised.

"Uh, pretty good Damien." He frowns, glancing down at his camera before lowering it a little more. "How's... dinner?"

"It's good," Damien chuckles. "Real good. Just came out here for a cigarette. You want one?"

Damien holds out his pack, the photographer staring at it for a second as he tensely holds his shoulders up around his ears. The sight almost makes Damien laugh. He used to regularly take a swing at these assholes, smash their cameras, give them the finger, and do his best to make their life a living hell like they did his. But he's got way too much to lose now.

He's gonna make this work.

"So, obviously you know my name. What's yours?"

"Robbie."

"Robbie, you look stressed. I promise I'm not gonna hit you, so have a fuckin' cigarette."

Robbie tentatively reaches for the pack and, after an agonizingly long pause, grabs a smoke and pops it into his mouth. Damien lights Robbie's first before his own, the two of them exhaling clouds of smoke into the air in silence for a while. He glances over his shoulder to see his friends staring at him through the glass. They all look varying degrees of tense and concerned. The big vein in Troy's head looks like it's about to burst at any second, Johnny clearly having managed to keep him still in his seat.

"So," He begins. "How long have you been doing this? Photography, the whole tabloid beat, all that."

"About a year," Robbie replies, still clearly a bit confused, but sounding more comfortable. "Why do you ask?"

"Just curious. How's the job?"

Robbie shrugs.

"It pays the bills. My wife's in college, so she's not working, and we have a kid now." He looks at the sidewalk, at least a small bit of shame burning on his face. "The more exclusive the pictures, the bigger the paycheck. You get it."

"Yeah, I get the idea. You like the job?" Damien asks.

"I mean, I'd like to be a reporter. This is step one."

Damien nods.

"Reporter sounds good. Maybe I can help with that."

"What do you mean?" Robbie asks.

"Look, I'm sure you've noticed I'm trying to show my girl a good time tonight, right? It's her birthday, and she's not used to all of–" he gestures broadly with his hands. "All of this. So I'll make you a deal. You get five minutes to ask me anything you want, about her, about me, about us. You get to take all the pictures you need of me out here, and of them– only through the window– and when you're done you're gonna take this…" He fishes his wallet out, slipping three hundred bucks into Robbie's hand. "And you're gonna take your wife out for dinner, tonight, tomorrow, whatever you like, but after those five minutes you're gonna leave us alone."

Robbie blinks.

"You're bribing me?"

"Not at all. Think of it as an exclusive interview. I don't give them out to just anyone. Sure, normally you'd be paying me for a thing like this, but I'm getting something out of it too, right?"

Robbie looks dumbfounded, but only for a moment, straightening up and pulling a notebook out of his bag in a single motion.

"How long have you two actually been together?"

Damien grins, blowing a smoke ring.

"Couple months now."

"Is it true the label hired her to make you guys look good?"

He laughs.

"Robbie, if we hired someone to make us look good, how soon do you think that'd leak and defeat the whole purpose? Nah, they reached out to us, and it took some convincing for the higher ups at the label to even consider it. These are easy, ask me another one."

"Did you two know each other before the tour?"

"Come on, man. You wanna be a reporter? Really dig for something,"

Robbie's face is flushed, his body tense as he rushes to scribble things down. It's not really fair to him, he's totally unprepared, but he might be able to use this as a springboard into something better. Worst case scenario, it gets him off their backs for the rest of the night.

"Do you love her?"

The question catches Damien off guard, and he lowers his gaze, meeting Robbie's eyes for the first time during the questioning.

"She's everything to me."

Robbie smiles as he writes it down.

"I've been following you guys for a long time, been to a few shows. I'm pretty sure I can tell when you're talking shit, and this isn't that."

Damien glances back inside the restaurant. Phoebe's eyes are still on him. She tilts her head with a curious smile, and he nods at her. Out of the corner of his eye, he sees Robbie raise his camera, prepped to take a picture.

"Well, love brings out the best in you, right Robbie?"

He turns back to the photographer, shooting him his best smile.

"Alright kid, you got three more minutes, better make the best of 'em."

Pour Some Sugar on Me

PHOEBE

This place is nothing like she pictured it. For some reason, she'd imagined a cabaret with cozy velvet seats, soft lighting, and quiet but sensual conversation carrying on in the background. Maybe there would be a few dancers swinging around poles while servers in nothing but their underwear brought them fancy drinks.

But she couldn't have pictured anything like this.

Everything smells sharp, like it's been perfumed in sweat, leather, and sex. Meathooks on thick chains hang from the ceiling and the entire place is bathed in red light. The dark walls look like they're pulsing with need, matching the beating of her heart.

She doesn't know where to look first. It's all so new. So tempting.

Everything about this place is primal.

Old pornos play on loops as people mingle and writhe on the dancefloor in various stages of undress, music pounding so loud that it's hard to think, much less take everything in. It's sinful. It's dirty.

It's total freedom.

Everyone here seems as comfortable with themselves as they are with each other; it's like they can really let loose here. She can see why he would have been drawn to a place like this.

Damien pulls her out of the way as bodies brush up against them, heading toward the bar. He adjusts the bag on his shoulder and squeezes her hand, flashing her a big grin and looking almost as awestruck as she feels, like his body is brimming with excitement.

She purposefully left Damien's kinks out of the article, merely describing him as intense and enthusiastic when it came to their relationship. There's no way she could print the things that they've done. It's their filthy little secret, one of the last things that'll be only theirs once her work is published.

Phoebe licks her lips, finding herself craving a drink as she spots a woman with her legs spread on a couch, her hand confidently placed on a head of dark hair.

"What do you think?" Damien's gravelly purr makes her hair stand on end.

"It's good." She clears her throat, managing to tear her eyes away, not wanting to look creepy. "It's a lot."

Phoebe swallows hard, her heart thundering as her eye is drawn to the bag hanging off his shoulder. It's black leather, discreet enough to not garner any suspicion unless you've been around him for long enough. He never carries a bag, least of all one like that. When she asked what was in it back in the taxi he just gave her a little smirk and told the driver the address of the club.

Damien's hand has been resting on the small of her back as she's been taking everything in, but he's slowly started to slide it down, drifting toward her ass. Her eyes remain fixed on the woman, who now has her head thrown back, moaning over the heavy bass.

I want that.

"We've got all night to take it in, babydoll."

She nods, greedily taking in her surroundings, but there's a nagging thought that's been working its way past all the excitement. One she can't ignore. Damien told her this place doesn't ask for names, anonymity in these cases is important after all, but circumstances are different when you're famous. Someone's got to know who he is. At least there's a chance.

"Are you sure it's safe to be here? I mean, with you being... well, you."

It's not like a place like this could taint his image, he sells himself as a bad boy after all, but she's not so sure if the label would be happy with one of its biggest stars being photographed in a sex club. Not after they've just pulled themselves out of their little ditch.

But Damien just laughs, completely unconcerned.

"My guess is a lot of the people you're gonna see are stock brokers, lawyers, judges— shit like that. Some of them don't have the space in their busy schedules to really be themselves, so they come to places like this. One of the reasons for the bag checks is so that nobody comes in here with a camera. Nobody is going to write about us in the paper tomorrow, and even if they did there wouldn't be any evidence."

"Okay." She finds herself breathing a little more calmly. "I trust you."

"That's all I ask, babydoll. You wanna grab a drink and take a walk around? See what people really get up to here?"

She grins.

"You bet I do."

As they walk around Phoebe absorbs the basics of the club. There are three floors to this place: the main floor has a bar, and seems mainly meant for dancing and lighter activities, with some closed booths for people to... mingle.

The floor above them is the exhibition area, filled with rooms to watch– or to be watched in. The thought of it sends a little buzz through her body, an almost perfect mix of fear and excitement. She's not sure if she's ready for something like that yet, but she doubts the idea will leave her mind anytime soon.

Finally, the basement, AKA The Dungeon. It's for... the more intense variety of play. She has a feeling that's where Damien is shooting to end up tonight, but as far as she's concerned it all sounds intriguing enough to give a look.

First though, they've got to get themselves a bit of liquid courage. Damien orders a double whiskey, and remembers her signature G&T without even having to ask.

"So, what do you say we start from the top and work our way down?"

Phoebe smiles nervously, taking his hand with a nod, and he leads her through the sea of sweaty bodies and up a set of stairs.

The top floor is relatively empty, with a few people lounging and chatting in small booths that look regular enough to be found in a standard pub. For a moment she's confused, wondering where the hell everyone is on what's supposed to be the exhibitionist floor, that is, until she sees a couple of people walk through a conspicuous set of open doors.

"Those are the voyeur rooms," Damien tells her. "You wanna check it out?"

He drains his drink in a few gulps and abandons it on a table nearby. He can probably tell just by looking at her. It looks so secretive, so tempting, and she doesn't even need to answer, simply taking his hand.

They enter a dark hallway, lit by a sort of soft red lighting, but she only has a moment to consider the ambience before her attention is snapped straight ahead with the crack of a whip against skin. The agonized moan that follows is like a prelude, screams of ecstasy pouring from the open doors on either side of the hall. The weighty air gets even heavier as they walk, and Phoebe thinks she might be sweating even more than her glass by the end of this.

"An open door is an invitation," Damien tells her.

But it's not just the rooms, there are also people mingling in the halls. One man is leaning up against the wall with his partner on his knees, sucking him off. A woman watches them from afar, her hand down her panties and a drink at her lips. She winks as the two of them pass by, her eyes lingering on them for the briefest of seconds before she turns her attention back to something far more interesting.

Phoebe finds her gaze wandering, left and right, behind her and ahead again, not quite sure where to look, but Damien leads confidently forward, to a large room at the end of the hall. It's like a little theater inside, complete with seating for any and everyone who wants to watch. They sit on an empty bench, a little ways into the room but still further back from the other couples enthusiastically looking on.

At the front of the room is a woman with her arms above her head, handcuffed to a large chain hanging from the ceiling– not unlike the ones back down on the main floor. She's blindfolded, a thick leather collar around her neck, and a ball gag in her mouth. Her golden hair is tousled, like someone's been all over it; wrenching it, pulling her around...

The man with her is circling, wearing nothing but a pair of black leather briefs with riding crop clutched in his hand, a calculating look on his face. The woman's head twists from right to left and back again as he stalks around her like a shark, trying to figure out exactly where the next strike might come from.

Phoebe spots welts on the woman's stomach and breasts, but it's also impossible to miss her damp inner-thighs, covered with sweat. Or maybe her own juices, it's frustratingly impossible to tell from this far back and Phoebe's already feeling the itch to move in closer. The woman's hips buck as if they have a mind of their own, her partner laughing and leaning in to whisper something in her ear. She can't hear it, but it doesn't matter.

Her imagination does the work.

In her mind, it's her and Damien in that room, surrounded by onlookers just beyond her own senses. The smell of his cologne slips into her nostrils, the sharp and intense pain from the riding crop stings her backside.

Then her thigh.

Her breasts.

Her pussy.

His gravelly voice taunts her, and she finds herself so desperate that squeezing her thighs together might make her come.

You think you deserve my cock?

Phoebe forces herself back into the moment, taking a sip of her drink and using the opportunity to steal a glance down at Damien's pants, finding the bulge she's hoping to see. Back up to his face though, she finds his eyes are burning, his chest heaving as that familiar red creeps into his earlobes.

"Aren't they fucking hot?" He leans over. "Look at her. You see the way she's shivering? All he needs to do is just be there, that's all it takes."

He's even more into it than she thought.

"I feel like I'm watching something I shouldn't be."

Damien goes silent as the man gets right down in front of his partner, not wanting to interrupt the show as he spreads her lips to the audience's explicit approval. Phoebe shudders, taking another big sip of her drink before pressing the glass to her chest, but the ice can only do so much against the fire blazing inside her. They've only been here for a few minutes and she's pretty sure she's going to leave a stain on the bench. In any other circumstance, she'd be far too humiliated to stick around, but here, like this? She can't deny how much she loves it.

"Well, that's the point," he continues, his eyes still locked on the show.

"You're watching complete vulnerability, but in a form we've always been told is wrong, even dirty. Some people see this lifestyle as disgusting, sure, but more than that they see it as dangerous. What they don't realize is how much care and compassion goes into it, because that's the thing: it's about trust. If she says their safe word at any point during the scene, he stops. That's a real partnership. He may look like he's in charge right now, but she has the power."

"It's emotionally freeing."

There's still so much that she has to learn about this, but her curiosity has always been her best quality.

"For both parties," Damien replies. "People who don't understand domination see it as cruel, only about the pain, but that's not it, at least not for everyone. The thing I see the most when I look at them is trust. I've always wanted someone to trust me the way she must trust him."

Phoebe turns to him, taking in everything about him all at once: his eyes, his lips, the shape of those arms beneath his sleeves, the curve of his thighs... the entirety of the man she's found herself bound to.

"Someone does."

In front of them the woman yelps out, her partner walking behind her after the sharp crack of the riding crop rings out through the room. He pulls his briefs down, rubbing his straining cock against her ass.

Phoebe lets out a quivering breath, her nipples poking out under her dress, raw and painfully sensitive. Every time she shifts, even with just the tiniest rustle of the fabric, the sensations are so strong she's forced to squeeze her thighs together.

And Damien's taken notice, wrapping one arm around her, playfully toying with the strap on her dress.

"So, this turns you on?" He asks, almost laughing. But it doesn't sound mocking at all, it's more like excitement bubbling up. It seems, just like her, he's trying his best to control himself.

She reaches under her dress, slipping her fingers into her dripping cunt before pulling them out again, and dangling them in front of his face.

"What do you think?"

He grasps her wrist and sucks her fingers clean, one by one, until he finally releases the last digit with a pop.

"So, do you think this sort of thing would be your style?" He asks.

"Tell me what you have in mind."

The question is only part of the play, and that Damien Bell Cheshire grin tells her all she needs to know.

Phoebe exhales, feeling Damien's fingers still toying with the strap on her dress again, gliding it up and down her skin. Back at the front, the man is kneeling in front of his partner, licking her pussy greedily as she groans into the ball gag. Every time they turn up the heat, he follows suit.

"Downstairs in the dungeon. A private room, and a St. Andrew's Cross."

"A saint– what?" She barely gets the words out, only half listening as she struggles to hold herself together.

"It's shaped like a big X, with wrist and ankle restraints. Once you're strapped into it you'll be totally in my control." He kisses up and down her neck. "I could do *anything* to you."

She shivers, eyes flicking down to the bag at his feet as she keeps her breath as steady as she can.

"How about you tell me what's in that bag?"

"How about I take us downstairs and show you?" His mouth is hot on her neck. "Discovery's part of the fun, right? Besides, you know what I want: You're gonna beg to be punished, beg for my cock. I want you to whine for my mouth to be all over that pretty little pussy."

Her eyes flick back to the couple, the man, having switched to a flogger, is dragging it along his partner's skin. Her muffled moans bounce off of the walls as he begins to strike her, again and again. There's something so intoxicating about the sounds, the way her chest heaves with every hit. Watching her tormented by all that pleasure mixed with pain... It almost feels like a religious experience.

And Phoebe wants that. All of it.

"Alright Damien. Downstairs, now."

Hungry Eyes

DAMIEN

He expected Phoebe to look more unsure, but she has a playful smile on her face as they hit the bottom floor, stopping for a moment and taking in the sights around her. The sound of whips, moans, and the rattle of chains fill the room as the distinct smell of sex permeates the air.

It's a wide open space with people tied to chairs, bent over surgical tables being spanked, and onlookers milling around watching. Some of them are fucking, others are touching themselves, and it sounds like they're all having the time of their lives.

Phoebe gasps, pointing to one of three crosses positioned around the room. Two of them are vacant, but the third is occupied, thick leather straps around the man's wrists and ankles and a ball gag in his mouth, his partner enthusiastically sucking his cock. The restrained man rocks in desperation, a look twisted between bliss and agony contorting on his face as they watch.

Damien gives the room a quick sweep, quickly noticing another man tied to a chair just left of the first, clamps on his nipples hooked up to some sort of battery, and a blindfold over his eyes. His domme struts around him in nothing but a pair of thigh-high leather boots, dragging a riding crop up across his shoulders as she moves. She stops in front of him and swats his swollen cock, his yelp, a shot of pure electricity that shoots straight through Damien. He licks his lips, his eyes slipping over to see Phoebe's chest heaving.

He grabs her hand, guiding her toward a private room and shutting the door behind him. There's a large cross in the corner along with a large black couch beside. She's practically giddy, looking around like a kid in a candy store. He's not sure if she's ever been this excited for something.

"This is amazing…"

He grasps her waist, pulling her against him and placing a soft kiss on her lips as the muffled sounds of screams and the cracks of leather against flesh echo through the door.

"I'm glad you like it. I just wanted to thank you for trusting me with this, I know it's a big deal and I–"

"I always trust you, Damien."

Those words mean everything to him; it's all he needs to hear to begin.

"I'm going to undress you."

"Yes, sir."

He unzips the back of her dress, sliding the straps off her shoulders until the whole ensemble falls to a puddle at her feet.

She's not wearing panties or a bra, only a pair of thigh-high stockings that dig into her skin just tightly enough to create a tiny bulge where they end. He wraps his arms around her waist, already wanting to caress every inch of her body he can get his hands on.

"Is there anything you want me to do?" He whispers.

"Well, what have you got in that bag?" She purrs. "You only turn 24 once, right? I'm feeling adventurous."

Damien grins.

"Well, to start with, I've got a vibrator, a blindfold and some bindings. There's also a riding crop, and a cock ring."

She turns around, frowning.

"What's a cock ring for?"

He chuckles.

"Keeps me from coming too fast. I wanna take my time with you."

He gently circles her nipple with the tip of his finger, watching it harden beneath his touch. Damien has loved teaching her about this part of his world, but admittedly he's still learning a lot about it, and about himself. Really, they've been learning together— their wants, their kinks, and their limits; he feels connected to her in a way that he never has with anyone else. All of this is what lets him be vulnerable, sometimes in ways that still scare him a little, but he wants her to keep seeing beyond the image he's created, beyond the money and the fame... because he knows she cares about him just as much as he does about her.

"I'll walk you through everything just like I did the first time, but I need to know if there's anything that you *don't* want."

"Electrocution is my only limit," she replies, glancing back at the door.

Damien grabs Phoebe's hand, gently kissing her knuckles.

"We won't get that intense, don't worry." He keeps her hand in his, tipping her chin up with the other so she's looking right in his eyes. "But more important than that, remember, even if we decide to do something tonight, you say daisy and I stop. Open communication, no shame, no fear."

"Yes, sir," she whispers, winding him up in her arms and letting her whole weight hang off him. "I love you."

"I love you, babydoll," he breathes. "More and more every day."

There's a moment where Damien wonders if they couldn't just stay like this, staring into each other's eyes the whole evening, but another ecstatic yelp from outside snaps him out of the hypnotic moment.

"Okay, well, we should probably get kinky. That's what we're here for, right?"

She snorts.

"Yeah, I should slap you in the face or something."

"You know, that's not a bad idea."

Phoebe helps him strip down to nothing, briefly getting on her knees to wrap her lips around his half-hard dick. He lets her swirl her tongue around the tip before gently pulling her back and tipping her chin up so their eyes can meet.

"Patience, babydoll."

Damien grabs some lube and the cock ring from his bag, carefully rolling it on as Phoebe, still kneeling, watches on.

"Do you wear it often?"

Her eyes are flickering with interest.

"Not often, no. But enough to know it makes things more intense for me."

She gently folds their clothes, placing them next to the cross before standing to face him.

"You want me this way?"

Her voice is sweet like honey, but with a curious edge to it. Now it's his turn to worship her.

"I want you every way."

She giggles as he backs her up against the wall, spreading her legs wide enough to have access to anything he needs. Damien slides the cuffs around her ankles and secures them, setting the key down next to the cross just out of her reach. Once her ankles are restrained, he works his way up her body, lips ghosting inch by inch up her silky skin.

He wants to make sure she feels safe before they get started. He's never been the *really* rough type of dominant with his partners. He likes to watch them melt, to crumble through careful implementation of a gentle kind of domination. Their pleasure is the thing that really gets him off; seeing someone swallowed up by their own ecstasy, watching them come over and over again, screaming his name and knowing that he's the person making their skin flush... *that's* what puts him over the edge.

He glides his lips over hers as he secures her right wrist, and then her left. The gentle click of the cuffs makes his cock twitch and he can't help but grind against her thigh.

"Are you ready?"

Her smile is just as big as his.

"Yes, sir."

"That's my girl."

He glides the crop across the palm of his hand, her breath quickening as he gives it a sharp smack against his own skin to test. The Dominatrix he met in Paris gave him some pointers, told him to avoid the lower back and the kidneys if he were ever to hit someone on the cross. At the time, he wasn't completely sure why the rules were important, but he's rarely listened more intently than he did that night, the thick ribbons of silvery smoke seeping from her lips with every word. Everything about her was captivating, and more than a little dangerous.

Even back then he knew he wanted to be like that.

Damien drags the crop up Phoebe's thigh, watching intently as the goosebumps form. Anticipation hangs thick in the air and curiosity stretches across her face. He's aching to turn her around on that cross and fuck her from behind.

But that can wait.

This is his favorite part.

Damien spends a couple minutes toying with her, sliding the thick leather across her belly, down her other thigh, and along the underside of her breasts. Her nipples are hard and he can't help but lean in and flick them with his tongue, her soft exhale sending a shiver down his spine.

He lightly swats her thigh, watching with amusement as her body jumps. The chains keeping her bound to the cross jingle lightly as he drags the crop between her thighs, her hips rolling against the leather.

"Desperate, huh?" He leans in. "If you're a good girl, I'll give you everything you need."

She only smiles in response.

"Again."

He wets his lips and swats her other thigh, but harder this time. Phoebe lets out a new sound for the evening, a mix of a whine and something raspier as she wiggles against her bindings.

"More?"

Damien drags the crop across her nipples.

"Please, sir," she breathes.

She cries out as he swats her breast, and Damien reaches between her thighs, smiling when he's greeted with wetness. He glides his fingers right between her pussy lips, and his mouth waters as he pictures every little thing he could do to her.

She's swallowing her moans, tiny gulping sounds filling the air between them, her breath reminding him of a rushing river. He slides the crop across her throat and her body quivers against it like a humming-bird's wings. She's trembling from the adrenaline, tiny diamonds of sweat forming on her forehead, and the sound of her mewling for him only making him harder.

"You like that?"

Delicately, he pushes his fingers inside of her dripping cunt and teases her, massaging that spot that makes her hands curl into tight fists. He slows his fingers as she writhes, her head rolling to the side.

"Use your words, sweet thing."

"I– I love it, give me more! I need more!"

"Hmm... I wanna have some more fun with you first."

He pulls his fingers out of her and pushes them between her lips.

"Taste yourself."

Phoebe moans, her eyelids fluttering as she swirls her tongue around them, licking them clean.

"I'm gonna tease you until you can't take it anymore, you little slut."

She writhes again, moaning louder as he pulls his fingers out from her mouth, ghosting his lips over hers. He can taste her on his tongue; he can smell her desperation all mixed in with the sweat and excitement in the air.

Damien takes a step back, letting the tip of the crop rest just above her throbbing clit. He watches as her tongue darts out to wet her lips, her voice rattling as she speaks.

"Hit me there."

He's a little surprised, not quite expecting her to be ready to go so far so quickly.

"Are you sure you want that?"

"Mmm, more than anything."

With a flick of his wrist, the crop makes a razor sharp cracking sound, and Phoebe's cry shoots through the room. Damien can feel his heart seize for a brief moment, terrified that he'd done too much, pushed her too hard, but then she laughs. The texture of her voice sends shivers down his spine.

"One more," she groans.

"Damn, you really liked that. Maybe you really *are* a little slut, babydoll."

He hits her again and she yanks against the restraints, growling like a caged beast. Her cunt is raw and red, her muscles twitching as he discards the riding crop and drops down to his knees. He glides his fingers through the folds of her pussy, rolling her clit between his fingers.

"I just want a little taste."

She struggles against her restraints, whimpering and begging for more pressure as he leans in and drags his tongue daintily across her clit.

He doesn't give her what she wants.

There'll be plenty of time for begging later.

Minutes pass as the circles become little flicks against her clit, feeling it swell more and more. If she weren't restrained, he's pretty sure she'd be down on her knees right about now. That, or straddling him with her hands around his neck. But here and now she's completely at his mercy, and he can tell that she's right on the edge.

"Damien!" She gasps. "Damien, I'm—"

Phoebe cries out as he pulls away, the chains thunking against the wood as she writhes helplessly.

"No! Nononono!" She wails, her eyes so frantic she looks like she might lose her mind. "Please, Damien– Sir! I need it, whatever you want I'll do it, just please–"

He stands, gripping her chin firmly as he smiles.

"Patience, babydoll. We've got a long ways to go yet."

Need You Tonight

PHOEBE

Her heart is pounding so hard it's like she's just run a marathon for the first time in a decade. The smell of sweat– hers, his, and everyone else's, it all clings to her nostrils. If it weren't for these restraints holding her up, she'd be on her hands and knees right now, still begging for him to fuck her.

He bends over and rifles through his bag, pulling out a two-pronged, slightly curved vibrator with thick ridges along the shaft and two "ears" on the smaller prong. A breathy gasp escapes her lips as she watches him check its battery pack.

"What's that?"

"It's called a Rabbit."

He points to the thick, curved shaft.

"This long part goes inside you, and these little ears vibrate..." He grins. "Against your clit. So, you wanna try?"

She nods eagerly. There's an ache so deep inside of her she's not sure even this thing could satiate it, but she's willing to give it a shot.

"I need to come."

Damien flashes her that wicked smile she's come to love so much.

"You know the rules, you get to come when I say you come." He cups her cheek and presses his forehead against hers. "Now, breathe."

Phoebe drags in a shaky breath through her nose, and she can feel Damien inhale along with her. He's watching her, studying her face, the rise and fall of her chest. He nods, giving her an affirmative pat on the head as her breathing becomes more measured.

"Now that we've calmed you down a bit, tell me what you want."

He's so good at these games, miles ahead of her in experience, but she's not going to let him get the better of her. She's going to drag every last bit of pleasure out of him tonight.

"As you can give me."

She feels something brush against her clit, a warm soft silicone making her throb in anticipation. Damien makes keeping cool increasingly difficult as she breathes through the adrenaline, with each kiss on her neck or nip at her ear adding to her distress. She almost regrets them getting a private room, having an audience would make this even more fun.

"I'm going to turn this on in a few seconds. You're not to come without my permission. Do you understand?"

"Y– yes, sir."

She's rewarded with a gentle kiss.

"That's my girl."

Even in full control like he is, Damien's bringing a softness that feels a bit foreign here, but she clings to it; she craves it nearly as much as the warmth that radiates off his skin as he touches her.

But then he presses the button, and everything shifts. She can feel her lips part involuntarily as she lets out a sharp moan, wiggling her hips wildly to get more friction– anything to satiate the overwhelming quakes of desire rumbling inside her. He's just teasing her, keeping the pressure light on purpose as he watches her every move, but it's all she can do to keep from shouting out. She can only imagine what her face looks like as the vibrations roll through her.

"Keep breathing," he whispers, his voice completely calm.

She stares him down, focusing as much as possible on his obnoxiously cool and collected face, anything to keep herself distracted. But the grin, alongside the tiny tilt of his head, lets her know he's on to her. He slides the curved end of the toy inside, and she clenches tightly around it. It's not as thick as he is, but the ridges bring an unexpected sensation, a violent shiver running over her nerves. Damien kisses her cheek again, one hand on her waist to help her relax, or maybe to keep her still, while his free hand pushes the vibrator in a tiny bit further.

"Relax, babydoll. I've got you."

Phoebe sucks in another breath as she feels the tiny silicone ears rest against her swollen clit, drumming into it in a manic rhythm. She wiggles against it, laughter bubbling up from her throat as Damien sucks on her neck.

"Good?"

She tries to speak, but only manages to let out a small hum of approval before he turns the toy up a little higher, beginning to thrust it in and out of her swollen pussy. She lurches back, tipping her head toward the ceiling as ridge after ridge rubs against her.

"You have no idea how much this turns me on. Watching you like this, completely helpless." He groans in her ear. "I'm going to fuck you until you can't walk."

He cranks the vibrator up further, and Phoebe feels like she may have reached her limit. It's like every muscle in her body clenches at the same time, her body going rigid.

"I'm gonna come!" She moans.

She's aching to topple over, ready to get lost in every little bit of what he's offering, but even in her addled state she knows he's not going to give her that satisfaction. She knows the rules to this game.

"No, you're not!" He sings, elongating the words in a taunting tone that somehow turns her on even more.

Sweat trickles down her spine and adrenaline pulses through her. She feels like she's slowly trekking up the biggest drop on a rollercoaster. The closer she gets to the top, the more intensely she feels everything. Her thighs quiver and her back arches.

"Damien, please!"

Her voice comes out in a pathetic squeak, nearly broken. He thrusts the toy faster and faster until her hips are bucking against it, pleasure building until she feels like she can't take it anymore.

"Oh, god! I'm coming! I'm so–"

As expected, Damien pulls the toy out of her and the big, lightning strike of a climax she hoped for fizzles out into nothing but a dull buzzing. The denial drags itself through her, sinking into her bones as she lets out a wail of frustration, trying pathetically to free herself from her restraints.

He clicks the vibrator off, licking it clean and giving her a mocking grin.

"What the fuck?!"

"You disobeyed me. You came without my permission."

"Barely," she snarls, her voice still shaking.

Phoebe nearly collapses as he uncuffs her, but Damien catches her in his arms, brushing the back of his hand across her cheek.

"I think you need to be punished, babydoll."

He turns her around and only restraints her arms this time. Her face is pushed up against the sweat-covered leather of the cross. She watches as he picks up the riding crop and flips it in his hand, humming softly.

"Really should have brought a paddle," he mutters to himself.

"You have a belt, don't you?"

Damien smiles to himself, proud that she's taking the initiative like this. He quickly abandons the riding crop and picks up his dress pants, yanking the belt from the loops and folding it in his hand. She watches with rapt attention as his fingers wrap around the thick silver buckle, losing sight of him as he moves behind her.

"You count to five. Just like the first time we did this, okay?"

She can feel a hand rest on her waist, steadying her.

"I thought this was supposed to be a punishment," she teases. "You're just giving me what I want."

The jolt of pain rockets through her as his belt strikes her ass, her sharp intake of breath the perfect prelude to the stinging sensation that follows.

"Even if you like the pain, remember: bad girls don't get to come. Now *count* for me."

She clenches her stomach, gritting her teeth and bracing herself for the inevitable strike. Her eyes slip shut as she tries to focus on the sounds around her, just barely catching the whoosh of the belt cutting through the air before the loud crack– like a gunshot– as it strikes her ass.

Phoebe lets out a strangled cry.

"One!"

"What color?" Damien asks.

She's already having to get her breathing in check, calming herself down before she answers.

"Green."

He hits her again, just as hard as the last time if not harder. Her hands are clenched into tight fists, her fingernails digging deep into her palms, but already the pleasure is beginning to build again, that familiar electrical buzzing gathering inside her.

"Two–" She chokes. "Green, keep going."

And another strike.

Phoebe presses her forehead against the now slimy leather. Her heart is in her throat and she can feel the welts growing on her ass, her skin burning. She's pretty sure she won't be able to sit down tomorrow, but it's worth it.

Damien presses himself up against her, the belt grazing her hip as he kisses her neck.

"You sure you can keep going?"

"Yes," she groans. "Harder this time."

She hears the leather cut through the air, followed by another sharp sting on her backside. Her muscles twitch and the chains binding her wrists to the cross clatter against it as she lets out a noise that's closer to a howl than anything else.

"Three!"

The sound of the thick buckle hitting cement makes her body slump with relief, glancing down to see the belt discarded on the floor. Damien gently grasps her hips and tilts them back, dragging his cock through her folds.

"Just like this," he whispers as he slowly sinks himself into her throbbing pussy.

Phoebe whines, relishing the languid and gentle pace. They have a primal connection, a shared yearning that can't be satisfied any other way than this. The love Damien has for her is something she's never experienced before, and she'd chase that high forever.

"More," she groans.

"You're a needy little slut, aren't you?"

She turns her head and presses her cheek against the leather.

"I thought that's what you wanted," she says, her tone teetering between mocking and playful.

She's clenching around him, and each time he hits her G-spot, she struggles to keep herself in check. She can't take another punishment, even though she's pretty sure he would love to dish it out. The thought of being edged with no relief in sight is too much for her to take right now.

Damien's thrusts are starting to grow more chaotic, and she can hear him letting out soft grunts as he tries to maintain some semblance of control. She smiles, licking her parched lips.

"You wanna come?" He growls.

Her body is teetering on the edge of climax and all she can muster is a nod. Damien grabs her hair and yanks it hard.

"I'm gonna count down from five, and you're going to come by the time I hit one." He pounds into her harder, as if he's daring her to come right that second. "Can you do that for me?"

"Y– yes, sir."

"That's my girl. Now..." He punctuates each number with another agonizingly rough thrust. "Five... four... three..."

Everything primal buried inside of her is bursting out of that little cage she's built herself over the years, turning her into someone she wouldn't have recognized even two months ago.

"Two," he purrs, swatting her ass. Her knees buckle as every sound that's not his voice begins to bleed out of the air, ending up as little more than radio static.

"One and a half..."

She lets out an agonized laugh.

"You fucking asshole."

Damien gives her ass another sharp smack, aiming right for the same spot that's still swollen from his belt. Pleasure and pain swirl together and Phoebe tenses to keep herself from falling apart.

"No backtalk," he growls.

He ups his relentless pace, hips slamming into her so hard that the cross actually starts to thud against the wall. Phoebe cries out, struggling to control herself, just as Damien lets out his own whimper.

God, just fucking say it.

And then she hears it: the word she needs to let go.

"One."

All she feels is bliss as a blanket of pure electric euphoria wraps around her. Damien keeps up the pace of his fingers, rubbing tight circles around her clit. With one final slam of his hips, he lets out a ragged moan. Her bones feel like they're made of rubber, her whole body damp from sweat as she shakes. Damien takes a few seconds to breathe, kissing her temple before he reaches up and uncuffs her, and she collapses into his arms for the second time that night.

"You okay?"

Phoebe nods, her head fuzzy.

"I'm great. Really fucking thirst, though."

He lifts her up, carrying her over to the couch and setting her down gingerly before grabbing his jacket and wrapping it around her. Euphoria gives way to exhaustion, but it's that rare kind that's more like a warm hug than anything else. It's the kind she feels after finishing a long day of work and knowing she can finally just let go.

Damien digs into his bag and pulls out a water bottle, handing it over. She's never been thirstier in her life and guzzles the entire thing in one go. He opens another for her, barely having it ready by the time she's finished the first. She drinks greedily, but thinks better of it before she's finished, passing the half-full bottle back to him.

Damien takes a large swig.

"So, how do you feel?"

She frowns, struggling for a moment to find the right words. Her mind is hazy, all she wants to do is close her eyes and rest, but her lips curl into a lazy smile as she stares up at him.

"Like this is the best birthday I've ever had."

The Lovecats

PHOEBE

"How do you lose your keys so often?" Phoebe laughs as her own set clatter in the lock. "This is just like back on tour."

"I didn't lose them, I just misplaced them."

"And now you can't find them," she teases as they step inside. "Almost like they're... lost."

"It's an important distinction," he replies. "Anyway, you won't be shocked to know this isn't the first time I've locked myself out of my house."

"Is it the hundredth?"

He gently pinches her waist, playfully growling in her ear before pressing her up against the wall.

"Are you asking me to punish you again, Miss Miller?"

She giggles, giving him a quick peck on the nose before slipping under his outstretched arm.

"As much as I love the sound of that, we've been burning the candle at both ends for a bit too long. I'll give you a quick tour and we can crash." She strokes his cheek. "Hrm, I guess you won't have fresh clothes for tomorrow."

"Nah, I'll shower and deal." He leans in, grasping her hands. "Now show me Château Miller."

Phoebe scoffs, leading him through the tiny entrance hall and into the living room.

"Garbage pit is a little more accurate."

Her apartment is a disaster, clothes strewn all over the floor from when she was packing, about a dozen notebooks piled on top of her desk, and her coffee mug still sitting unwashed in the sink from that day she told Brian the truth. She didn't quite remember how bad she'd let things get.

"God, this is embarrassing."

"Look Pheebs, this is what my hotel rooms looked like when I didn't expect you'd be stopping by." He shrugs. "You've got nothing to be embarrassed about. I'll still love you, even if you fling your panties everywhere."

"I think that's part of *why* you love me."

"Guilty as charged, now let's see the rest of the apartment."

She leads him into the small kitchen, already cringing with embarrassment at the state of it, flicking on the light and praying that no cockroaches are hanging out on the floor. Much to her relief, it's relatively clean save for the few crushed doritos next to the sink. She thought she swept those up.

Damien doesn't even seem to notice. Instead, he points at a cupboard hanging off its hinges and Phoebe cringes. Fuck, this place is a disaster.

"You want me to fix that?"

"Nah, I think it's charming."

She takes him back into the living room, pointing at her desk near the small window. It's covered in papers and empty coffee cups. And again, she swore she left this place in better condition.

"That's where the magic happens."

"Fantastic. Not as nice as your new office, but still pretty great." Damien winks at her. "If I do say so myself."

Phoebe notices that her answering machine light is blinking. She's still a little hazy from the club and wanders over. Three new messages. Definitely her mom. She presses the play button and listens to the tape grind.

"Phoebe, it's your mother. I don't want to take up too much of your time, but I'm organizing our New Year's brunch and I need to know if you're making an appearance this year, thanks sweetie, love you!"

Phoebe sighs. It really is nice to hear the warmth in her mother's voice, and she feels bad for putting off returning her calls for so long. It's not that she doesn't want to talk to her, she's just been so busy.

The machine crackles, beeping again.

"Phoebe, are you home yet? I'm worried about you, sweetheart." Her tone is coated in honey, but this time there's an undercurrent of anxiety and irritation that makes Phoebe's heart jump a little. *"I guess you're still off with that rock band."*

"I don't like the way she said that," Damien groans as he moves aside a pile of clothes to sit on the couch.

"Anyway, it's fine, please just call me, Phoebe. Your father and I need a head count for brunch– oh! I was talking to my friend Patty about you! She said that if you're interested, she could get you into that secretarial school. You could put those typing skills to good use and get yourself a decent salary. Just something to keep in mind. Anyway, give me a call back ASAP."

"Jesus," Damien mutters. "Secretary school? You're already a pro writer."

"It's not– she's just trying to be helpful."

This isn't how she wanted Damien to be 'introduced' to her mother.

Another beep, the last message on the machine.

"Phoebe, I've been trying to get a hold of you for an entire week now, and nobody can tell me where you are. I'm just worried, sweetie, you always call back so quickly and I hope nothing bad has happened to you." She lets out a heavy sigh. *"I'm hoping I've just slipped your mind and you'll get back to me as soon as you can. I can deal with getting forgotten, but just... call me when you get this, please."*

"She's a peach, isn't she?"

"I'm sorry," Phoebe mumbles, suddenly much more focused on picking up some of the errant mess. Anything to get her mind off that embarrassment.

"Why are you sorry? You're not the asshole here Pheebs, she's the one who–"

"Don't call her that," Phoebe bites back.

He doesn't even know her mom. All he's heard is these messages, and maybe a couple things she's said. Things she regrets.

"Just... please don't call her that. She means well."

Damien puts his hands up in surrender.

"You're right, I'm sorry. That was out of line."

She sits down next to him, suddenly completely exhausted, leaning into his shoulder as he twirls her hair between his fingers. The silence is nice, even soothing, but she still feels the need to explain things.

"She grew up in a different time, you know? I don't think she ever got to be as independent as I was, or really come into her own. And she had to grow up *fast*. She had Michael when she was only 19. I think it changed her perspective on things." She shakes her head. "But I know she cares. None of it's on purpose."

Her mother doesn't really talk about this stuff, and her father never felt comfortable enough to share more than a couple words on the subject, but she's pretty sure it's an accurate picture. It's the best she could do piecing it together on her own.

Damien nods slowly, staring straight ahead as he listens. She's rarely seen him look this uncomfortable before, like he's caught between two completely separate compulsions. The two of them have had a few bumps, but nothing they couldn't handle. But the look in his eyes scares her a little.

She's seen it before.

"Hey, I just– you know that the plan is to be in Paris around New Year's, right?"

"I know." She picks at the faded scar on her knee, not wanting to make eye contact. "This is just a family tradition, that's probably why she got so intense about it."

"Yeah, I remember you mentioning it. So what's the tradition?"

"Well, Michael goes to his in-laws and I usually go to Janis's parents' house for Christmas because neither of us want to get stuck Upstate in the snow. So, New Year's Brunch is the compromise."

"Sounds like you don't even want to go," Damien remarks with a chuckle.

He looks relieved, and for some reason that sets her off a little.

"No, I do! I thought that it would be nice to introduce you— I mean, I'm meeting your parents and they're—"

"I guess I'm just extra defensive because my dad gives me so much shit about the band, and everything that comes along with it. But Pheebs, you have a great job–"

"And I can let her see that." She's more determined now, locking eyes with him. "My brother and his wife are going to be there, and their kids, and I want her to see..." She fiddles with the dog tags around her neck.

"See what?" Damien asks.

"This life I'm building for myself, the friends I've made, and the fact that I'm writing this big important cover story. She can see that I'm stable, like Michael, and–"

"You don't need to keep comparing yourself to your brother, Pheebs. You're two totally different people on two different paths. If she can't see that, that's on her." He brushes her hair away from her face and cups her cheek. "I dunno, from what I can tell it sounds like we might not even be welcome in that house."

She shakes her head. That's not true. Sure, it was tense sometimes, but that's every house. Nobody's perfect. It wasn't her fault, and it wasn't her parents, it was just the way things were.

"I left when I was 18 because I wanted to get out on my own; it didn't have anything to do with my mom."

She remembers her mother fussing over her when she left, telling her she could take a few more years, that she could go to college Upstate and stay close to home. That's what Michael did, so why not her? But Phoebe wanted to get out on her own and experience life on her terms. She wanted the chance to let the world change her, and her mother couldn't understand that.

"Wouldn't you rather spend New Year's in Paris?" Damien asks, wrapping an arm around her. "We could run off and it'd be just the two of us. We'd walk along the Seine and I'd take you out for dinner, we'd watch the Eiffel Tower light up and then I'd fuck you on the hotel balcony... you know, real romantic shit."

She giggles as his kisses become little nips and bites, sending sparks across her skin.

"That does sound nice, but..."

"Just think about it, okay? I'm not saying you have to turn your mom down, but this is a pretty big deal and there's no reason to take it off the table, right?"

She's never seen him try to avoid something this intensely before.

Does he really hate the idea of meeting her family so much? Just from a couple messages? It all seems like such an overreaction.

"Damien, I'd really like you to meet my parents. It's important to me, and New Year's Brunch is important to them. You can do that for me, can't you?"

Damien pulls her in close, turning her around as he begins to massage her shoulders. He must be sensing the tension in the air.

"Look, you know I'll do anything for you Pheebs, but you don't have to give her an answer right now, do you?" He asks. "New Year's is a long way away. How about you call her back in the morning, you can tell her we're hoping to make it, and we'll take it from there."

Phoebe rests her head on his chest, listening to his heartbeat. She knows her mother can be difficult, even frustrating at times, but Damien hasn't seen how kind she can be. She used to throw these huge birthday parties for her and her brother; she'd spend all day baking, decorating, and making sure every detail was picture perfect. That's how she shows people she loves them, with a big event and a whole lot of effort.

For now though, she's too tired to keep trying to convince him.

"I'm gonna have to tell her about Paris either way," she mumbles into his chest, inhaling his comforting scent.

"Here's an idea, what if *I* call her and tell her." Phoebe can feel her shoulders shake before she even realizes she's laughing at him. "No? That's not a good idea?"

"You're not meeting my mother over the phone!"

"Why not? You know I'm lovely over the airwaves."

"Because there's a more than zero-percent chance you'd hang up on her." She glances off toward the phone, her imagination starting to spin. "Or call her something..."

Damien snickers, his nose scrunching up.

"Fine, fine. Well we should go to bed. I gotta get up early to be in the studio. Speaking of, tomorrow, you wanna come with?"

She shakes her head as he helps her off of the couch, leading him to the bedroom. It doesn't look much better than the living room, but she's happily surprised to see her bed is made. It's just the miracle she needed.

"Normally I'd love to, but I've gotta get to work on the article." A nervous energy starts to build, as if saying the words somehow made it all real. It's got to get done, and soon. She's been putting this final stretch off for way too long. "I actually think I need to just... spend the next week or so locked to my desk."

She lifts her head, that nervous energy quickly turning to panic in her sleep-deprived state.

"It's not that I don't love you, or going to the studio, but–"

"You have a job to do," he replies, rubbing his nose against hers until she's forced to smile again. "I get it. How about this: You come to my place! I'll cook for you every night, bring you whatever you need, and you can write in your new office with Maverick. I bet she's a great assistant."

That's all it takes. All her panic melts away with his simple promise.

"Can you teach her how to make coffee?" Phoebe chuckles.

"I think the lack of thumbs might be an issue for her, but she's gone up against steeper odds in the past."

"Perhaps her one and only flaw." Phoebe lets out a loud yawn as she strips off her dress and tosses it into the hamper. "I'm gonna brush my teeth."

She heads for the bathroom, flicking on the light and choosing to ignore the roach that scurries underneath the counter. Quickly, Phoebe puts away the makeup scattered around the space, doing her best to make it look at least presentable. She hopes he's not judging her too harshly, regardless of what he said. They just live so differently.

Phoebe squeezes some toothpaste onto her toothbrush and shoves it in her mouth, already a week ahead in her mind as she fantasizes about the finished article. In her imagination, it's amazing– the best thing she's ever written. That's the worst part, it's so easy to focus on the end product instead of the process. She has to get through this block, otherwise it's all just smoke.

When she glances up at the mirror, Damien is leaning up against the doorframe behind her, framed perfectly in nothing but his briefs, a dorky smile on his face. He looks her up and down, his eyes lingering on the curve of her ass.

Phoebe raises a brow as she spits some toothpaste into the sink. She's too tired to fuck him right now, but she's happy enough just to feel wanted.

"What's up?"

"Nothing." His smile gets wider and he takes a step toward her, reaching out. "Just thinking about how... domestic this all feels."

She rinses her mouth out and taps her toothbrush four times on the ceramic. It's something she's been doing since she was a kid. She doesn't know why. Four just feels like the 'right' number.

"Domestic?"

"Yeah, like living together and shit." Her stomach flutters as Damien snatches the toothbrush out of her hand, bumping her gently with his hip. "I gotta brush my teeth. Shove over, gorgeous."

"Damien, that's mine!"

He stares at her like she has two heads.

"Pheebs, I've had my fingers in your mouth, I've had my *dick* in your mouth, that happened literally a couple hours ago. You're getting tied in knots over sharing a toothbrush?"

She rolls her eyes. She likes that toothbrush. There's no way she's going to let this be a regular thing.

"I'll get you one for my apartment, how's that?"

"Or, and hear me out, you could bring yours to my place," he replies as he squeezes out some toothpaste. "Permanently."

She can feel the air in the room thin as she catches herself on the counter. They haven't even met each other's parents yet. Hell, they've barely been together for three months, and he wants to live together? She eases herself onto the edge of the tub, chewing on her lip as he casually brushes his teeth.

"Are you asking me what I think you're asking?"

He spits some toothpaste into the sink and runs the tap, taking his time before turning to her with a determined look in his eyes.

"What I'm saying is that I've really liked waking up next to you for the past couple months. Kinda gotten used to it, if I'm being honest. And hey, you have your office there now, and a lot of your clothes... and Maverick is a *big* Phoebe Miller fan."

"Oh, she told you that, did she?"

A smile tugs at the corners of her mouth. She'd love to get out of this apartment, eventually. Her goal, if she ever got promoted, was to move into a really nice place that's close to work. Now, there's a half naked rock star in her bathroom suggesting that they live together in his huge fucking house.

"She did. Yelled it right in my face before she puked up a hairball. The hairball was unrelated to her raving about you, just so you know."

Phoebe stares into his eyes, her heartbeat picking up with every second. He's cracking jokes, but she's sure that he's serious. And he's right, Damien's house has felt more like a home than her own apartment this last week. It would be nice. It would be really fucking nice. He rinses her toothbrush off casually, dropping it back into her little ceramic mug and lowering himself to his knees right in front of her.

"I'm not asking for an answer right now, okay? But everything I said... it's all true. This is what I want. It's how I feel."

Then, without a moment's pause, he scoops her up and carries her back to the bedroom, putting her down only to let her crawl into bed as he shuts the lights off. He slides in beside her, wrapping her up in his embrace. Soft kisses litter her shoulder and the back of her neck as he hums against her skin. It takes her almost a whole minute to realize he's humming *Happy Birthday*.

Phoebe beams as she fades slowly into a deep peaceful sleep. Never in her wildest fantasies did she ever think her life would turn out like this.

Girls on Film

DAMIEN

The morning sun glaring through the window makes Damien groan, squinting and turning away as he laments forgetting his sunglasses. It killed him to walk out the door alone. It always does, even if it's just for a few hours. A year ago he'd have said it was disgusting, that *he's* been disgusting since he met her, falling all over her like a teenage boy. But fuck that guy, he wouldn't have known what was good for him if it hit him in the face.

He's scribbling in his notebook at the back of the train to the studio, letting his mind wander. He'd managed to ignore the giggling girls just off to his left for the first chunk of the ride, but it's a losing battle. They look like they're maybe around 16 or 17, both wearing matched private school uniforms— he recognizes the crest on their sweaters; they go to the same school he used to. They notice his eyes on them, quickly using one of their backpacks as a makeshift shield to avoid eye contact.

He'd probably be the same way if he saw someone he admired out in public. Actually, he's sure he would. Once, he saw Robert Plant at the Limelight and got so nervous he started downing shots of whiskey one after the other. By the time he had the confidence to walk up to the guy, he couldn't even string a full sentence together. Luckily, Shaun pulled him away before he could make a complete ass of himself; told him there'd always be a next time.

Damien winks at the girls, signing his name on two pages in his notebook, accompanied by a big heart. He rips the pages out and tucks the book back into his jacket, remaining as inconspicuous as possible, and waiting until just before his stop to make his move. Both girls stare at him like their brains are malfunctioning when they notice him walk over, and that's when the stammering starts.

"Ohmygod." All he hears is a rush of breath and garbled noises coming out of the first one. "I have all your albums— I mean your album—"

"We didn't mean to make you feel weird," the other girl butts in.

"You didn't." He hands them the autographs and waves as the doors open. "That was probably the most respectful fan interaction I've had all year. Remember ladies, keep classy and stay in school!"

The air is crisp and refreshing, and Damien finds himself in a much better mood than he expected, yet as he makes his way toward the studio, he can't shake the feeling that he's being watched. At first he thinks the girls may have followed him out, but a quick check over his shoulder kills that idea completely. Being followed isn't uncommon considering who he is, but it creeps him out nonetheless. More than likely it's just a photographer hiding somewhere, waiting to leap out, but maybe he's just paranoid.

That's also a possibility.

"Damien!"

An unfamiliar voice cuts through the air, setting him even more on-edge as he whirls around. It takes him a moment, but before long he places the owner, a man with shaggy hair and thick glasses jogging toward him. He looks young, but not too much so, maybe a few years younger than Phoebe. There's a notebook tucked underneath his arm and a camera hanging around his neck.

"Ken Russell, Us Weekly."

Of course.

Damien's body tenses, but he steadies himself. He's trying to be calmer, more cooperative; the more of them he has on his side, the better it'll be for the two of them when Chris drops the other shoe.

"Hey man," he sighs, slowing his stride to let him catch up. "How's it goin'?"

"Good! Well, great now. You recording today?"

"Yep, heading over now actually."

"New album, right? I went to that show last week, the last-minute one? Had no idea who was gonna hit the stage but I'm so glad it was Revolver. You guys were fucking great!"

Damien grins as Ken matches his stride, and the two head toward the studio. The dude doesn't seem so bad, turns out some of these folks might be worth talking to after all.

"Thanks, I appreciate it. It was kind of a make-or-break show for us, so I'm glad it went over so well."

"Hey, no problem. I've been a huge fan of you guys for a while. I even remember some of the shows back when you played those dive bars in the beginning. Shit, that was a good time," Ken laughs.

Damien smirks to himself.

"Yeah, those were some wild fuckin' nights."

Maybe not *every* single journalist was a complete shithead. Odds are some of them had to actually like music, after all. It's just hard to separate the good ones from the horde of assholes.

"Hey, so no girlfriend with you today? I've seen her around a bit recently, seems pretty cool."

He grits his teeth. He knew this was coming, but it's a fair question. He did mention Phoebe at the show, they've taken the steps to make things public, and it's not like they have to keep things secret anymore.

"Nah, not today. She's working."

There was a certain kind of safety in knowing they weren't asking questions about her. It was a protected part of his life, and hers. Now that's all off the table, he's taking it on himself to protect her as much as he can. Just like he promised he would.

"It's Phoebe, right? Phoebe Miller?"

"That's her." He can hear the warmth flood his voice. "She writes for Titanium."

"Yeah, I looked her up!" Ken laughs. "Did all my research, read a bunch of her stuff, too. You guys are lucky to have her, she turns out some great copy."

Damien snorts, wondering exactly what *lucky to have her* means to someone like Ken. But, the guy's right, he is lucky. If he hadn't met Phoebe, he'd have kept burning through a lineup of groupies and finished the tour just that little bit more hollowed out. Death by inches, they say, but instead he's got this whole new life to look forward to.

"She lives in Willamsburg, right? Near Bedford?"

Damien stops in his tracks, Ken taking a couple extra steps before realizing and turning around. Did this asshole follow him? He was probably standing outside of Phoebe's apartment waiting for them to come out. He's just like that fucker from the other night. He expected this, sure, but part of him was hoping it would be different this time around.

"Did you follow me from there?"

Ken shakes his head, quickly raising his hands.

"N– no." Nervous laughter bubbles up from his throat. "No, man. I just saw you from–"

Damien takes a step toward him and Ken backs up, his throat bobbing.

"Listen to me," He puts a hand on the man's shoulder, feeling the muscle twitch beneath his fingers. "It's Ken, right? I'm not gonna hit you Ken, that's not me anymore. I just... wanna say something."

"I swear, I wasn't–"

"You're young, and you seem pretty new at all this. Eager to please, want to get a big scoop right out of the gates, right?"

Damien gets closer, keeping him still with a firm grip, all while Ken remains completely silent. Phoebe doesn't need some kid hanging around her apartment taking pictures and following her to and from work, and *he* sure as shit doesn't need some curious reporter trying to find out which apartment she lives in.

"I get that this is your job, and I'm learning to respect that. To respect your profession. But I don't want you hanging around my girlfriend's apartment anymore. You want someone to take pictures of, you take pictures of me. You wanna follow me to work and have a conversation about music and the album? I'm cool with that, we can have a fun chat, on the record or off." Damien puts more pressure on his shoulder, just enough to be slightly uncomfortable. "But she didn't ask for this. She's one of you guys, not one of us, and I want you to treat her like it. I want her to feel safe. So just to make things completely clear, Ken: she's *off limits*, get me?"

"Y– yeah. Yeah, of– of course, Damien."

"Great!" He lets his expression slip back to pleasantly casual. "You can write all this down if you think it might help you guys remember the rules. In fact, you should probably tell your buddies at Us Weekly the same thing." He shoots Ken a warm smile, letting the tiniest bit of aggressive edge show as he releases his shoulder with a final sharp squeeze. "Great talk. I'm looking forward to chatting again soon, Ken."

He brushes past the man without another word, picking up the pace and striding toward the studio as he digs his cigarettes out of his pocket. His hand is shaking, and he almost drops the pack on the pavement, thinking better of it and deciding to wait until he hits the studio to light one up.

This is going to be the rest of their lives, and that's *if* they can stick out this shitstorm. The bigger the band gets, the more of them follow. Sure, there's more security and preparation that comes along with it, but they're going to have to find their freedom where they can.

Damien tries to steady himself, thinking of all the worst possible ways things could go down. Even now, with the Chris situation and the new interest from the tabloids, she's already taking more heat than he intended, and it's only going to get worse. What if it changes them? What if she leaves? It all seemed so simple just a month ago.

He pushes the door to the studio open, any positive feelings he left the apartment with totally evaporated. His anger at Ken has already faded into a murky sense of apathy that makes him feel sick more than anything else.

"Hey, Damien!" Erin chirps from the front desk, giving him a quick little wave.

He grunts and tries to walk past her, not wanting to get into a conversation with anyone until he's had a chance to decompress. Erin, unfortunately, clearly has other plans, and she steps out to block his path.

"Move," he snarls, much more aggressively than he intended.

She's decked out in a Black Sabbath t-shirt, jeans, and combat boots that look like they could destroy his shins if he pisses her off. More important than any of that, she doesn't move an inch.

"Erin, I'm serious."

"No dice, big guy." She pops her gum and Damien grits his teeth. "Not until you tell me what's going on."

"Nothing's going on, I'm fine."

"You're grumpy." She tilts her head with a frown. "You don't have that usual sparkle in those baby blues."

He sighs. There's no way he can endure this right now, not without saying some things he'll likely regret later. He has to focus, to get back in the right headspace before he hits the mic. Even after the positive reaction from Allan, they're still under pressure to get the album into a workable state, let alone finished on time. No one needs Damien's personal life screwing all of that up.

"Erin, I just wanna get into the studio, you know how much we still have to get done."

"Of course I do, and that's why you're going to tell me what happened, so I can help. I can't imagine it's a problem with you and Pheebs, right?"

He shakes his head, leaning to the side to get a glimpse at the studio down the hall. He's never been this eager to start work before, but anything's better than impromptu therapy. He can save it all for the mic.

"We're fine. She's at home working, it's all going great."

She snickers, shaking her head.

"You're such a shitty liar. *Something* happened, otherwise you'd be walking up to me with that smug-ass Damien Bell smirk. You look like a sourpuss right now."

"Erin, I'm not–"

"You are!"

She grabs him by the sleeve of his jacket, pulling him toward an empty studio a couple feet away.

"Johnny's gonna get suspicious," he mumbles.

"Oh, please," she scoffs, folding her arms. "Don't flatter yourself, Bell. The only thing Johnny'd be worried about if we disappeared together is me kicking your ass."

Inside the room, with the door closed and locked, her expression grows soft again.

"Now please, tell me what's up."

Damien lets out a breath, sinking down onto the couch in the corner, his shoulders slumping in resignation as he realizes that there's no way out of this without spilling his guts. He loves Erin, but she's so much more open than the rest of them, always wanting them to talk about their feelings, always wanting to help solve any and every issue. It's exhausting.

"Great, you've figured it out faster than usual, so spill."

He sighs and runs a hand through his hair. This kind of shit shouldn't even faze him anymore.

"Some guy from Us Weekly followed me after I left Phoebe's apartment, at least I'm pretty sure he did. Totally fucking invasive. They know where she lives, they could be there right now."

Erin scoffs, her face immediately a mix of empathy and disgust. She knows exactly what Phoebe's going through, and how bad it could get.

"The other night, Johnny and I were out for dinner and some fucking pap just came up to our table, tried to pull up a chair like we were old friends. We've been dealing with it on overdrive since Denver. One of them was outside of our apartment when Johnny came back from the tour, knew exactly when to be there, just waiting to get a shot of the two of us."

She glowers, grinding her teeth as she paces around the room.

"You know, when Johnny and I decided to do this, to really do this, I was nervous but figured it would be mostly fine. Nobody would really give a shit who I was, right? Why would they? Now all of a sudden, it's like I have to look over my shoulder any time I'm going out, just to see if someone's trying to take a picture."

Damien shrugs, not quite sure what to say.

"If it helps, I haven't seen you guys in any magazines yet."

She grins.

"Yeah, but you don't look inside of them, do you? My mom found one the other day at the grocery store, with a whole page analyzing our body language. It was bizarre. They even picked apart my outfit. I was just wearing jeans and a t-shirt, the most normal thing you could think of, but apparently that means I'm 'sloppy and don't care about how my fiancé perceives me.' What a crock of shit."

Damien rolls his eyes.

"Those hacks get paid to pump out trash, pennies to a word. They'll make anything up to fill a page."

"Well, *duh*," Erin snorts.

Damien fishes his cigarettes out of his pocket and offers one up.

"That's what I'm saying, Damien, this shit's all ridiculous. It's the stupidest crap you're gonna see in print, and there's a never ending flow of it. I'm not saying you shouldn't care, of course you should care! It fucking sucks! But it doesn't mean anything, nothing real. It doesn't reflect on you, or Phoebe, or any of us."

Damien sits there in silence for a moment, considering Erin's words. She's right, of course, but he's still not sure if it's made any of this feel better. Maybe it wasn't supposed to. Sometimes you just have to think about what really matters, and let all the rest of it fall away.

"I think you look cool," Damien offers. "Jeans and a t-shirt is rock 'n' roll as fuck."

Erin chuckles with a shrug. There's a faraway look in her eyes as she stares straight ahead, blowing a big smoke ring. She's got a lot on her shoulders. Her job at the studio, dealing with Johnny being on the road all the time, and now the press on top of it.

"You know, there's a huge double standard when it comes to how you guys are covered versus how people like me or Phoebe are covered in the press," Erin murmurs. Her slight Irish accent always gets a little more pronounced when she's angry. "You lot are Revolver! You're the next big thing on a good day, or a monumental trainwreck on a bad day. Me though? I'm Johnny Reed's girlfriend. What's my job, what are my hobbies, where am I from? Fuck, they don't even ask my favourite band, they just assume it's you guys. It's like I'm a fucking accessory."

Damien nods. He's not stupid, he's seen it. It even used to happen with Ophelia in the early days. Journalists spent more time asking her about fashion and makeup than they did about the music.

"Anyway, I'm sure you know this shit. People say that being followed or hassled in public comes with the territory when you're famous, but it shouldn't have to be like that. We've created a whole damn industry of putting people up on pedestals and tracking their every move. It's socially acceptable voyeurism."

"It's stalking," Damien snorts.

She nods.

"Pheebs should go unlisted in the phone book," Erin tells him, taking another drag. "That'll help a little. We had it all set up before my name dropped, and now we only get the most obsessive people that make the connection."

Damien clears his throat. He'd actually been thinking a lot about the living situation. It hadn't really left his head all week. All month, if he was being honest with himself.

"I was thinking about moving her into my place. My number's already unlisted, I'm not even in the phone book." He takes a long drag. "I'll feel better with her close by."

Erin raises a brow.

"That's a *big* step, buddy. Usually people do shit like meet each other's parents first, date for more than a couple of months..."

Damien groans, rocking back in his seat.

"Okay, *mom*. What would you suggest?"

Sometimes, it feels like she and Johnny are the only ones who really have their shit together in terms of what the rest of their lives are going to look like. Damien always avoided thinking about the future before he met Phoebe. He always sort of assumed he'd burn out long before it'd matter, but now... it doesn't scare him, it excites him.

"Have you talked to her about this?"

"Sort of, yeah. I told her we don't have to think about it right now, but—"

She pokes him in the ribs, a big goofy smile on her face.

"*But* I know you, Damien Bell. You won't leave this alone. No chance in hell."

He finishes his cigarette, crushing it in a nearby ashtray and watching the embers smolder and die amongst the ash.

"Well, I would feel better if I knew people weren't trying to break into her apartment. You should see the place! The cupboard doors are falling off the fuckin' hinges, man, so who knows how good the locks are, if they work at all."

What if one of those tabloid guys got into her building? Or worse, an unhinged fan? She'd be safer at his place.

"Look, if you've talked to her about it, give her time. She's got a lot of shit on her plate right now, *and* she's got that looming deadline."

"I know, you're right, but—"

"And *you've* got an album to record so that *I* can have a free vacation in Paris." She bumps Damien playfully with her shoulder. "Don't you ever think about me and my needs, Bell? So selfish."

Damien nods, rubbing his stubble as he feigns a serious expression.

"You're right, you're an equal part of this relationship, and I should know better."

He wraps an arm around her shoulder as they sit in silence for a while. She's right, he's got to focus. He can finish the album, Phoebe can finish the article, and then they can worry about everything else.

"What would I do without you and your sage advice, Campbell?"

"Get arrested, probably." She pats his leg. "You know things are gonna get better when this is all over and done with, yeah?"

"Yeah," he murmurs, truly believing it for the first time in a while. "I do."

Dear Prudence

DAMIEN

DAY TWO, TUESDAY

"Fuuuuuuck!"

Phoebe's bellows have been echoing through the halls for the past hour or so, as Damien's been working in the kitchen.

His initial plan for the evening was to make them a nice relaxing meal, and then to take her to bed, but when he came home the energy in her office was nothing short of chaotic. Damien wipes his hands on a dish towel and pokes his head out of the kitchen.

"You need anything, babydoll?"

"A new brain!" She shouts. "You got one in the fridge?"

"Sorry, fresh out. Used it up at the studio," he teases.

Her laughter is a little hollow, but he'll take it. He's never seen her on a deadline before, and it's a lot scarier than he imagined.

He grabs a glass out of the cupboard and pours her a generous amount of wine, carrying it to her office where he finds her hunched over her typewriter. She looks absolutely defeated, her head in her hands, and balled up pieces of paper scattered all over her desk and the floor. He noticed a couple of paper balls in the hallway when he first came in; she must have been playing with Maverick when he came home. Now she's probably trying to make up for lost time.

Damien puts the glass down on her desk and wraps his arms around her.

"Maybe you should take a break. Dinner's almost ready."

"I don't have time to take a break," she sighs, frustration lacing her words. "I've barely written a damn thing all day."

"I think these tell a different story," he mutters, gesturing down at the crumpled pieces of paper all around her. "You must have written at least... 20 pages? Jesus, was this all today?"

"Yeah, and that'd be great if they weren't all terrible. I can't even settle on a goddamn title," she groans, throwing herself back in her chair and looking up at him. "This fucking sucks."

His heart aches for her. It's the first time they've hit any sort of speed bump he couldn't at least help with a little bit. And maybe there is something he could do, who knows, but he doesn't know what it could possibly be.

"Come on, Pheebs, take a break, then you can come back in with a fresh perspective."

"Is that an order?"

Her face is stoney, and he can't tell if the question is playful or serious.

"Let's call it... a suggestion," he replies. "I made chicken and those little roasted potatoes you love, I promise you'll feel at least a little bit better."

"Wait." She snatches up a little stack of papers sitting next to her type-writer. "Can you read these? It doesn't have to be right this second, but I... I need to know what you think. The other drafts weren't good, and... well you've seen what happened to them. I don't know how I feel about this batch yet."

The uncertainty in her eyes makes him want to swoop in and rescue her, but she's the only person who can write this story. And what would he even be saving her from?

"Hand it over, gorgeous."

She places the papers in his hands and he leans up against her desk, scan-ning through them. The article starts out in LA, with her walking into the hotel room and meeting the band for the very first time. He smiles as memories of the day all come rushing back. The way her hand felt when he shook it, the way she looked at him, a little timid and unsure, and the way he couldn't stop thinking about her even after he'd wandered back down to the bar. She clearly had felt the same, considering the follow-up conversation.

But none of that's in there. There's a few mentions of the spark between them, but not much else. Her narrative is strong, even a little poetic, but there's so much missing. He glances over at her to see her fiddling with a stray thread on her pajama pants.

"I like it," he announces.

"*Like?*"

"Well, I could love it."

He's kind of afraid to offer his honest opinion, even though he knows it's what she needs. It's such a stupid thing to be worried about, especially with how obvious he's being.

"Damien, I want actual feedback, not coddling bullshit."

"Okay, okay." He clears his throat. "The writing is good, I don't know what you're talking about when you say this is terrible."

"But there's something missing, right?" She raps her knuckles on her desk, a mildly irritated gesture.

Of course she sees it too.

"I don't know, I think the spark between you and I is sort of absent in the article, it seems so honest about everything else."

She frowns, glaring at him as her mouth twitches in irritation, but it's only a moment before it all melts away into a playful smirk.

"Yeah, don't worry, that's what I thought too."

He exhales as silently as he can, letting out the breath he had been holding. Thank god she was just fucking with him.

"I just don't know how much of *us* to put in here. I want some things to be private, but even more than that, I want to make sure I'm not turning it into a story about my boyfriend, right?"

Damien pushes himself off of the desk, playing up his thinking-face as he paces around the room.

"Well, in this case, you might have to go bigger. You don't have to talk about all of it, but I think the best way to get into your audience's hearts would be a little more... detail. What about telling them how nervous you were to meet me, how cool I was, stuff like that. They should be picturing you with those cartoon heart-eyes by the end of it all, that'd be a big success I'd say."

She bumps him with her shoulder, that playful grin still on her face. He's been wondering where this Phoebe went. For the past 24 hours, she'd been more a ball of stress than a person.

"That stuff comes later when we *actually* hook up."

"Make sure to write me with a giant dick," he teases. "I want explicit details, measurements, everything."

He was worried that making fun of the situation may have backfired, but it seems like it worked out. At the very least he's got her laughing now. That's one step on the way out of her slump.

"Oh, it'll be the biggest ever described in print, but don't forget I have to save some juicy details for my tell-all book. I have to fleece you somehow, after all."

"That's what I like to hear, Miller, you got those long-term financial plans. Glad I found the right person to carry me through life."

He picks up her wine glass and motions to the door.

"Come on. You need to eat and I wanna hang out with my girlfriend; at least one hour per night, those are the rules set by the good lord, or so the scriptures say."

Back in the kitchen Damien pulls a chair out for her, pouring her a glass of wine before returning to plate the food.

"So how was the studio?" Phoebe asks as he scoops roasted potatoes and fresh vegetables onto their plates.

"Pretty good today," he replies. "Shaun and I re-worked some tunes. We're making real progress, but we still need to hit that big breakthrough."

"Gee, I wonder what that's like," she mutters into her glass as Damien passes a plate to her with a sympathetic look.

"Sorry."

Phoebe shakes her head and chuckles.

"Don't be, I was just being a jerk," she sighs as she cuts into her chicken and takes a bite. "It's just a little catharsis, I'm glad things at the studio are going well."

He sort of feels bad, but he's just as surprised as anyone by how easy it all got after that initial hurdle with Liam's notes. The last couple days they've walked into the studio, creativity just flowed between the four of them like it was the most natural thing in the world. Meanwhile, Phoebe's back here struggling to put words on paper.

He reaches over and grasps her hand. She looks worn out already, only two days into the process.

"You'll get there, Pheebs, even if it doesn't feel like it right now, I know you will."

"Maybe some of your creative genius will rub off on me," she lets out another long sigh. "I'm going to have to start a new draft tonight, so that'll be fun."

He frowns.

"You've been writing all day, shouldn't you take a break? Reset, try again tomorrow."

"Yeah, well you saw the results of my labor," she laughs. "A bunch of new cat toys for Maverick, and one less day of buffer-time left."

Damien wouldn't describe Phoebe as carefree, but this is a totally different side to her that he's going to have to get to know. She definitely struggles when she hits that wall, a familiar feeling that he's used to in his own work.

He reaches over and grasps her hand.

"If you let yourself obsess over this you're just gonna spiral. You'll never get to a place where you can be happy with what you're writing. Nothing'll be good enough."

She puts her fork down, pulling her hand back softly and rubbing her eyes.

"I don't want to be happy with it, I just want it to be *right*."

She really is exhausted.

He knows how important this is to her, and how hard she works for the things that really matter. She's always scribbling in her notebook, taking photos, gathering information, and looking for new angles to attack a story from. There's no doubt she has more dirt on all of them than any other journalist could possibly get, enough that she could knock this thing out of the park if she wanted to swerve that way. He trusts her with all of it. They all do. But that's where the difficulty comes in: she's imposed the penalty of ethics on herself.

"It'll turn out good," he assures her. "It'll turn out right. *But,* for that to happen, you need to give yourself a little bit of grace, Pheebs."

She squeezes his hand.

"Thanks for the pep talk, fearless leader."

"Hey, I provide it all: inspirational speeches, erotic distractions, and to top it off, I'm your own personal chef."

Phoebe raises her glass to him.

"Great, because I think I'll be needing all of the above."

DAY FOUR, THURSDAY

Damien sits at the piano downstairs, his fingers gliding over the keys as he works through the notes that Liam gave him the previous night. He gave them the day off to regroup and rest, and Damien's been chained to the instrument ever since, tweaking lyrics and scribbling down notes while Phoebe does her own work one floor above.

The last time he checked in on her she had her fancy red pen in a vice grip, making notes on her most recent draft as Maverick lay passed out next to her typewriter. She had that crease between her brow, the one that let him know not to bother her under any circumstances.

Down at the piano he hums a couple bars in accompaniment, smiling as he stops playing to make some extra notes next to the lyrics.

Violins come in here?

Liam said he wanted more richness in the song, and they'd decided on some strings. It was just a matter of how many, where, and how strong they came in.

Test between these bars, possible extension.

"Damien?"

He turns in time to catch Phoebe pushing the door open just a crack, a mischievous look in her eyes. He's pretty sure he knows the look, the same one she gave him back in the recording studio when they made their little tape.

She saunters toward him in nothing but a pair of silk pajama-shorts and a tank top. Damien inhales deeply, closing his notebook as her hand glides along his back. A shiver shoots through him as she leans over to kiss him on the cheek. There's no way she didn't notice his reaction.

"You mentioned offering sexy distractions the other day," she purrs. "I think I could use one."

It's only been a couple of days since they've had the chance to fuck, but in such close proximity it's felt like an eternity.

"I did mention that was part of my service package," he chuckles. "You need a break, babydoll?"

Her hair is all over the place, and that plus the little bit of smeared mascara underneath her eyes gives her a very messy, sexy kind of look. She flashes him a faux pout as her hand slides into his sweatpants and she strokes him, gentle and slow, until he's hard as a rock.

"I need to clear my head," she breathes. "And you can help with that."

"Mmhmm," he purrs. "Climb up on the piano."

She stops, pulling her hand back in mild surprise.

"You have a bedroom, Damien."

"Nah, see I've done the math in my head. We won't make it to the bedroom, so this'll have to do."

"Damien—"

He tilts his head ever so slightly.

"Strip."

She smiles, shaking her head to herself as she shimmies out her shorts.

Damien licks his lips, eager to give her the distraction she so desperately deserves. He gets to his feet, grabbing her by the waist, lifting her up, and placing her on the top of the piano. Her legs brush against some of the keys as she gets comfortable, making some little cacophonous sounds, but he couldn't give less of a shit.

"I've always wanted to do this."

He sits back down at the piano bench and lifts both of her legs, positioning them so they're resting slung over his shoulders.

"This exactly? Seems extremely... specific."

"Call it a bucket list item," he shudders, savoring the warmth of her skin against his palms. "Now, let me take care of you. Like I promised."

With one hand, he begins to play the melody of the song he was just rehearsing, slowly placing gentle kisses up her thighs, not wanting to miss an inch of her soft, milky skin.

Phoebe gasps, her hand already grasping at his hair as he works his way up until– Just like that, he's nestled right where he wants to be. He exhales, letting his warm breath tease her pussy, and he laughs when she lets out a whimper, tugging a little harder on his hair.

"Patience," he whispers.

Her reply is a frustrated growl.

"You always make this so difficult."

"I do," he murmurs whimsically, dragging his nose between her folds and stopping just short of licking her clit. He wishes he could bottle the sounds she makes when he toys with her like this. "I'll make it up to you, though."

He knows she's aching for him, he can feel it, but Damien takes his time toying with her anyway. He bites down on her inner thigh, on the very edge between gentle and violent, pressing down until she keens. He sucks hard enough to leave a bruise, relishing the way her body writhes against his touch.

He continues like this until he's pretty certain she's used to it, then slides his tongue along her clit, keeping the pressure just light enough to drive her into a frenzy as he goes to town. Phoebe's thighs are up around his ears, shaking but still squeezing hard. He laps at her swollen bud, feeling it quiver. She's desperate, and he loves it, but he forces himself to remember that this is about her, not him.

Damien groans, stroking himself faster as he wraps his lips around her clit. Fuck, he loves this. Listening to the purely animal sounds that she makes is better than any song he's ever heard. He devours her like she's his last meal, the whole thing making his cock ache and his hips buck, needing more.

Needing more of her.

His fingers stumble over the keys, sloppily, like they're working separately from his body. It sounds like shit, but that's what makes it the perfect chaotic accompaniment to Phoebe's moans and grunts.

"Fuck." Her voice shakes. "God, Damien!"

Damien's own strokes match the speed of his tongue as it pushes and swirls around her clit. His muscles begin to burn as his lust starts to consume him; he can't keep playing anymore.

The hand that was devoted to the piano keys shoots between her legs, almost without a conscious thought on his part, and he pushes two fingers inside her, crooking them a little until he's stroking her G-spot. He works it until all he can hear are strings of incoherent words and grunts. His skin tingles, goosebumps rising on his arms, his back, his neck; he can tell that he's right on the edge, close enough that he could topple over at any time.

But that's not the job.

He needs to push *her* over first.

Damien can't get enough of this, the sight of her completely at his mercy driving him even further, faster than he expected. Hell, he might be able to convince her to take the rest of the day off so he can carry her up to the bedroom and *really* distract her. He could tie her up and make her forget about the whole damn article.

Damien pulls back, letting his fingers do the work as Phoebe groans at the absence of his mouth.

"Please." Her voice breaks. "Please make me come! I'll be so, so good!"

Even after just a couple days without it, he's missed hearing those words. He's missed hearing that desperate tone in her voice. He's missed all of this.

Damien dives back in, feverish as he flicks his tongue against her clit. Her pussy squeezes his fingers as her thighs lock his head in place. Damien shudders, clenching his muscles in an attempt to hold back his climax, but he's losing control. He can tell it won't work for long. Her cries get louder and louder, his own groans vibrating against her as he wraps his lips back around her clit and sucks as hard as he can.

"Damien! Oh fuck, *oh fuck!*"

That's the sound he needs to hear.

He works his cock in quick strokes as he presses his fingers firmly against her G-spot, and Phoebe rewards him by screaming his name as she topples over the edge. The moment he knows she's finished, he finally lets his own climax take over, shooting all over his hand and a bit onto the piano. He can feel his eyes slip shut as little aftershocks shoot through him, and she slips a little ways off the piano, leaning forward against him as her muscles finally relax. It's only a moment before he starts lapping at her again, lightly and without much conscious thought, until she pushes his head away with a groan.

"I can't come anymore Damien," she laughs. "Fuck."

He opens his eyes, getting his bearings again as he watches her lift herself back up to a sitting position on the piano. Her eyelids flutter and her chest heaves as everything starts to catch up with her.

"So," he chuckles, feeling a little giddy in the afterglow. "How was that for clearing your head?"

She exhales, lips curling into a blissful smile.

"I'll be sure to leave a glowing review."

I'm Still Standing

PHOEBE
DAY ONE, MONDAY MORNING

"Here you are, my love," Damien murmurs, setting a giant mug of coffee and a plate down on her desk. "Breakfast is served."

It's 8:00 am. Damien's been up since 6:00, tidying her office, making coffee, and cooking breakfast.

"Perfectly poached eggs– if I do say so myself– on top of sourdough toast, extra crispy bacon–"

"You remembered my favorite!"

"Of course! And a fruit smiley face." He grins at her. "Not bad for a rock star, huh?"

Phoebe looks down to see the plate elegantly arranged. There's even a tiny jar of jam tucked next to her toast. It's so sweet, and the fruit smiley face looks so pretty she almost doesn't want to eat it. Damien massages her shoulders and she smiles, enjoying being taken care of like this. Usually, she grabs a donut for breakfast and then forgets to drink water for the rest of the day.

"Thank you. I'm gonna need all the fuel I can get."

Her plan is to have a rough draft finished by Thursday, so that she can spend the rest of the week making small tweaks and changes, all the polish that needs to go into something like this. By the following Monday, it'll be faxed to Brian and out of her hands.

The beautiful view of Damien's backyard is a nice change of pace from her usual scenery, a fire-escape and some brick across from her own cramped apartment, and she gets to hang out with Maverick all day as an extra bonus. It's pretty close to the ideal environment to finish her work. That is, it would be if she could get her ass in gear.

It's been a Herculean task so far.

"There's lunch in the fridge, too. It's my ma's macaroni and cheese recipe."

Damien's voice centers her back in the moment.

"Damien, please. You're doing way too much, I can make my own food."

"No chance. I said I'd take care of you, and I meant it."

He ruffles her messy hair, grabbing his jacket off of the couch and shrugging it on.

"Make some magic, babydoll. If you need anything, call the studio, alright?"

She smiles as he pops a cigarette between his lips. There's still something so surreal about Damien Bell cooking her breakfast. This is *not* the same man she met in LA.

"You're too good to me."

Damien winks at her.

"But it's still not as good as you deserve. I'll be back around 5:00 with dinner, so don't bother yourself with that."

He blows her a kiss, and with that he's out the door.

Phoebe has a week to get this done. She's finished four drafts already, but none of them have felt right. The details are too intimate in some, and portray the band as caricature in others. Every time she feels like she's getting close, a quick read back through the pages reveals a big problem, old or brand new, and she's back to square one.

In the planning phase, shifting notes around and working out the bones of the piece, everything feels so much simpler. No matter how long she's been doing this, she still has the magical idea that all her words will translate easily from the bones to the body, perfect from the moment it starts to take shape. It's never been true, but somehow the thought still poisons her progress.

Phoebe shuffles the pages of her latest draft. Reading them out-of-order is an old trick she learned back in school. It allows you to engage with the work outside of the pre-existing constraints you've formed in your head, disconnecting from the structure and pace you've come to expect, and letting mistakes jump out right away.

And, of course, they do.

Clunky sentences that don't flow properly into each other, typos, and the scattered nature of her ideas plague her as she moves from page to page. It reads like she's trying to force puzzle pieces together that don't fit.

"What the fuck was I thinking?"

With a defeated sigh, she tosses the pages aside, letting them flutter to the floor as she feeds another blank page into her typewriter.

Maverick pads over, briefly intrigued by the crinkling mess of paper on the ground. All it takes is a couple swats of her paw before she gets bored of the new toys, though, and she hops up onto the desk. Phoebe leans back in her chair, giving the cat's chin a loving scratch as she stares at the blank page. Even just the beginning of it all, every thought she had, every feeling, the way he made her heart race... how can she contain that in the limited space she has?

She was so sure of everything when she pitched the new angle to Brian, and now she wishes she could go back in time and give herself a good smack. There's just too much to work with, too many key aspects and heartfelt anecdotes, and she doesn't know what to omit. It all feels important, and that's because it *is*. It was the most important month of her life.

"You got yourself into this," she mutters. "Now, you've gotta write your way out."

Phoebe cracks her knuckles, Maverick jumping down off the desk as she lets her hands hover over the keys in yet another moment of doubt. But then the clack of her keys fills the room, and word after word makes its way onto the page, slowly filling her with a little more determination.

She's going to get this finished.

There's really no other option.

She has to do this.

DAY THREE, WEDNESDAY AFTERNOON

"Phoebe, you've gotta give me something."

She scritches behind Maverick's ears, watching her stretch out as long as possible on Phoebe's lap. It's been like a ritual the last few days, the thing she does to get her mind off the impending doom that's looming over her. It hasn't really worked, but the cat's so cute she doesn't really care.

The whole day has been a wash: writing, reading, re-writing, and ending up just hating every word that's sitting in front of her.

"Brian, I have four pages, and you know what? You can have them, I'd sooner throw them at someone then be forced to read them over again."

"That's not what I wanted to hear this afternoon," he chuckles. *"What's going on?"*

Maybe she bit off more than she could chew, even with this ideal writing situation, she's still struggling.

"I need a deadline extension," she replies.

Maverick hops up on the desk, her tail flicking back and forth as she glances at a toy mouse sitting off to the side and headbutts Phoebe's hand insistently.

Come to think of it, she did make some impressive progress yesterday. Around midday, when she crumpled up a particularly terrible page and tossed it behind her, she made an amazing discovery: Maverick liked to play fetch. It was the perfect distraction, and took up more of the day than she'd like to admit. Damien came home to balls of paper littered around the office and a tuckered out kitten.

"Look, can't give you an extension," Brian laughs. *"You've had months to get this together, and it's already slated. We don't have anything good enough to replace it!"*

"I know, I know, I just need–"

"Phoebe, you came into my office guns blazing, with a brand new outline and some good ideas. You've got a great piece somewhere in all those notes, all you have to do is buckle down and write it."

She rolls her eyes hard enough that she's half-worried that he may have somehow noticed through the phone. It's so much easier said than done, and this is the biggest thing she's ever written in terms of both volume and scale. Every time she starts to make progress she gets sidetracked again and again by little moments and stories that she's desperate to weave in, but she has to pick and choose. The whole magazine can't be about her and this tour; Revolver's big, but they're not *that* big.

"I get it. This is just the first time I've really had final-say on anything. I've never been left to my own devices before, and now I have so many notes and interviews and pictures..."

The last time she had writer's block like this, it was because she couldn't tell the truth. Now there's too much of it to tell.

"You don't have to use it all," he assures her, that fatherly gentleness clear in his voice. *"Take today to figure out what's really important and what contributes to the story. That's all you do today, alright? No working on anything else. Then, tomorrow, sit your ass down and write me that draft."*

"Okay," she groans. "Alright, I'll do it."

"I've gotta be firm with you, kiddo. You're in the big leagues now, and that means tight deadlines. I want to get it to the editors next week so that they can fact check everything." He pauses for a moment. *"Just remember, you can't edit a blank page."*

Maverick paws at her to toss the mouse and Phoebe pitches it down the hall, smiling as the cat skitters after it. She slides on the hardwood and misses entirely, bumping into a wall. Phoebe has to hold back her laughter. The last thing she needs is him thinking she's not taking this thing seriously.

"Thanks, Brian."

"No problem, Phoebe. You've got this."

She hangs up the phone, plopping herself down on the floor and just laying there, staring at the ceiling.

"All you have to do is get it done, Phoebe. That's it. It doesn't have to be perfect."

But it does have to be perfect, because she's so close to her subject matter that she can't...

"Ugh!"

Phoebe presses the heels of her hands over her eyes, rubbing them until she sees spots. Something drops onto her chest and she feels Maverick pawing at her arm again. With a sigh, she grabs the kitten and holds her up in the air.

"Sorry Mav, no more fetch for a little while. You 'n me have been slacking off too much, it's time to buckle down and get serious."

Phoebe gets up, Maverick tucked passively under her arm, and heads into the kitchen for another pot of coffee. As the coffee maker whirs up she sits, staring out the window in vain hope that inspiration will suddenly hit. She'd love to just take some time to appreciate the gold and red leaves sprinkled around the backyard, or the little squirrels rushing up the trees, but as the smell of rich coffee hits her nostrils, and Phoebe watches the pot slowly start to fill up, Brian's words echo in her head:

"Just remember, you can't edit a blank page."

She's going to get this finished.

There's really no other option.

She has to do this.

DAY FIVE, FRIDAY NIGHT

"I thought you said you were going to let me work tonight!" Phoebe laughs as Damien pulls her into the bathroom. "You already made great use of my time yesterday."

"Hey, you asked for it," he reminds her. "And from the way you were moaning, I think we can safely say you enjoyed it."

"I did," she chuckles, her cheeks pink as she thinks back on how good his stubble felt between her thighs. He was the perfect distraction, clearing her head and readying her for a full mental reset, but once she sat back down at her desk it was like every new thought evaporated.

So today, it seems like he's trying a different technique.

The scent of rich vanilla wafts up to her from the bubble bath as the water rushes into the tub. He's strategically placed candles throughout the room, and has champagne set out for the two of them, cooling in a bucket of ice. He did say he would make sure she was taken care of while she worked this week, and let no one say Damien Bell is a liar. Tragically, despite it all, she's still feeling that nagging sensation digging into the back of her neck. She hasn't worked hard enough today. She hasn't made enough progress.

"Hey there, space case." He slides himself in front of her, forcing her out of her self-conscious spiral. "You worked all day today, and then all through dinner. You need to take breaks, can't have you burning out!"

He's right, of course, and she knows it, but the problem is most of this week basically ended up being a "break." The only difference is she didn't get any rest or peace of mind out of it. Damien's house is ripe with distractions, and lately it feels like focusing is near-impossible. She even dragged her typewriter downstairs into his studio for a bit when he was away, in the hope that she could get some inspiration from the surroundings.

It didn't work. She just wound up digging through old Revolver demos, finding even more material to struggle with cramming into the article.

On the flipside, things with Damien are on an upward swing. Everything he's told her about their session makes it sound like the album is going smoothly. She can't help but be a little jealous as he tells her about each problem they're ironing out, one by one. She was sort of hoping they'd be struggling together. Having someone to commiserate with would make things easier.

"Come here," he purrs, pulling her into his arms as the rushing water fills the room up with soothing steam. He tugs gently on the hem of the giant NYU sweater she's been wearing the past two days. "This needs to come off."

Phoebe lets him undress her.

He kisses the tip of her nose, her cheeks, her lips, the light caress of his hands and the careful pressure of his lips on her skin bringing out a smile. Maybe she really does need a break, even if she doesn't feel like she deserves it. She's got three and a half pages written, and they're not *total* shit.

Damien looks her up and down, a warm smile sitting still on his face for a moment before he sheds his own clothes. He helps her climb into the massive clawfoot tub, sitting behind her as she sinks into the hot water. She sighs, her muscles immediately loosening as her whole body greedily absorbs the heat. Damien wastes no time, reaching off to the side and pouring her a glass of champagne.

"For you, my love."

"Thanks, I think I might need it."

She takes a sip, closing her eyes as the contrast of the two competing temperatures wakes her whole body up. Damien takes the initiative, beginning to massage her as she relaxes, and immediately she can feel her blood start to rush.

"Holy shit, that feels *amazing*."

"You're tense as hell, Pheebs," he chuckles. "It's like mixing cement."

"That's what I get for hunkering over a typewriter all day," she mutters.

He continues the massage in silence for a couple minutes, with Phoebe taking advantage of every second of peace she can squeeze out of this lovely situation. She knows what he's going to ask, but that doesn't make it any less agonizing to answer.

"So," he starts smoothly, trying as hard as he can to sound natural and unassuming. "How's the work going?"

"Terrible," she laughs, taking a quick sip of champagne. The bubbles burn her throat just a bit, and she winces as he presses against a tender spot underneath her shoulder blade.

"Terrible? The stuff I read last night was great! You've gotta be less hard on yourself."

"I still hate the introduction, it feels so cold and removed... It reads like an itinerary with some quotes thrown in. Like I'm just writing to get something done. Like I have no connection to the material."

She groans. It feels like she's been going over the same shit day after day, flip-flopping from one problem to the other.

"I don't know, maybe I'm overthinking things, or maybe I really am too close to you guys and it's fucking everything up. One day there's too much to say, and the next I'm overcompensating and it all feels like a boring checklist."

"Well, you can't get away from me now. I know where you live, Miller."

She snickers, glancing back at him to find his eyes dancing around the room. She can see the wheels turning in his head.

"What are you thinking?"

"I was just wondering... if you go back to the reason why you wanted this assignment in the first place, before we met, before everything, do you think that might help you connect with what you're writing?"

She frowns.

"What do you mean?"

"I mean... what did you expect way back at the start, right when you first got on that plane?"

"That you'd all hate me," she laughs. "That it'd be like pulling teeth, and that I'd never get a story out of you."

"So, go with that," Damien chuckles. "That's your introduction right there, and then you can spend a whole page talking about how the incredibly sexy, mysterious lead singer completely subverted your expectations."

She snorts, careful not to choke on her champagne.

"It sounds like you just want more time in my story."

"Maaaaybe," he sings. "Just think about it, though. Not that shit about me, but going back to the start. Maybe that'll break you out of this funk."

She watches the bubbles float along the top of the water. It's not a bad idea at all. She could really dig into Damien's tough guy act, and how it all falls away when he's around his friends and the people he loves. She could feature each bandmate and how different they are from public expectations; from her own expectations.

Her first instinct is to jump out of the bath and run back downstairs to her notebook, but that's exactly what hasn't been working. Instead, she lets the new ideas grow in the back of her mind, rolling around as she soaks in the ambience. The article doesn't have to be complicated. She can boil it down to the big emotions, the things that will really make an impact. She can give them a look at the man behind the rockstar persona, about their relationship, and about the family he's made. That could be it.

This could be it.

"You okay, babydoll?" He asks, his hand brushing softly through her hair.

"Yeah, I am."

She sighs. She'd contend with the story tomorrow, armed with this new direction, but for now she's content to just exist; safe and sound, all wrapped up in this moment.

"How about you tell me more about the shiny new album."

Private Eyes

PHOEBE

THREE WEEKS LATER

There's something intangible in the air as Phoebe steps out of the house, notably for the first time all week, tasting the cool and crisp November wind on her skin. She buttons up her long black coat, already regretting her choice of mini-skirt and crop top as her bare legs prickle with goosebumps. What's that thing people say about suffering for style? Whatever the expression is, she feels like she must be living it.

Yesterday, her article hit the newsstands, but she didn't seek it out right away. Instead, she spent the day curled up on Damien's couch, hiding from the world while they watched shitty daytime TV under the blankets. No talk of the band or the story, just Damien and Phoebe.

It was exactly what she needed, but that was yesterday.

Now it's time to face the music.

When she called into the office Brian said he had news for her, but he refused to elaborate. Said he had to talk to her in person. Why do bosses always do that? They can't just tell you the news, they have to have a whole meeting about it. And of course, that meeting is always some time in the afternoon, you know, whenever they've got the time. Giving *you* all the time in the world to stress the fuck out.

All she can think about is how everyone is going to react. Did she over-estimate her own abilities? Is the article even good? She's so exposed now that it's all out in the open, far more than when she and Damien first announced their relationship.

And she did it to herself.

Phoebe walks quickly through small crowds of people, dodging around corners as she slips away from literally no one, finally stopping at a little bodega to pick up a coffee, and hopefully a blueberry muffin as big as her face. But as she's fishing for change in the bottom of her purse, she suddenly feels eyes on her. It's different now, different from the no-one that she was trying to give the slip. She spots a photographer immediately as she cranes her neck, snapping pictures of her through the window. It's just like at her birthday, except this time there's no Damien here to handle things.

With a sigh, Phoebe pays for her breakfast, shoves the muffin into her bag, and pretends she doesn't notice the man as she exits the bodega. It's just a few more blocks to the train station, she can handle it.

Or at least she thinks she can, right up until the violent clack of the camera shutter, and his footsteps closing in, put her even further on edge. There isn't even that usual little part of her that wants to tell him to fuck off in the moment. All she wants to do is get to the office.

Her senses seem even more intense.

Phoebe picks up the pace. He matches her.

She turns a corner quickly. He's right there behind her.

She tries to ignore him. The grind of the film advancing is sharp.

He's getting closer. She can feel it, and even see him in the corner of her eye. Finally, when she steps to the side to get around someone walking the other way, he takes the opportunity to sidle up in front of her, walking backwards as he continues snapping away.

"Does that ever get old?" She asks, exasperated.

"Tell you what, if you want to stop and pose for a few shots, I'll get lost," he offers with a grin.

Phoebe shakes her head, lengthening her stride and forcing him to step off to the side. She's not a goddamn zoo animal, and she shouldn't have to make a deal like that just to avoid getting harassed out in public.

"Hey, word of advice? You should probably get used to this sort of stuff," he shouts from behind her, picking up the pace.

She storms toward the train station, certain he's hot on her heels. She's freezing, somehow covered in sweat at the same time, her clothes suddenly feeling far too tight. Every breath feels like a new shard of glass is embedding itself in her lungs.

"Deep breaths," she tells herself. "You're fine. You're gonna be fine."

The entire way down the stairs, she begs her body to keep it together — at least until she's safe in the train car, near a seat or something she can lean up against. Her legs feel like they're quivering more with each step and she's terrified she's going to slip.

She hates that it would make a fucking great picture.

Thankfully, she makes it to the landing without incident, glancing back over her shoulder to find the photographer still standing at the top of the stairs, his camera raised. Phoebe rushes for the turnstiles. Maybe he doesn't have subway fare.

She drops some tokens into the turnstile and it clicks, but when she tries to push through, it won't budge.

Her stomach churns and she tries again. Nothing.

"Fuck!"

She pushes on the bar.

Nothing.

Her breath gets shallower and her throat feels like it's closing. She keeps glancing behind her, but she can't see him anymore. Maybe he fucked off. But now people are rushing down the stairs like a waterfall and she can barely get a breath in. It's like she's drowning.

Focus.

She repeats the word over and over again, her hand shaking as she drops in another token.

The turnstile refuses to give and she kicks it out of sheer frustration.

"Goddammit!"

And when she cranes her neck, the photographer is still there, a little further down the stairs, still snapping away.

"Here." One of the subway attendants opens up a big metal door for her. "They've been giving everyone hell all morning."

She rushes for it, the attendant ushering her through.

"Thank you," she manages to choke out.

She's so embarrassed that she quickly walks to the furthest edge of the platform where she can be alone. Maybe she was overreacting, maybe she should have just ignored him, or told him off, but there was something about the entire situation, being all alone and having no way to actually fight him off if she needed to. Something about the idea that anyone could be following her at any time.

She shivers, feeling the sweat trickle down her spine before she slumps against the wall, letting out a huge exhausted breath as the fear bleeds out of her system along with all that adrenaline.

She can survive this.

If she wants to be with him, she has to.

With her heart in her throat, she knocks on the door to Brian's office. She didn't even have time to fully recover from the photographer incident before she found herself in a bit of a daze, standing right out front.

"Come in!" Brian calls.

Phoebe pushes open the door, finding him sitting at his desk, hunched over with his phone in one hand, and scribbling furiously onto a legal pad with the other.

"Uh-huh. What time? Sure, sure."

He glances up at her and nods, a pleasantly familiar smile on his face.

Sit down, he mouths, gesturing to an open bottle of open champagne and two glasses on his desk.

"She's here, I'll call you back, Bill– yeah, yeah. I'll ask her. Okay, great. Talk soon." He hangs up the phone and rushes toward her, wrapping her up in a big hug.

Phoebe giggles, all of the remaining anxiety in her body flying out the window. It wasn't likely, but now she knows she's definitely not getting fired, which is a good start.

"Congratulations, kiddo!" He steps back and takes her in, his grin cheeky and playful. "It's a big hit! Everyone's calling to talk about the elusive Phoebe Miller who *stayed home* on publication day."

"Now, why would anyone want to be in the office for that? You get all weird and huggy."

"Sometimes you're a real jackass, you know that Miller?" Brian chuckles. "C'mere, take a seat, we have some things to discuss."

She follows him to his desk where he pours some champagne into a little crystal scotch glass, and another for himself. Brian raises his drink, eyes glittering behind his reading glasses.

"I brought out the good stuff because, Phoebe Miller, you are about to put Titanium on the map."

"What do you mean?" Phoebe laughs as they clink glasses. It's 10:00am, but that doesn't seem to matter to him, and after the morning she's had, it's definitely appreciated.

Brian stares at his glass for a moment, nodding as he savors the flavor before reaching into his desk drawer and pulling their brand new issue out.

"Take a look."

He slides it toward her and she snatches it up, more excited than she expected to see it complete. There on the cover is one of her pictures, the first one she took way back in Vegas, the one that truly captured everything she loved about the band. Right out in front is Damien, gripping the microphone as he howls at the crowd. Shaun and Johnny play back to back off to his side as Ophelia clashes her drumsticks high above her head. Above all of that, front and center, is the title:

REVOLVER: LOVE, LUST, AND ROCK 'N' ROLL

She flips through the pages, still not believing it's the feature story. It really is surreal seeing months of her doubt, sweat, and tears all laid out in front of her. She'd read the damn thing over so many times that she knows every single phrase, every punctuation mark, but seeing it like this is, even just those first few words...

You don't go on a tour with a rock band expecting to fall in love..."

It just feels so completely different.

"You did good, Pheebs– better than good. The issue's flying off the stands. Apparently we're getting re-orders already."

She glances up with a look of disbelief. He's exaggerating, obviously. Just being nice. She remembers back when he said something similar when she published her first album review.

"Okay, Brian," She fires back as she sips her champagne. "And I'm sure that was the president on the phone thanking me personally."

"I'm not lying, Phoebe!" He laughs. "I've been getting phone calls from other pubs and even some stations all morning asking if they can have a sit-down with Phoebe Miller. Hell, someone from over at The Midnight Hour called and said Carter Daley wants to have you on as soon as possible."

Phoebe nearly chokes as the bubbly liquid slides down her throat.

"Me? On TV?"

"Yep. They read the story, and they loved it."

"Why don't they just talk to Damien?" She asks. "Or any of them, really. I just wrote the damn thing."

"Because it's as much your story as it is theirs. I haven't told them anything yet, and you're absolutely free to turn them down, but I think you should give it some thought at least."

She sits back in her seat, gently cradling her glass in both hands, her confrontation with the paparazzi this morning still fresh in her mind. This whole thing could feed into Chris's narrative, his claim that she's done this to make Damien look good. Or worse, to enrich herself.

"I mean, I'm not so great with interviews, Brian. You remember my job interview, right?"

"Yeah," Brian laughs. "You were a disaster. I think you called me Ben. After I corrected you. Twice."

She winces, covering her face with her hands. It was three times.

"Fuck!"

"Water under the bridge, kid, and look at it this way: I hired you."

She groans.

"No, really Phoebe, look how it turned out! You're clearly not the same person you were back then, so what are you so worried about?"

She leans back in her chair, lowering her hands with a sigh.

"I'd like to talk to Damien about it first. And the rest of them. They're all involved in this, and I don't want to jump the gun."

"Completely fair," Brian takes another swig of his champagne. "Can you let me know by tonight?"

"Why tonight?"

"They want you for this Friday's broadcast."

God, it's and it's already fucking Wednesday. She was hoping to put it off for at *least* a week, hoping that maybe the studio would think better of the request in the meantime.

"I... yeah, I can do that."

"Great. Great! Well, with that out of the way, I'd also like to talk to you about writing some more pieces. No more album reviews, unless you want to keep doing some of those on the side, bigger stuff like this." He taps his finger against the magazine. "You proved yourself big time with this one, Phoebe. You turned what was a pretty standard pitch into something special, and your writing blew me away; I want to help you grow that talent of yours, get you to really stretch your creative muscles."

Brian shakes his head, frowning a little at himself.

"Ah, sorry I'm rambling. Look Phoebe, I want to give you a salary bump and a promotion. We're moving you up to staff writer, if you want it that is."

Phoebe's jaw falls open and a strange, garbled sound tumbles out of her mouth. This is it, exactly what she's been working for, what she's been fighting for since she stumbled into this job two years ago.

She can barely keep it together as tears mist her eyes, and she tries to shield her face with her glass.

"Phoebe, why–" Brian chuckles, reaching over and putting his arm around her. "Why are you crying, kid?"

"Because this is all so nice, and wonderful, and I know I deserve it, I do, but I'm just... really shitty at accepting compliments I guess?"

"Phoebe, look at me." Brian leans over and takes off his reading glasses. "You've worked hard for this, so please, enjoy the moment." She barely manages to swallow the lump in her throat. "And seriously, take the damn promotion."

She laughs, sniffling a little as she pulls herself together.

"Oh, I was going to."

"Hey Brian, is Phoebe in here?" A knock at the door interrupts them, one of the interns poking his head inside. "Sorry for interrupting, but Phoebe's brother's on the line."

Oh god, it's probably about fucking brunch. Her mother must have pressured Michael to call her.

"We'll talk shop later," Brian says cheerily, downing the rest of his glass. "And remember, let me know about that show by tonight!"

Phoebe heads back to her own little office, staring at the blinking light on her phone. Michael doesn't call her much, he's more of a birthday card with a good joke in it kind of guy, so it's hard not to be worried.

After putting it off as long as she can, she flops down into her chair.

"Hey, Michael?"

"Phoebe! How's it going?"

"Good!" She smiles, winding the cord around her finger. "Really good, actually."

"Well of course it is! I'm just calling to say that Tara and I picked up your new issue! Actually, I bought four copies for the office too. I've been telling everyone that my baby sister's famous."

"God, you're such a dork!" She laughs as she shakes her leg under the desk, unable to control her giddiness.

"Nah, I think that's still you."

"Probably, yeah." She taps the table, all of her nervous energy desperate to go somewhere. "How did you even find out that I– Oh! I got a big promotion, too! Well, not *big* big, I'm not an editor or anything, but it's a—"

"Hey, don't do that whole selling yourself short thing! A cover story and a promotion? That's a huge deal!"

She puffs out her chest, the pride swelling inside her.

"I'm a staff writer now, oh and I might be on TV on Friday."

"Pheebs!" Michael practically squeals. *"That's— seriously?! TV?! Way to bury the lede, Jesus!"*

"Yeah, I couldn't believe it either," she chuckles.

Honestly, she still can't believe any of this.

"My little sister's gonna be a big star!"

She can picture his crooked smile, recalling the way he used to grab her by the shoulders and shake her when he was so excited for something he never knew what to do with his hands.

"I don't know about that. I still don't even know if I'm gonna take the TV gig. It seems like it might be a lot."

"You have to, Pheebs! You should be soaking up all of the accolades and praise that you get. I read the article. It's great! The pictures are amazing, and you all look like you fit together. And from the writing... man, I can tell how much you love that guy— and how much he loves you. I'm proud of you, Pheebs. You've always followed your heart and done what makes you happy." He pauses and she hears him take a sip of coffee. Phoebe follows suit with her champagne. *"Speaking of, when do we get to meet him?"*

And there it is, the anxiety flooding back.

They still haven't fully had that talk.

"I don't know, uh... he's taking me to Paris for Christmas, so I'm not sure if we'll be back for the big brunch. Flights are going to be crazy, and..."

The past three weeks have been all about the story, and New Year's Brunch has kind of fallen by the wayside. Maybe they could invite her mom and dad to Damien's place for dinner.

*"Well, obviously we'd love to see you, and I'd love to meet Damien, so if you do end up making it, the door's always open. But if you wanna stay in Paris, which makes me not **at all** jealous of you, that's fine too. You're not beholden to mom and dad... But they do love you."*

Phoebe sighs and drains what's left of her champagne, savoring the little burn of the bubbles on the back of her throat.

"Yeah, I know."

She's sure it's not his intent, but it still feels a little like a guilt trip.

"I gotta go, but I love you, Phoebe. And I'm so proud of you."

Her face is hot and her head buzzes from the combination of pure excitement and the champagne running through her system.

"I love you too."

"And I want to see you on TV, okay? We'll record it! You're gonna knock it out of the park."

She chuckles.

"Thanks, Mike."

As she hangs up, all she can think about is Damien. He's absolutely going to freak out when he hears the news. She can picture it, him picking her up and hauling her over his shoulder to– well, maybe that's a little dramatic, but it seems like something he'd do. The biggest and best thing she's ever written is sitting on every news stand in the city, after all.

Three months ago, she was eating canned ravioli over her sink, struggling with the deadline for a piece that was going straight to the back of the magazine. Now, she's living with rock stars, getting interviewed on live TV, and going to fucking Paris for Christmas.

Damien was right, 24 *is* a pretty big year.

Break My Stride

DAMIEN

He's always hated photoshoots, and nothing about this photographer dancing back and forth in front of him is likely to change that. It's a fact he's certain would surprise most people who heard it, especially given his public image, but they've just never sat right with him; it all feels so fake. But, just like any kid knows how to pretend to like those shitty socks his grandma gets him for Christmas, Damien knows how to force it. He hams everything up, always ready to take things to 11 at a moment's notice as he lets that rockstar persona take over. It's a little distressing how often that turns out to be the best move, shaving more and more of himself away for convenience... but it certainly makes tolerating things a whole lot easier when you're already playing pretend.

"Damien, I need a little more Bowie!" Liam calls out, dipping into view from behind the photographer.

"Ziggy Stardust or Thin White Duke?" Damien asks.

"Oooh!" Liam taps his chin. "Let's say Duke."

"You got it," he replies, doing his best to figure out what the *fuck* he just half-mockingly suggested.

"The rest of you are good," Liam calls. "Except— can we get hair and makeup on Johnny? That shaggy mane keeps falling in your eyes."

Johnny pushes his hair back, trying to handle it on his own, but the stylist is there in seconds, spraying his locks in place as the rest of the band takes a quick breather in between shots.

Lately Damien's been distracted, feeling more nervous than ever before about putting their music back out into the world. This album feels so personal. It sounds a little cheesy, but it's so much more about *them,* with each band member putting a real piece of themselves into the music. That's not where his worries end, though. The sound is different too, with the usual weight, but a lot more melodic than their past work. There's more gravity to the lyrics, and Liam helped him bring out a new depth to his voice that he's still not quite used to. He does like the new sound though, the whole band does, and luckily so does Liam. *That's* the part that really matters.

Liam spent the past few days tweaking what needed tweaking, and coaching where he could, but most importantly he's almost done putting his own personal touches on the tracks in the mix. The entire thing has come out as a cohesive story, carrying both a musical theme and a narrative from start to finish. He would have doubted it if you told him a week ago, but it's even better than their first album.

"A few more shots and then we're breaking for lunch!" The photographer calls. "We'll do an outfit change when we come back, go a few more rounds, and then you're free to go! But for now, Damien, can I get you at the front for this shot?"

Ophelia leans up behind him as a flashbulb goes off.

"I got to read Phoebe's article. She's pretty great, even makes you sound eloquent, at least when you're trapped in print."

"Yeah, she cut a lot of the swear words," Damien chuckles.

Ophelia grins.

"And to think, the last thing Damien Bell wanted on that tour was another journalist kicking up dirt. How does it feel to be wrong on pretty much every level?"

He wraps his arm around her and ruffles her hair, ignoring the off-set glare from the stylist.

"It's a new feeling, I'll admit. Hopefully it's the first and last time I'm ever wrong."

A few dozen more clicks and a couple explosions of flashbulbs and the photographer finally calls it for lunch.

"Thank god."

Damien slumps his shoulders, the near-immediate hit of exhaustion taking him by surprise as they make their way back to the dressing room.

"You know, I gotta say, I have a really good feeling about this record."

Shaun looks shockingly alert, seemingly sharing none of the fatigue that's threatening to drag Damien to the floor.

"Yeah?" Ophelia asks. "What about it? Not that I disagree."

"Our sound has sort of evolved along with us. The whole thing is just more... complete. I think we've really matured!"

"Don't tell Troy that," Ophelia snorts. "We'd never hear the end of it."

That's all Damien's ever wanted, to push his craft to the limit, to show their fans something new, something meaningful. The fact that it gets harder with each successive album wasn't something he really thought about before now, but he's grateful they were able to make it happen. At least he hopes they did. Liam seems confident, but it's hard to know how something will hit before it actually hits.

Johnny reaches the dressing room first, swinging the door open but immediately taking a step back, his hand over his heart.

"Oh my goodness gracious! If it isn't famous journalist, Phoebe Miller!"

Phoebe is sitting on the counter of the room with a lollipop in her mouth, and a *big* smile on her face. She's in a black crop top, a little pink and yellow floral mini skirt, and a pair of sneakers with that luscious dark hair flowing down her back. Her meeting with Brian must have gone well, because she looks even more confident than usual.

"No autographs, please!" She laughs as she pulls the candy out of her mouth and shoots a knowing look at Damien.

"How was your meeting?"

"Well, I talked to Brian, and amongst a host of other things... I'm gonna be on TV!"

"TV?!" Johnny rushes over with a big grin on his face. "For your story?"

Holy shit. He knew the article was going to be good, but he didn't know it was going to be TV worthy.

The group descends on her like a pack of wild animals, ruffling her hair and giving her other playful little congratulatory bobs or jabs as they whoop and cheer. Over the past three weeks he's gotten pretty used to that serious crease that's been forming between her eyebrows, or listening to her swear under her breath while she writes. It's nice to see her smile so freely again.

"Alright, alright, so here's what's up: someone from this show called The Midnight Hour contacted Brian and... the short version is they want to interview me. Thing is, we haven't agreed yet. I wanted to talk to all of you first since I know they're going to ask about the band, the tour, Damien and I..."

Her eyes that've been bouncing around between the lot of them slide over and lock onto him, a little nervous twitch of her mouth punctuating the moment. She looks like she's asking permission, but doesn't quite know how to go about it. Thing is, she doesn't need it. It's her work, her story, her words. He's just a feature in it. They all are.

He grasps her hand and brings it up to his lips for a kiss.

"Well, I for one'll be backstage watching you, babydoll."

She lets out a quick breath, smiling with obvious relief.

"Really? And you guys are okay with it too?"

No single voice overtakes another as they all agree in cacophonous unison, returning to their congratulations only to be interrupted.

"Hey, idiots!" Troy shouts from the doorway. "I would say your lunch is getting cold, but really it's getting eaten by me and Liam—"

He notices Phoebe, barely changing his tone as he turns to her.

"Miller, you got those liner note pictures for me? We're getting close to the deadline."

"In my bag!" She replies, carefully sliding out an envelope and handing it to him after checking for bends and cresses. "I've got prints in there, along with the negatives. They came out nicely, but your people can do whatever they need with them."

"Well, it's great to see *someone* around here has a real work ethic."

He looks around the room with a frown, seemingly just now realizing the celebratory mood he'd walked into.

"So, what's everyone so overjoyed about? You've been burning the candle at both ends all week, you're supposed to be exhausted. It's freaking me out!"

"Pheebs is gonna be on TV!" Ophelia squeals, immediately holding up her hands with an apologetic look on her face. "Sorry, sorry, I'm not trying to steal your thunder. I'm just excited for you!"

"TV, huh? Well, welcome to the big leagues, Miller." Troy leans against the doorframe with a smirk on his face. "When and where?"

"Friday, on The Midnight Hour." Phoebe takes a deep breath, steadying herself. "I told Brian I wanted to clear it with you guys first."

Troy scoffs, trying to play it off with a little bit of disinterest, but he's smiling from ear to ear. If Damien were a betting man, he'd put down at least 100 bucks to say Troy's proud of her.

The funny part is Troy would absolutely take that bet, no matter how dire.

"It's your article, Miller. You don't have to clear anything with us. Hell, it'll be good publicity for the new album as well, Allan's going to eat that shit up. Everything's coming up Revolver!"

He pats the doorframe, nodding to himself as Damien watches the gears turn in his head.

"C'mon. You kids need to eat, and cancel your Friday plans! You're all coming to the studio for Phoebe's interview, no exceptions. She's been in our corner this whole time, it's our turn to be there for her."

The room is full of whoops and hollering, everyone chattering away as they file into the hallway, loud and distracted enough for Damien to shut the door behind them without being noticed.

"What are you doing?"

Phoebe cocks her head coyly as Damien makes his way over to her, his hand sliding around her waist.

"Giving you a congratulatory gift." Her smile widens as tension crackles between them. "I think you deserve one, don't you?"

"You're gonna buy me another collar?" She teases. "Or a ball gag?"

"I think that lollipop in your hand will work just fine. Remember Vegas? Nice and quiet."

"How could I forget?"

He leans in close to her, wetting his lips as adrenaline pulses through him. He wishes he had time to *really* play with it.

"Hey, uh... are you guys boning in there?" Johnny's voice rings out from behind the door. "I forgot my cigarettes!"

"You need 'em right now?" Damien snaps.

"Yeah, Damien! I fuckin' do! Do you think this room is only for banging your girlfriend?"

"Today it fuckin' is!"

Johnny pounds on the door.

"Let me in, dickhead!"

Damien and Phoebe try to stifle their laughter, failing miserably.

"We really should go get lunch," Phoebe grins. "Maybe that can satiate your appetite until we get back to your place."

It's My Life

DAMIEN
NBC STUDIOS

The green room is abuzz with excitement as everyone settles into their seats. They're all here, the whole band plus Troy, Liam, Janis, Erin, and Brian all crammed into a tiny room, filled to the brim with chairs, snacks, and a couple buzzing screens with a direct feed to the set.

The producers initially asked if any of them wanted to sit in the audience, but Damien cut that idea down quickly. The chances of any of them making an ass out of themselves the second Phoebe stepped onto the stage was far too high to take the risk. And of course, by 'them' he really meant him. He'd rather cheer her on from back here, letting all of the attention rest on her. It's her big moment after all, getting to talk about her work on national fucking television.

Damien sips at his beer and stares straight at the TV, not wanting to miss a single second, even though the show hasn't even started yet.

"She's gonna be great, man. You can chill out."

Damien glances off to his side and finds Janis standing there, hands on her hips and a wide grin on her face.

"Oh, no Jan it's fine, I'm not nervous– do I look nervous?"

"Well, to *me* you look like you're sweating a *little* more than usual, but I don't know you super well. Maybe you're just a really moist kinda guy?"

Damien chuckles and wipes his clammy palms on his jeans. Okay, maybe he's a little nervous, but it's not stemming from any fear– it's more like how a kid feels on Christmas morning, counting down the minutes until he can finally open his gifts. It's her chance to make a name for herself, prove that she's more than just a rockstar's girlfriend. She's gonna show the world exactly who Phoebe fucking Miller is, and he can't wait for everyone to fall in love with her just like he has.

"Yeah, Miller's gonna be fine," Troy grumbles as he pops the cap off on his own bottle. "She's smart, she's personable, she's even kinda funny–"

"She's *very* funny," Damien cuts in. "You just don't understand humor."

Damien fiddles with the bottle cap in his hand, briefly considering how easy it'd be to flick it right at Troy's big shiny forehead.

"Hey! Guys, it's starting!" Shaun shouts, cranking up the volume on the TV. "Everyone shut up and sit down!"

Silence descends on the room, replaced by the canned sounds of the show's theme song while the title card flies into frame. Damien is zoned in, his head a little fuzzy, kind of like the way it felt the first time he sang in front of an audience. It's like he's not really in his body, a surreal feeling that's only increased by the sound coming both from TV, and at the same time, a slight audio leak through the walls of the green room.

He reaches into his pocket for his cigarettes, lighting one up as Carter Daley walks into frame, flashing those blinding made-for-TV veneers, emphasizing a smile that somehow looks even more fake.

Damien's seen the show a couple of times while flipping through the channels, but he's never watched a whole episode; he's never really had a reason to stick it out. Now, though? He's enthralled. You couldn't pull him away from the screen with an entire crew of security guards.

Carter motions for the audience to settle, nodding his head as he bobs around the stage.

"Welcome, welcome! So glad you could all be here because we're doing something a little bit different tonight, a little... special." He shoots that obnoxious grin all around the room, soaking in the cheers and applause from the audience. "All right, all right, now Sharon? Be a dear and hand me that magazine, will you?"

He reaches out of frame, pulling a copy of Titanium right in front of the camera. As they fix the focus, Damien feels a warm wave of pride roll over his body. They chose a great one for the cover, a picture Phoebe took in the dressing room right before one of their shows. It's a candid photo, one of the four of them onstage from one of the first times Phoebe shot them at a show.

"*Damn*, I love that one," Ophelia shouts. "My hair looks amazing, how'd I even do that?"

"It's all Phoebe's composition," Damien murmurs. "She combed through tons of pictures trying to find the best one. Took her ages."

"Now," Carter announces, pulling the audience's attention back to him. "I got wind of this article a little early and that's why we knew we *had* to get the author on the show. I don't know if all of you out there have had a chance to dive into it yet, but it's not your average story. This... is a love story." He lets the audience's 'oohs' linger for a moment before continuing. "Now don't get me wrong, it's not just the sort of love between two people, there's clearly a passion for these people, this band and their music, but the real trick of it all is this journalist not only got a hell of a story, but she also got one hell of a man in the process!"

Damien gives a little nod of approval to no one in particular.

"Hell yeah she did."

"So, without further ado, we are *very* excited to welcome to our stage, for the first but hopefully not the last time, Miss Phoebe Miller!"

More cheesy canned music blares as the camera pans to the side, Phoebe stepping out from behind a dark curtain like she's emerging right out of obscurity into the spotlight. She's dressed in a smart maroon pantsuit, matched with black heels that make her look a lot taller than she actually is. Her hair is perfectly curled, the tips of her locks flowing down her back.

She waves at the audience as Carter strides toward her, taking her hand and leading her to the setting area in the middle of the set. There isn't a single inkling of nerves on her. Her face is calm, her stride completely confident as she makes her way to her seat. Damien finds himself leaning even closer to the screen, his cigarette quickly stuffed between his lips as he claps as loudly as he can.

"That's my fuckin' girlfriend!"

Janis tugs on his sleeve and he steps back, turning around to see everyone else already sitting down on the couch, and he joins them with a sheepish little look on his face.

"She looks so good," Erin remarks. "Very professional."

"Thanks," Ophelia chuckles. "That suit's mine. She's owning that look way better than I ever did, though, so I can't take all the credit."

Damien shushes them, and the room falls silent as Carter and Phoebe find their seats. She folds her hands in her lap, settling into the new setting along with her brand new role. Now, with things so close to really beginning, Damien can tell that nerves are starting to settle in. She scratches at her nail polish, smiling a little too readily and a little too wide. But she'll be fine, he knows it and so should she. All she has to do is answer a few questions, play to the audience a bit, and bask in the spotlight.

"So, Phoebe, can I call you Phoebe? I've been told this is your first time on television, and I want to assure you that you have nothing to worry about. We're going to ease you into this, make it a great first experience."

"Thanks," Phoebe laughs. "When I got the call I was pretty surprised, and I have to admit I never really got past that step. I'm still a little nervous."

"Aw, well that's quite alright, isn't it folks?" The audience applauds, a few whoops and cheers jumping out from the rest. "Just take your time answering the questions, we don't want you to feel rushed. We can always bump Andew McCarthy. I'm sure he won't mind!"

"Oh, no!" Phoebe laughs, holding up her hand. "He's probably a hell of a lot more interesting than me!"

"Well, let me tell you, we don't normally have journalists on this show," Carter replies. "But when we got ahold of your article, I was so blown away that we figured we'd give your boss a call to see if you were interested. From what I understand, historically getting this kind of coverage on Revolver has been *really* tough, so it's no simple feat!"

"Oh, well thank you Carter, that's really sweet." Phoebe blushes, tucking a lock of hair behind her ear. "I'm just glad our story resonated with everyone, it was a lot of work, but people seem to like it."

Carter leans in close, really getting into his TV persona.

"They sure do, and I think there's a few questions everyone would love some answers to! How did you get into this situation in the first place, and how exactly did the idea of this story come to be? This doesn't seem like your typical assignment, so was it your idea from the get-go?"

"Actually, in the beginning it really did start out as just a normal assignment," Phoebe laughs. "Go in, keep your distance, and get the real truth about Revolver, and of course, the elusive Damien Bell. As you can imagine, though, I realized pretty quickly that I was going to have to take a... different approach once I met with the band."

She's already looking more comfortable, and Carter mirrors her energy, exuding more warmth than scrutiny. Damien still wishes he could be there holding her hand, but she really doesn't need him for this.

"Our producer gave me a rundown on your background before this. You were writing album reviews, right? And there was one article on a band called... Delirium?"

"Yeah. I'd done a few smaller things but I'd never tackled anything like this." She's really hit her stride now, her body language showing off that confidence she had in the very beginning. "I actually begged my boss for the story when he put it up for grabs because I was already such a huge fan of Revolver, ever since their first album came out. I figured if there was anyone who could crack their little shield of silence, it'd be someone who genuinely loves their music."

"Let's dive more into that, if you don't mind: their music, what do you love about it?"

"Well, they're always experimenting, the balance of each member shifting song-to-song. You know how they say the Beatles were mostly Lennon and McCartney? Revolver may seem like it's just Damien on the surface, but really it's all of them. Ophelia, Shaun and Johnny all contribute their own important pieces, and that goes a long way into crafting truly memorable music. But, to put it simply: they know what they want to do, and they don't compromise on their vision. What comes from that is pure poetry."

"She's so much more eloquent than you," Troy chuckles.

Damien silently flips him off, choosing to take the high road this time and ignore him. He's right, but he didn't have to say it out loud.

"Well then, I think another question we'd all love an answer to is how you and Damien wound up together!" Carter's smile still hasn't left his face. It's like a goddamn mask. "Because from everything I've seen, he's been pretty elusive when it comes to journalists. To go from persona non-grata to falling madly in love is quite the leap!"

"This shit's all in the article!" Johnny shouts at the screen. "It's like you didn't even read it, asshole."

Janis shakes her head.

"He wants to hear it from the horse's mouth. There's a good chance some of the audience hasn't even heard of any of this yet, and these late night shows are always looking for a soundbite."

Damien knows how this stuff goes, Carter has to cover all of his bases, which means asking questions that aren't necessarily interesting to begin with. And Janis is right, a lot of his viewers probably haven't read the story yet, but they will once this is over.

"Well, I was determined to be professional, and I like to think I kept that going in whatever capacity I could, but there was an obvious chemistry between us, and after a while we just couldn't ignore it anymore."

Phoebe is barely holding back her smile, keeping things cool and collected for the camera, but it's infectious, and he finds himself grinning like an idiot at the screen.

"At first, Damien was a little rough around the edges, he actually didn't seem to like me at all, even professionally. You can imagine how awkward it would be if one of your main interview subjects just decided to freeze you out, so I realized early on I needed him to feel comfortable talking to me before anything else could get done. So sure, we didn't get off on the right foot, but it didn't take too long to find our pace."

He still feels bad about giving her such a hard time back then. First, she was an interloper, just another journo out to get a scoop at their expense. Then, she was the forbidden fruit, something he wanted just because he couldn't have it. For a while there he figured her could just fuck it out of his system, so he decided to go all in on the 'Damien Bell: Rockstar' persona, but the more the universe pushed them together, the more he knew he wanted far more than that. It was just a matter of finding out if she felt the same way.

"So, did something happen right then and there?" Carter asks.

"No, no," Phoebe laughs. "He was actually very cautious. Journalists can be invasive, I'm sure anyone can understand that getting bombarded with personal questions day after day can really grind away at you over time. We're not always there to make our subjects look good, either, so it makes sense to be wary. Ideally, though, we're there to tell the truth, and that's what I hope I've been able to bring to everyone out there. It's something I was only able to do because of the way we warmed up to each other, and not just the two of us, the whole band. In the end all it took was for us to get out of our own way. Well, that and being stuck in a hotel room together."

"That was one of my favorite parts of the story," Carter chuckles.

Someone in the audience whistles and Phoebe giggles, the camera zooming in on her as she blushes a little.

"Mine too." Her eyes get wide and she leans forward, like the audience isn't even part of the conversation. "Oh, but you know what? Damien actually told me he had every issue of Titanium at home, with all of my album reviews in them from way before we met. It turned out to be true!"

"Oh, you fact checked that, did you?" Carter laughs.

"Went straight to the source!"

Phoebe tosses the crowd a flirtatious wink, and Damien feels his blood rushing. It feels like he's falling in love with her all over again.

"So he fell for you before he even knew what you looked like?" Carter takes a sip out of his big, black mug. "That's pretty romantic, no?"

He gestures to the camera, a small round of applause echoing through the room as Phoebe beams out at them.

"The thing everyone should know about Damien, and I hope he doesn't mind me saying this: there's an expectation of him that gets cycled in all the papers, and it just doesn't fit in with the person that I know. He's guarded, sure, like any of us would be in his place, but when you really get to know him he's the sweetest guy. He loves his friends, he loves his art, and he loves his fans." She takes a deep breath. "He's just much more of a private person than anyone would expect, and the two of us being forced to go public like this ended up being difficult in more than a couple ways."

When he was younger, this kind of thing getting revealed to the public would have humiliated him. He never wanted to be seen as soft, to be seen as weak enough that some random asshole could get at him with just a few carefully placed jabs. But things have changed. She changed them. Or maybe she brought them back to the way they're supposed to be.

"You say the public scrutiny is making things harder, would you care to elaborate on that? This could be your chance to reach out, let the world know what it's like."

He can see the wheels spinning in her head, searching for the right words.

"For a while, everything between us was a very carefully kept secret, and back then our relationship was just... ours. Now on the one hand, everyone knowing about us is quite freeing, and I do really love that we don't have to hide, but on the other, our life's everyone's business now. I've never been followed by photographers before, so that's a new thing for me, but Damien's been amazing helping me through it."

"Well, the two of you are big news these days. I have to imagine you've started being approached by fans out in public as well?"

"Yeah. The fans have actually been really sweet. It's the press I can't control."

And there her posture changes, just a little, her expression suddenly a tiny bit unsure, and Damien can tell exactly what she's thinking:

Should I have said that?

Carter leans toward her, his cheap suit glistening beneath the studio lights as he digs something out from under his desk. Damien's heart leaps into his throat as the camera zooms in on the cover.

ALL FOR SHOW? INSIDE DAMIEN BELL AND PHOEBE MILLER'S RELATIONSHIP

"So, I'm sure it's nonsense, but what do you have to say to the people who are claiming the label paid you, specifically to provide good press for the band?"

Phoebe blinks.

"Wh—"

He frowns, looking briefly uncomfortable as he glances off-set. Probably to his producer or something. Maybe they thought she knew.

"I'm sorry Miss Miller, this wasn't meant to be awkward. This story came out just after yours, and it paints the two of you and your relationship in a very different light. We just assumed you'd want an opportunity to deal with this publicly."

Phoebe's lips are tight, stretched into a thin line. All of the color seems to be draining from her face, but her body language doesn't change. Her eyes just look more intense, like she wants to reach over and smack Carter in his perfect fucking teeth.

It had to have been Chris. He found a way to get at them.

Damien *knew* that little worm had been too quiet for too damn long. Of course he couldn't just leave it alone.

"Son of a bitch!" Troy gets to his feet with a roar. "How the hell did we not know about this?! And them! They turn a perfectly pleasant interview into a fucking police interrogation for some goddamn ratings— You all wait here, I'm getting a copy of that magazine."

Troy hurls a grape at the TV, the thing he just happens to have in his hands at the moment. It bounces off of the screen and rolls onto the floor as he stomps out of the room, Phoebe's voice pulling Damien's attention back to the television.

"To be honest, Carter, I haven't read it yet, but I suppose these days anyone can say anything they want and claim that it's true. I've always been of the opinion that it's a good idea to support yourself with facts, sources, and evidence, but I suppose other people have different ideas on the topic."

Damien's heart is thumping in his chest and everyone is on edge. The wry smile on Phoebe's face is surpassed only by the sheer amount of venom in her eyes.

"I'm confident in my relationship with Damien, and the accuracy of how everything was portrayed in the article. As to the accusation that I was hired to be his girlfriend? I was put on the project because I was the best person for the job. If my piece reads as a love-letter to him and the band, that's because it is one. Every word of it is the truth, and I stand by it. I always will."

This time the cheers are audible even through the wall as the audience stands, and Damien is on his feet along with them, pumping his fist in the air.

"Fuck yeah! That's my girl!"

Carter claps his hands together with excitement.

"I'm glad we got to put that to bed."

He tosses the magazine behind him comically, the crowd laughing along.

"So, with that unpleasantness out of the way, what can we expect from you in the future?" Carter asks. "Any other big projects you can share with us?"

"Well, I just got a promotion, so things are still up in the air, but you'll be the first one to know, Carter."

"You've got my number! Ooh, actually don't tell Damien I said that!"

The audience laughs again. Jesus Christ, is this the guy's entire schtick?

"Well, before we finish off for the evening, I actually have one more surprise for the audience." He reaches down under his desk a final time, pulling out a copy of their new album. Phoebe beams as the crowd goes nuts, clapping along with them.

"It's fresh off the presses, in fact they just brought it by the studio this morning, I think this may very well be the first copy of Revolver's brand new album in the wild! For any of you with bad eyesight, this one's called 'Babydoll,' and I've been told by some very reliable sources it's going to be an absolute smash hit!"

He leans it up so that the camera can get a good shot, turning back to Phoebe.

"Now I have heard, Phoebe, that there may just be more than a couple songs on this album that were inspired by you! I don't want to overstep my bounds, but can you confirm that here for us today?"

"My boyfriend's a romantic," she chuckles. "What can I say?"

"Well that's that then!" Carter stands, taking Phoebe's hand and helping her to her feet. "The record releases on December 3rd, so make sure to grab a copy for yourself, for your kids, and what the heck, why not grab one for your next-door neighbor! Before that, though, make sure you get yourself the newest issue of Titanium! Amazing work, Phoebe, and thank you so much for joining us tonight— Phoebe Miller, ladies and gentlemen!"

The applause thunder through the walls as the feed cuts to commercial, the last shot lingering on Phoebe while she waves at the audience as the music plays them out.

"That's my girl."

Always on My Mind

Carter Daley *almost* got to her. He had that look in his eyes, like the question he really wanted to ask had been sitting on the tip of his tongue the whole time. Phoebe *knows* that look, she's seen it in her colleagues. She's absolutely certain other people have seen it in her as well.

"What do you have to say to the people who are claiming the label paid you, specifically to provide good press for the band?"

As her brain wrapped itself around the words she found herself shaking in her seat, stretching for the right answer. Just when she was starting to relax into the interview, Carter decided to surprise her, and it worked. She'd never felt so blindsided by something in her life.

For a moment there, she hated him. It's the kind of gotcha journalism that she specifically made the effort to lean away from. But she can't deny it's effective; knocking someone off guard at just the right moment is often the best way to get them to reveal some hidden truths. The downside, of course, is when it's all over you've incinerated the bridge between you. Carter, at least, seemed a little surprised that she didn't know. Maybe his producers gave him bad info. Maybe he just made an assumption. Either way, it didn't really matter, because a gotcha only works if there's a secret there to reveal.

There's nothing to hide anymore. The thing Chris wanted, probably even more than a hit article to overtake her own, was for her to make a fool out of herself in public. But he'd miscalculated.

By playing his hand like this he's completely disarmed himself, and now he's going to be even more irrelevant than he's ever been before.

"Is there anything else you need?" The PA asks as they approach the green room.

"Not unless you can slip my friend in to meet Andrew McCarthy," Phoebe replies wryly.

The girl laughs.

"I can do a lot of things, but I don't know about that."

She's a young woman, probably no older than 18, with short blonde hair and a round face. She's wearing light blue jeans and bright red sneakers. She kind of reminds Phoebe of herself when she was that age.

Phoebe wonders, for a moment, what would have happened if she'd done what her mother wanted. Gone to Stanford, got a 'stable' job, went to secretarial school... That version of her would have never chased her ambitions like this. It would have crumbled out there on that stage. But that's not her. Not anymore.

"It's fine. I'll let her down gently."

She opens the door to the dressing room and steps inside, walking straight into a giant Revolver group hug accompanied by a hell of a lot of cheering. Her heart swells, her legs shaking with relief as she beams at them. And then Damien pushes his way in, wrapping his arms around her. She melts into his embrace with kiss after kiss, holding him as tight as she can.

"You did good, *so* good. You fucking nailed it, Babydoll."

Damien steps back to give her some space, and she's able to take in her surroundings for the first time, spotting a big bouquet of pink and white roses on the table. She scoops them up, finding her name scribbled on a little tag in her brother's handwriting. There's even a bottle of champagne sitting there, sealed and waiting for celebration. It's lovely to know her family actually heard about her work. Maybe they were even watching.

And it's then that she spots the copy of the Enquirer in Troy's hands.

"Is that it?"

"That was a dirty goddamn trick Carter pulled."

He hands her the magazine and she studies the cover as he rambles on about the scummy host. She scoffs, they didn't even pick a good picture of the two of them, but maybe that was the point.

"I really hope you told that asshole off once you got backstage," he finishes.

"Nope," she sighs. "I figured it wasn't worth it. What's it say, anyway? Did you get a chance to read it?"

"Yes, and it's mostly just weak speculation," Brian chimes in. "But you should know he did write about your... altercation. It's possible it can be fact checked with his medical records."

Phoebe idly flips through it, trying to keep the anger that's bubbling inside her down.

There's a whole section on how the label *might have* paid Phoebe to go after Damien, and give the band good press. He doesn't drop any real names, just *a source close to the band*. It may as well say he pulled it right out of his ass. Anxiety starts to creep in as she reaches the section on the attack. She shouldn't have taken that swing at him, no matter how angry he made her. It's the one thing he can hold over her, and the one thing she'll always regret.

The finale is some candid paparazzi photos of them walking around New York hand in hand, and even pictures from the restaurant on her birthday. Her stomach jumps and she quickly flips through the rest of the article to make sure nobody got a shot of them going into The Vault. Much to her relief, there's nothing. But each photo is accompanied by a caption 'analyzing' their body language to see if they're faking it.

She starts to laugh.

"I can't believe people buy this shit." She drops the magazine onto the table, feeling Damien's arm snake around her waist. "Alright, I'm done with this. I'm not letting him fuck my night up."

"Atta girl." He gives her a peck on the cheek. "You handled that shit so well. I'm serious, it was way better than anything I would have done."

"Yeah, he's not lying." Troy sighs. "Bell would have jumped over that desk the second things took an even slightly negative turn. Tomorrow morning's paper would read: *Carter Daley Beaten to Death With Rolled Up Magazine*."

He glances at Brian before turning to Phoebe.

"We can try to get The Enquirer to retract it. I know some people over there."

"What for?" Phoebe snorts. "It's out there now, so at this point asking for a retraction would look far worse for us to anyone who's on the fence."

Nothing she could say now would fix an opinion that's already been formed. Gossip sells, especially when it's something juicy like this. If Chris got a hell of a good paycheck for playing the game, good for him, but it's not going any further than this. She's done letting other people affect the trajectory of her life.

Damien takes her hands in his, bringing her back to earth.

"We'll go away for Thanksgiving weekend. My folks have a pool house and we can stay in there, disconnect completely. We don't need to stick around to see how the rest of this turns out."

"As much as it pains me to say it, Damien's right," Troy chimes in. "I have no doubt that there'll be photographers waiting outside of his place tonight after a bomb like that got dropped. They'll probably follow you home." He shakes his head. "To pull something like that so soon before the album drops? He had to have planned that."

"What a shithead," Ophelia growls. "He's got nothing on you, Pheebs. You wrote poetry, and he wrote the equivalent of graffiti on a locker."

"Yeah, but unfortunately this graffiti might do some damage," Troy replies. "Shit's gonna hit the fan with his article, especially after Carter actually gave that fuckhead some play. You really did handle it like a champ, Miller."

She smiles. Chris can say whatever he wants, but copies of Titanium are still flying off the shelves. Nothing he says is going to change any of that.

"So what do we do?" Johnny asks. "About Chris's article?"

"Nothing," Phoebe announces, stepping up before Troy can even say anything. "It was always going to drop sooner or later, and while it's going to give us some more attention than we want, Carter actually gave me the perfect opportunity to show the world just how little it matters to me." She sighs. "If he thought he had anything actionable, he'd have called a lawyer already, so all we have to do is ride it out."

Before she flew back to New York, she was terrified of this kind of thing happening, but now that it's here? She's not going to hide anymore, and more than that, she refuses to be intimidated.

"I think Phoebe's got the right idea. Who cares what this dude says about your relationship?" Shaun jumps in. "Besides, everyone always says any publicity is good publicity, right? Sure, Chris might get The Enquirer a sales bump because of this, but so did Titanium... and when the record drops, so will we."

Damien shoots him some finger guns.

"You know, that's not a bad way of looking at it, Slater. Remember when I punched that photographer and we broke our personal record for sales that week?"

Troy groans.

"God, don't remind me. It's the most conflicted I've ever been."

"Didn't you get divorced at some point?"

"Powell, I swear to god..."

Phoebe bumps her shoulder against Damien, getting his attention. She has no intention of hiding from their problems, but still, time away from all of this sounds like a dream.

"You know, if we start packing the minute we get home, we could make it to your parent's place a bit early."

Damien beams.

"I'll call my ma tonight. We can head out in the morning."

They still haven't really talked about the situation with her own parents, but one thing at a time. If things at the Bell household go well, maybe it'll be the push he needs to open up to the idea of meeting her family. Either way, she'll have to call her mom sooner rather than later.

One crisis at a time.

"Okay!" Ophelia laughs. "Enough of all this crap! It's Phoebe's big night, so let's celebrate! Pheebs, we got dinner reservations at this great Italian joint, it's right by your place!"

"In Williamsburg?"

Phoebe can't imagine Ophelia means the pizza place; it doesn't exactly have seating after all. It's mostly just a good place to go when you're hammered at 4am and really need to shovel something hot and greasy in your mouth while you lean against a wall.

"No," Ophelia laughs. "In SoHo! I guess I just assumed you guys were living together, you're always over there."

That's another thing they have to talk about. But that can wait, too.

Liam carries over the bottle of champagne, popping the cork as everyone fans out to grab their little plastic cups. Damien stays behind and nuzzles against her and she takes a moment just to breathe, letting the scent of his cologne overwhelm her.

They hang out in the green room, watching the other guests while they sip champagne. Ophelia and Janis swoon over Andrew McCarthy while Phoebe listens to snippets of conversations. Eventually, Brian comes to sit down next to her, bumping her with his shoulder.

"You did really great out there, kid." He sighs. "For what it's worth, that was a dirty trick they pulled."

She shrugs, refusing to let it get to her. She deserves to be celebrating tonight.

"I can't let that shit get to me, right?"

"That's right," Brian remarks with a smile. "Do me a favor, and don't think about it in Paris, okay?"

"Trust me," she chuckles over her champagne. "I won't be."

"Good." He takes a breath. "But... I *will* need you to pitch me something new soon."

"Already?" She groans, not wanting to seem ungrateful, but she did literally just finish the biggest story of her life.

Brian chuckles and moves to ruffle her hair, but seems to think better of it, settling for clinking his glass against hers.

"No rest for the wicked, kid." He smiles. "Seriously, though. I'm proud of you. You're a hell of a writer and you deserve this night."

"You're coming with us to dinner, right?" She asks.

"Wouldn't miss it for the world."

Their little party comes to an end when Carter announces his last guest. As they're getting their coats on to head to the restaurant, Damien grabs Phoebe by the wrist and pulls her close.

"Hey. You were *incredible* tonight," he breathes. "Gorgeous, articulate, and you held your own."

"I don't even remember what I said."

The biggest moment of her career came and went in the blink of an eye and as far as she's concerned, she was floating out of her body the entire time. It was so fucking surreal, one of those moments she'd always thought about but assumed she'd never actually experience.

"Trust me, you did everything right— and coming from someone who does everything wrong, you know it's the truth."

Phoebe shakes her head, smiling warmly as she places a hand on his chest.

"No," she sighs.

"Not everything."

Dr. Feelgood

PHOEBE

"Morning, Sleeping Beauty," Damien murmurs, giving her thigh a gentle squeeze.

Phoebe's eyes open slowly and she sucks in a deep breath, taking in her surroundings with a big stretch.

"Oh god, how long was I asleep?"

"About 45 minutes. I stopped to feed Maverick and realized you were out cold. It was so cute, your head was all tilted back and your mouth was wide open. You were definitely snoring."

She rolls her eyes and yawns, her body still trying to wake up. It's so warm in this car. The last thing she remembers doing was leaning up against the window and she was out like a light.

"I'm sure that was attractive."

Damien had woken her up pretty early that day, the two of them getting ready together before he rushed out of the house with a mysterious comment about some surprise or other. The plan had been to make it up to his parent's house a little earlier than they originally planned, staying until Monday before heading straight to the airport to join the rest of the band on their way to Paris, so Phoebe had to pack her heavy duty winter clothes as well.

She recalls sitting on her suitcase, waiting with Maverick's cat carrier outside his apartment for whatever *surprise* Damien had in store, and getting *just* cold enough to consider heading back inside when a shiny black Mustang roared up in front of her. It had taken her a minute to put two and two together, rolling her eyes in annoyance at the noise before the door popped open and a grinning Damien beckoned her inside. He said it was his dad's, that he got it as part of some sort of bonding experience, one of the only truly successful father-son endeavors the two of them had. Now, he drives it up every Thanksgiving.

"Damn, you look fucking gorgeous, Pheebs."

Damien's free hand slides over her thigh, as the car's engine roars beneath them, resting just far enough to the side to still be harmless. For now.

She's a tiny bit grumpy, but the cool breeze is a decent substitute for coffee, blasting her hair back as she smiles. They've got a while until they can stop for lunch, needing to make it a certain distance before 12 to guarantee skipping past some potential trouble spots for traffic.

And so they drive like that in silence for a while, Damien glancing over at her out of the corner of his eye every so often. Before too long she can feel his hand climb a little higher up her thigh, and then higher still, until it's just about slipping under her dress, but then a moment later he only lets out a disappointed sigh, and she glances over to see him looking at least a little bit diminished.

"What?" Phoebe laughs. "What's wrong?"

"You wore panties," he mopes.

Phoebe scrunches her face up with incredulity. Sometimes it's hard to take her man seriously.

"Damien, I'm meeting your parents. For the first time. I wasn't going to wander into their house without any underwear on."

He gnaws at his lip, failing to hold back that wicked smile.

"You know, while you were asleep? I was thinking about Paris."

"Yeah? And what *exactly* was on your mind? Or is it another surprise about Oscar Wilde? You're not renting his funeral clothes too, are you?"

One of the ways Troy had pitched the trip was by telling them their hotel had been rather famous, or infamous, for being the place Oscar Wlde had died. She's pretty certain he had only intended it as a fun little fringe detail, but Damien had latched onto it immediately, ensuring the two of them were booked in the exact room he had stayed in. Somehow, the idea of their own little private romps in the proximity of such a talented and notoriously scandalous author had really got its hooks into Damien's mind.

His fingertips graze just overtop of her panties, her body responding almost instantly, and she quickly rolls up the window as a full-body shiver rocks through her.

"No, no," he chuckles. "It doesn't have to be a secret if you don't want it to be. But are you sure you really wanna know?"

Phoebe grasps his wrist and pulls it away for a moment, lifting her dress and slipping her panties down her legs.

"Eyes on the road, Bell." She places his hand back on her thigh, letting it begin to wander all over again. "And don't you dare stop talking."

When it comes to him, she wants to know everything.

"Well, I was thinking... maybe when we're out there, *you* could dominate *me*." He clears his throat, his voice wavering a little. "I can't stop thinking about how good you'd look in nothing but a pair of heels, forcing me onto my knees, making me worship you." He bites his lip. "I could crawl for you, like a dog."

His fingers glide over her clit, lightly brushing into it but no more than that, and she pops the button on his jeans open in turn. Damien grunts all while keeping his eyes fixed on the road. She wraps her fingers around him, tugging his cock free and stroking him slowly as she pictures his little scenario.

"You're so wet," he rasps, the blush in his cheeks growing brighter as he struggles to keep focused.

"Tell me more."

"I had this fantasy– Jesus *Christ*, just like that, babydoll–" He grunts, his grip around the steering wheel tightening. "I had this fantasy that you tied me to the bed and teased me for hours until my cock was aching. And then you rode me and the whole time you wouldn't let me come— not until you got off over and over again, as many times as you wanted."

Seeing him turned on like this is driving her crazy, and she'd like nothing more than to grab the wheel and pull the car over herself. Instead, Phoebe unbuckles her seatbelt, shifting slightly in preparation and dipping her head. Damien looks down, his hand still playing between her legs.

"Now Pheebs, what do you think you're doing?"

She looks up at him, her mouth just inches from the tip of his cock. Her heart is pounding in her chest as she digs deep for that kind of confident cockiness *he's* brought to almost every sexual encounter they've had.

"I'm taking charge, Bell, just like you wanted. Now, be a good boy and put both hands on the steering wheel. We don't want to be breaking any laws, do we?"

Damien pulls his hand out from between her thighs, leaving her aching, but she can wait. She swirls her tongue around the head of his cock, lapping up the little beads of precum. He was more excited than she thought.

"Keep talking, Bell."

What she really wants more than anything right now is to hear him moan.

"I wanna— *fuck*—" She wraps her lips around him before he can even get another word out, curling her tongue around the head of his cock. "Goddammit, babydoll."

Phoebe releases him, letting her saliva dribble down onto his dick.

"I said keep talking. If you're a good boy and I like what I hear, maybe I'll let you come in my mouth, we'll see how I feel."

He groans.

"I wanna try something brand new for both of us in Paris." She takes him all the way down her throat and Damien lets out a contented sigh. "Thought about this thing I've wanted to try forever... There's a sort of harness, straps onto your hips, and you can attach a dildo to it."

She's not sure if she's choking because of his cock, or the idea he's proposing, but either way she refuses to come up for air.

"Oh, *god*, babydoll," he groans, one of his hands briefly wandering down to her head before he remembers the rules and snaps it back to the steering wheel. "I want you to fuck me with your own cock."

She's soaked, the combination of her own sweat and arousal making her thighs almost stick together, and then she hears the squeal of tires. The car lurches as Damien pulls them over to the side of the road, grabbing a handful of her hair as he yanks her off of him. He's parked them just off the highway, the car's hazard lights blinking in front of a clearing of trees. They're not really far enough out of sight to avoid the eyes of every potential passerby, but they're obscured enough that they might get away with it. At least they're not tempting fate on the highway.

He stares her down, his gaze hardened with naked lust.

"Get out of the car."

"What?"

Damien flashes her a devilish smirk that makes her legs turn to jelly.

"Don't make me tell you twice."

He opens his door and climbs out, with Phoebe stumbling out her own side after him. He's standing right in front of the hood, completely confident in himself as he pulls down his jeans.

"Get over here. I'm gonna bend you over this hood and give you exactly what you need."

It's quiet out here, save for the sound of the odd car passing, and the silence combined with gentle afternoon chill is giving Phoebe goosebumps as Damien stares her down. He tilts his head to the side as she saunters toward him, his eyes darting all over her body as he watches her every move.

"You want me to take all of this off," she taunts. "Sir?"

The tension between them shifts and crackles into something fiery, tense just like the first night in that hotel in Portland. Something about being challenged like this is really turning him on.

Damien spins her around, pushing her down onto the hood of the car and giving her ass a hard enough smack that she can hear it reverberate into the surroundings. She hears the tell-tale jingle of his belt buckle, followed by the sudden feeling of thick leather snaking around her neck, and her jaw goes slack. He's careful, pulling just a little– *just* hard enough to make her head start to spin without causing any real harm.

"Careful, babydoll. Remember, some people drive with their windows open so I need you to stay nice and quiet for me." He kicks her feet apart as her heart thrums all the way up in her throat. "Daisy, remember?"

There's nothing for a moment, but the second she nods she can feel him grip the belt harder, using it as leverage as he pushes inside her with one powerful thrust. Phoebe can feel the belt straining against her windpipe, enough to restrict blood flow as she wheezes and chokes for air. He's rougher than she expected, his hips crashing against hers as she claws at the hood of the car.

"Tell me– Tell me more about your fantasy."

The words are a struggle to get out, each one rough and ragged.

"Well, when we get to Paris, I want you to flip the script on me," he rasps. "I'm gonna give myself up to you completely."

There's a beautiful irony to the situation, listening to him describe one of his deepest desires, his hope of being dominated, all as he slams her up against the hood of his car, choking her in the cool morning air. It's the first time he's verbalized this specific desire, this need, and she knows it has to take a lot of courage to be vulnerable enough to say the words out loud, even when he's in total control like this.

"Whaddya say, babydoll? You wanna fuck me? Spank me? Make me yours?"

Her skin prickles, more and more goosebumps spreading across her body with every word.

"Yes, sir," she chokes. "Anything for you."

Her legs wobble as he drives her closer to the brink with each thrust. The belt gets a little tighter and he reaches around with one hand to flick her clit. She's extra sensitive, and each pulse of his fingers on her swollen bud drives her wild.

Phoebe's moans grow louder, not caring who hears them, her eyes rolling back as a wave of pleasure overtakes her and she walks that beautiful line between pure tension and her climax.

"I can feel you tightening up on me." He smacks her ass again, forcing a wild yelp from her lips. "You gonna come for me?"

She slams her hand on the hood of the car, another aching moan echoing through the air. She's already trembling, only a few minutes in and she feels like she's barely gonna be able to hold on for much longer.

"I asked you a question," Damien sings.

Something about this fucking man always keeps her on her toes.

"Yes!" She cries out, straining every muscle in her body as she struggles to keep from collapsing. "Damien, I'm–"

Her eyes squeeze shut, barely registering the sounds she's making as coming from her own mouth; all she feels is wave after wave of pleasure as Damien slowly loosens the belt around her neck.

"How about one more, whaddaya say?" He purrs. "C'mon, babydoll, one more, just for me."

She's still lingering in that agonizingly perfect in-between, her first climax just beginning to fade as the second overtakes her, but this time Damien's thrusts continue to speed up as he crashes into her. With one final grunt he collapses on top of her, pushing her hard into the hood of the car as he comes with a deep guttural groan.

The tightness around her neck that had already loosened all but vanishes as the belt falls onto the hood of the car, and all Phoebe hears is the sound of heavy breathing. She's still too shaky to move, feeling him stroking her lower back the way he's done so many times before, the times when he hasn't known quite what to say but still wanted to show her how much he cares.

When Damien pulls out he instantly wraps her up in his arms, turning her to face him with a warm smile. He nuzzles against her and she breathes, taking in the cool air along with that scent of leather and spice that's become so comforting these last few months.

"You good?"

"That was amazing," she breathes, her body still weak and wobbly. "I think that you might have–"

"You kids decent?"

A voice cuts through the silence, the sound setting her immediately on edge as they spring apart and scramble to cover themselves back up. Phoebe yanks her dress down her hips as Damien shoves his cock back into his pants, grabbing her hand and tugging her toward the door.

"Come on, Pheebs, let's go."

"Not so fast!"

A man emerges from around the little bit of brush. His thick brows pinched together and his mouth turned down in a deep and disapproving grimace as he takes in the scene.

Phoebe freezes. A cop's the last thing they need in their lives right about now.

"Someone called the station, said they heard a woman screaming. I happened to be in the area, wanted to check in and make sure everything was okay."

He raises his brow.

"I'm assuming you kids didn't know there are houses behind those trees?"

Shit.

"No, officer," Damien replies, shoving his hands in his pockets. "We just pulled over to have lunch, that's all. We can head out right away."

Phoebe tugs her dress down a little more as humiliation's claws rake up the back of her neck and across her cheeks, lighting them up.

"I gotta write you kids a ticket. This is indecent exposure, you know."

"Oh, come on!" Damien barks. "Just look at us, do we look exposed to you?"

"You prefer a ticket, or a night in jail?" The cop drawls, pulling a notepad out of his pocket. "Lot of you whack jobs out and about whenever there's a holiday, so I figure I'm doing us both a favor by getting back to my job as quick as I can, but if you *want* a tour of the precinct–"

Damien raises his hands.

"Look, we're leaving and we're not coming back, okay? You won't be seeing us again."

"Sorry, lovebirds. It doesn't work like that."

He clicks his pen and starts scribbling on his notepad, and Phoebe's almost certain she can see a little flash of a grin on his face.

"Now hurry up, I need to see some IDs if we're gonna get you back on your way."

Poster Child

DAMIEN

"**I** cannot *believe* we got a ticket."

Phoebe sighs as he pulls into his parents' driveway. She's been running it over in her head for the last half hour or so, bringing it up every few minutes. She's clearly still embarrassed.

"And we're late."

"Trust me, babydoll, if my mom sets the start time for 5:00, it's because she knows I'm not rolling up until at least 6:30. She's used to this."

"Is she used to you getting tickets for public indecency, too? You almost got arrested. Actually, you know what? Don't answer that."

Damien chuckles. The cop let them off light with a 175 dollar fine and a warning. It had been something he'd wanted to try for a while now, and the cost was absolutely worth it. Meanwhile, as he was reveling in their newly made memories, Phoebe had spent her time covering the belt marks on her neck with powder, and ended up throwing on a little scarf for good measure.

"Since when did you become such a prude?"

Phoebe whacks him in the gut and Damien laughs.

"Okay, okay, I admit that might have been a bit out of line."

"Damn right it was— what are you doing with that ticket anyway?"

"Maybe I'll show it to my mom." He tucks the ticket into his pocket. "She can put it up on the fridge."

"I wouldn't put it past you, you're always proud of any little 'bad boy' badge you can get your hands on."

He smirks. The funny thing is his mom probably wouldn't bat an eye, but Phoebe doesn't know that. It wouldn't be a reflection on her, just another one of his stupid stunts that he's pulled over the years. All that said, there's no reason to think his parents won't love her.

His mom was so excited when he called and told her he was bringing someone to Thanksgiving dinner. It was all, *what's her favorite food? Does she drink red wine or white wine? Does she have pajamas? I could run out and buy some for her!*"

He leans over and puts a hand on her thigh breaking their collective silence as they sit in the driveway.

"They're going to *love* you, you know that right?" He looks into her eyes and sees a bundle of nerves, twisting and turning as that brain of hers comes up with a number of horrible scenarios that could ruin everything at the drop of a hat. "Hey, tell me you believe me."

She manages a pained smile, though she probably thought it looked legit.

"I believe you."

Phoebe Miller could convince a crime boss to give up his evil ways if she really needed to, but if it comes to her own sense of self-worth? It really seems to depend on the day.

Damien slips out of the car, quickly scooting around the side to open her door for her. She smiles, looking a little bit calmer as he takes her hand and helps her out. They unload their bags, Maverick's carrier resting on the hood of the car as the two of them stand staring at the house. Sometimes, he misses the old brownstone back in Brooklyn. He grew up there, even smoked his first cigarette in that house; hell, he and Ava got drunk there for the first time in their lives, sneaking some of his dad's vodka until Damien threw up in the bathroom sink. But there were other memories too, some of them less than ideal.

"Ready?" He asks with a reassuring smile.

"Yeah. Let's do this."

The two of them head down the cobblestone driveway, past a perfectly manicured lawn and garden, and up the steps to the old door. Damien grabs the ancient copper knocker and bangs it against the wood, and immediately starts to ring the bell over and over again. Phoebe looks mortified, giving him a whack on the back.

"Damien, my god, stop! We're guests!"

"Nah, it's fine Pheebs, Ma loves–"

"Damien James Bell!" His mother's bellowing voice echoes from inside, and he can feel Phoebe shrink behind him. "You'd better cut that out *right now*, you hear me?"

The front door whips open, and there she is: Rosaline Bell in all her glory, a big sweating glass of chardonnay locked in her death-grip. Her fingernails are painted green, a nice balance to her billowy blue blouse and matching dress pants. She's never been one to *truly* dress up, but she'd rather be caught dead than be dressed beneath an occasion.

"When are you gonna grow out of that?"

She stands stock-still, blocking the doorway with a steely glare.

Damien sucks on his teeth, scrunching up his face in a faux-look of deep concentration before leaning in and giving her a kiss on the cheek.

"I was thinking the 12th of never? Does that work for you?"

Rosaline rolls her eyes and wraps her arms around him.

"God, you're such a pain in my ass."

"I love you too, ma."

She steps back, giving him the once-over.

"You're an hour late, but I suppose I shouldn't have expected things to be any different. You look hungry, are you hungry?"

"Oh! Yeah, a little. We got... uh—"

"A flat tire," Phoebe cuts in, stepping up to his side with a warm smile.

Rosaline gasps, blessedly abandoning her scrutiny of him.

"You must be Phoebe!" She dramatically places a hand on her chest, almost posing in the moment. Damien sighs; she's always been this way, making a bigger deal out of everything than she needs to. "We've heard *so* much about you, dear, but Damien didn't tell us how pretty you were!"

"Yes I did," Damien grumbles. "I said, and I quote: *'she's a total babe, number one on the top-10 babes list for sure,'* you just have a memory like a sieve."

"Oh, shut up, Damien," Rosaline gives him a light whack on the head, her expression lightening more and more by the second.

She's obviously excited to meet Phoebe. She'd even asked him if he could bring her around earlier, but he didn't want to push things too quickly. Thanksgiving's a good neutral time, no real pressure, but a perfect opportunity to slot right into the family.

Damien gestures to his mother as he grabs Phoebe's bags.

"Well, it's a little awkward now after a few minutes of standing out in the cold, but Phoebe, this is my mom Rosaline. Mom, Phoebe."

She shoots him a look, but decides to spend her energy on Phoebe instead, going in for a big hug.

"It's *lovely* to meet you, sweetheart, but Damien's right, we have to get you two inside."

Damien glances back, watching the chardonnay in her glass threaten to spill out onto Phoebe's back in the embrace.

"Good to meet you too, Mrs. Bell," she manages to grunt out, obviously surprised by the strength of the hug.

That's one thing about his mom you never forget after meeting her. She takes her hugs seriously.

"Oh, please. Call me Rosie, now come in, come in!"

Damien pries the chardonnay from his mother's fingers, taking a sip while she's busy fussing over Phoebe's outfit on their way inside.

"This is so lovely! Is it cashmere?"

"I don't know, I borrowed it," Phoebe confesses with a nervous chuckle.

"Well, it's gorgeous, dear. You both look so cute."

Damien smiles to himself as he drags suitcases one by one through the threshold, putting the wine glass on the floor as he opens up Maverick's carrier. She trots up the stairs with a belligerent yowl as Damien shuts the door, shrugging off his jacket and quickly putting it in the closet before his mom gets a chance to fuss over them.

So far, so good.

He knew his mom would love her.

"Well well well, is that world class asshole, Damien Bell I smell?"

His sister stands dramatically, hands on hips at the top of the stairs as Maverick nuzzles around her legs. Her short, curly black hair is a chaotic mess around her head, backcombed all the way to hell. She's wearing a long black lace dress, one he's never seen before, with big bell sleeves. She even has a black dog collar on, if there was any doubt of her fashion sense. He can smell the hairspray and perfume wafting off of her as she walks down the stairs.

"Look at you! It's like you're dressed for a ritual sacrifice!" Damien exclaims. "Maverick's not up for grabs, you know."

She laughs, the cat following her step by step like they were inseparable. Ava always did have a way with animals.

"I missed you, you fuckin' jerk."

"I missed you too." He ruffles her hair and she recoils, trying to fix whatever damage he'd done to her ridiculous hairdo. "But please, tell me, what's Anton LaVey like in person?"

She punches him in the gut and he lurches over, letting out a feigned painful groan. Damien adores Ava, and pretty much always has. They fought like animals when they were young, but he fondly remembers each and every one of their shared late-night drives when they were teenagers, and they've only gotten closer as time's gone by. There isn't another person he'd rather have as a sister.

Ava pats his cheek and walks right past him, paying no attention to his antics. Her long black dress trails on the floor behind her dramatically as she holds out a hand to Phoebe.

"Hi, I'm Ava, Damien's sister. He hasn't told me *anything* about you, but don't worry, it's not because of you, it's because he *never* calls. You'd think he'd check in with his own flesh and blood once in a while, but I guess he's just too good for me now."

"Come *ooonn*, Ava," Damien groans.

Phoebe's struggling to hold in her laughter, clearly still unsure of her place in all of these pre-established dynamics, and Damien gives her a quick affirmative nod.

"It's nice to meet you, Ava. He actually *has* told me a lot about you."

Before the conversation can continue, his mom glides back into the hallway and ushers them forward, always desperate to get everyone to where they're supposed to be. She's always said every room has a purpose.

"Come on, come on, into the parlor! Your father's in there."

Rosaline leads the way, Phoebe falling in step beside him with a big grin on her face.

"A parlor? Fancy fancy."

"It's a second living room, really. Mom just likes to sound cultured."

"A second living room *is* fancy," Phoebe chuckles. "And your mom seems lovely."

"She's pretty great, always out to please. My dad's a little more judgmental, so get ready."

He's not sure if it's just how unreliable memory is, how it shifts over time, but it feels like the room hasn't changed since he left the house back when he was 18. Victorian furniture, vases always filled with fresh flowers, and… yep, the mini-bar built into the far wall.

Rosaline wasn't sure about keeping it, and they considered tearing it down multiple times, but Damien's dad prides himself on his willpower. Plus, it helps that they only really stock the thing during the holidays.

A few of Ava's pieces hang on the walls, along with a framed and sealed printing of Revolver's first record.

There are four wine glasses sitting on a large coffee table along with tiny sandwiches, vegetables, and macaroons, his father's own glass of seltzer off to the side.

"Damien!" His father booms from the expansive leather sofa.

He can feel his spine instinctively straighten, but he flashes his best charming smile in response, hoping it will offset whatever might be going on behind those eyes.

"Hey, dad."

Outwardly, George Bell has always been the complete opposite of him, most often dressed in a crisp white shirt with the sleeves carefully folded up to his elbows. His dark hair is cropped close to his head, his blue eyes forever hardened from his two tours of Vietnam. He looks across the room at them, present in the moment, but nowhere near as warm and jovial as his mom. It really does seem impossible for him to simply *be in a room* with other people, to relax and just… exist. He's always observing, always ready.

George pushes himself off the couch with a grunt and heads straight toward Phoebe, his hand prepped for a proper shake.

"You must be the mysterious Phoebe that Damien's been hiding away. It's truly a pleasure to meet you."

As Phoebe steps forward, Damien falters for a moment, noticing the slight gap in her scarf revealing the edge of a *very* red mark on her neck.

"Nice to meet you too. You have a lovely home."

"Oh, it's all Rosaline," George replies as he glances around, the slightest inkling of a smile on his face.

Damien quickly wraps his arm around Phoebe and fiddles with the high collar on her sweater dress to obscure the mark. She blushes, but says nothing as he gives her a quick peck on the cheek.

George raises his eyebrows, his expression a little more stern as he turns his attention back to Damien.

"You're late, son."

"Yeah, sorry, we had some, uh... car trouble." He grins and reaches into his pocket to pull out the ticket. "Can I put this on the fridge? How about next to one of my old shitty drawings from school?"

George frowns at him, his eyes bouncing from the ticket, to Damien and back again. Phoebe groans.

"I'm so sorry, sir," she murmurs. "He's just—"

"Oh, I'm very familiar with his antics by now." George scowls at Damien. "He pulls something like this every year."

His dad's always been a stickler for rules. It's something the military ground into him, and something he tried for years to grind into his children. Turns out some people are harder to train than others.

"Sit, sit!" Rosaline coos, breaking the tension between them. "You can talk amongst yourselves once we're all comfortable. I'll be in and out, getting the turkey ready, so feel free to snack while you're waiting."

Damien moves to the table, slipping past his dad and pulling a seat out for Phoebe.

"You want a drink?" Damien asks as she sits.

"Yeah, uh, is there wine?"

She looks like she's in a bit of a daze.

"Pour her some of that Sauv Blanc we got from Napa!" Rosaline chirps from the kitchen, the clatter of silverware intermittently filling the air. "It's excellent! The best I've had in years."

"Sure, I'll just look for the bottle that has all that printed on the label," Damien mutters.

He wanders over to the wine fridge, rooting around until he finds the bottle he's pretty sure she was talking about.

"So, Phoebe, I understand that you met Damien on tour?" George asks.

Phoebe nods, gratefully accepting the glass Damien offers her.

"I got assigned to write a piece on them for Titanium– actually, I kind of begged for it. But it worked out pretty well."

"I'll say, you were great on the Midnight Hour," Rosaline calls from the kitchen. "We all watched it the other night!"

"And mom bought out every copy of your magazine from the news stand," Ava chuckles. "She's been giving them out to friends whenever she goes to play bridge."

"Well, I just want to be supportive!" Rosaline replies, puttering into the room to put out sets of forks, each with imperceptibly tiny differences, at each seat. "It's wonderful work, Phoebe."

"We're used to reading about him throwing guitars off of balconies, or getting *tickets*," George mumbles as he takes a bite of his sandwich. "It was a nice change of pace."

There it is. He was waiting for something like this from his dad, even if sometimes he deserves it. George has always wanted Damien to clean up his act, telling him again and again that he can't run around like a drunken idiot forever. Phoebe didn't paint him as an Angel, but this is probably the first time his dad's seen him portrayed in an even vaguely positive light in the press.

"Dad," Ava warns, glaring at him. "Not the time."

Damien picks at his fingernails as George scoffs and sips his seltzer. No matter how famous he gets, his dad's right there to humble his ass. It's a sobering experience, but it hurts just the same.

"Oh, I'm just teasing. Damien knows that. Like I said, it was a nice change of pace. Unless Phoebe omitted all of his bad behavior, it sounds like the boy's turned over a new leaf."

"He was on his best behavior the whole tour," Phoebe assures him. "Actually, I'd read a lot of those articles too, and so I was really surprised to find out he was nothing like they all claimed."

She gives Damien's thigh a gentle squeeze, leaning against his shoulder as his mother takes a temporary seat next to them.

"The way you wrote about Damien, it was like when he was a little boy all over again. He was always so emotive and sensitive, bouncing around the house and singing all the time— we'll have to show you baby pictures! But the story, it was beautiful, Phoebe, just beautiful." Damien braces himself, seeing the mist forming in her eyes. She's the crier in the family, never ashamed to show people exactly how she feels. "It felt like... like I was getting to know my son all over again."

"Yeah, you almost made my brother sound like a real human being, which felt *very* weird," Ava teases.

"Alright, Cruella, maybe tone it down a little." He snorts.

"Cruella? Really? You look like Tommy Lee, brought to you by Kmart."

Damien grabs a cheese cube with the intent on tossing it at Ava, but Phoebe is quick to pluck it from his fingers and set it back onto his plate, seeing right through him.

"Alright, alright, behave yourself," she laughs.

"They're *always* like this," George grumbles.

A bell dings from in the kitchen and his mom jumps back to her feet.

"Shoot, I got so caught up with our guest that I forgot about the turkey– George, will you give me a hand, darling?"

"Of course."

Ava quickly takes her dad's spot the moment they're out of the room, her eyes volleying between Phoebe and Damien. Phoebe sips her wine, offering a warm, calming smile. She doesn't seem as nervous as she did when she first walked into the house, already finding her own place in the family dynamic.

"Phoebe, now that we're free from the vice-grip of parental authority, on a scale of one to ten, how awkward has it been meeting the Bells so far?"

"Hrm..." Phoebe pops a cheese-cube into her mouth. "A solid three. But I think that's mostly nerves on my end. It feels a bit different from the Thanksgivings I'm used to, but you guys have been great."

Damien wonders what dinners at her place are like, trying to picture

Thanksgiving at the Miller household with basically zero information as Ava continues.

"Sorry about dad, by the way. He wasn't allowed to touch the snacks until you two got here. Those cucumber sandwiches are his favorite, and I think he's a little grumpy at Damien for his tardiness." She grins slyly at Phoebe. "So, is the ticket the only reason you're late?"

Damien's eyes flick to the kitchen door, double-checking that it's closed. His dad's hearing isn't the greatest these days, but he'd prefer to avoid confrontation. When he's confident their conversation is well enough insulated, his face breaks into a huge grin.

"Sort of," Damien replies. "It's for public indecency, but I don't think dad read that part."

"Wow, Damien. Still no sense of shame?"

He grins, hoping to get a little more of a rise out of her, but Ava only rolls her eyes.

"Well, I guess mom and dad *did* meet at that orgy in the '60s, so they can't really talk."

"I'm sorry... they met at a what?!" Phoebe leans forward, looking suddenly more invested than she had been since they arrived. "Am I being pranked? You're trying to get in my head, make me act super weird around them?"

Damien solemnly puts a hand over his heart and Ava follows suit, an action they'd practiced many times before, but Phoebe still looks like she doesn't believe a word of it.

"Scout's honor. Really, we're not shitting you."

"Yeah, it's true, Auntie Shirley told us," Ava sighs. "You ply her with enough Shiraz and she'll tell you all the family secrets. Really, she'll probably tell you without the booze, but it speeds things up."

"That's how I found out *you* were the favorite twin," Damien replies, only somewhat bitterly.

Ava lets out the world's biggest sigh as she sips her wine.

"I'm *her* favorite for a reason. You pushed Joseph into the pool when you were ten and she's never forgiven you."

"Well, he shouldn't have been a dick!"

"But mom and dad don't have a favorite," Ava says with a laugh. "Fame's made you delusional."

"This coming from the favorite," Damien grumbles, shoving a macaroon into his mouth.

"Oh, stop. They love you."

"They love me, but the one dad is *proud of* is you," Damien mutters. "I could never figure out why."

"Well, if you spent your time writing those mystery novels he likes to read instead of writhing around in makeup and leather pants, he might find you more relatable," she teases.

"Ah, but there's the rub, dear sister. I *love* writhing around in makeup and leather pants!"

Phoebe snorts, choking on her wine, but Ava seems completely unfazed.

"It really doesn't matter what they think, Damien. You're thriving! A job you love, a gorgeous girlfriend... What more could you ask for?"

He can feel himself start to tear up, quickly taking a big swig from his glass of wine. Ava's always been in his corner, but it somehow hits him harder when he hears her say it out loud.

"Deep down I know they really do just want you to be happy, but that doesn't mean they're going to understand you any better, especially if you keep yourself at arms-reach all the time."

Phoebe's hand brushes against his as he nods, somewhat absently, at Ava's words. She might be right, maybe he could do a little bit of the work to shoring things up with his parents. Maybe he could try harder to get them to understand his art.

Or him.

"Kids?" His mom calls. "Dinner's gonna be in five minutes, wash your hands and sit at the table!"

"We're not five, ma!" Damien shouts.

The kitchen door slides open and she leans up against the doorway, her eyes narrowed and both arms crossed, but there's a playful smile on her face.

"Just do as you're told, Mr. Rockstar. I brought you into this world and I can—"

"Yeah, yeah, take me out," Damien groans, watching Ava lead Phoebe to the bathroom.

As he tries to slip past his mother she grasps his chin, forcing him to stop in his tracks.

"Don't you forget it."

Her eyes scan his face, probably taking the opportunity to make sure he's gotten enough sleep before finally letting him go. No matter how old he gets, she's never cooled it with the mothering shit.

Secretly, he kind of likes it.

"My oh my, how long have you been with this girl again?"

She likes Phoebe, he can see it in her eyes.

"A couple months. Feels like forever, though."

"I can tell. You two have that look about you." She gives his cheek a gentle tap. "She's lovely, Damien. It seems like you finally have it all figured out."

He smiles, relief setting in along with a swelling warmth inside him. He knew his mom would love Phoebe, it's impossible not to fall in love with her after all, but hearing it from her lips...

"Yeah, I– I think this is it ma," he shakes his head, surprised to finally be saying it out loud. "I think she's the one."

Young Americans

PHOEBE

The table is piled high with food. Turkey, stuffing, potatoes, and vegetables are passed around as jovial conversation bounces around between them. His dad is the only quiet one, observing his son intently, but Damien's been too focused on her to notice.

All night he's tried to be the best possible version of himself, pulling out Phoebe's chair for her, making sure her wine is topped up, and carefully checking in with a glance to make sure nothing's making her uncomfortable. It's still crazy to her how he can be the most ridiculous, outrageous, borderline obnoxious clown one minute, and then the next, he's Mr. Darcy.

"So, Phoebe, where'd you grow up?" George asks as they all take a break, relaxing before seconds.

"Brooklyn. Actually I've pretty much lived there my whole life."

"Oh, that's lovely! We raised the kids there, for their early years at least."

"Pheebs and I figured out that we used to go to the same bar," Damien replies. "We just never ran into each other until the tour."

"That's fate for you," Ava chimes in. "Damien says it's ridiculous, but there are too many coincidences not to believe in that stuff, at least a little."

"Believe in what, bullshit?" Damien teases, taking a bite of turkey and sticking out his tongue. Ava reaches across the table, trying to smack him.

"Damien, stop acting like a demon at the table, please," Rosaline says flatly.

Phoebe glances over to George, who continues on as if he didn't see it at all.

The way Damien described his parents is so different from what she's been actually seeing. Part of her wonders why he wasn't honest with her. Was it to keep up that impenetrable bravado that he had when she first met him? That Damien seems like a completely different person compared to the one sitting beside her. But maybe that's not it at all. Maybe, in his mind, they don't accept his lifestyle. Maybe he really does think they don't understand him. Admittedly, she's only known them for a short amount of time, but from what she can tell that simply isn't true.

"So Phoebe," Rosaline chimes in, swerving the conversation to something Ava and Damien can't fight about. "What made you want to get into journalism? It seems like it must be really competitive."

Her mother brought up something similar when she expressed interest in the field, bringing out all the red-flags and reasons it was going to be a terrible profession to get into. Phoebe gears herself up with her standard answer, ready to defend her choices, even wondering if Rosaline might've caught wind of some of that very competition in the form of Chris's article.

"It's definitely a bit competitive, yes, but I've carved out a bit of a niche for myself. There aren't quite as many journalists covering the music industry, at least not in the circles I'm working in. Besides, I've always loved music, and writing about it came naturally to me after a while. I remember my journalism professors wanted to push me into focusing on something more impactful, politics was top of the list, but I've always been of the mind that art is inherently political anyway."

Phoebe can see Ava nodding enthusiastically out of the corner of her eye, but is also surprised to see she's caught George's attention as he sits up a little straighter.

"How so?" he asks.

Damien squeezes her hand under the table, but she's fine, and only rubs her thumb over his calmly. His father's tone isn't abrupt or dismissive, more genuinely curious than anything, and it's a conversation Phoebe's always willing to have.

"In a lot of ways, actually. The simplest example is how art can bring light to social issues, intentionally, to talk about them in a way that's accessible to people and that they can understand. Think of it like how some writers communicate important ideas with metaphor, then you translate that into visuals, or music. It gets even more complex when you think about how our own interpretation of art comes into play. We can observe something that has no intended political or social meaning, and still get those aspects out of it. Art reflects both the artist and the audience; the act of viewing it alone forces interpretation onto it, and interpretation has its own bias, including the political."

George nods slowly.

Phoebe can't tell if he's impressed, annoyed, or simply disinterested in her answer, but at the very least he's not telling her she's an idiot. She absolutely wants to impress his parents, but these kinds of questions always feel like a job interview. No matter how interested in the topic she is, some amount of joy gets robbed from it when you're competing to be accepted.

"Do you do any other writing?" Ava asks. "Like, not other stories for the magazine. Other types of writing."

"Oh, I used to write a lot of fiction," Phoebe replies. "Lots of different kinds of stuff, but that was when I was a kid."

"I kind of thought so," Ava replies. "It felt like there was a bit of that in your Revolver article."

"Really?"

"Oh, but not like... I'm not saying it felt like fiction, just more that I could see the bones of a fiction writer in it, you know what I mean?"

She didn't, but she'd take the compliment anyway.

"So, lots of fiction? What did you write?"

"Sci-fi," Phoebe chuckles. "I was a big Star Trek geek. Went through a huge obsession as a kid."

"Seriously?" Damien snickers. "You never told me that."

She blushes. It feels surprising that there's still a lot they don't know about each other, but much less so when she remembers they've only been together for a short while. The fact that she still has a miniature version of the Enterprise sitting in the back of her closet doesn't really come up in your average conversation.

Damien kisses her on the cheek.

"Such a cute dork."

"Don't let him push you around," Ava teases. "Damien was a Lord of the Rings geek *and* a band geek. He played the trombone."

"I actually knew that," Phoebe giggles. "You called it--"

"A tromboner!"

Damien, Ava, and Phoebe all say the ridiculous word in unison.

"Yeah, well, Ava was goth long before everyone started beating up goth kids in school. Used to tell people she was a *creature of the night*, had an entire bedroom wall covered in vampire movie posters— even the shitty ones."

Ava shrugs her shoulders. None of this is even remotely embarrassing to her; she's effortlessly cool, just like her brother.

"Why pay for a poster when they're getting thrown out at the theater? Anyway, I turned it all into a bunch of art in my teens. Waste not."

"Oh, I remember Damien mentioning you were an artist," Phoebe says, grateful for any opportunity to steer the conversation away from her. "So the posters probably ended up as a collage, right? Do you also paint, or..."

"I do a bit of everything, but these days I'm into abstract sculpture. I started out doing realistic busts, and I still do those on commission from time to time, but I kind of like just working with raw materials and seeing what I can make. Sometimes I have an objective, or like a statement of intent in my head, and work around that. Other times, I'm just fucking around in the studio."

"She was always pulling things apart and putting them back together again when she was young," George rumbles between sips of his sparkling water. "So when she became an artist, we weren't surprised."

"I take pictures, too— that reminds me, the photos for the article... you took those, right?"

"I did, yeah."

"They're good. Real intimate."

"Thanks, I've always loved photography. Never had the chance to go pro, but I've figured out a lot on my own."

Phoebe taps her finger on the table, thinking to herself for a second before launching back in.

"So, photographer, sculptor, and I've seen some of your other work on the walls; you've clearly got a real passion for all of it; what made *you* want to become an artist?"

Damien grins as Phoebe catches herself slightly too late to change course. It's hard to get away from her instincts, but one of the reasons why she loves what she does is her inherent curiosity about people. It opens up a lot of situations, lets her really dive into who people are, but it can also be *really* fucking awkward.

"Sorry, sometimes I can't turn off the ol' journalist brain."

Ava smiles, shaking her head.

"Getting two words in edgewise when Damien's at home is a rarity in itself, and now someone's actually asking me about *me*? Let's just say I could get used to this."

George nods.

"I feel like I'm sitting at a proper dinner table for once. Having this kind of decorum is a nice change of pace."

"See, babydoll?" Damien chuckles. "You brought civility into the Bell household, my dad actually used the word *decorum* in a sentence."

George cracks a smile, a real smile, for the first time all night as he looks over at Damien. In that single frame of time Phoebe gets a glimpse of a much happier relationship between father and son, before both men become painfully aware of the awkwardness and slip back to their removed default state.

Ava clears her throat, pulling Phoebe's attention back to her line of questioning from before.

"With the art stuff, it's kind of like dad said earlier, I liked to pull things apart and put them back together, but always in a different way. If I'm remembering right I think these two wanted me to be an engineer, but I really sucked at math, so I took up sculpting instead. It's pretty funny, because there's actually an annoying amount of math involved in this stuff too, but I make do. I've got a studio in Williamsburg and—"

Phoebe perks up at the familiar name.

"No way! I live in Williamsburg!"

"Well, not for long," Damien mutters as he shoves some more potato into his mouth.

Phoebe swallows hard and Ava raises a brow.

"What was that?"

"Nothing," Damien replies.

"Bullshit. I heard that with my own ears. Did you say 'not for long?'"

Damien clears his throat while Phoebe takes a sip of wine as the entire table descends into an awkward silence. Her stomach twists. She wasn't expecting him to bring it up at dinner. Her first dinner with his parents. Her first time *meeting* his parents.

"I just meant that... Well, you all already knew we basically lived together in those hotels and shit for most of the tour, and Ava helped design the office I built for Phoebe. We're talking about it, that's all."

"Are *we* talking about it, or are *you* talking about it?" Rosaline asks, her eyes on Phoebe, checking in to make sure that this is a mutual discussion. "Because this one is rather prone to... *grand* gestures. I'm sure you know that by now."

Phoebe puts her hand over Damien's underneath the table. He's damn lucky she's here to save his ass.

"Damien's right, we've been basically living together since Portland. It just got so hectic with the article, the TV show, Thanksgiving and everything else, that sometimes it's just easier to stay at Damien's place. It's so close to the studio and my job... But it'll be a mutual decision when we make it."

She can't read George's expression at all, but Ava is all smiles. Rosaline is practically beaming.

"And it's still just a discussion, ma. We know it's fast, if that's what you're worried about."

"Worried? I just wanted to make sure Phoebe was involved in the discussion too. As long as you've talked it out and you're not rushing into things, *too* quickly, I'm all for it."

And the night continued on like that, little moments of George coming out of his shell, Ava's enthusiastic admonishment of the brother she clearly adored, and Rosaline's motherly doting all intermingled with Damien's tender little caresses of her hand.

She was ready for almost anything, nervous but prepared for the harshest resistance to their relationship all the way down to a passive indifference but nothing could have prepared her for this. Despite everything Damien had warned her about, regardless of how quickly their relationship came together, and how right his parents may have been to question any and every aspect of it, none of that had happened. Instead, she was accepted into their lives without issue, no questions asked.

Well, not *no* questions.

Phoebe wakes to burnt orange and pink light spilling through the gauzy curtains and turns, struggling to find the clock in an unfamiliar room.

7:00am.

She groans. She's almost never up this early, especially when she's with Damien, but they had an early night last night. The two of them had crashed pretty much the second their heads hit the pillow.

She rolls onto her back, her mind immediately starting to wander. From work, to here, to Paris, and back again.

To her mom.

Shit. She still has to call her mom.

She rolls over, dread pooling in her stomach, as she eyes the clock again.

7:02am.

Her parents have an answering machine. She could just leave a message. But what would she say? They haven't talked about New Years at all since she brought it up. Not really. And what if her mom answered and she had nothing concrete to tell her?

Jesus.

She could put it off a bit longer.

Paris is coming up very soon, and with it comes a *very* long flight. There'd be nothing to distract them, nowhere to go to get away from the question. But maybe she can give her mom a tentative answer before then.

Quietly, she slips out of bed, craning her neck to confirm Damien is still sleeping soundly. She grabs the phone off the dresser and carries it into the bathroom, shutting the door behind her and dialing her parents as quietly as she can. Eventually, blessedly, the answering machine picks up.

"You've reached the Millers! Leave a message!"

Phoebe finds herself bracing against the counter, tensing as she's called to task with a beep.

"Hey, mom. It's me. Um, I'm not... sure about New Years. Things are kind of up in the air right now, but I can let you know soon?" She clears her throat, anxiety bubbling up. "We're going to Paris– um, Damien is taking me to Paris."

Shitshitshit. This isn't how she wanted to tell her mom, but she's already opened her mouth.

"He's the guy I've been seeing, the lead singer of the band I was writing about. I don't know if you read my new article– but oh hey, I was on TV! So that's... that's pretty cool. Um, okay. Yeah, sorry I haven't called. It's just been crazy with work and everything. I love you, and I promise I'll call you next week, as soon as I know if we'll be able to make it. Okay, bye, mom."

Phoebe exhales, the long breath shaky and fragile. At least now she can go to Paris somewhat guilt free. Back in their room Damien's rolled over, his plush lips parted as he breathes deeply. The blanket is draped around his waist leaving his toned chest and abs exposed.

Fuck.

She slips back into the bed, rolling to her side and reaching out, gently running her nails along his skin. Damien whimpers, and she can see the shape of his cock shift beneath the sheets.

She leans in with a kiss.

"Are you awake?"

"Half," he murmurs. Her hand slides lower, beneath the blanket, and a big lazy grin of recognition spreads across his face. "Morning, babydoll."

His voice is soft smoke, wispy and addictive, and Phoebe finds that she can't help herself.

"Morning."

She hooks her fingers into his briefs and tugs them down until his cock slaps against his abs. His eyes are still half-closed as she straddles him, shimmying down his body to get in position before dragging her tongue up his shaft, base to tip. Damien's back arches and a gravelly moan erupts out of him; she loves the way his voice sounds first thing in the morning, husky and low in her ear.

His fingers find a home in her messy hair as his eyes flutter open.

"Fuuuck, come *on*," he half-laughs, his voice so low she can feel it reverberating in the base of her spine.

"What's the matter, Bell? You can dish it out, but you can't take it?"

Damien's eyes are heavy, half with exhaustion and half with lust, as he licks his lips.

"You're being a brat. You know what happens to bad little girls."

Phoebe spits on his cock and teases the tip, swirling her tongue around it until she's rewarded with a thick bead of precum. She takes her time, working him until he's writhing beneath her. He lets out a groan as she finally takes him all the way down her throat, his fingers grasping at her hair.

"Good girl. Let me fuck that pretty little mouth."

Phoebe reaches between her legs to flick her clit, and she's surprised at how much wetness greets her fingertips. Damien's pace picks up, the tip of his cock hitting the back of her throat with each thrust.

There's a deep, carnal bliss spreading through her as she lets him use her, saliva dribbling from her mouth. Then, without warning, he pulls her off of him, grabbing her by the waist and flipping her over, bearing down on her until she's pinned beneath him. She feels her legs acting on their own, ensnaring his waist as he pushes into her with a single fluid motion.

"I knew you'd be fuckin' soaked." His lips brush her ear. "You like being used like this, babydoll? You're my little toy."

An explosion of euphoria spins her thoughts into a blur as he fucks her, his thick fingers wrapped firmly around her wrists in a perfect embrace.

"Say it," he growls. "Be a good girl and tell me the truth."

"I love being used," she manages to force out in the midst of his violent thrusts. "I want to be your toy!"

"Mmn, so obedient..."

He's driving her right to the brink, faster than usual, and with no care for his meticulously paced punishments or pleasurable delays of gratification. Phoebe's whole body quakes beneath him as he dips his head, capturing her lips in a kiss so messy and violent she thinks it'll surely leave a bruise.

"I'm yours."

The words send him into a frenzy, and moments into his newly aggressive pace she can already feel her muscles coiling in preparation for release. She's barely aware of Damien's hips stilling as he comes with a grunt, her own orgasm sending her body into wild convulsions, like she's a bird caught up in an unweatherable maelstrom of pleasure; she's battered, exhausted, and radiating bliss.

But it's not over and she knows it, feeling his stubble scrape her inner thighs as his tongue lashes against her clit. Phoebe covers her mouth, hoping to keep the rest of the household from hearing the sounds she's certain she's about to make, one climax leading straight toward the next.

"You've got one more in you, right sweets?"

He slips his fingers inside of her, stroking her G-spot until she's struggling to hold on. She's a fucking mess, bleary-eyed and trembling. Her final orgasm of the early morning crashing into her like a freight train. When she comes back to her senses, she finds him above her, looking down with a warm fondness in his eyes. He's already regained his breath, looking cool and collected while she feels like she just did a goddamn triathlon.

Phoebe flips herself onto her side, slowly bringing her breathing back in line as Damien hums a little tune beside her. When they first got together they'd probably have had a whole conversation at this point, a big long talk about how amazing things were, or where it was all going. Now though, it had all become standard; this is the kind of thing she could expect on a regular basis, and she couldn't be more excited for this exact kind of 'normal' her life had become.

Boys Don't Cry

DAMIEN

Damien nurses a mug of coffee as bacon crackles in the kitchen behind him. His dad is in charge of breakfast most mornings, a fair tradeoff when his mom cooks up such ostentatious dinners.

"Okay, okay, this is a good one. Look at his little marching band uniform!" His mom has been gushing over childhood photos for what's coming up on an hour now, and every few pictures or so he glances over at Phoebe, ready to rescue her from the most boring activity he can imagine. Unfortunately for him, she can't seem to get enough of it.

Phoebe beams as she holds up a super dorky picture of him in the seventh grade. Braces, slicked back hair, holding his trombone with a huge grin.

"Damien, this should have gone in the article! How could you keep this stuff from me?"

"No fucking way." He shakes his head. "I have an image to maintain."

"Oh, come on, Damien!" Ava giggles. "Don't you want the public to see the real you?"

He groans, getting to his feet.

"I'm gonna go help dad with breakfast."

The whole countertop is a mess of spilled egg whites and smattered bacon grease, his dad completely focused on the meal. Well, anything to get out of looking at any more childhood photos; he grabs a cloth, tapping his dad on the shoulder to let him know he's there.

"What happened to clean as you go?"

"Do as I say, not as I do," his dad retorts.

Damien grins, sidling up beside him close enough to smell his dad's aftershave as he begins to wipe down the counter. Aqua Velva. The smell brings him right back to his teenage years again, seeing his dad at the same kitchen table, pouring whiskey into his coffee mug in the mornings as his cigarette burned away in the ashtray in front of him.

It's hard for him to admit, but Damien's proud of the man in front of him. He's come an extremely long way.

"They're giving you a rough time out there, huh?"

Damien shrugs.

"Nothing I can't handle."

George turns down the burner and motions to the kitchen table.

"Why don't you sit for a minute?"

Damien frowns, split between his deep-seated compulsion to do as his father says, and his long-held need to push back as much as possible against the old man.

"Am I in trouble?"

"For god's sake, Damien, you're 26 years old. I couldn't ground you if I tried. Go on, sit." He pats the chair beside him.

"What for?" Damien asks.

"Why are you always so combative?" George snaps.

"God, I wonder where the hell it could've come from?"

George sighs, a little smile breaking out on his face.

"A rock star *and* a comedian. How did we get so lucky?"

Damien wrings the cloth between his hands, staring down at his feet. It's always been like this between them, at least as long as he can remember, a little tense and rocky. Well, maybe more than a little. Other than barking orders, the man was never very good at communication, but he's definitely tried over the years. The problem is he's honestly terrible at it, and it always freaks everyone out.

"Okay, I'm going to sit, and you can join me if you like."

Damien holds out for a good 20 seconds before he gives in, slowly sliding into a seat. There's no getting out of this.

George cocks his head, poking at the emblem on the sweater Damien's wearing.

"Looks good on you."

Damien glances down, a little confused until he realizes he'd thrown on one of his dad's old military sweaters in a hurry when they were called down for breakfast.

"I'm not really US Army material, remember?" Damien says, a little too defiantly. "We talked about this."

Any mention of George's dream of Damien to join the military still makes him furious. They fought bitterly over it, George always holding to the belief it would be exactly what he needed to get the focus and discipline he was missing in life, but Damien refused. He wasn't going to end up with the same demons, so he went his own way.

It always felt like George never really forgave him for that.

"No, that's not what I– Damien, I know you never had any interest in joining the military." He grabs his coffee cup and clutches it tight in his hands, staring down at it like there's something inside that might grant him the courage to say what he hasn't been able to. "I heard Ava in the parlor last night. I want you to know I wasn't eavesdropping, you're just all so loud... Anyway, she was talking about how we don't understand you — either of you. And I heard how you think I'm more proud of Ava than I am of you."

"Dad, I don't want to—"

"But *I* do," George's voice cuts through his refusal like a hot knife through butter. The man may be a little anti-social, but he knows how to control a conversation when he needs to. "Damien, for a long time your mother and I were worried about your behavior. The fights, the tabloids, smashing guitars in the middle of the street... and the drinking? You know first-hand how much that can ruin someone. I'll be honest with you, it really scared me, and it scared your mother too."

His throat clenches as George stares across the table at him with tears in his eyes. Damien has to look away as his own eyes start to sting.

"It's not that we're not proud of everything you've accomplished. We were watching you go down the same destructive path that I did, and it was terrifying."

"So you keep up with my little shenanigans, then, do you?"

"Of *course* I do. I worry about you."

Damien turns back to him, ready with a comeback that never leaves his lips. His dad's eyes are red, his lip quivering as he struggles to hold himself together. George Bell never lets people see him like this. *Never.*

"Dad–"

"Damien, I need you to know that I love you."

He's not which of them looks more surprised by those words.

George is a stoic and serious person, a man of knowingly disapproving glances and very few words. And he's a man who hasn't said those words to his son in many, many years.

Damien sits in stunned silence, absolutely unsure of what to say.

"I just need you to know, as far as the music goes, your mother and I *are* proud of you. You've been on TV, you pack the nightclubs, and the other day Rosie told me you sold out a whole stadium. You've always had a gift, ever since you were a little boy, and... your mother and I never meant for you to feel like we were pitting you and Ava against each other. I'm sorry if that's the way it felt."

Damien blinks, dumbfounded. He moves to speak, but finds himself just frowning, shaking his head to himself before pushing through it.

"I think this is the first real talk we've had in a decade. Outside of that screaming match about baseball after we fixed up the Mustang, at least."

George grins.

"I noticed you drove her here. I thought you might have sold her. Glad you didn't."

"Had to show you I can take care of some things," Damien mutters, gazing off behind his father with an absent look. "Besides, it's nice to have her around. Reminds me of some of the few good times, baseball aside."

"Damien—"

"You know it's true dad," he laughs. "I think it started getting bad that night I came down and found you with that bottle of whiskey, at this very table. You'd just punched a hole in the wall earlier that day, and Ava and I drove out to the beach because you and mom were fighting."

"I remember," George whispers. "There were a lot of days just like that, and they all sort of blend together, but I remember that one."

"I know."

"I never really apologized to you for that. I guess I just hoped that if I stayed sober, that could be enough. When you said you wanted to start a band at 17, I got scared. I mean really goddamn scared, Damien, because we all know what that stuff can lead to. I thought I was always acting in a way that would be best for you, but I didn't even bother to ask *why* you wanted it. I just assumed you'd fall down the same pit I did."

They sit in silence, Damien tapping his fingers against the table. He's trying to center himself, to rebuild his confident presumptions of their toxic relationship as it's completely torn down in front of him, but it's a hopeless endeavor. Better to let it fall down, and start to build it up again.

"I wish we'd had this conversation years ago."

His father nods.

"Seeing you with Phoebe last night, seeing how happy the two of you are, it made me regret not being more involved in your life."

"You could always call," Damien offers, much too quickly.

"And you could give me your tour itinerary," George counters.

It's true. He's the one that's constantly on the move, not them.

"Fair enough."

His dad lets out a sigh and sips his coffee.

"I mean it, though. It's really good to see you happy, Damien. Love looks good on you."

He can feel his whole head flush. He's not particularly easy to embarrass, but hearing this sort of stuff from his dad is still completely new to him.

"Yeah, that's what I thought. She's real special, huh? You don't bring a lot of girls home. I think I could count the number on one hand, Phoebe included."

Damien shifts in his seat.

"It's not that I didn't want to bring some of the others home to meet you guys, it's that... Well, they usually ditch before I can ask. Sometimes *when* I ask. It's not easy being dragged into the public out of nowhere. I don't think any of them were ready for it, even if they said they were. With Phoebe though, I think we've mostly got it figured out. We've talked it through a lot."

"You might not believe it, but that was the key to me fixing things with your mom, staying open. Talking to each other about the important things."

"*Everything*," Damien mutters. "There's nothing I wouldn't share with Pheebs. She makes me want to wake up every morning and be better than I was the day before."

His father nods.

"I noticed you stopped getting into trouble in the papers a little while back. Your mother and I figured that your manager finally put the fear of god into you, but it looks like it was a girl that did it."

"It was a bit of both," Damien admits. "In fact, Phoebe's story sort of happened because the studio was looking for a way to get some press on us that wasn't just a laundry list of the shit I'd been doing."

His dad chuckles, standing to check on the food, his back to Damien as he continues.

"So it really is serious with Phoebe, then? You've only been together for..."

"About two months."

Damien nods to himself, a little private moment of reassurance that he doesn't really need.

"She's forever."

He knows she is.

"I had a feeling," George replies. "It's the way you look at her, like she's the sunrise and the sunset."

"Damn dad, that's actually pretty poetic."

George laughs to himself, pulling the pan off the burner and setting it aside to cool as he digs into his pocket. He pulls something out as he makes his way back to the table, placing it down and covering it with his hand as he sits.

"This may not be something you'll need any time soon," he mumbles, his eyes a little misty. "And I don't want you to feel pressured to use it if you have something else in mind, but... Well, it was always my hope that you'd find someone who makes you smile the way you did last night. I knew she was special because I still look at your mother the same way."

Damien's head drops and a soft sob slips from his lips. He wants to do everything right, to take care of Phoebe to the best of his ability, the way she deserves.

The hand on his shoulder almost breaks him as he holds back the tears.

"She's bringing out the best in you, son, and I think you're doing that for her too."

"I hope so," Damien sniffles as he wipes his eyes. "I love her so much, dad, it's..."

He trails off and sighs. The lyricist, unable to find the right words.

"It drives you crazy, doesn't it?"

"God, you have no idea. Nothing I write matches up with these feelings whirling around inside me. I've been trying, but I can't even scratch the surface."

His dad opens his hand, and Damien's eye is drawn to it instantly: a subtle gold band sits there, with a beautifully cut ruby surrounded by tiny white diamonds housed on top. The light hanging over the table catches the stone, making it sparkle and shine in different ways with every passing second.

"This was your grandma's engagement ring. Not sure if you've ever seen it. I woke up early and polished it up."

All four of Damien's grandparents have long-since passed away, but he has a faded memory of this ring sitting on his grandmother's finger. She wore it all the way until the end.

"Your grandpa saved up every single dime he had to buy this for her. Took him years, to hear him tell it. I remembered dad telling me how he knew he wanted to marry my mother. You know what he said?" George clears his throat. "He said she made him want to be a better man. One day, when you're both ready, I'd love you to be able to put this ring on that girl's finger."

Neither man can hold back anymore, tears flowing freely down both of their cheeks as Damien laughs. The two stand, embracing for the first time in far too long.

"Thank you, it's..."

"You're a good man, Damien. You always have been."

They hold each other for quite a while, a good few minutes before his dad finally breaks away, chuckling with a gesture toward the stove.

"Alright, now that's out of the way, you want to help me with the rest of this?"

Damien wipes his eyes with his sleeve, chuckling to himself.

"Anything to avoid looking at more of those baby pictures."

"Oh, that's what chased you in here, is it? Don't worry, I'll bust out the one of Ava throwing that temper tantrum at Disneyland," George replies, patting him on the shoulder. "We've got plenty of ammo for the both of you."

The next few minutes are carried on in silence, the two of them working side by side as Damien chops fruit and his father preps pancakes and bacon. Any other year he'd be happy to let the silence seep back in again, returning them to their normally distant relationship, but that's all changed. There's no going back, and he wouldn't even if he could.

"Hey, so I don't know if you knew this, but we're recording a new album."

His father nods slowly, focusing intently on preparing their food.

"I did hear something– well, I read about it. How's that going?"

"Not bad, hoping it's better than the first one. It was great, but we're always looking to improve, you know? Anyway, the studio's flying us to Paris for the release party in December, and I'm bringing Pheebs along."

George raises his eyebrows and smiles, and Damien can't help but wonder if the two of them each came up with the same idea.

"You didn't hear it from me, but I bet that ring would look awfully nice all lit up by the Eiffel Tower."

It's another few minutes of work before everything is done, but when they finally emerge they have enough pancakes and fruit to feed an army, and are met with a resounding cheer.

"Finally!" Ava claps her hands together in mock-prayer. "It was like torture out here. Not only am I starving, but after you left mom found the box with *my* pictures in it. Truly a horror I'll never get over."

Damien rolls his eyes, giving her a little ruffle of her hair before he makes his way over to his seat.

"You a pancake fan, Phoebe?" George asks, offering the plate.

"Definitely," she chirps.

Damien takes his seat and wastes no time in pulling her toward him, giving her a passionate kiss on the lips. She blushes, pulling away and looking a little flustered, but happy.

He takes a long breath.

"Okay, let's do New Year's with your folks."

Her whole face lights up as she lets out a little squeak of surprise.

"You're sure?"

"Yeah." He nods. "This went so well, against every one of my expectations, and like... I wanna meet them. It's important that they see how crazy I am about you."

Phoebe hugs him tight, leaning into him as she lets out a big contented sigh.

"I'm so excited for you to meet them, I'll call my mom right away!"

"Anything for you, Babydoll," he whispers into her ear as he runs a hand through her hair. "Besides, it's only fair that I get to see *your* stupid baby pictures next."

Make Your Own Kind of Music

PHOEBE

"You good, Miller?" Damien asks.

Phoebe manages a forced smile as she drags her eyes from the window. She's never been a great flier, always doing her best on flights where she can distract herself with work. Knowing just how long the flight is going to be makes it so much worse; at least with New York to LAX and back again it's usually over before she has *too much* of a chance to get into panic mode. But the worst part was always the waiting.

"Takeoff and landing just kind of freak me out. It's always so loud, and the rattling... all of it just kind of gets to me."

Damien links his fingers with hers, massaging her hand with his thumb.

"Well, I'm here this time, and nothing bad's gonna happen to you."

The closer they get to takeoff, the faster her heart thumps. She's never been on a flight longer than five hours before. There's so much that could go wrong.

"Tell me the dumbest thing you ever did," she mutters, closing her eyes.

"What?" Damien chuckles.

"I need something to take my mind off of this."

"Oh! Okay, that's easy. When we were in Europe the last time,

Ophelia and I dropped acid after our first show of the tour. When it didn't hit right away we came up with the fantastic idea to start walking around Athens until it did. We'd never done acid before, right? So we had no idea what it's gonna be like. So, we're walking and we're walking and then we see this *massive* fountain, and Ophelia says, 'Wouldn't it be hilarious to pour a bunch of bubble-bath shit in there?' And, of course, I thought, *fuck yeah it would!* I couldn't get the thought out of my head. So, we run back to the hotel and pretend we're a couple so that we can ask for as much bubble bath as we can get, even told them it was our anniversary."

"Like... the little bottles?" Phoebe laughs, you'd think she'd be ready for pretty much any story he could come up with, but somehow this was beyond her expectations. "You loaded up on tiny bottles of bubble-bath?"

"Yeah, and they were *so* fuckin' small we fit a dozen into Phi's bag. I bet one bottle would have done the trick, but we just took as many as she'd give us." He shakes his head, smiling with a funny mix of what looks like pride and embarrassment. "We ran back to the fountain and just started pouring them one by one into the water. And then..."

He pauses, groaning as he rubs his eyes with his palms.

"And then...?" There's no way she's letting the story end on a cliffhanger like that.

"And then, well... What do you do with bubble-bath? We stripped down and jumped in."

A month ago she might not have believed that story. It sounds like such bullshit, like he came up with it on the spot to seem like a goofy rebel, but now? She can picture the two of them clear as day, jumping up and down and screaming with laughter as bubbles fly everywhere. It makes her wish she'd known him back then.

"What happened after that?"

"Well, from my perspective at least, it was just Phi and I, right? We're totally in the zone. Of course, the plaza was full of people, and they were understandably... scandalized. Anyway, a cop swung on by, but by then we were so far into the trip we had no clue what was going on anymore. Tried to hide in the mass of bubbles, but we were laughing so hard it couldn't have done any good. When he got in close we burst right out of the water and fuckin' sprinted back to the hotel. Never got caught, or so we thought."

He sighs and chuckles to himself.

"Turns out Troy got wind of what was going on a little while after we left with the bubble-bath and rounded us up halfway back to the hotel. Intercepted the cop, paid everything off, and made sure no one in the press got wind of who exactly caused the public scene. I think he was busy that whole day tying up loose ends; cost a pretty penny too, but we were on stage the next night."

She blinks incredulously, shaking her head as she tries to keep from breaking down laughing, but Damien only tilts his head, pointing off to the left. She follows his finger to find the view out the window much less treacherous than before. They're already pretty far up in the air, New York getting smaller and smaller as they ascend.

Phoebe lets out her breath, feeling her body begin to relax as Damien rubs her shoulders.

"Better?"

"Yeah, much." She leans her head over, resting it on his chest. "Thank you."

"Anytime, babydoll."

Soon, the flight attendants come around, offering food and drinks. They eat a late dinner, have a few glasses of wine, and start to settle in for their eight hour flight.

There's not much to do on a red eye except sleep, and all of the adrenaline from the takeoff is finally slipping away after a couple of restless hours. She closes her eyes, sliding her Walkman out of her bag and putting on her headphones, content to slip into unconsciousness to Bowie's impeccable voice.

But it's only a few minutes of that before she can feel Damien shifting beside her, restless. And then again, and again. One minute, he's scribbling in his notebook, the next he's drumming on his thighs, and then flipping through the in-flight magazine. Her mind rockets back to that night on the tour bus, when neither of them could sleep. Her legs squeeze together at the memory.

They can't have sex on the plane.

They *cannot* have sex on the plane.

She takes a deep breath and attempts to drift off again, trying every trick in the book, but just as she starts to feel herself slipping away, her headphones are slid off of her ears, Damien's breath on her neck.

"You wanna play a little game, babydoll?"

By now, she knows the kinds of games Damien likes to play, especially when they're In public. There's a moment where she considers just staying still, pretending to be asleep, but curiosity gets the better of her and she turns her head enough to take in the devilish look on his face.

"Is this a game that's going to get us into trouble?"

Damien digs into his pocket and pulls out a small white pill.

"You tell me."

How the hell did he get through security with that?

"Damien, what...?"

"It's just a bit of ecstasy, and besides, it looks like any other pill. Anyway I got it from Liam, said he and his husband took some at a concert and within an hour, they were all over each other. Had to head to the bathroom, if you get my drift."

He's keeping his voice really low, rumbling softly in her ear. Even he knows it's not the smartest idea to project that you're carrying drugs on a plane. And of course, her immediate reaction is to tell him he's being crazy, but somehow being around him makes her want to experiment.

To take some real risks.

"Okay, but what's it do? Besides Liam's anecdotal sex stuff?"

"Makes you feel all warm and fuzzy," Damien's voice is laced with sex, drawing her in already with almost no effort. "Colors are brighter, textures are more intense..." He sucks on her neck, and she can feel the bulge in his jeans start to press against her leg. "I was thinking we could split it and see who has to... handle themselves first. It is a *long* flight to Paris, after all."

They could get caught. They probably *will* get caught. But that's the fun part. Besides, if she turns him down he'll be holding the drugs when they hit Paris. This way, at least no one will be able to find anything on them.

With a smirk, Damien bites down on half of the tablet and leans in toward her, passing it across to her on his tongue. The moment it hits her mouth she can feel herself shiver with excitement, and she knocks it back with a swig of wine, as quickly as she can. Damien swallows his raw, quirking a brow at her as she stares back across at him.

"How long does it take to kick in?"

"Liam said about half an hour. Apparently they're strong, so half each was probably the best call."

Phoebe nods, reaching down and pulls a book out of her bag, turning on the soft overhead light and doing her best to keep calm and collected. She finds the spot that she bookmarked with a thin piece of receipt paper. She's been reading this book for two months and she's only on page four chapters in. She's been so focused on writing that she hasn't had the chance to read anything.

Damien's hand slips underneath the blanket on her lap and glides up her thigh, giving it a quick squeeze.

"Stop that," she whispers.

"Stop what?"

"You know what," she murmurs, turning her attention back to her book. "It drives me crazy."

His hand slides higher.

"Well, there's definitely something else I'd rather be doing."

She keeps reading, despite his... active hand, but there's not a hope in hell that she's going to absorb a single word. He slips between her legs, his fingers massaging her slowly over her panites. Phoebe breathes deeply, her hips rolling into his touch against her will. She's probably read the same sentence at least ten times.

"You're gonna lose."

His snicker lights her up, a perfect mix of irritation and arousal making her wish she could bite back at him.

"Shut the hell up, I'm trying to focus."

"Aww," he coos. "You're mad at me?"

"What do you think?"

"Well, I'll tell you what I *know*: you're already wet enough that you might need to pay the airline for a new seat."

He's such an arrogant prick, but that's half the fun. Besides, he makes her come harder than any other man she's been with. Even on her best day, knowing exactly what turns her on, she can't measure up to him in that area.

Damien continues to torment her as she struggles to keep as calm as she can, but by the time about twenty minutes has passed she can tell her attention is starting to wander even more than before. The words on the page shift, muddling up into thoughts of him: the way he pins her to the bed, tongue lashing against her as he makes her beg for mercy, the feeling as she struggles against whatever binding he's decided to use.

His fingers torment her, carefully paced to keep her from coming right then and there, but more than enough to make her squirm. Her only hope is that the stewardess isn't planning to come by again any time soon.

And then she has to wonder, have his lips always been this silky? Have his fingers always sparked against her skin like this? Phoebe tries her best to focus on something else. Anything else. She runs her fingers over the pages of her book, zoning in on them over everything else.

She's not even reading anymore, just flipping through the book, marveling at the texture of the pages. They're somehow both silky and rough under her touch, and she's not sure how she's never noticed such a perplexing phenomenon before.

"Isn't it weird how we don't think about what we touch?"

"Hmm?"

He's miles away, too busy working on driving her crazy to even listen. She could ask him for his wallet and he'd probably hand it over– but to be fair he'd probably do that on a normal day, too.

"Do you ever think about how good some things feel?" She runs her whole hand down page after page, swearing she can feel each individual letter like they're raised right off the paper.

Damien stops his own activities, staring over at her with a bewildered expression for a moment before he starts to snicker, his nose scrunching up with glee.

"Why are you laughing?"

Phoebe frowns, even more annoyed that he's not taking her seriously.

"Oh, no Pheebs, I'm not laughing at you–"

"Yes you are!"

Damien grasps her face and brushes her cheek, his shoulders still shaking with those suppressed giggles.

"I promise I'm not, it's just... I think it might be working."

She doesn't feel high, but now that she thinks of it, all the colors on the plane are much more intense. Even Damien's eyes are brighter, more vibrant if that's even possible. She begins to laugh, too.

"You're so pretty it makes me mad sometimes," she breathes.

"What?!"

"No other man on earth is as pretty as you, and I think you know it."

Why the fuck did she say that? It looks like her fucking filter's long gone.

"Does it make you wanna give in?"

"No. I'm gonna win this."

"I don't think that's gonna happen."

Her brain is overloading with sensation. Tingles creep up and down her body, over every inch of her skin.

"Fuck me," she whispers, leaning into him in dizzying desperation. "It's too much."

Damien doesn't waste a single moment, gripping her chin tightly and forcing her to look him straight in the eyes.

"Bathroom. Three minutes. Do *not* be late."

Phoebe flashes him what she hopes is a sultry smile, but at this point there's a chance it could look like anything.

"Oh, I don't plan on getting distracted this time."

He's off like a shot, unbuckling his seatbelt and rushing for the bathroom as she tries to look as inconspicuous as possible. She glances around, shaking with adrenaline and... well, whatever the hell was in that pill.

Almost everyone on the plane is asleep, save for the few passengers reading beneath their overhead lights, and the only sound in the cabin is the muffled roar of the engines. It's a little eerie, so quiet she swears she can hear the pages in her book shuffle even now that it's closed shut.

But it's okay, she can do this. It's exactly like that night on the bus. All she has to do is get in there, where they're completely hidden away.

And then she just needs to keep quiet.

Phoebe glances at her watch, shocked to find that it's already been a bit over the three minutes he'd told her to wait, tumbling out of her seat and keeping her eyes fixed straight ahead as she walks step by step to the bathroom.

With every foot a new terrifying thought jumps into her head: Are any strangers looking at her? Do they all know? Will any of the others notice? Will a flight attendant figure out what she's doing, and stop her?

Shit, does this stuff make you more paranoid, too?

But she reaches the bathroom, and as far as she can tell no one's watching her as she quickly makes a few sharp knocks. The door opens and Damien yanks her inside, covering her mouth as he pushes her up against the wall. She hears the click of the lock and his lips are on her immediately, aiming to finish what they started in their seats.

"I'm in charge. Understand?"

He keeps diving back in with little nips and kisses, not giving her a moment of time to adjust, and so Phoebe only nods, so wrapped up in the feeling of his lips against her skin that she can't even find the words to respond.

"You're such a good girl."

Her body is aching to be touched, and the moment his hands run up her waist she has to bite back a loud moan. He pulls her arms behind her back, slipping a hand up behind her head and tugging at her hair tie, watching in the little mirror of their cramped hiding spot as her hair tumbles down. She feels powerless as he bends over the tiny counter, sliding her hair tie over her wrists, and twisting it around until they're held together nice and tight.

"Mm, I like you like this" he purrs. "Stuck in here with me, nowhere to run."

His eyes dig into her like knives.

"I'm gonna fuck you as long as I want, however I want."

She can hear the sound of his zipper sliding down, and before she knows it her dress is being pushed up past her waist; she can feel Damien press his cock against her ass, rubbing it up and down her pantyhose. She keeps watching everything unfold in the mirror, completely unable to do anything but fall into the experience as she's consumed by the pleasure.

"Holy shit, this feels good." He laughs. "How the hell does this feel so good?"

Damien pushes down the straps of her dress, roughly caressing and squeezing her breasts, making sure to tug her nipples just long enough to make her eyelids flutter. He already looks like he's on the verge of losing control, like every time she's seen him fully give in to his lust, perfectly rough and brutal. He steps back, takes a big grip of her pantyhose, and rips them apart at the seam.

"I want to see you beg," he orders, his voice dropping down to a low whisper. "You're so pretty when you beg for me."

Phoebe gasps, feeling the new rush of cold recycled air against her backside. Trying to keep herself together.

"Sir, please..."

"You can do better than that," he growls, his hot breath on her neck as he grabs her hips hard enough to leave a bruise. "Come on, sweetness. Tell me what you want. Show me how good you are with words."

She grits her teeth.

"Dammit, Damien, fuck me like you own me."

He smiles, nodding as he spreads her legs, reaching around her front and gliding his fingers between her pussy lips.

"You're dripping for me," he whispers. "That's a good start."

He pops the fingers into his mouth and sucks them clean, his rings glittering in the buzzing light of the bathroom.

"Are you gonna keep teasing me, or do what you promised?"

Damien readjusts his grip, pushing his way inside her as she lets out a soft whine, in lieu of the moan that got so dangerously close to escaping her lips. He begins to move his hips slowly, at least to start, as though he's savoring every bit of their amplified sensations that he can.

Phoebe's heart is pounding, praying there's not someone standing outside the door, but that thought is quickly whisked away as Damien's hips start to move faster.

Damien's hands glide up her waist and he cups a breast, the rough crush of his grip sending shocks through her body. Phoebe's head drops, but he doesn't let her rest, wrapping his free hand around her throat and forcing her head back up; watching her reflection get fucked by him.

At this point, she's so sensitive that she swears she can feel every curve and bulge of his cock. Her legs tremble as Damien's grip on her throat gets tighter, squeezing the sides of her neck just right to make her feel faint without losing her balance. Even in this compromised position, so precariously balanced between discovery and physical bliss, she somehow still feels safe in his arms. Tears stream down her cheeks as he drives her closer and closer to her peak, each amplified sensation fighting for dominance in her mind as everything starts to go white.

"I know, baby," he coos. "You wanna come all over me, don't you?"

"Yes," she whines. "Oh god, yes."

A sharp slap to her ass almost makes her yell out, and she glances at the door, expecting it to burst open at any moment. Somehow, through it all, he doesn't stop.

He doesn't even slow down.

"What's my name?" He heaves, his breathing heavy and rough. "Say my name!"

"Damien," she rasps, forcing herself not to scream with everything shred of willpower she has left. "DamienDamienDamien*Damien*!"

"Atta fuckin' girl," he groans. "I really thought *I* was gonna last longer but look at *you*. You're falling apart just for me, aren't you? You gotta be so fucking close right now."

She bites the inside of her cheek, struggling to hold it together as she nods, but Damien doesn't even hesitate as he reaches around to dominate her clit.

"There she is, my filthy little slut."

And that's all it takes.

Her knees knock against the counter as she almost smashes face first into the mirror. Her breath fogs up the glass as he holds her in place, shuddering violently as he slams into her faster and faster.

She can see him in the mirror, his head tilted back, the veins straining on the sides of his neck as he swallows the moan he so desperately wants to let out, making a muffled humming sound in its place. He grabs her bound wrists, using them as leverage to fuck her even harder, each thrust slamming her forward before he drags her back onto his raging cock.

Finally, she can feel him shudder, tensing up as he slams her forward with all the force he can muster. She looks up just in time to see him shivering through his climax, his hips moving languidly as he comes down with deep shuddering breaths.

She only has the time to take a few measured breaths of her own before he unties her wrists and pulls out of her, leaving her empty and aching. Even after all of that, she would probably go again if he asked her to.

Damien grabs some paper towel out of the dispenser and runs it underneath warm water as Phoebe takes off her boots, bumping against him in that incredibly tight space while she peels off her pantyhose and shoves them into the trash. When they get out of here, there's no way they're not getting some side-looks, but it's better not to walk out with the evidence still clinging to her legs.

"Why do I feel like I'm gonna be too horny to let us actually make the time to explore Europe?"

She watches as he lowers himself to his knees, wiping down her thighs. It's still stunning how quickly he can swap from domineering to the sweetest, most adorable man she's ever known, and she's not sure if she'll ever get over these little gestures, the ones that show her how much he loves her.

Phoebe grins, looking at the two of them crushed against each other in the mirror. They'll have all the time in the world for sweet gestures, for the quiet little moments they get to share, and for all the other stuff as well.

"Don't worry Bell, you're not the only one who has no shame. I'd fuck you in the Vatican if we got the chance."

Come and Get Your Love

DAMIEN

Their arrival was quiet and calm. Nobody was waiting for them outside of the airport, no sneaky photographers carefully hidden behind oversized potted-plants, no fans running up for an impromptu signature, nothing.

When they got into Paris they crashed hard, not even truly getting the chance to enjoy the fact that they're staying in the most romantic city in the world, in Oscar Wilde's room no less. They ended up sleeping a bit into the afternoon on their first real day in the city, grabbing some brunch from a cute little café across the street before they made their way to the Louvre.

It was the only thing the group all agreed they simply had to do before they left, with Phoebe being particularly interested in the trip. She said she was hoping to get inspired, that it would help get her in the headspace to write something new. Now, about an hour into their visit, Damien's still not sure if it's working, but at the very least she seems to be enjoying herself while his mind wanders elsewhere.

Their big release party is only two days away, and they've all agreed they're going to do as much touristy stuff as possible before then, but he's found himself distracted by this new sort of tension crackling in the air. He's not sure if it's the anticipation of the album, or the fact that he's got an engagement ring sitting in his jacket pocket, just waiting to be used, but whatever it is, it's making him feel giddy.

Something about Paris just feels right.

Damien watches Phoebe pace back and forth, her head craned as she takes in everything about a statue she's found herself particularly interested in. He'd heard of it before: Psyche Revived by Cupid's Kiss. The soft, cream-colored marble glows in the golden light, Cupid's wings stretching confidently toward the sky while Psyche stretches up to meet his embrace. There's a heartbreaking desperation to the pose, oddly fluid and full of life for something made of stone.

More than any of the art though, Damien finds his gaze consistently drawn back to her. She's bathed in the same golden light as the piece itself, dressed in a Led Zeppelin t-shirt and a long skirt with cherry red sneakers, her face bright and curious as she takes shots of every piece she can.

He's been watching her the whole morning, finding his mind wandering to the future he sees for two of them. Everything he wants is laid out in front of him: a hit record, a Grammy or two, and a beautiful wife with an incredible career— maybe she'd even climb her way up to be Editor in Chief at Titanium. Or she could start her own publication, why not? She's brilliant.

They're only ever in a single room for so long before their curiosity gets the better of them and they move on. This time it's a room full of paintings, and Phoebe's taking her time, reading the little signs accompanying each piece. He should be enjoying this place, really engaging with the art, but he's too busy watching her take it all in.

"Dude, do you get any of these paintings?" Johnny asks.

"What do you mean *get* the paintings?" Damien chuckles.

"I just don't understand this kind of art." Johnny gestures to a mildly abstract painting with a bewildered expression. "Like, they're nice and all, and I think some of them look cool, but why are these specific paintings in here? What makes them so special?"

"Some of them have historical significance," Phoebe cuts in as she wanders back toward them. She kisses Damien on the cheek, flashing a warm smile before turning back to Johnny. "And some of them are here because they're the paintings that started major artistic movements; changed the landscape."

Damien smiles. It's always so cool seeing Phoebe in her element.

Johnny slings his arm around Erin and grins.

"They should put us in here, then. We changed the landscape."

"Yeah, I think we made it hornier, and drunker," Ophelia laughs. "Besides, we'd be in the Rock 'n' Roll Hall of Fame, not in here with all the dusty old paintings."

"See, I already knew this shit." Damien gestures at the paintings. "I could have answered that question."

"Oh yeah?" Janis walks over, pointing at the large painting of a dog lying in a field, surrounded by greenery. "Who painted that and why?"

Damien puts his hands on his hips.

"That?" He asks. "That was done by me, uh... yesterday. See, it's a literal interpretation—"

So he may have been exaggerating a little. He has no fucking idea about any of this shit, and not being able to read French definitely cuts in on his ability to crib his notes.

"It's Louis the XIV's dog, man." Shaun chimes in. "It says right there."

Damien rolls his eyes.

"Come on! Let me have one joke!"

"Nah, I decided my Christmas present to myself is calling out as many of your terrible jokes as possible."

"Aww, last year you said they were horrible! I got downgraded to terrible!" Damien tries to pinch his cheek and Shaun swats him away, laughing.

Johnny strokes his chin, still staring at the painting.

"I think I get it now! Famous dog. I like this."

The group keeps wandering around, and Damien can't tell if he's jetlagged or just distracted. He remembers coming here on their first European tour and really taking it all in, even sitting down to write in front of a couple of pieces. But now all he can feel is the weight of the engagement ring in his pocket.

Where the hell can he propose to her? He could bring her back here at night, after dinner, and find her favorite painting... or should he do it somewhere more private?

Damien watches as Phoebe stops in front of another installation, taking the opportunity to nuzzle right up next to her.

The Raft of the Medusa. The main feature is a shipwreck, with survivors stretching out their arms in what looks to him like pain and desperation. Phoebe seems moved by it and nearly reaches out to brush her fingers along the canvas, but she seems to think better of it.

"I've seen these paintings in books, but never up close." She looks up at him, a big smile on her face. "I can tell you're not as into this as I am, so thanks for indulging me."

He grins.

"I'll indulge *anything* you want."

"Wow, it only took you…" She checks her watch. "Ten hours to show Paris your perverted side."

"A whole ten?" He asks, wincing a little. "Damn, I'm losing my touch."

"Slowing down in your old age, I'd say."

This little back-and-forth jabbing is exactly the distraction he needs right now; with each extended moment of silence he feels more and more compelled to drop to one knee. But it's not the right time. Not yet. They need to be alone. It needs to be intimate. Special.

And, even if the chances are extremely low, Damien Bell isn't particularly keen on getting rejected in one of the most public locations in the world.

"Hey, you guys wanna see this Mona Lisa chick?"

Erin snickers, whacking Johnny in the arm.

"The Mona Lisa is not just some chick!"

"Well, she *is* a girl, right?"

Phoebe rolls her eyes as Damien struggles to keep it together. Shaun, on the other hand, doesn't seem fazed at all.

"I'm not the biggest Da Vinci guy, and there's actually a painting over there I've wanted to check out: The Wedding Feast at Cana. There's almost nobody around it, at least compared to the overrated wonder over there, so you can get up real close."

"Sounds good to me!" Johnny chirps, grabbing Erin's hand as the two wander off behind Shaun and Ophelia.

Damien notices that Phoebe is purposely lagging behind the group, her fingers entwined in his. When their friends round the corner, she tugs him back, trying to bite back a smile. Damien quirks a brow, his eyes searching hers as he matches her smile with his own.

"Wow, Miller, that's quite the look. What's up?"

"I was thinking... I've *been* thinking... since the plane." She looks around, teeth digging into her lip. "Later, sometime soon. I– I want to try dominating you."

His heart picks up. She's flushed, but looks surprisingly confident; she's obviously telling the truth, it's definitely been on her mind.

"Yeah?"

"Yeah," Phoebe's eyes darken as she stands back, the blush staining her skin like watercolor paint. She drops her voice to just above a whisper, playing with the zipper of his jacket as her husky tone sends tingles all over his skin. "I can't stop thinking about what you'd look like on your knees. Begging for me on all fours."

Her kiss is hungrier than usual, an unspoken demand. His biggest fantasy feels like it's consuming him and he's never been more desperate to get on his knees and beg her to take him back to the hotel.

But then she tears her mouth away, her lips already swollen, her pink lipstick a little smeared. Damien wipes it away with his thumb.

"Well, that's one hell of a proposal. How about tonight?"

"Tonight would be lovely." She places a hand on his cheek, her thumb gliding over his stubble. "Don't shave... I like it rough."

Damien's face heats up. There's something about this woman when she takes control that makes him want her even more.

"I wouldn't even think of it."

She swallows, glancing around for a moment, self-consciousness suddenly creeping back into her demeanor.

"Do you... have everything we need?"

He nods.

"Yeah, all of it. After it came up I figured it'd be best to be prepared."

Her body is brimming with excitement, and he can tell the anticipation is already getting to her. Hell, he's no different. He wants to take her back to the hotel room right now, but he's going to be taking a backseat on this one. For the rest of the day, she calls the shots.

"Hey, love birds!" Shaun calls. "You can canoodle later! We haven't hit our intellectual quota yet, and that means there's more culture to absorb!"

"Wow, I didn't realize someone was standing in for Troy!" Damien chides.

Shaun feigns offense, placing a hand over his chest.

"Such *slander*! I thought we were friends! Have you already forgotten my unbelievable sacrifice back on the plane?"

Damien grins, taking Phoebe's hand as she leads him back toward the group.

"You're right, of course. I will be forever grateful for the second dessert."

Shaun bumps against him playfully with his shoulder.

"Oh, before I forget, Ophelia said she saw a flyer for some sort of Christmas carnival happening near the hotel. You guys wanna grab some lunch and check it out? Apparently there's a Ferris wheel."

Phoebe's eyes light up and she nods.

"I love Ferris wheels! Ooh, I wonder if there's a special name for them in French?"

Damien feels a small pang of disappointment knowing they won't be rushing back to the hotel to fulfill one of his biggest fantasies, but for once, he can be patient.

The rest of The Louvre was lovely, and there's no denying how impressive the collections they had on display were, but Damien can't help but feel like the sight in front of him is the better of the two. It's far more than his expectation of a cute little Ferris wheel and a couple of booths, this is *the* Christmas market. It's like the whole goddamn holiday exploded onto this single place and time.

He's never been a big Christmas guy. Maybe it's the commercialization of the whole thing, or the fact that his mom always seemed so fucking stressed about cooking a bird. But today? He's feeling more than a little of that Christmas spirit.

The scene is perfect: The Christmas lights are on in full force, the sun just beginning to set as people file around different little booths and holiday-themed vendors. The entire market is filled with people trying all sorts of different foods and drinks, all while bundled up in their coats and scarves. Carolers' songs drift through the air as local artisans sell homemade jewelry, clothes, and gifts, and there's even a fucking skating rink, filled to bursting.

Phoebe walks up beside him, handing over a steaming cup of mulled wine. He takes a whiff, catching a mix of nutmeg, cinnamon, and that intense citrus that's impossible to miss.

"Here, try some! It's great."

Damien takes a big swig, immediately regretting his overconfidence as the mouthful of cinnamon sends him into a coughing fit.

Phoebe lets out a nervous laugh mixed with a yelp, leaning over and patting him on the back.

"Whoah, alright. You good, rock star?"

"Yeah," he coughs, trying his hardest not to sound like a child. "That stuff's *strong!*"

She waits for a moment, ensuring he's alright before patting him playfully on the cheek.

"Alright Superman, looks like you've got a weakness after all."

She tosses him a coy little look as she turns and walks ahead, her pace slow and intentioned, enough that the sway of her hips is impossible to ignore.

A thrill rushes through him as he rushes to catch up to her, offering her his hand as they continue to stroll through the market. Phoebe tugs at his coat as they come across the Ferris Wheel, sitting at the end of their path, lit up and slowly spinning like it's destined to be the finale of their little adventure.

"Wanna ride it with me?"

"Of course!" Damien chuckles. "I may have not been on one since I was a kid, but even *I* know it's not polite to let a girl ride alone."

She smiles, staring off at the glowing ride looking like someone lost in their memories.

"They're my favorite. I used to go out to Coney Island at night all the time during the summer. I'd ride the Wonder Wheel for hours."

"What for?" Damien asks.

He'd never really been a theme park guy himself. When he was growing up most of his thrills still came from more illicit places.

She shrugs, still transfixed.

"It cleared my head. Helped with writer's block."

He's seen her making lists in her notebooks a lot lately, almost every day since the big TV interview, narrowing down her options with each page. She's clearly been struggling with it again. With what to write next.

He leans in, flashing her a wicked grin.

"Well, if this big ol' wheel doesn't do the trick, I got something else that's guaranteed to help."

Phoebe shakes her head, giving him a pitying smile as she pulls him toward the ride. They get through the line quickly, climbing onto one of the cars, Damien grimacing as the attendant pushes the big metal bar down. He squirms a little before accepting he simply won't be getting comfortable, settling for pulling her in close, his arm wrapped around her shoulder.

He can hear whoops and squeals of joy from below as the ride lurches, lifting them slowly into the air along with some slightly static-y and overly familiar Christmas music. He's pretty certain he's heard O Come All Ye Faithful more times in the past hour than in his entire life.

"You're quiet," Phoebe remarks, pulling her camera out of her bag to get a shot of the sparkling lights of the city.

Damien's heart races a little. There's no way she could possibly have found out about the ring. It's been in his pocket the entire time, he only ever took it out back in the hotel to look at it, but he was alone in the bathroom. Could she have felt it through his coat? No, there's no chance.

"Me?" He laughs with a little bit too much force. "That doesn't sound right, I'm always flapping my lips, you know that!"

"Uh-huh." She takes another shot of something off in the distance. "But every once in a while you get real quiet. You've been doing it the whole trip. Something on your mind?"

He shakes his head.

How much I want to ask you to...

"Nah, nothin' in particular. Just shocked by how much I've been enjoying Paris with my best girl." He smirks, thanking whatever force gave him the perfect out. "And also, maybe I'm a little busy thinking about what you're gonna do to me tonight."

The Ferris wheel stops with a jolt, the seat lurching and leaning a little bit more than could be called comfortable. Luckily, it's the perfect opportunity for him to double check to make sure the ring is still safe in his pocket.

And there it is.

He tries not to exhale too loudly.

"I've been thinking about it too," she admits.

"Yeah? And what've you come up with?"

She turns to him, lowering her camera and letting him see the look in her eyes. He can feel his throat tighten, watching her stare straight into his soul. Her fingers glide up his thigh, digging in as she leans in as close to his face as the safety bar will let her. His breath hitches in his chest as she steals a kiss that quickly turns fierce and passionate. She slips her arms around his neck, breaking the kiss but holding him still, trapped in her hungry gaze.

"I want you. With nothing but a collar around your neck. To start, I want to see you crawl. You don't get to do anything unless I tell you. You'll lick my pussy from down on the floor, exactly the way I say."

Is this what she's been daydreaming about while she was looking at fucking sculptures all morning? Or at lunch when she was staring wistfully into the distance? Damien feels like she could consume him at any moment, and he'd welcome it in a heartbeat. He's so hard he thinks he might combust, and it's not made any better when she tugs down his zipper.

"Phoebe–"

She leans over, slipping it out from under his boxers and spits on the tip. She begins stroking him slowly.

Painfully.

It's like she's savoring every agonizing stroke.

Watching him closely as his eyelids flutter and he squirms in their shared seat. At first, he thought she might be out of her depth, that he'd pushed her into something he might not be totally prepared for, but it's the complete opposite. She's fully immersed in the fantasy, and he's discovering that alone is hotter than anything he could possibly conjure up in his mind.

Phoebe's thumb glides along the head of his cock, and he aches, desperate to be deep inside of her, to watch her ride him while she does whatever she wants to him. Never has he wanted to give himself to someone the way he wants to give himself to her, but love makes you do things you never thought you would.

Her strokes are rough and quick, almost like the way he would jerk himself off. Warm breath fans his face and she lets out a little moan. The rush of cold air on his cock feels fucking good when its met with the warmth of her hand. He lets out another whine that makes her laugh.

"That's a good boy. You wanna come for me? All over your jeans on the Ferris Wheel?"

She claims his lips in another feverish kiss, her hand speeding up. Fuck, he's close. Fuck the mulled wine, the way she touches him is all the warmth he needs. His hips buck and he's losing control. How does she do this in just a few strokes?

And just when he feels the pressure building, she stops and swipes the bead of precum that's clinging to the tip of his cock, licking it off of her thumb with a dazzling smile.

"Not yet, Bell, not here. When you come, I want you to be able to scream as loud as you need to."

Pink Moon

PHOEBE

After her little game on the Ferris wheel, Damien was chomping at the bit to get back to the hotel, but Phoebe made the decision to let him sweat it out a little longer. They went on a few more rides and she tortured him a bit more. Nothing crazy, just whispering in her ear about how she was going to make him hers tonight. It might have been cruel to let him walk around with a raging hard-on for another couple of hours, but the tension building up is her favorite part about all of this.

And she has to admit, there's nothing sexier than seeing Damien Bell tugging at the sleeve of her jacket, silently begging her to take him back to the hotel room.

Phoebe slides the key into the lock as Damien watches from behind, his obvious eagerness radiating off of him.

"I'm surprised you're not pawing at me," she chuckles. "Any other day and I'd be on the bed the second we were through the door."

"You're in charge," he replies cooly as they step inside.

It's such a simple phrase, but it's intoxicating.

Phoebe grabs him by the collar of his shirt even before she hears the door click shut, kissing him hard as she pushes him up against the wall. He lets out a moan of anticipation as she unzips his jeans and loosely wraps her hand around his cock. He's putty in her hands, kissing her back desperately as she strokes him, alternating between firm, full length motions and the lightest little brushes against his cock. If she learned anything from the Ferris wheel, it's that he can stand more than a little bit of torment. God knows he's dished out enough of his own.

"Tell me what you want tonight," she whispers, nibbling on his ear.

Damien lets out a ragged breath, staring at her like he's hanging on her every word.

"Anything. Everything."

She chuckles as she glides her thumb over the head of his cock.

"I want specifics, Bell. Don't get shy on me now."

She can feel the full-body shiver run through him.

"First... I want you to tie me to that bed, Mistress."

Mistress. She likes the way it sounds as it rolls off his tongue; it's the same feeling she gets when he moans her name .

"What else?" She asks, her voice dripping with honey. "I know you're more creative than that."

"I want you to use me. Slap me, pull my hair. And when I beg you to let me come, I want you to tell me no as many times as you want to. Everything about tonight is up to you."

Phoebe steps back, placing a hand on his chest and smiles. She takes in the combined strength and softness of his features, picturing the exact look of his muscles tensing just under his clothes; imagining how beautiful he's going to look crawling for her tonight.

"Go get cleaned up. I'll get everything ready."

Damien kisses her and heads straight for the bathroom, keeping the door open just a crack and leaving things only half to her imagination. Phoebe takes in her surroundings for a moment, psyching herself up as she sheds her clothes, deciding to wear nothing but a pair of lacy black panties and a set of heels. She wants him to be able to see as much of her body as possible, and more importantly not be able to touch it until she gives him explicit permission.

She stands in front of a large full-length mirror as she slides her feet into her heels. His gift of her dainty new collar sparkles in the light, naturally drawing attention to her neckline, and all the naked skin surrounding it. Her eyes glide over the off-white stretch marks that adorn her breasts, the tops of her thighs, and around her waist. These things that used to make her feel so self-conscious pale in comparison to her newfound confidence; she's never felt more comfortable, more powerful than she does now.

There are still the little thoughts, brief but pointed: she finds herself wondering if she'd be able to live up to his expectations of her. Would she be commanding enough? Could she actually give him this thing he'd fantasized about for years? But those worries that used to have the kind of teeth that could dig in and tear away at her are now easily calmed.

"None of that anymore," she whispers. "The hottest man in the world is getting ready for you to dominate him, and you're gonna do it. You're gonna rock his fucking world."

She lays out his collar, the rope, the harness, and all the rest out on the bed. The act of preparation is calming, ritualistic in a way that soothes her buzzing nerves. She may not know exactly what she's doing, but she saw that look in his eyes on the Ferris wheel, reveled in the power she had in that moment; controlling exactly what he could feel, and when.

And then the sound of the shower abruptly ends, and every one of her self-assuring words flies out of her head. Quickly, she dims the lights, shutting the curtains and easing herself into the closest chair. She crosses a leg over the other, posing herself in a way she assumes a professional would, straightening her posture and tilting her chin up like she owns the room. The moonlight spills in, lighting her from behind and adding to the ambience, all along to the sounds of the city in the background.

At least she hopes it does.

Damien steps out of the bathroom, the tips of his hair still damp as a bit of water trickles down his gorgeous chest. He's chosen not to wear his rings or his signature silver bangles, looking a little more naked without them. Maybe he wants to give her full access to him, to his least guarded self. Just Damien, not the image he projects.

Phoebe's eyes dance up his body, staring at his chiseled abs, his toned thighs, and lingering a little too long on his half-erect cock... but it's the look on his face that really makes her sweat. Those crystal-blue eyes staring right at her, the rest of his body is coiled, tense, and waiting for instruction.

Sometimes she forgets how fucking *pretty* he is.

She draws in a long, labored breath. This is it then, she's in charge now.

"Tell me everything I can do to you, give me the list."

Damien shakes his head.

"You're in charge, Mistress."

She feels her little hairs stand on end.

"Limits?" She asks, trying to keep composed.

"I want as much as you can give me. Don't worry, I know the safe word."

He trusts himself, but more important than that he clearly trusts her as well. Phoebe casually gestures to the thick black collar on the bed with a single hand, refusing to move from her perfected pose on the chair, keeping her eyes locked on him.

"Put it on."

"Yes, Mistress."

Phoebe's already soaking through her panties, and the rich tenor of his voice is a jolt of electricity straight to her most sensitive places. She smiles to herself, remembering minutes ago when she thought it might be him who would have trouble keeping himself in-check, when it turns out she's the one already going to great lengths to hold herself back from shoving him onto the bed and fucking him senseless.

Damien walks with purpose toward the bed, slowly brushing his fingers against the collar. He playfully drags it against his skin, all the way up his chest before expertly securing it around his neck. She's surprised by how much it suits him, when days ago all she could picture of that collar was the feeling of it tight around her own neck as he choked her. He's thrown all that bravado and swagger aside for the night to be the perfect submissive.

"On your knees."

She uncrosses her legs, hoping he can't hear how loudly her heart is thumping in her chest as she spreads them. She doesn't have any plans, running entirely on instinct to guide her in the right direction. But she has to guide him as well.

Damien doesn't say a word, lowering himself onto his haunches, his palms resting firmly on his muscular thighs as he stares up at her, awaiting instructions. If she can't show him real confidence, neither of them will be able to get the most out of this. She tips her head back, acting like the hotel chair she's sitting in is the grandest throne either of them has ever seen.

She owns everything in this room, and that includes him.

"Crawl to me, pretty boy."

His cock is fully erect, and the sight of it hanging between his legs as he slinks toward her on all fours is enough to make her hand begin to wander. As his fingers sink into the maroon carpet, she slowly teases her clit, carefully alternating between wide, circular motions and light direct strokes.

Even on all fours he seems to stalk toward her, his pale eyes darkening the closer he gets. The muscles in his arms and back flex and ripple under the skin, the soft moonlight shining off what's left of the water that's still clinging to him. He finally reaches her, dutifully placing both hands on her thighs in preparation, but she leans forward, wrapping her fingers around his throat before he can begin.

"Did I say you could touch?"

"No, Mistress."

He grins, breaking character for a moment as the look on his face practically screams *you're nailing this*.

"Good." She slides her fingers out from her panties, carefully tracing his lips. "Now show me how sorry you are."

She relishes this newfound feeling of power she has, watching him shudder as his tongue slides around each digit.

"That's my good boy."

Her entire body is electrified, trying to decide what she wants to do next. What would feel the best? She can see his cock throb between his thighs, precum gathering at the tip as his breathing gets heavier and heavier. She wants everything all at once.

"Do you like that? Hearing that you're a good boy?"

He nods, meeting her gaze with an animalistic expression. Damien's eyes are hungry and focused, practically staring her cunt down as slowly wets his lips.

"I want to taste you."

His jaw is slack, and he leans in closer, warm breath fanning against her thighs, but she puts a hand in his face, pushing him back.

"Mmm, really? That's the best you can do?"

"Please, I need you..."

His voice is tight, like it's being stretched far too thin with anticipation.

"Please what? Have you already lost your manners?"

"Please, Mistress. Let me make you feel good."

There it is again, the urge to tackle him to the floor and fuck him right this second— maybe taking him by surprise would still count, maybe it would still be something she could do in her new role.

Phoebe leans forward, letting her lips hover just beyond his, torturing him in the same way that he's done to her so many times before.

"Take my panties off."

Damien is all too eager, hooking his fingers into the waistband and tugging them down her hips as she lifts herself off of the chair. He runs the fabric through his fingers, careful not to knock off her heels, all while looking at her inquisitively as he slides them past her feet. Phoebe's so used to him taking charge that it takes her a couple of seconds to realize what the look means.

"I'm sure you can make good use of them."

His eyes shimmer and he takes the initiative, wrapping the flimsy lace around the base of his cock, stroking himself lightly. She reaches out and grabs a handful of dark hair, pulling him toward her aching cunt.

"Now, don't you think it's about time you thank me for everything I've done for you tonight?" she purrs. "Show me how grateful you are."

Damien groans, diving in with zero hesitation, like he's been waiting for this moment his entire life. He immediately finds the perfect position, working her clit with the tip of his tongue, savoring her. Phoebe's head falls back and a quiet, satisfied sigh slips out from her lips.

"That's it. Slow. Just like that."

Before long he hits a particularly sensitive spot and she cries out, Damien taking full advantage as he swirls his tongue in languid circles, putting just enough pressure on her clit to make her shiver.

"Right there... *oh fuck!*"

He pushes his tongue inside of her cunt, hands wrapping around her thighs and lifting them up onto his shoulders as Phoebe sinks deeper into the chair. It feels like every one of her senses is heightened. The traffic on the streets below is louder, the light breeze from the window shockingly cool on her skin, and even the dimmed lights of their room are like bursts of sunlight. Even with all of that, all she can think about is how soft he is, almost velvety, riding the wave of pleasure as he devours her. But she doesn't want to come like this.

It's far too soon.

With a tug, he's off of her.

"Not so fast, puppy."

"But what if I don't want to stop?"

A smirk tugs at one corner of his mouth as Phoebe holds his head in her hands, a bit unsure about what to do with his insubordination.

But he solves that problem quickly, his eyes flashing with passion.

Giving her permission.

Phoebe draws herself up out of her chair as Damien gets onto his knees in front of her. She swings her hand back and slaps him across his left cheek, her breath catching in her chest as his head snaps to the right. Immediately she's mortified that she misjudged the situation, that she hit him too hard and ruined the moment.

Then he fucking *moans*, turning back to face her with a cocky grin.

She leans in close, looping her finger through the silver ring in his collar, and tugs him toward her.

"What color?" She asks.

"Bright fucking green," he replies, letting out a small giggle as Phoebe rubs her nose against his.

It's a little moment of tenderness that makes things that much fucking hotter between them, but when it fades, she takes the reins again.

"That all you got?"

"Get on the bed. On your back."

"Yes, Mistress."

Damien scrambles to his feet and flings himself onto the bed as she trails lazily behind. He spreads his arms and legs, ready for anything.

"Such a good boy."

Phoebe grabs the first spool of rope and saunters to the corner of the bed. She ignores him and his little whimpers, deciding instead to focus on the rope as she starts to loop it around his wrists, just like she'd seen him do on her. Damien raises his eyebrows, grinning up at her.

"You remembered how to tie the knot."

Phoebe struts to the other side of the bed, plucking up the second spool of rope and preparing another knot.

"I'm *very* smart, Bell."

She gives him a quick kiss on the forehead, pulling away as he tries to lean in for more, securing his other wrist instead.

"How is it?"

"Perfect," he pants.

She's fucking nailing this.

Her eyes glide up and down his naked body, tilting her head as she watches a thick bead of precum roll down his cock, her panties still bunched up around the base. She slides them off, keeping them close by. If he gets too mouthy, she can always find another use for them.

Damien's face is warm and relaxed, his eyes alight with anticipation as she climbs onto the bed, straddling his hips. With one finger, she delicately traces the engorged tip of his cock, and he moans as his head jolts back into the mattress. She crawls up his body, raking her fingernails across his chest as she lets her dripping cunt hover over him.

"I bet you'd like to fuck me, wouldn't you?" She taunts. "You want me to ride you until you're coming so fucking hard, you're losing your mind."

She can see his throat bob as he swallows, his mouth twitching in anticipation, unsure if he should respond or not. She places her hand on his chest, just over his heart, feeling it thrum quickly beneath her touch.

"You want to be inside me, don't you?"

He lets out a strangled sound, something raw and animalistic, and she hooks her finger through his collar again, yanking it and pulling him close enough that their noses touch. His breath comes out in a frenzied, staccato rhythm, ecstatic glee dancing in his eyes.

He's devouring every second of the agony she's putting him through.

"Are you going to answer me? Or do I have to teach you another lesson?"

Those words surprise her, but it's easier than she expected to lean into it, embracing this new side of her identity.

"Please, Mistress," Damien begs. "I want to be a good boy for you."

Electricity crackles between them. She can feel it on her skin.

She grips his chin with her free hand, gently forcing his lips to part with her thumb. She's embodying him, the version that he's brought to the bedroom so many times before.

"Stick out your tongue."

Phoebe leans over him, letting a wad of her spit drip from her mouth and land straight on it. He groans as he laps it up.

"There's a good boy."

She lifts her hips triumphantly, taking her time to lower herself slowly onto his cock. His thickness always surprises her, but she makes sure to stay in control. That heady mix of pleasure and a little bit of pain is too powerful to ignore and she feels herself shiver, Damien matching it with one of his own as she fully sinks down onto him.

"You want more, don't you?"

He grunts, his feet slipping against the sheets as he squirms out of sheer frustration. For all the times he's edged her, taunted, and slowly pulled her climax out of her until she was almost in tears, well... payback's a bitch. Even though he looks like he's on the verge of combustion, he's clearly enjoying it, tiny beads of sweat peppering his forehead and the bridge of his nose as his breathing gets even heavier.

Slowly, agonizingly so, Phoebe rocks her body back and forth as she massages her G-spot with his cock.

"You're all mine tonight," she moans. "And I'm gonna use you like the toy you are."

"Jesus Christ," he whines, his eyelids fluttering as he tries to keep under control.

"Mm, I learned from the best."

It feels so good— the way he fills her and stretches her, the way he looks at her like she's the most amazing creature he's ever seen. Damien doesn't need to be the one touching her to worship her; she can feel it in every breath, and hear it in every whimper.

That familiar heat rises up from the depths of her belly, and her legs begin to tremble as she continues to bounce on his cock. She twists, reaching behind her for her panties as he groans, taking the opportunity to shove them in his mouth.

"You be a good little slut and come when I tell you to come, not before," she snaps. "Nod if you understand."

Damien's muffled moan fills the room as nods excitedly, trying and failing to keep some manner of control over himself. She gently brushes his cheek with the back of her hand, feeling his thick lashes flutter against her.

"*Very* good."

Damien finally finds some purchase with his legs, bucking up and hitting her G-spot and sending her into a sudden fit of ecstasy, digging her fingernails into his skin until she threatens to draw blood. The climax is as intense as it is blinding, but her body doesn't stop, plunging down on him as hard as she can. She's sure the two of them are making some of the loudest sounds they ever have in their lives, but she can no longer make out who is who in their tangle of bliss, riding for what feels like forever through wave after wave of pleasure.

When she comes to her senses she's slumped down on top of him, Damien with her panties still between his teeth.

She pulls them out as she slides off of him, feeling him shudder.

"Oh, you didn't come after all, did you?"

"I know the rules," he groans. "But if you kept going, I might have."

"Well, even if you barely made it, you still did as you were told, so I think you deserve a reward."

His eyes light up.

"You're going to..."

Phoebe flashes him a wicked grin as he trails off, walking over to the nightstand where the final few toys he brought along with them lay in wait.

"Only if you beg for it."

Renegade

DAMIEN

If there's one thing Damien loves more than music, it's being right.

He *knew* Phoebe had a fucking beast inside of her, and now that he's seen it, he wants to see more.

He thought he was going to have to walk her through this, but she's done so fucking well, and he can't help but admire her confident strut as she slinks around in nothing but her heels.

"Please, babydoll," he whines. "I need you."

Phoebe arches a brow, leaning over the edge of the bed and Damien's toes curl, his whole body aching to release the desire that's wrapping around his spine like a vine.

"I'm sorry, I'm almost certain we discussed what you're to call me tonight." She tilts her head, her eyes flashing as she looks down at his pathetic form. He's starting to think she might have been paying more attention to his tactics than he initially thought. "So, try again."

"Mistress," he chokes. "Please, Mistress. I need your cock."

"Much better."

It was stupid of him to think she was still this innocent, inexperienced girl next door. She took to all the kink stuff like a duck to water, and it seems like however far he takes her, they never find a real limit.

With that said, though, he's been struggling a little, trying to focus on anything but how much his cock hurts as it strains in the cool air. He almost came when she was riding him, and clenched his muscles so hard he thought he was going to pop something as he held himself back from coming.

Sure, maybe it's not a bad way to die, but there's no way he's gonna let himself go before he gets to experience what's coming next.

The moonlight sneaking through the curtains illuminates her face, giving her skin a golden sheen, her warm eyes shimmering as she slips into the harness. It fits her like a glove, the two thick leather straps digging lightly into her hips as she gets used to the weight. Phoebe picks the dildo up off the bed and firmly tucks it into the slot between her legs, making sure it's secure before she turns to look herself over in the mirror. He can see how powerful she feels, her chest heaving as she smiles at her own image, glancing over at him for a moment, and back again. Tonight, she owns him. And she knows it.

His eyes dance up and down the gentle curve of her ass, her pillowy thighs that poke out of the tops of her stockings, and that curtain of dark hair that falls down her back. But when she turns to face him, all he can focus on is that thick pink dildo hanging between her legs.

She struts around to the side of the bed, the counterfeit cock bobbing with each step until it's right in front of his face. Phoebe grips his hair tight.

"Open your mouth."

Jesus Christ.

He finds himself choking, tears stinging his eyes as the cock slides past his lips and down his throat, but he feels her gentle hand on the back of his neck; she's right there to guide him.

"Relax your throat and breathe through your nose."

When he follows her command, there's almost no resistance; he feels like he might be able to take the strapon whole. She's the expert, after all, could teach classes on the subject, and he's rewarded by a hand on his cheek, and a gentle moan.

"That's a good boy."

Phoebe strokes his hair, gazing down at him lovingly as she slowly shifts her hips forward. Even in his compromised position, his eyes straining as he stares up at her, he can't help marvel. She's ethereal in this light, the soft orange from the sunset making her skin glow like the flame on a candle.

"I think you deserve a reward."

She pulls her cock from his mouth, leaving his throat hollow and just a little raw as she bends down to kiss him. He wants to make her happy, wants to worship her. But she has other plans.

Phoebe walks the distance slowly, swishing her hips from side to side playfully as she rounds the bed before climbing up and positioning herself between his legs. She leans over to the side-table, carefully grabbing the bottle of lube and popping the cap open. She starts to pour some out on the dildo, smearing it around in preparation, but Damien shakes his head, clicking his tongue to catch her attention.

She freezes, a bit of her confidence lost in the moment of perceived criticism.

"What?"

"Nothing to worry about, just... fingers first, and lots of lube." He smiles. "I'll tell you when I'm ready for more."

Her brow furrows, looking a bit embarrassed as she squeezes some more of the liquid onto her hand, and Damien can't help but flush as she holds up her fingers with an inquisitive look.

"Is this enough?"

She's so *fucking* cute.

"You'll need more once you get going." He drags in a breath. "I want you to make sure I'm nice and lubed up."

He lifts up his legs so that his thighs are flush with his abdomen. Damien has never felt so fucking vulnerable in his life, watching the confidence return as Phoebe lick her lips, squirting the excess lube onto her fingers.

The moment she touches him Damien lets out a little yelp of surprise, shivering as she circles his asshole, making it slick. It's a brand new sensation for him, taking more than a few seconds to get used to it, but before too long he can feel his cock twitching.

"Good?"

Her voice is soft but sultry, like a knife slowly tearing through silk.

"Yeah," he moans. "Fuck yeah, more than good."

"Alright, then it's time for you to give me a color."

"Green. Definitely green."

Phoebe continues to tease him, the two of them breathing in almost perfect tandem. She massages him until he's almost fully relaxed, just a little bit of the tension left from how new the sensations are, and he tilts his head, flashing her an encouraging smile.

"Alright, you can put a finger in."

She nods, wordlessly preparing for her first real foray into this kind of play, her brow furrowed yet again in heavy concentration. The first push makes him cry out as he struggles against his restraints, startling her a little bit, but it's not that she's done anything wrong. He's just so fucking horny his head is swimming. Buzzing.

"Breathe," she coos, recovering quickly from her surprise to slowly slide her finger further in. She's nothing but gentle. Comforting. "You're okay. I've got you."

Slow and deliberate.

"Feels good. You're doing so good."

A confident smile flickers across her face.

"I'm supposed to be saying that to you."

And then Phoebe crooks a finger, pressing it against his prostate, and Damien hears a sound leave his mouth that he's never heard before. He's not even sure that she's realized what she's hit, but there's no way she's missed his reaction as he spasms along to her every movement.

Her eyes are a forest fire, and he's ready to be burned.

"Well then, who am I?" She purrs.

"Mistress," he groans. "Another one."

She tilts her head with a mix of mockery and tenderness.

"You're sure? I'm not certain you're ready for that."

"I am, I'm ready," he grunts. "I'm so fucking ready."

She nods, prepping him with only the slightest push of her second finger as a hiss leaves his mouth. He clenches his teeth at the sensation, the slightest sting giving way to pleasure, and she takes more initiative, pouring the lube right onto his asshole. His body trembles, his short and sharp gasps turning to longer moans as Phoebe plants little kisses on the insides of his thighs. Her expression is soft, murmuring gentle affirmations as she fucks him at a controlled, methodical pace.

He struggles to swallow, his throat dry as she smiles down at him.

"That's it... you're taking my fingers wonderfully, just breathe."

His eyes roll back as his cock throbs and strains, but she never touches it, the anticipation just making him crave her that much more. With the mix of emotions rushing through him he feels like he could cry at any moment. She's been so sweet; even when he brought up his fantasy, this fantasy, she never laughed at him, never said it was strange. She was just curious. She's *always* been curious. It might just be the thing he loves the most about her.

"Alright, I think I'm ready."

She removes her fingers slowly, picking up the lube and drizzling a generous amount onto the strap-on. Their combined anticipation is palpable, hanging thick in the air, and he tries to calm himself the best he can. The more relaxed he is, the easier this will be.

Phoebe drapes his legs over her shoulders, only struggling a little bit with the logistics. It's exactly the way *he* loves to fuck *her*, being in the perfect position of domination; of control. Here, in the reversed spot, he savors the gentle kisses she leaves on his leg as she lines herself up, the tip of the silicone cock brushing against his asshole.

"I've got you, okay? Keep up those deep breaths for me, gorgeous."

Damien nods, and then she's inside him, every nerve feeling like a frayed wire, exploding with electricity and pain. The sensations are sharp and intense as she stretches him much wider than before. He grabs onto the sheets, twisting them hard as he acclimates to the new feelings, but after a few heavy breaths it starts to feel good— no, *great.*

"More," he begs.

He relishes the sensation of her fingernails digging into his thighs as she pushes further, watching her eyes dance down his torso and rest hungrily on his aching cock. Damien feels his lips part automatically as she fills him up more, his mouth hanging loose as he twitches and shakes around her thick cock. She smiles at him lovingly, pouring a generous amount of lube onto his cock and wrapping her hand around the base.

"Think you can take it?"

It's more than just a question, the edge in her voice making it sound like a challenge she's laying down.

"Y– yes," he moans, closing his eyes to focus on nothing but the sound of her voice, and the pure feeling of pleasure running through him. "Fucking give it to me."

She takes her time, her hips moving languidly as she slides her hand nice and slow, up and down.

"Jesus, babydoll!"

"Mm, look at how well you take me."

He cries out as she bumps up against his prostate, his eyes snapping open to see her in all her glory. Her cheeks are flushed and she begins to moan along with him, her hips picking up speed as the slick sound of the lubricant fills the spaces between their moans and sighs.

"Are you coming?" He asks in between grunts.

She shakes her head.

"Not yet. The strap—" she's stammering, lips parting. Holy fuck. This is so much hotter than he imagined. "Every time I move, it rubs me — *oh*! Feels so fucking *good*."

The last word escapes her lips like a gasp for air, and Damien takes the opportunity to remind himself to breathe.

"Are you close?"

She's clearly struggling to hold it together.

"Harder, Mistress! I just need a little more!"

"Tell me you're mine," she moans.

"I'm yours!" He can feel his balls tighten, his stomach clenching as he tries to stave off his climax for as long as he can.

"Tell me how it feels, how much you love taking my cock."

She thrusts into him harder, rougher, giving him exactly what he asked for. Sweat trickles down his temples as his toes curl, their combined moans making for the most beautiful music, and it's all he can hear beyond the sound of their bodies pounding against one another.

"Your cock, it's— It's—"

Sometimes when they're fucking he doesn't know where her body stops and where his begins, and that's never been more true than now. It's just the two of them melting into each other here.

For some reason his mind suddenly picks out an old memory, one of Johnny telling him sex was so much better when you're in love. Damien made fun of him for it, told him he was full of shit, that he was just saying it because he missed the bachelor life.

But that motherfucker was right.

She puts her whole body into it as he reaches his peak, and he cries out as she sinks her teeth into his thigh. Pain blends with pleasure so well that it sends him into an electric spiral, tugging so hard on his restraints that the headboard thunks against the wall.

A wave of euphoria washes over him and he cries out, his voice strangled and raw. It's intense, the feeling more a blissful release than normal as it ripples through him. It's the same sort of sensation, but different; he can feel *everything*. As cum spurts onto his chest, his euphoria melts away into total relaxation. He looks up at Phoebe, who's stilled, her head tipped back as she shivers in place.

A sense of freedom he's never felt before starts to overtake him, tears streaming down his temples as Phoebe pulls out. She looks so beautiful as she takes off the harness, letting it fall limply on the floor with a light thump before crawling up into bed with him.

"Careful, I've got cum on my—"

"I don't care," she murmurs, wrapping her arms around him.

Damien nuzzles against her chest, feeling his throat tighten as he tries to stay in control. He squeezes his eyes shut, and she strokes the back of his head as their legs intertwine.

"Are you okay?" She whispers.

"Yeah." He sniffles, looking up at her.

Phoebe stares at him, a mixture of puzzled and concerned.

"You're crying."

"It's a good cry." He chuckles, the tears streaming freely down his face. "You were incredible, Pheebs. You did everything right."

"I just tried to be like you," she grins.

"Would you... Would you wanna do it again?"

She nods.

"Absolutely. I had a lot of fun."

"Me too, Pheebs." The feeling of relief mixes with everything else that's been piling up, and he suddenly feels all the exhaustion hit at once. "Me too."

He feels so vulnerable like this, and yet, being here in her arms, with this quiet that lingers between them... it's the safest he's ever felt.

"I'm gonna order us champagne and run a bath," she says, caressing his neck softly.

He smiles. She even remembered the most important part of all of this.

"Extra bubbles, please."

"You read my mind."

Gently, she rolls off of him and gets to her feet, taking his hand and helping him up. For the first time in their relationship, he's the one with the shaky legs after the deed is done, stumbling a little on the way to the bath.

As she runs the water, the question he's been wanting to ask keeps running through his head, lingering just below his tongue as it chokes him. He should ask her. Right now. It would be perfect. It feels right.

She slips past him and he stops her, reaching out for her hand. She turns to look at him and he finds his mouth open, ready and willing to say everything that needs to be said, but he stops himself at the last second.

"Are you sure you're okay?"

A puzzled expression is spreading across her face.

Not yet. Maybe the party? That's when he should do it. Now it might seem impulsive, like he thought of it in the heat of the moment, still reeling from the blissful afterglow. She'd never believe it was real if he asked her now. No, the party was it. It had to be right.

"Never better," he smiles at her, pulling out as much false sincerity as he can muster. "When you order champagne, don't get the Dom Perignon. It's a ripoff."

She still looks concerned for a moment longer, but the expression breaks against her laughter before she gives him a quick peck on the nose.

"How about you climb into that bath and I'll bring you a list. We'll order whatever you want."

He smiles back at her, crushing down the screaming desire to tell her just how he feels right this moment.

"You know exactly how to take care of me."

As she bounds out of the room, he can't stop thinking about how lucky he is that she walked into his life.

That's why he has to do this right.

One of These Nights

DAMIEN
RELEASE PARTY NIGHT

"I look like a fuckin' dork," Johnny mutters.

Damien's lounging on the couch with his dress shirt still open and his bowtie sitting lazily around his neck as he watches his friend. Johnny's been looking at himself in the mirror for a few minutes straight now, finding something new to worry about every couple seconds or so. He's pretty anxious about the album release tonight, but so is everyone else. They just know how to handle it better.

"Hey, quit knocking the outfits. Those are nice suits, because tonight you're gonna be nice kids." Troy barks, snapping his fingers as he points at the two of them. "And no fighting. If those things get ripped, I don't get my deposit back."

"Who says we're gonna fight?" Johnny asks. "I've been on my best behavior. I can't say the same for this asshole."

"Don't worry, I've got my eye on them," Liam chimes in, lighting a cigarette.

Liam's been dressed since the rest of the guys arrived in Troy's room, looking professional but cool in his tailored navy suit, black tie, and ornate silver cufflinks. His black dress pants don't have a single wrinkle, and even his shiny patent leather shoes are catching the light in just the right way as he puffs on his cigarette. He couldn't dress down if he tried.

Damien's been holding it together, but he keeps finding his mind wandering to the release party. How are people going to respond to the new songs? The new sound? Will they even *want* something new? Each and every person that piles into that ballroom downstairs is going to hear their album for the first time, and no matter how much work they've put it, how sure they are that it's the best thing they've ever done, there's always a chance it just doesn't hit with the crowd; that's what's most terrifying.

And he's been hiding that fear well, but the real nerves he's been feeling have a completely different source.

Tonight is *the night,* the opportunity he's been waiting for, and the anticipation is choking him. He's been quieter than usual for the past couple of days, while they've been exploring the cafés and museums of the city and spending their nights out clubbing with the band. She's obviously taken notice, and in turn he's tried his best not to freak her out, to convince her everything's normal. But it's not normal.

The words have to be perfect.

Damien sinks back into his own anxieties, the weight of the ring in his pocket making it feel more like an anvil at this point, and he looks around the room; anything to keep his mind from spiraling.

Shaun is lounging near the window, completely calm as he plays his guitar. Liam's flipping through a magazine, his cigarette resting in his hand, only looking up from time to time at the sound of Johnny's grunts. Troy probably looks the most stressed out of all of them, smoking furiously and pacing back and forth near the doorway. Damien's sure he's making everyone anxious, but bringing it up would almost certainly make things worse.

And then there's Johnny, still struggling with his bowtie. Suits and ties aren't really Damien's expertise, but his dad forced him to wear them to church growing up, so he knows a thing or two about them.

"I can't watch this atrocity anymore. Just let me do it," Liam sighs, making his way over to Johnny.

"I'm closer," Damien cuts in, rolling over and getting to his feet before Liam can make the distance.

"Bell, you dress like an eighth grader fell into a sales rack at Saks Fifth Avenue. Let me do it."

But just before either of them reaches Johnny, Troy steps in, panic flashing in his eyes.

"Bell? What the hell is that?"

Damien blinks, unsure what's got Troy so spooked.

"What's what?"

"I think he means *that*."

Damien follows Shaun's finger to the floor where, just barely obscured by the shag carpet, he sees his grandmother's engagement ring glinting in the light.

Shit.

His stomach clenches, and he silently curses whoever invented the shallow pockets they put into suits as he crouches down and scoops it up.

"It's nothing. It's mine. Don't worry about it."

Smooth. Very smooth.

"That," Shaun says with a raised brow, "is a *very expensive* looking nothing."

"Damien, is that..."

Troy's staring right at the pocket Damien slipped the ring into, dumbfounded.

"I said it's nothing!" He snaps. "Let's just get ready."

Suddenly this whole thing, the proposal, the ring... it all feels all wrong. He can already hear the shit they're going to give him. What a stupid idea.

"No, I think we need to have a talk first." Shaun puts a hand on Damien's shoulder. "You're going Olympic-sized again, dude. This is, what, your first vacation together, and you're already going to propose?"

"Technically it's a work trip, not even a vacation," Johnny chimes in.

"Exactly! What the hell are you thinking?"

"I don't know!" Damien exclaims, flinging his arms in the air as he starts to pace around the room. "I had this big talk with my dad at Thanksgiving about how much she means to me, and I know that shit sounds cliché and maybe I'm one big fuckin' cliché, but I don't give a shit! I haven't been able to stop thinking about it since we got on the plane."

He takes the ring out of his pocket, his eyes stinging with tears.

"Every time I look at her I start thinking about what the rest of our lives are gonna be like. Every version of the future where I'm happy has her in it, so I thought... Why wait?"

Sweat trickles down the back of Damien's neck. Shaun's face is twisted up with a mixture of bemusement and worry, Troy's eyes are filled with trepidation, while Liam's stands a little removed, off to the side.

And then there's Johnny, staring right at him with a big toothy grin, and motioning for Damien to follow him out onto the balcony.

"Let's talk."

"Johnny, we don't have time—"

Johnny turns to Troy and holds up a hand.

"It's *our* release party, and what, you've never heard of being fashionably late? They can wait a little longer down there, I wanna talk to my brother."

Johnny and Damien slip past the French doors leading out onto a large patio, stepping outside into the dying sunlight. The winter chill immediately shoots goosebumps across his skin.

Johnny digs his cigarettes out of his pants pocket, handing Damien one as the fading sun paints streaks of pink and purple along the clouds. The two men stand in silence for a moment, leaning up against the balcony railing as they each take a drag.

"Not that it matters what any of us say, but I think it's a great idea."

Relief rushes through him. At least one person doesn't think he's a fool.

"It's fuckin' insane but... it's you. I know you, man, and I know this is for real. Now, that said, I just want you to remember, you gave me shit over telling Erin I loved her like three days after we met—"

Damien shakes his head.

"That was a joke, man. I didn't—"

"No, listen to me." Johnny's voice is firm. "There's no roadmap for loving someone. We're all either going in blind or we're basing everything on some self-help book, what our parents tell us, shit like that, but *no one* knows what they're doing. So you're winging it, sure, but anyone can see exactly where your heart's at the second you start talking about Phoebe."

He's right. Their whole relationship has been chaos, pretty much every plan they've made has had to be sidelined or changed or dropped completely, but they've had each other through it all.

"I used to think I'd fallen in love before, but this is so..." Damien sighs. "It's just not the same. It's something completely different."

"Why do you think I proposed to Erin? It wasn't about locking anything down, or doing what we were supposed to do. I gave her that ring because she's the love of my life, and I knew no one could make me as happy as she does."

Damien's chin trembles as he fights back the tears.

"That's how I feel about Pheebs. I wanna wake up next to her every morning. I wanna cook dinner for her, and watch her hunched over that typewriter. I want the fights and the struggles and I want her on her best days just as much as on her worst..."

Johnny claps him on the shoulder.

"Well, it sounds like you know exactly what to do."

After all that support and affirmation, Damien's surprised he's still...

"I'm scared."

"Yeah, of course you are. It's scary," Johnny rasps. "But that's life, bud. You gotta take risks. Carpe diem that shit."

"Yeah I... Actually I was thinking of doing it tonight."

Johnny squeezes his shoulder.

"Then go and fucking get your girl, dude. Dibs on groomsman, by the way."

"Really?" He snorts. "You're not even the best man in your own fantasy?"

"Aim low, and you often get pleasantly surprised."

"True, it could be worse, I could make you the usher."

As if on-cue, Troy raps on the window, his face twisted up with incredulity as he jams a finger into his watch over and over.

Ah well, so much for the heart-to-heart. It looks like duty calls.

⁓

"Your bowtie is all crooked," Phoebe mutters as she fusses over his suit.

"Yeah," he puts on his most pitiable face. "Johnny tried to beat me up."

"Well, how'd that go for you?" Phoebe asks with a little smirk. "Because I only date winners."

The crowd outside sounds a little gentler than he's used to, but then again, it's a release party, not a concert.

"It was a tie," he murmurs.

They've had no time to actually enjoy themselves, but that'll come later. Right now, he's focused on getting through this small set, and on to the much more important task at hand.

"We'll say you won."

"Thanks, babydoll."

She slips a black hair tie out of her purse and clenches it between her teeth, reaching up to tame his unruly locks before slipping behind him and securing it all into a small ponytail.

"There," she breathes. "Gorgeous."

"I thought you liked my shaggy 'do," he chuckles.

"I love every part of you," She wraps her arms around his waist. "But now you've got a James Bond thing going on, with the slicked back hair and this suit... real sexy."

"Ohhh! Hey, Shaun! You hear that? I look like James Bond!"

"Yeah, maybe if he went on a week-long bender," Shaun fires back.

Damien smiles, looking around at his friends as they go about their final prep, smoothing out their outfits. It might be the most professional they've ever looked, but it's *definitely* the most uncomfortable Damien has ever felt in his clothes.

"Okay, kids!" Troy calls from the stage. "You ready?"

Troy's nerves seem to have faded as the band makes their way toward the stage. He squeezes Damien's shoulder as they gather around him.

"You kids look great in black and red."

Shaun puffs out his chest.

"I look great in everything."

The stage lights dim and Troy steps out, disappearing behind a curtain. Shaun's tuning his guitar as Ophelia goes wild, spinning both her drumsticks into the air and catching them again. Johnny can't contain his nervous energy, bouncing up and down like a boxer getting ready for a fight, but Damien only hangs his head, taking in measured, deep breaths. It's rare that he wants to muscle through a show to get to the end, especially such an important one, but getting Phoebe alone feels so much more important.

"Good evening, ladies and gentlemen! My name is Troy Sullivan. Most of you in this room know me for my work managing the absolute hooligans that are going to be gracing this stage in about a minute—"

Johnny catches Damien's eye and walks over as Troy's speech rattles on.

"So, haven't chickened out yet? Still gonna do it?"

"Yup."

"Do what?" Ophelia asks, sitting up a little taller at her drum kit.

"Damien's gonna—"

"Ladies and gentlemen, please welcome... Revolver!"

Troy rushes backstage, the roar of the crowd following behind him as he ushers them out to the frenzy. The whole room is gorgeous, with people dressed to the nines and drinking from the most expensive glasses Damien's ever seen. He takes in the room, noting blown up versions of Phoebe's photos from the liner notes on the walls, the whole place looking like an art installation devoted entirely to the band.

Damien's heart pounds as he grabs the mic, beaming out at the crowd.

"Bonjour, Paris!" He spots Phoebe in the back of the room with a drink in her hand, his smile widening even further as all that giddiness hits him at once. "That's about the only French I know, so enjoy it. We're gonna play you four tracks from our brand new record, and uh... well, this album is real special, because I wrote all of these songs for my girl. Can't wait for you to hear them."

Ophelia's drumsticks crack together four times, crashing down onto her kit right as Damien lets out a deep, primal howl to start the first song. They're going big right out of the gate, with something more aggressive, a little closer to their old sound before they change it up.

It's only a few bars in and the crowd is already loving it, and he's loving them. It feels just like when he was back on tour, and he knows that he wants to do this for as long as his body and the fans will let him.

Burning Love

PHOEBE

He's been quiet the last couple of days. Every so often, she'll catch him staring at her for a really long time. The first time he did it, she got a little nervous. Was he keeping something from her? Had something gone wrong? But that didn't feel right, the guy built her an office and took her to meet his parents a couple months after meeting her. The old Phoebe might have taken the nerve-wracking train of thought right off of a cliff, but the new Phoebe is more curious than anything. Maybe she can pry something out of him.

That's her job, after all.

After Revolver's second song wows the crowd just as expected, she taps Janis on the shoulder, nodding toward the exit with an inquisitive look. She nods, and the two take their drinks and head out to an enclosed area, immediately refreshed by the brisk open air. The lush little garden is filled with perfectly manicured rose bushes and trees, but as Phoebe steps toward them to get a closer look, something wet lands on the back of her neck. She looks up to see little snowflakes dancing down from the black-ened sky as Janis holds out her hand, catching a couple of them.

"Hey!" She laughs. "First snow of the season!"

The night is quiet, save for the music pulsing in the background, and the errant conversations of a couple men in the distance, chatting as they smoke some cigars. The two women reach a little gazebo, carefully climbing the steps to enjoy a bit of cover from the light snowfall. Phoebe stares back at the hotel, watching people trickle in and out of the back door as Janis sips her drink with a knowing look in her eyes.

"So, what's going on?"

Phoebe takes a deep breath. Even a couple months ago she might've tried to pretend things were fine, but so much has changed.

"Do you think Damien's been a bit weird? Since we got here?"

"You've gotta be a lot more specific," Janis chuckles. "That guy is the epitome of weird. Or maybe freaky is the right word, don't think we haven't heard you two through the walls."

Phoebe rolls her eyes and lights a cigarette, handing the pack over to Janis. The first rush of nicotine doesn't even do much for her nerves anymore, but she's too deep into this habit to quit now.

"It just feels like he's been quieter."

Janis shrugs.

"Maybe a little, but Pheebs, you're not catastrophizing, are you? There's no way he's hiding anything bad from you. He adores you."

"I know that," she replies, shaking her head. "And I'm not, I just... I don't know, I guess I'm not used to this. He's been so open with me, at least since we sorted things out during the tour."

Janis looks just as clueless as Phoebe feels.

"Maybe he's gonna ask you to move in with him," she offers.

"He's already asked," Phoebe laughs. "I haven't given him an answer."

"Oh, do you not want to? Because from where I'm sitting you guys seem pretty serious."

"No, I do!" Phoebe exclaims. "We haven't been together that long, though, you know? I guess it just feels fast. I want to wait until he meets my parents at least."

"Love moves at its own pace," Janis replies, nodding sagely. "You can't really control it. Just look at me, you think I was planning to be in a throuple with two people you were doing a story on? Just ask yourself a few questions: does he make you happy? Do you feel like he respects you? Do you see a future with him?"

Phoebe smiles. Lazy mornings in bed, birthdays, Christmases, little parties, a ring on her finger, maybe kids one day... She's thought about it all.

"Yes." Her heart beats faster. "It's just... we haven't really talked about where we're going to take things– you know, as a couple."

"You should have that talk, then. Maybe his brain's running in the same circles as yours."

"You think so?" Phoebe asks.

She's only 24. She's never been this serious about a guy before, nor has she been this invested in a relationship.

"Yes!" Janis laughs. "Look, normally I might caution you against this kind of stuff, but if you're definitely looking at long-term... I think him offering to let you move in is a pretty clear sign he's in the same headspace. You really do kind of suck at this communication thing, Pheebs."

"I know," Phoebe sighs. "I think I'm just afraid to rock the boat."

Her childhood made her a natural people pleaser. If she was doing her best to make everyone happy, then nobody was upset with her. But that's not how the real world works. She's been working as hard as possible not to be a doormat, one step at a time.

"Well, take it from me, sometimes you've gotta wobble the boat a little. You love Damien and he loves you, that much is clear. If you tell him what you need, I'm sure he'll give it to you."

"Maybe you're right, but..." She coughs, clearing her throat. "So, how's it going with Ophelia and Shaun?"

Janis grins.

"You'll do anything to get out of talking about this, won't you?"

"What else is there to say?!" Phoebe laughs. "I'll bring it up to him. I kinda have to, or it'll drive me nuts."

Janis sticks out her pinky.

"Gotta promise."

Phoebe rolls her eyes as the two of them lock pinky fingers and shake.

"Promise."

"Alright, you've earned the deets! The three of us are really good. I don't know how it's all going to turn out, but they both fulfill my needs in different ways, and I think I do the same for them. I care about them both a lot."

"Is it overwhelming?" Phoebe asks.

Janis shakes her head.

"Nah. Shaun and Ophelia know each other so well. They've basically been together since they were just out of high school, far as I can tell, off and on at least. They're great about answering my questions and I never feel afraid to tell them what I want or what I need. Honestly, it's the best relationship I've ever been in."

"I'm happy for you, Jan. The communication thing is crucial. I think Damien and I would have fallen apart without it."

"It is pretty great," Janis says with a contented sigh. "And you have it too, all of this silent Damien stuff aside. That guy would bend over backwards for you. Remember what he said to Chris?"

Phoebe straightens up, puffing out her chest and putting on her meanest glare as she slides into her Damien impression.

"You come after my girl and you're gonna be leaving on a fuckin' stretcher, you understand?"

"Oh my god! That was literally him!" Janis looks a little shocked, but more amused than anything. "Yeah, that dude was ready to throw down for you. Maybe even go to jail. Gotta admit, it was pretty hot."

She doesn't typically fawn over that kind of thing, but Janis is right, it *was* hot.

"The other day Shaun was even saying that you guys look like you've been married for ten years already." Janis stirs her drink and then takes a generous gulp. "I see it too."

"It seems like that sometimes," Phoebe watches her breath float up into the cold air. "The past two months have felt more like two years, and not just because of all the shit that's gone down."

When she first started this whole thing with Damien she never pictured any of this, never had a hope in the world things would end up the way they did. Maybe that's a good thing. It means life still has the ability to take her by complete surprise from time to time.

"Hey," Janice puts her hand over Phoebe's, giving it a little squeeze. "You're not alone in any of this."

"I know. Thanks for being here, Jan."

Janis raises her glass.

"Hey, I'd love to say I came here for you, but if I'm being honest I am *all about* taking a vacation from work to bang hot rock stars."

Suddenly, Phoebe hears the sound of footsteps crunching on gravel, turning in anticipation even before she hears his voice.

"Pheebs?"

Damien appears out of the darkness with a big smile, cheeks flushed and his forehead glistening with sweat. His suit jacket is draped over his shoulder despite the cold weather, and he's unbuttoned his dress shirt a little, totally abandoning his bowtie.

"She's over here!" Janis calls, before dropping her voice for Phoebe "Don't worry, I'll take my leave and let you two do your thing."

"Do our *thing*?"

Janis rolls her eyes.

"It's like you don't even know that man at all."

Damien skips up the stairs to the gazebo, buzzing from what she has to assume was a very successful set.

"Well well well, I was just looking for one hottie, but I found two!"

Janis giggles and tucks a strand of hair behind her ear.

"I don't know how you ended up so charming, Bell, but please don't ever stop complimenting me."

"I literally can't. It's a disorder at this point, I think." He grins. "But hey, Shaun and Ophelia are looking for someone to do shots with and I dropped your name. I think they may have heard of you."

Janis wraps an arm around Phoebe, her friend leaning in close enough that she can smell juniper and lime from the cocktail on her breath.

"Make sure you tell him," she whispers.

"Tell me what?" Damien laughs.

"Oop, good ears, Bell! Gotta go!"

Janis skitters back into the hotel, patting Damien on the shoulder as she slips by. Phoebe's cheeks flush, and Damien tilts his head, walking up the steps toward her.

"Tell me what, babydoll?"

"Nothing. Jan's just had a few too many drinks."

"You sure?"

She looks out at the garden, the lightly falling snow now having coated the flowers and trees in a soft dusting of white. She knows exactly what she needs to say, she just has to open her mouth and say it. That's always been the hard part.

"Pheebs, remember our last fight? We said we'd talk about–"

"Why have you been so quiet?" She asks.

"I haven't–"

"Yes, you have. You keep staring at me, and when I ask you what's up you don't say anything. Or you tell me it's nothing." She reaches out, brushing away a strand of hair that's fallen in his eyes. "I know it's not nothing."

"Pheebs, everything's fine," he laughs, his hands jammed in his pockets. "I've just been thinking about you– well us, and what it all means."

Shit. Maybe Janice was right. He wants an answer about moving in together.

"Oh, Damien, I know I haven't given you an answer about moving in together, but I just wanted you to meet my parents first. You understand, right? That step is important to me."

"No, Pheebs, I get it!"

His gaze is so intense, his eyes so soft and inviting, she finds herself fighting not to get lost in them.

"Okay, I just– I just want them to see how happy I am; that I'm with someone I see a future with."

She's surprised to see her remark catch him off guard.

"A future?"

"Yes," she breathes. "I'm... I'm in this for the long term."

He's only stunned for a moment, but all of that quickly melts into a warm smile.

"Pheebs, we're absolutely doing New Year's brunch with your parents. I'll be polite. Hell, I'll wear a tux, a top hat and monocle, or whatever the fuck your mom wants me to do."

"She doesn't want you to be the Monopoly man, Damien," Phoebe giggles, picturing the ridiculous image. "But maybe for Halloween."

"Well, I'd do it if that's what it took! I'm sorry I waited so long to give you an answer about meeting your family. You didn't deserve that. I was... being selfish." He looks and sounds so brutally sincere it takes her off guard. Somehow she was expecting him to just spin off into another goofy speech, but he's going in hard. "I *love you*, Phoebe Miller. And you're right, I have been quiet. That future with the two of us? That's all I've been thinking about; because I've been trying to figure out how the fuck to do... *this*."

He slides his hand into his pocket as Phoebe's heart slams into a staccato rhythm.

"You remember that morning when my mom and Ava were showing off my baby pictures?"

"Yeah. I remember."

"When I went into the kitchen to help my dad with breakfast we got to talking. Lots of stuff, father-son, kind of humiliating really– you don't need to know the details. The thing that matters is... well, he gave me something. I was planning something big, to figure out a perfect time, but the second we got on that plane I knew I wouldn't be able to wait it out."

Slowly, he slides his hand out of his pocket, a beautiful ring nestled in the center of it. She doesn't know if it's the cold or the circumstance, but all of the sudden she's shivering like crazy as he lowers himself onto one knee.

"Damien, what are you doing?"

"Something really stupid if it doesn't go the way I'm hoping," he laughs through newly formed tears, his body shaking right along with hers.

Phoebe feels like everything around them has faded to black; the only thing she can see is him, and that ring in his hand.

"My grandpa said my grandma made him want to be a better man, said it was the reason he married her. I never knew that growing up. My dad only told me when we were alone in the room, and he did it because I told him the same thing about you. Every morning, I want to do more for you. Be more for you. I want to give you the whole entire world, because that's what you deserve. That's how much you mean to me."

Phoebe covers her mouth with both hands.

"I need you to know that you can turn me down, but it doesn't mean I won't ask you again in six months, a year, two, three, four... god, I'll wait ten fucking years if that's what it takes."

She laughs, brimming with a joy that's tinged only with the tiniest bit of fear.

"I'll wait for you forever, Pheebs. I want to live with you, and fight with you, and get old with you, and fuck you—" He grimaces. "I shouldn't have said fuck- uh, make love- no, that's..."

She crouches down, bringing them eye to eye. She can feel her heart in her throat as her eyes well up with tears.

"I'm fucking this up."

"No," she whispers. "No you're not."

Damien stares at her as she presses her forehead against his.

"You see me, Damien. You've shown me so many parts of myself that I'd never have found on my own. In the short time I've known you, I feel like I've come so much closer to being the me I've always wanted to be. And fuck, maybe this is all gonna blow up in our faces, but I refuse to picture a future that doesn't have you in it."

She's never been more sure of anything in her fucking life.

"I want to marry you."

He lets out a deep sob as he flings his arms around her, the thunk of the ring falling onto the gazebo floorboards startling them both. Damien jumps up and untangles himself from her, searching blindly as tears rush down his face.

"Fuck! I didn't mean to do that." He kisses his fingertips and raises them up to the sky. "Sorry, grandma! And sorry again for cursing!"

There's a brief moment of panic as Damien fumbles around for the ring while Phoebe waits, pressing a hand on her chest to calm her thumping heart, but he finds it quickly, snatching it up and beaming as he slides it onto her finger.

"Oh, thank god. I wasn't sure it was going to fit."

They stare at each other for what seems like an eternity, Phoebe feeling like she might have to pinch herself to make sure this isn't a dream, but it's the ring that brings her back to reality.

It's the most beautiful thing she's ever worn.

From a distance, the sound of a camera shutter startles them both, and they raise their heads just in time to catch a photographer scurrying back down the path toward the hotel. She can feel the panic begin to fill her, but as she looks back to Damien there's only calm contentment in his eyes,

"Let him go." He grasps her hands, holding them tight. "This is all I care about right now."

Free Bird

PHOEBE

The bartender back in the hotel was kind enough to let her use the phone in the staff room. He was a little tentative, but relented when she told him it was to call her family and let them know she was engaged.

Phoebe holds the receiver in one hand, not knowing exactly how the conversation is going to go. It's about 5:00pm in New York, so her mom should be home. Dinner's always at 6:30, the second her dad walks in the door from work, so there shouldn't be a chance she'll miss them.

Damien is sat down next to her, sipping on a glass of scotch as she dials. He looks a little tense, but probably nowhere near as much as she does. Either way, she wants him to be here– at least for moral support, but maybe to talk to her parents.

And this time, he didn't even argue.

With every ring, every second she doesn't hear someone's voice on the other end of the line, she gets more and more nervous. Maybe her mom had a bridge game tonight? Or it could be her book club. Wait, does she still do book club? She did when Phoebe was a kid, but it's been so long. Samantha Miller's always loved to host parties, taking any opportunity to schedule another event in her home to show it off. Maybe she's just too busy to answer.

As she's prepping to leave a message, annoyed to have missed connecting yet again, the line finally clicks.

"Hello?"

She lights up, excitement and anxiety perfectly blended in the slight waver of her voice.

"Mom!" Phoebe exclaims. "Mom, it's me!"

"Phoebe? Oh, Phoebe, I've been trying to call you! Where are you?"

"Paris, mom. I left you a message, you didn't get it?"

"A message?" She sounds confused, but at least she's not mad. *"Oh, shoot. Your father must have fiddled with the machine again. You know, I keep telling him to stop doing that! He should know not to touch it by now, never figured out what half the buttons do."*

Phoebe chuckles.

"Yeah, sounds like dad."

"So, what are you doing in Paris? Are you working?" She gasps. *"On no, you didn't lose your job, did you? You know, I read this article in the New Yorker that said that all of these creative jobs are dying, that people need to focus more on practical careers that have longevity! You could always go to secretarial school if this falls through— did you get my message about that?"*

Phoebe's eyes slide over to Damien. He's heard every word, but he's kept still, staring straight ahead.

"Mom, I still have my job. Actually, I got a promotion! And I was even on TV!"

"TV? What for? For something good, I hope!"

Phoebe chuckles nervously, doing her best to push past her anxiety.

"Yeah, it was something good mom. But um, listen, I have some news."

"Oh, Phoebe, are you coming to brunch? You're not spending the whole month in Paris, are you? It's got to be so expensive, and being away from your family for New Years?"

"Jesus," Damien mutters into his glass.

"We're definitely coming, mom. That was in the message dad erased."

"Wait, we? Who's we?"

"Me and my boyfriend. His name's Damien, and... well, he's the lead singer for a band. Actually, it's one that I wrote about. We've been together for a few months, since their last tour and..."

She takes a deep breath. It's now or never.

"Actually, he proposed to me tonight."

There's heavy silence on the other end of the line but she holds it together. At least for a good half a minute before she digs her teeth into her lip so hard she tastes blood.

"Mom? Are you still there?"

"Yes..." Her mother's voice sounds distant. *"Engaged, that's... wow, Phoebe."*

"Yeah." She smiles at the memory, still fresh in her mind. Every detail is crystal clear, down to exactly how the snow looked as it fell around them. "It was so romantic."

"Hmm."

Phoebe can practically hear the disappointment dripping through the phone. She knows how it sounds; obviously it seems really fast to anyone who wasn't there. It probably sounds crazy, and it makes total sense that her mother would be worried about her. But she's the happiest she's ever been, fully embracing the next steps. Besides, her parents got married right out of high school after dating for six months– it's not like her mom really has a leg to stand on here.

"You'll get to meet him!" She promises. "You'll love him, mom. He's sweet and charming and... he makes me happy."

"It's just awfully fast, isn't it? I was watching Donahue the other day and he had this lawyer on who said that divorce rates are through the roof– oh, and the birth rate?!" She scoffs. *"People just don't care about family like they used to. Everyone's so focused on themselves these days."*

Phoebe clears her throat.

Her mom listens to daytime TV the way some people listen to sermons. Every sentence is gospel.

"I just thought you'd be happy for me."

"I am, sweetheart." Her voice grows higher in pitch, but there's a slight disconnect, like the emotion isn't really there. *"It's wonderful, truly. Does he have money? It's important that he takes care of you. Especially finan- cially. These rock stars, they spend all their money so fast. Does he have an accountant?"*

Damien's clutching his glass like he wants to crush it in his fist.

"Of course he takes care of me, mom."

"Oh, so you said you'll be here on New Year's?"

"Yes," Phoebe replies. "Of course we will."

"Wonderful. Listen, I have to get going. I've got a roast in the oven. I'll see you when you get back, okay, sweetheart?"

"Okay, mom."

The line goes dead and Phoebe leans back.

"I thought she'd be pissed." She sighs. "That went better than I thought."

He chuckles.

"She asked you if I had money."

"Damien," Phoebe warns. "We're not doing this right now."

"I know, I know." He takes a long breath, probably pulling himself out of snark-mode. "She's just being a mom, right? Mine can do the same shit sometimes. But remember what I said, tuxedo, tophat, monocle... whatever she wants me to wear. Monopoly man is still on the table."

"You know, It might ease her fears about you running out of money."

"Or make them worse," Damien snickers. "Depends on how expensive the suit looks."

Damien wraps her in a warm embrace, just holding her there in silence for a while.

"I can't believe we're engaged."

"I know, it's a lovely feeling." She glances at the floor, taking a big breath. "But how long do you think we have until it gets out into the wild?"

"A couple days, at best. Someone definitely saw us tonight, but who knows what exactly they got on film. Anyway, I can get Troy to talk to the label; send something out to the press so we get to control how it gets out there. We should enjoy the quiet while we can, though, just keep it between the lot of us."

Phoebe slips the ring off of her finger and places it on her other hand with a sad smile.

"Wish we didn't have to do this."

"We really don't," Damien replies, draining what's left of his drink. "But the release party would definitely morph into an engagement party real quick if word got out."

Phoebe shrugs.

"I mean, everything's already set up, right? Free party."

Damien chuckles.

"Hey, despite what your mom thinks, I've got the money to throw us a real one. Hell, we could rent out the Louvre. They love me over there."

She rolls her eyes with a smile.

"Do they?"

"Come on!" He exclaims, taking her hand and leading her to the door. "It's me, after all. All I'd need to do is slip them a couple hundred and flirt a bit, they'd shut the whole thing down the second they got a glimpse of these baby-blues."

"Wow, so I get you *and* your delusions for the rest of my life, huh? What a deal."

"That's right, Miller. And remember the ancient holy rule of engagements: no take backsies."

Phoebe steals a kiss, slipping around him and skipping back into the main hall as he jogs to catch up.

No. Not a single part of her would ever want to take this back.

It's been quiet. A little too quiet after three days of waiting, but Phoebe would rather not jinx it. For now, she's enjoying the thrill of being engaged.

Today they decided the morning would be all for seeing Notre Dame, their planned path taking them right along the Seine. The view is spectacular, with fresh snow covering the ground, all the way up the tops of the buildings as well. A few minutes back they ducked into a little shop to pick up more film. That was her excuse, at least. The real goal was to snatch up a little tourism book, because apparently Damien Bell doesn't believe in the need for maps.

Over the last few days Phoebe's found that she can't take enough pictures in this city, something new to be enthralled by around every single corner, be it architecture, fashion, or just people out in their day-to-day routine. There's just something so special about this place.

Maybe they could come back here and get married, have a little honeymoon in the French countryside. Her parents have never been to Paris before, at least as far as she knows. It'd be a nice trip for everyone, and despite what her mom said about it being too expensive, Phoebe's pretty sure she'd love it here.

Damien yawns, and she chuckles behind her camera, snapping away.

"Bored, or tired?"

"Just tired," he replies, glancing down at his coffee cup with a frown. "I don't think this stuff's doing the job. I thought it was supposed to be better in France, right? Isn't this supposed to be the land of bread and coffee?"

"Well, it tastes better," she laughs. "But I don't think that comes along with more buzz for your buck, my love."

He grumbles to himself, taking a sip as Phoebe snaps yet another picture of him, perfectly in focus with the cathedral looming in the background. The architecture is exquisite, almost jaw-dropping, and only more so when they finally get up close. She doesn't really know where to start, her eyes flicking back and forth over each detail.

Damien, on the other hand, quickly zeroes in on the one thing he'd obviously love the most, pointing straight up to the roof of the building.

"Check those out!"

The gargoyle he's locked onto looks as gruesome as it is gorgeous, its head cradled in its own hands. She pulls out her little guidebook, flipping through to the big section on the cathedral, pretty certain she's found the exact same gargoyle to show him. The photo is detailed, the creature's tongue sticking out like it's ready to spit down on anyone who dares stand below it.

"That's this guy! Check out what he looks like up close."

Damien leans in, quirking a brow.

"Huh. Looks a bit like Troy."

She snickers, bumping him with her shoulder.

"Apparently it's called a stryge. They're bad omens that feed on human flesh and blood. Better watch your back."

His face lights up in a moment, looking much more excited.

"Think they sell replicas? I could put one in Troy's office, imagine his face when he sees it!"

"I think he'd hit you with it."

The inside of the cathedral is even more stunning than the outside.

High, vaulted ceilings, chandeliers casting down warm light from overhead, massive stone pillars and black & white checkered floors all spread throughout, the ornate stained glass windows providing a kaleidoscope of colors that refract and land on everything in view. Even Damien looks a little awestruck as they take everything in.

"Holy... fucking... shii—"

"Damien!" She hisses. "If there's anywhere you should be watching your mouth..."

He turns to her, his shoulders already shaking as he fights against the oncoming snickers.

"Babydoll, I don't know if you remember, but the last time we were in God's house, you had my di–"

Phoebe stomps on his foot, shaking her head and dragging him off behind a small tour group. Unfortunately, the guide seems to only be speaking French, but there's still something fun about listening to the cadence of their voice as they point out different fixtures of the building.

Phoebe sighs, letting all of this beauty wash over her.

"This place is amazing."

She's snapping pictures every few feet as they walk, wondering how many funerals, masses, christenings, and whatever else this building might have seen. How much joy and sorrow, how much humanity filled these walls over the centuries since it was built.

"Do you... think people actually get married here?"

"Nah," Damien replies. "Too many tourists darting in and out, I think they'd mess things up. And imagine what you'd have to pay to make it worth their while to shut things down for a whole day?" He tilts his head, a tiny grin creeping across his lips. "Wait, why? You wanna come back here and rent a big church? Do the whole traditional thing?"

Phoebe hums, slipping her fingers into his open hand. She's never really thought about what her dream wedding would look like, only little details. She'd always pictured a gorgeous dress, and she'd need some of her friends there, maybe some of her close family, but really she'd be fine getting married anywhere.

"I'm not really super traditional."

"Me neither," he laughs. "I'd marry you today in someone's backyard. I don't give a shit."

Phoebe stops in her tracks, glancing down at her engagement ring sitting on the wrong finger. She spins it around, her heartbeat picking up as her mind begins to race.

"What if... what if we did?" She asks.

"Did what?"

"Got married. Today."

Damien starts to laugh, pressing his hand to her forehead.

"Are you feeling okay, babydoll? What about the planning, what about our families?"

"I mean... We can have another ceremony back home," she replies. "I'm feeling great. Better than great, actually, and I think you are too. So we should do it. We should get married."

He stares at her, a mix of incredulity and excitement painting his face.

"You want to get married, three days after we got engaged? Damn, Miller, I thought I was the impulsive one!"

She stands stock-still, letting the tour group wander off ahead of them as she caresses his palm with her thumb.

"I've never been this sure about anything before. The trip has been incredible, better than anything I could have imagined, and I don't mind waiting but... It just feels right. I'm ready to take the next step, if you are."

Everything about this could go wrong, but deep down, she's sure it's the right step for them. They've been the very definition of impulsively chaotic since moment one, and since everything else has moved at the speed of light and worked out fine, why should this be any different?

Troy has had his head in his hands for what has to have been 5 minutes straight, mumbling to himself in disbelief. Liam, in contrast, is bouncing on the balls of his feet, clearly extremely excited with the idea. They decided to tell the two of them first, the moment they returned to the hotel, just in case there were some horrible logistical issues that needed to be talked through. Really, though, Phoebe was hoping to maybe get some help organizing this whole thing.

The goal is to get married in the hotel, find the nicest room they can, or maybe even do it out on the terrace, but they'll take what they can get.

Beyond that, they need a minister, but Damien said he's almost sure Liam told them all he was ordained back in the day. Apparently he's got the certificate hanging in his office.

It's like this was all meant to be.

"It's like you *want* me to have an embolism!" Troy finally looks up at them, so red in the face she feels like he could pop any moment. "I'm convinced that's it. You *cannot* give me a moment's peace, can you?. You know what I was doing before this? I was smoking a big cigar and eating soup. *Excellent soup!* That's what I wanted to do on this trip, not listen to two lunatics–"

"Troy–"

Phoebe tries to cut in but he waves his hand, silencing her immediately.

"I have no control," Troy continues, glancing helplessly around the room. "I'm the management, the one who *manages*, and I have no control! This is some sort of cosmic joke."

"Oh, come on Troy! Look at them!" Liam grins. "They're sickeningly in love. I think it's a marvelous idea."

"Seriously, Liam?!" Troy barks.

"Troy, please, and I say this with all the love and respect in the world... I think you need to take that stick out of your ass. It's been in there so long I'm worried about internal bleeding."

This is going far better than Phoebe expected. At the very least she was certain Liam would be telling them they were being too headstrong, so it's a pleasant surprise to see him... almost giddy about this? Troy, of course, is another story as he strokes his chin, staring at them for another uncomfortably long time before he speaks again.

"Alright. Okay. Just be real with me for a second. This isn't a joke?"

Damien puts his hand on his heart.

"Scout's honor."

Troy nods. And nods.

And then he keeps nodding, as if the act will make him feel better, but apparently it's not quite doing the trick.

"You know what? I don't believe you!" Troy insists. "You're fucking with me, you're always fucking with me so why would this be any different!

He groans, rubbing his eyes before he drops himself onto his bed.

"I didn't even bring my blood pressure pills with me because I was convinced that we were going to have a nice, *relaxing* getaway."

Damien squeezes Phoebe's hand.

"Troy, it's not a joke, we're sure about this. We talked it over and we're ready to jump in. Both feet."

"You just got engaged three days ago! Three days, Bell, come on!"

"People elope all the time," Phoebe argues. "When you know it feels right, you know it feels right."

Phoebe doesn't care how crazy this looks. Time is fucking relative, right? She wants to go back to New York as Phoebe Bell. Or Phoebe Miller-Bell. Or Phoebe Bell-Miller, or–

"We're doing it, Troy. And you can either help, or you can pout and ruin everyone's day. Which is it gonna be?"

Damien's tone is still snarky, but there's a bit of fire in his eyes. He looks serious enough about this that even Troy can probably tell it's not time to question his intentions.

Troy sighs and glances over to Liam.

"How fast can we get a real tuxedo for this clown?"

Signed, Sealed, Delivered

DAMIEN

The food is all laid out, carefully plated along with more bottles of champagne he'd ever have expected could fit in such a small space. They've transformed the bed into a big sofa, currently occupied by an expectedly casual looking Shaun. He's learning to play the wedding march on his guitar, because of course he is. They can't have a ceremony without music, right?

Outside, the sun is shining a golden honey hue, illuminating the terrace. It's such a gorgeous display that Damien wishes he could really enjoy it, struggling to ignore the knots forming in his stomach as he stares back at himself fixing his bowtie in the mirror.

"God, I'm more nervous for this wedding than any show, even one that could make or break us," he chuckles.

"Well, even a high-stakes show is something you know inside and out," Johnny offers. "This is... Well, it's big, dude."

Johnny's right, of course he is. Damien's never made this kind of commitment to someone before. In an hour or so he's going to be a husband, and their lives will be changed forever.

"So, have you guys talked about the future at all?" Johnny asks. "Get any further on that whole 'moving in' situation?"

"Not really, but we can figure it out. I didn't really know you were supposed to talk about stuff before the wedding. I was just excited."

"Wait, what were you doing in between suddenly deciding to get married and now?" Shaun asks. "You didn't talk about what the future's gonna be like at all?"

"We wing everything, dude." Damien sighs, wringing out his hands. "But alright, I'll bite: what should I have asked about?"

"Kids, definitely. Maybe how you're planning to handle finances..." Shaun trails off. "Like, is she planning to keep working, you know shit like that! Johnny, help me out here."

"How about where the two of you wanna live? Not just moving in, like, long term. Have you talked about how you handle conflict, and how it's working for you? Oh, here's a good one! How are you gonna handle being away from each other on tour? Is she coming with you every time, or..."

Fuck, maybe there were some things they should have hashed out.

"You and Erin talked about that stuff?"

"Yeah, dude," Johnny chuckles. "It was the conversation we had right before we got engaged. It's how we decided we were ready."

Damien exhales, his cheeks puffing out as he runs his hand through his hair.

"Shit... I didn't even think of any of this."

"Not a surprise," Liam replies as he flips a page in a magazine. "You're a bulldozer, Bell."

"Shut up, man!" Damien flips him off and Liam retorts by blowing him a kiss. "Wait, actually, did you and Brendan talk about this stuff?"

"Well, we can't get married," Liam replies. "Not legally. But, yes, we had a similar conversation prior to moving in together."

Maybe they've done this all wrong. He doesn't even know if Phoebe wants kids, or what her idea of their future looks like. Hell, he doesn't even have any of his *own* answers to all these questions. God, what if he was too focused on the wrong thing, only thinking about *his* big moment, *his* proposal.

"Okay, so do you think we should talk about it now?"

"Well, you're getting married in forty-five," Liam chuckles. "So, unless you're planning to back out, I think you might have to save it for the honeymoon."

"No fucking way I'm quitting now." It doesn't matter how everyone else did things, they're not him. He's ready for this. He's been ready for this since he had that talk with his dad. "I got this, things are gonna be fine. Now, where's Troy?"

"Getting the rings. He'll be back before the ceremony. Oh, before I forget, do you two have your vows prepared?"

Damien pauses, panicked all over again.

"I thought you were going to handle all that, you're our minister right?!"

Shaun pinches the bridge of his nose to keep from laughing and Johnny claps Damien on the back, flashing him an encouraging smile.

Liam, on the other hand, just has a bemused look on his face.

"I tell you what to repeat, yes, but did you two want to write anything of your own?"

"I..." He tugs at his bowtie. Suddenly it's fucking strangling him. "I don't... we didn't really talk— God, I gotta see her!"

He takes off toward the door and Liam calls after him.

"Groom's not supposed to see the bride before the wedding! It's tradition!"

"Yeah, well, fuck tradition!" Damien fires back as he whips the door open and sprints to the room down the hall.

Ophelia answers the door, a glass of champagne in her hand, and her hair meticulously curled, piled on top of her head with a few pieces framing her face. He's taken aback for a moment, not knowing quite what to say.

"Bell? What are you doing here, you know the rules."

"I have to see Pheebs." Damien brushes past her, giving her a quick pat on the cheek. "You look gorgeous, by the way."

Only a few feet in and he realizes he might have miscalculated: the room is empty save for some half-filled beer bottles and a bouquet of flowers.

"Janis and Erin went to pick up some more film and some more ciga-rettes. They'll be back in time," Ophelia replies. "What do you mean you have to see Pheebs?"

Her voice has a sharp edge to it as she stands in the doorway, sipping her glass of champagne. She's staring him down.

"Damien James Bell, you start talking right now, and don't you dare tell me you've got cold feet. I'm the only one here and If I'm the one who has to break Phoebe's heart, I'm throwing you out that fucking window myself."

Her voice is a soft hiss, but Damien can hear the blow dryer on top of it, coming from the bathroom. Phoebe must be in there.

"It's not cold feet." He sighs. "The guys just got in my head is all, I have to talk to her about our future."

"You had two hours to do that, bro," Ophelia laughs. "And at least a few days since the engagement."

"If one more person tells me I should have– Look, I was so fuckin' excited to get married that I forgot to ask, okay?"

Ophelia chuckles, sidling up and giving him a pat on the back as Damien takes a sobering breath.

"You look like you're gonna puke, big guy." She steps back and hands him her glass. "Take a drink, might get your mind off things."

He takes the drink with a grateful nod, knocking half of it back in a single go.

"She's in the bathroom?"

"You're not supposed to see the bride before the wedding, you know. It's bad luck."

Damien shifts awkwardly, shoving his hands in his pockets, not knowing quite how to handle this.

"Talk to me, D. Tell me what's really wrong."

"I don't know, Phi, I was just so excited for this whole thing I got us both jumping in without thinking. I want to do it right, make sure we don't start things off on the wrong foot, but now it feels like we're both heading off of this big, scary cliff. I mean, what the fuck do I even know about her?"

"What do you– Are you kidding me? You're ridiculous, I need you to know that. Sure, you dove into this quick, but that's because you're in love! All a wedding ends up being is a big party that you leave with a piece of paper, and all that piece of paper says is you want to be together forever."

She steps right up in front of him, pressing her finger into his nose.

"And that's what you want, right?"

"I do."

Ophelia smiles, adjusting his shirt collar.

"Love is a never-ending exploration of another person, and this is exactly how it was supposed to go down for you two. All the rest is the little shit, stuff you figure out as you go."

Trust Ophelia to have more insight than a fucking self-help book. She doesn't ramble on as much, either.

"Just take a second, finish that drink if you need to, and when you're ready, knock on the door. I'm gonna go next door and make sure that everything looks great, including the rest of the guys." She finishes with his shirt and gives him a kiss on the cheek. "If everyone looks as frazzled as you I've got my work cut out for me."

"Thanks, Phi."

"Any time– oh, and if you ever want to pay me back for this favor, I'm sure I could use a free wedding singer."

"Nah, I think I'm done with singing. I could break out my standup routine though, how's that sound?"

"Wow, yeah, that'd be a great way to get me to kill someone on my wedding day," she laughs, heading for the door. "Go get her, tiger."

Damien glances at the bathroom door, stalling as long as he can until he hears the blow dryer click off, quickly replaced by the sound of Phoebe's slightly off-key singing.

It's *Modern Love* by David Bowie, because of course it is.

He wraps his fingers around the door handle and pushes it open, finding her belting the lyrics into a can of hairspray. She looks beautiful, in a pale blue gown with tiny diamonds on the straps and bodice, the skirt clinging to her hips as she sways to the music.

Damien waits for her to finish, only starting his applause as the final note leaves her lips, catching Phoebe by surprise. She yelps, spinning on her heel and hurling the can of hairspray straight at him without a moment's pause. He'd like to think that on a less stressful day he might have dodged it, but he'll never know; today, at least, it cracks him right in the forehead.

"Ow! Pheebs, Jesus..."

"Sorry, oh god, Damien, I thought you were— Wait, why the fuck were you just standing in the doorway?!"

"I was listening to you sing!"

She rushes toward him, brows pinched together with concern.

"I'm *so* sorry," she mutters. "Oh god, did it hurt? I'm really sorry, I just- You shouldn't sneak up on people like that!"

Damien shrugs it off, content to see his reflection isn't covered in blood.

"You've got a hell of a pitch, Miller."

"Yeah, sure, I bet I could go pro. Now what are you doing here?"

Damien chuckles, his nerves flooding back in.

"I have to talk to you."

He really should have written some of those questions down. Kids, finances... What the hell else was there?

She's watching him carefully, tilting her head as worry eclipses her face.

"You wanna back out."

"No! Not at all, we just need to talk about some stuff."

His hands glide up her waist and he nuzzles against her cheek. She holds him so tenderly, her fingers playing with the hair at the nape of his neck.

"Damien, talk to me."

"We have to talk about the future- I mean, the guys asked about- and it just... it didn't even occur to me to talk about any of this shit." He takes a breath. "Pheebs, I'm freaking out."

"We're getting married in like 45 minutes," she laughs.

Damien thought of the two of them, *she* would be the nervous wreck and *he* would be the one to calm her down, but life has a way of surprising you.

"I know, and I still want to do that. Believe me, I do. I just love you so much, and I need to do this right." Damien takes a big breath, steadying himself. "Look, it's a bit messy, but I'm gonna ask you all the questions I can remember, and then we both answer honestly, alright?"

Her hands move down to rest on his belt and she stares at him, entirely calm.

"Like a lightning round in a game show."

"Exactly!" Damien exclaims, the buzz of excitement taking over from his earlier anxiety. "Okay, we'll do the big one first: Do you want kids?"

"Not right now, but eventually. I'd like to focus on my career first, and you should too. Make sure we're both where we want to be in life before we make a big leap like that."

She didn't even hesitate.

"Okay, cool. I— yeah, that's a great answer."

The gentle tugs and jingles of her toying with his belt makes his heart skip a beat.

"And... you feel the same?"

"Yeah," Damien breathes, his focus suddenly split between the questions and her busy hands. "We don't have to jump into that stuff right away."

"Of course not. But I *do* think we'd make pretty babies," she breathes as she slides the leather out of the belt loops. "When we're ready."

"Is this turning you on?"

It's a stupid question, Phoebe's hungry expression is threatening to devour him more every second.

"Seeing you in that suit, all helpless and anxious, it's kinda hot." She works the buttons on his dress pants and his mind goes blank. "You need to relax, Damien."

"Fuck, Pheebs, we gotta have this conversation."

"We are. I'm just clearing your head." She spits on her palm, stroking him nice and slow. "Keep talking to me."

Well, they said they wouldn't use sex as a replacement for communication, but they can do two things at once, right?

"How are you gonna handle me being on tour all the time?"

"Phone sex exists for a reason, Damien. And hey, we found out that we're *very* good at it."

She releases his cock and hops up on the bathroom counter, tugging him toward her. Her cheeks are flushed and her pupils expand as she continues to take her time with him, gliding her thumb over the tip.

"Ask another one."

"Fuck..."

"Come on... for me?"

He can't help himself, lifting her and hiking her dress up as he sucks on her neck.

"How are we going to... uh, when there's a conflict, how are gonna problem solve?"

Nailed it.

"I don't know... like this?" She pulls her panties aside and drags the tip of his cock between her soaking wet lips. "We're pretty good at this part, too."

She winds her legs around him and Damien sinks all the way into her with a slow, measured movement, each of them letting out their own sinful groan. It's just what he needs, something more than logic. Maybe he didn't actually need answers to all these questions; maybe he just needed a little bit of reassurance.

"I'm starting to think some of these questions are pretty dumb."

"You think so?" She moans, speeding up her own movement. "I think it's kind of cute that you're the one who wants to be prepared for once."

What started out slow and sensual quickly becomes frantic as the sound of Phoebe's moans fill his head. His fingers tangle with the dog tags around her neck, forcing her head back as he slams into her. He tugs on one of the crystal-encrusted straps of her dress with his teeth, pulling it down to reveal her gorgeous tits. He wraps his lips around one, sucking with gentle pulsing motions that match the speed of his hips.

"I fucking love you."

She shudders, keeping the pace as best she can.

"Show me, babydoll." He buries himself deep into the crook of her neck, sucking the biggest hickey he can manage into her skin. "Why don't you be a good girl and come for me."

His hands are everywhere, pinching her nipples, gripping her thighs like he's never going to touch her again, and finally tangling in that sea of gorgeous, dark curls. He gets to have this forever. Her softness, her intense vulnerability, her laughter, her brilliance... it's all his.

"I can't wait to make you my wife," he groans.

Phoebe's eyelids flutter as her climax ripples through her, her muscles twitching violently. A familiar buzzing sensation starts in the back of his skull, trickling down through his body like water. Within seconds, it's consumed him, and he's coming so fucking hard he can't help but slam a hand against the mirror as he cries out. His hips crash against her, feeling nothing but pure euphoria, as his lips brush against hers.

"I don't think I could ever stop kissing you," he breathes.

He takes a breath and pulls out of her, only relaxing for a moment before zipping up his pants and scrambling to grab some tissue to help her clean up. Damien helps adjust her dress, getting it all back in order before she turns around, her fingers gliding over her brand new swollen hickey as she smiles.

"Sorry," He chuckles, "Got a little carried away."

"I've never known you to apologize for marking me up, Bell."

Damien's arms snake around her waist, pulling her close as he kisses her bare shoulder.

"Okay, maybe I'm not *that* sorry." He plucks her collar off of the counter and fastens it around her neck, stepping back to admire his work. "There. Now it stands out even more."

She beams.

Damien can't take his eyes off of her. He presses his cheek against her shoulder blade and breathes deeply.

"Okay, one last question: should we open a joint checking account?"

Phoebe laughs, fixing a few final strands of hair in the mirror.

"Where did that come from?"

"Shaun said we should talk about finances." He replies, puffing his chest out. "I'm being proactive, getting my shit together, all that stuff adults are always going on about."

"We're gonna be okay, Damien. You know how I know?"

"How?"

He lifts his head, finding himself immediately calmed when he sees the serene expression on her face.

"Because it's us, and no matter what happens, we always make it through."

She looks so sure about this, and it makes him feel that much more confident that they're taking the right steps. The rest of the world may not see it that way, but fuck what they think.

"So don't rush. We've got all the time in the world to figure these things out together."

Born To Run

She really thought she'd be more nervous on her wedding day, but instead there's only a deep sense of calm washing over her.

The only part that's bothering her is it's all already going by too fast. Nobody told her things would be over in a heartbeat.

Thank God Erin's taking pictures.

Damien stands out on the terrace overlooking the city with Liam and Johnny at his side. Ophelia, Troy, and Janis made a little makeshift aisle for her to walk down, scattering pink and white rose petals on the floor. They even managed to scrounge up some candles to add that special golden glow to the room.

The shutter on her camera clicks and Erin takes a step back, giving the thumbs up.

"That's gonna be a good one." Erin says, snapping a picture of Ophelia and Janis as they ensure there isn't a hair out of place on Phoebe's head. "You guys, I think this might be the best you've ever looked."

"This'll keep those curls out of your gorgeous face," Janis murmurs as she secures a stray lock of hair with a hair pin. "I know he's already seen you today, but once you get up there, he's not gonna be able to stop looking at you."

Phoebe's heart thunders and she can feel her legs begin to wobble. She shouldn't be this nervous, it's just their friends after all. Just her friends, and his friends… watching them get married. God, they're getting married.

Phoebe glances at Janis, looking for any positive affirmation she can get.

"This isn't stupid, is it, doing it all like this?"

Should she have been less impulsive? She'd been feeling a kind of freedom in Paris that she's never really had in New York, at least not since they got back from the tour, and it just felt right. Here they can just be Damien and Phoebe, two random people in love. At least when he's not actively putting on a show.

"I mean, it is a bit, yeah," Janis laughs. "And this may be the two and a half beers I've had talking, but that's love, baby. You can't slow it down and you sure as hell can't stop it, stupid or not."

"Are we ready?"

Erin spins around and snaps a picture of Troy before he manages to cover his face with a practiced hand.

"Campbell, I've told you before, point that thing at me and you'll get it back in pieces!"

"Don't you dare," Phoebe laughs. "It's mine. And we're ready— oh, wait…"

In all of the chaos, she didn't even think about who was going to be walking her down the aisle.

"I think I already know the answer, but would you be the one to…?"

Janis squeaks and flings her arms around her.

"I thought you'd never ask, of course I will!"

Phoebe offers Janis her arm, her body alight with nerves as the two of them link elbows as Troy gives a sharp whistle and the chatter in the room settles down almost immediately. She watches in awe as Damien turns to face her from his spot on the terrace, his dark feathered hair blowing gently in the breeze. He rubs his hands together, blowing on them to keep warm, and she can't help but notice the tip of his nose is glowing red.

You look beautiful, he mouths.

Troy puffs out his chest as he steps forward, always excited to be the center of attention.

"Ladies and gentleman, talk show sensation, Phoebe Miller!"

Shaun starts to play his guitar, and Phoebe recognizes the melody immediately: *I'm on Fire*. Almost instantly the waterworks start, and Phoebe reaches up to wipe away her tears.

"Don't you dare cry all that makeup off," Janis whispers. "That shit was expensive."

She laughs, the joke only making more tears trickle down her cheeks, but when she looks over Janis is crying too.

"Oh my god. Hypocrite!"

"Look, I'm allowed to cry, my best friend's getting married!"

She can hear Erin snapping pictures, but she's barely taking in her surroundings, completely unaware of all the eyes on her as she looks to Damien. Her legs are trembling like leaves as she finds herself consumed by his gorgeous eyes, shimmering in the dying sunlight.

When they reach the threshold, Johnny extends his hand to help Phoebe and Janis make their way out onto the terrace. Shaun's guitar comes to a gentle pause, strumming the final notes right as Janis releases Phoebe with a kiss on the cheek.

And there he is, looking like a prince with his hair styled and swept carefully out of his face, dressed in a charcoal suit with a silver bow tie and white button-up.

Liam glances around before he clears his throat. He's dressed in a black suit, with a thick turtleneck underneath, his light brown skin glowing in the sunlight.

"My beautiful, beautiful friends..." Liam stretches out his arms. "We are gathered here today to celebrate the... admittedly very sudden union of Damien James Bell and Phoebe Lynn Miller. Each of you are here because you're important to Damien and Phoebe's journey– or in my case, you just happen to be a gorgeous man who's also an ordained minister. I cannot think of a better place to have this wedding than Paris, a place we've all been told a hundred times is the most romantic city in the world. Damien and Phoebe have each found the person who completes their little puzzle, and they share a bond that not many people have the fortune of experiencing. While I've only had the privilege of witnessing Damien and Phoebe's love for a short while, I can tell that this is a relationship built on mutual trust and respect."

Damien winks at her, his eyes glittering as Liam turns to face him.

"Now, do the future bride and groom wish to say a few words, or would you like to repeat after me?"

They didn't plan this part either, but Damien looks confident, pulling his shoulders back and standing tall.

"I think we're gonna wing it, right, Pheebs?"

"Seems to be working out so far," she grins.

Damien reaches out and grasps Phoebe's hands.

"Pheebs– er, Phoebe— I guess it should be Phoebe." He glances over at Liam for guidance, who chuckles, only shrugging his shoulders in response.

Sure, they don't have to have everything planned out to a T, and they don't know every single thing about each other, but why would they have to? A relationship would be so boring if there were no surprises in it. No matter how well you think you know someone, there's always something new to uncover, and that's part of the fun; it's the beauty of falling in love, finding the good parts, the ugly parts, and everything else along the way.

"Pheebs, the second I laid eyes on you, I knew exactly what I wanted. You had this shell around you and I know I was a dick to you in the beginning–"

Everyone laughs, but Damien shakes his head, some regret lingering in his eyes.

"No, it's true. You didn't deserve the shit I gave you. I don't even know if I should be saying this in our wedding vows, but I'm just speaking from the heart." He clears his throat and Phoebe feels a lump growing in hers. "But the more you opened up to me, the more I saw this brilliant woman who is so quick on her feet and so curious about the world around her. You had the exact energy that I look for in people. I remember that interview in Portland where it was just the two of us eating burgers on a shitty hotel bed, talking about music, and movies, and what bars we liked to hang out in. You were so fucking warm and so real. I think that's the day I fell for you."

He brings her hand up to his lips to kiss her engagement ring.

"We've only been together for a couple of months, but you've changed me. And maybe this is gonna blow up in both of our faces, but there's nobody else I'd rather have beside me during the fuckin' chaos. If I had to do this all over again, I'd do it the exact same way. You're my entire universe. Every time I look up at the stars, all I see is you."

Tears stream down her face, but off to the side she sees Johnny flicking away tears of his own.

"That's so lame, Bell," he chokes.

"Super dorky," Shaun agrees, his own eyes glistening as well.

Damien's speech seemed to hit all of them, with Janis and Ophelia sobbing behind her. She's shocked to see that even Troy is misty-eyed.

"That's it. That's all I got."

Liam turns to Phoebe and smirks.

"You wanna follow our resident Poet Laureate?"

"I don't know if I can," she chuckles. "But I'll try."

All she has to do is speak from the heart. It can't be that difficult, but as she strains and struggles to find the perfect words, they're simply not there. So, she closes her eyes and takes a calming breath, assured that she'll find them along the way.

"Damien, when I first met you, I thought you were a pompous, condescending asshole."

He grins, nodding along.

"I like it when she talks dirty to me."

She clears her throat, hoping to remind him that these are *her* vows.

"*But*... you surprised me. In a lot of ways. And it didn't take long for me to realize just how sweet you really are. Then, the more we got to know each other, the more I realized... I wanted to love you, to be loved by you. And the stronger our relationship got, the more I was willing to fight for it. All the press, all that bullshit they write about us... none of that matters to me anymore. You've changed me, opened me up to a world I've only ever dreamed of. And now I get to live in it every day with you. I love you, Damien. And I always will."

Damien lunges for her, arms outstretched, but Johnny yanks him back.

"Dude, you have to *wait*!" He hisses.

"Sorry," Damien mutters. "Sorry."

Phoebe laughs and turns to Liam.

"I don't think I've got anything else."

"That was perfect," Liam whispers. "Do we have the rings?"

"Oh, fuck, that's me. Hang on!"

Janis rushes inside and comes back a few seconds later, holding a box with two white gold wedding bands inside that she hands off to Liam. It's the first time Phoebe's seen them, and she can't for him to slip one onto her finger.

"Repeat after me. I, Phoebe Miller, present you, Damien Bell, with this symbol of our everlasting love."

"I, Phoebe Miller, present you, Damien Bell, with this symbol of our everlasting love." She manages to slide the ring on his finger despite her quaking hand.

"Damien, repeat after me. I, Damien Bell, present you, Phoebe Miller, with this symbol of our everlasting love."

He slides her wedding band onto her finger. His hands are clammy and cold, but she's not sure if it's from the snow that's begun to fall, or if it's just nerves.

"I, Damien Bell, present you, Phoebe Miller, with this symbol of our everlasting love."

Liam grins at them both, the light making his gray eyes glisten.

"By the power vested in me, and the beautiful city of Paris, I now pronounce you husband and wife... *Now*, you may kiss."

"Fuck yeah!"

Damien flings himself toward her, scooping her up off the ground and swinging her around as he kisses her. The rest of the world falls away and all she feels is him. Phoebe runs her fingers through his hair and he breaks the kiss, pressing his forehead against hers.

"I love you, babydoll."

They've both waited for a love like this their entire lives. They've dreamed about it, written about it, and sung about it. Now that it's in their grasp, neither of them ever wants to let it go.

"I love you too, Damien."

Cold As Ice

DAMIEN

UPSTATE NEW YORK, NEW YEAR'S DAY

She's been eerily silent the entire drive up from SoHo, all of the euphoria of their wedding and the whirlwind that was the rest of their Paris trip has worn off, and now the two of them are faced with a slightly more sobering reality.

They got back into the city two days ago, holing up in Damien's house and only leaving to go to the bodega or to get some groceries. It wasn't the plan, but once Damien caught some photographers following them around the grocery store he decided to grab a few days' worth of essentials and lock them down until the trip to Phoebe's parents' place for New Year's.

The trip itself has been its own source of mildly building anxiety for the both of them. Pretty much the first thing she did after they got in from their flight was call her mom and left a message to confirm they were still coming.

She never got a call back.

So, that's what led them here, sitting in Phoebe's parents' driveway wallowing in a slightly awkward silence.

Damien's eyes rake over the modest-looking peach and white Victorian home that towers over the street. It looks inviting, with a small rose garden and a perfectly manicured lawn. The shades have been pulled open to let some of the morning light in, but Damien can't see any signs of life.

"You okay?" Damien whispers.

He watches her chest rise and fall as she glances back over at him. She's been just sitting there, and it's clear that she's caught between an obvious desire to head on in and share her good news, and some underlying fear of what could go wrong.

"I'm just hoping this all works out okay."

"And if it doesn't?"

She lets out a long, heavy sigh, shaking her head.

"I really don't know. A few months ago I'd probably just roll over, but..."

"You're living life on your terms now Pheebs. Just remember, we play nice, and they'll play nice too."

Her lips find his cheek and he smiles. He hopes he can provide at least a few moments of warmth in the midst of all the anxiety that's weighing her down. Besides, just look at how well their Thanksgiving visit with his parents went, despite his expectations. How bad could it really be?

"I want to thank you ahead of time for coming with me. Just in case things get complicated and we get... distracted."

"Hey, you're my wife. It's my job to be here for you. I'm just sorry it took me so long to get my shit together over the visit."

It's another couple minutes before she's ready, but soon enough they're climbing out of the car and dragging out their bags of Christmas presents they picked up in Paris. French wine, perfume, some books, and of course some toys for her brother's kids. It's an expensive peace-offering, but it'll be worth it if it smooths things out.

Damien whistles in an impressed tone as they climb the stone steps to the front door, his eyes falling on a large copper knocker placed right in the center of the soft peach door. Phoebe reaches right past it for the doorbell and pushes it quickly before taking a step back, immediately grabbing his hand. He's not sure if it's the nerves, or to keep him from ramming on that door-knocker, but he can swear he feels the pulse racing all the way to her fingertips.

"Pheebs, you're gonna be fine." He gives the warmest, most calming smile he can muster. "It's gonna go great, I promise I'll be on my best behavior."

And they wait like that.

And they wait.

And wait.

And wait.

Damien taps his foot, leaning in for the doorbell again, but Phoebe stops him with a squeeze of his arm.

"She heard it, trust me. She's probably just still pissed it took so long for me to get back to her."

"Hey, I don't know the woman, but I feel like that's... a lot," he whispers.

"Yeah, well, that's my mom," she sighs. "Sometimes she's a lot."

Suddenly the door flies open, as if Samantha Miller heard her cue and rushed to the stage. She looks strikingly like Phoebe, but with much shorter, feathered hair that's been dyed a strawberry blonde color. She's got piercing black eyes and a longer nose than Phoebe, but they have the same lips, and almost the same smile.

The resemblance shouldn't surprise him, but does all the same.

Her eyes land on Damien first, and he stands as straight as he can as she looks him up and down, lingering briefly on the gift bags, Phoebe's hand on his arm, and finally right on his face. After consulting with Phoebe he had decided to wear a black button-up shirt and a pair of dark jeans, while Phoebe picked out Ophelia's dark blue sweater dress and matched it with black tights and boots, a leather jacket shrugged over her shoulders.

Just as he's preparing to explain whatever the woman decides to criticize, Damien's surprised to find her mother reach over and wrap her arms around the two of them, pulling them in close for a tight hug.

"It's so wonderful to see you, sweetheart!"

He feels his brows peak on his forehead, completely against his will as he processes what's happening, and Phoebe gently pats her mother on the back, looking equally confused.

"Oh, yeah, it's... it's good to see you too, mom!"

"Come in, come in!" Samantha chirps, turning around and floating back inside the house.

Damien looks at Phoebe, speaking in a bewildered whisper.

"So uh, what the fuck?"

A relieved smile creeps up, all her color flowing back into her face.

"I don't know, she... She seems like she's in a really good mood."

The caution in her voice is already slipping away, replaced with excitement. She's obviously really happy, and he's going to do everything he can to keep it that way.

As they step inside, Damien slips off Phoebe's coat, intent to make as good a first impression as possible.

"Where can I hang the coats, Mrs. Miller?"

"Oh, please, dear. Call me Samantha!"

The surprisingly cheery tone of her voice is still triggering his fight-or-flight, but he's almost certain it's all in his head. She's making the effort, and so he will too.

She takes their coats and hangs them, puttering around about as busy as anyone could in their own home with Phoebe following close behind.

"Mom, I was hoping we could talk about—"

"Pheebs?"

He turns to see a man with dark hair, slightly taller than he is, leaning up against the doorway with a book in his hand. He's in a light gray t-shirt and a pair of black slacks, looking as comfortable as can be, and something about his presence is immediately relaxing.

"Mike!"

She rushes toward him, but by the time she's in range he's thrown his arms around her, pulling her into a tight hug.

"Hiya, kiddo, and congratulations! Mom told me the news."

"Oh thank god, for a second there I thought *the news* had already spread on its own." Damien chuckles.

Her brother untangles himself from Phoebe walks over, offering his hand with a confident smile.

"I'm Michael."

"Damien."

"Yeah, I know. I'm sure you get this a lot but I'm a big fan, actually." He lets out an awkward chuckle. "That new album? *Wow*. I've been playing it pretty much non-stop since it dropped. Honestly I'm pretty sure the wife wants to kill me, so you might have to watch out for her."

Damien hooks his arm around Phoebe's waist, beaming.

"Thanks, man. If it helps share the blame around, your sister was my muse for pretty much the whole thing."

"Your father's in the living room, Phoebe." Samantha's still busying herself around the house, striding in and out of the other room. "You should go in and say hi, the two of you! I'm sure he's excited to meet this strapping young man."

When she's out of earshot Michael gives them both an apologetic smile.

"It was brave of you to show up today," he whispers. "She's been in maximum 'host-mode' all morning. You won't get a moment's peace until she's set you up with every possible accommodation."

Phoebe shakes her head, still looking a little bemused.

"I'm just happy she's in such a good mood. When I called her from Paris she was really bubbly until I told her about us getting engaged. She basically flatlined and changed the subject."

"Well, I don't know about that, but you two are all she's been talking about since we got here," Michael replies, glancing behind him and keeping his voice soft. "She's definitely got you on her mind."

Michael leads them down a long hallway that's filled with family photos. Seeing Phoebe at 10 years old, smiling awkwardly with the rest of the Miller clan... it's extremely cute. He does notice, though, that she always looks happiest in the photos with Michael. It's nice to see that even after all the years of feeling like she has to measure up to him in some way, they actually do get along really well.

Stepping into the cozy living room, with its crackling fireplace and warm, inviting decor, Damien finds himself a little more at ease. Plants sit in hanging-pots, dangling in front of some large windows that overlook the backyard, and a stack of magazines pepper the coffee table in the middle of the room, where a man he can only assume is Phoebe's father sits, leaning back in a stiff-looking green sofa. He has salt and pepper hair that's been slicked back, casually dressed in a thick-knitted navy sweater and dark slacks. He's looking up from his newspaper, his deep blue eyes fixed on Damien from just over the top of the page.

Damien reaches out his hand.

No better time than the present.

"Mr. Miller? I'm Damien Bell. It's a pleasure to meet you, sir."

Silence fills the room, and Damien can already feel the tension building, crushing him. Maybe her parents hate him already. Maybe he's missed his chance to make a good impression. But he can't give in that easily. Anything it takes to make this all work out.

The man eyes Damien's ring-adorned hand with trepidation for a few more seconds before dropping his newspaper, grasping it firmly with a curt shake.

"Damien, yes, it's nice to meet you, I'm Louis Miller." His voice is a little bit pinched, but Damien can't sense any overt distaste in it. And then there's his disarmingly warm smile. "I have to be honest, son, I thought you'd be showing up in a mohawk, leather pants, and nothing else, so this is quite the pleasant surprise."

"Dad," Phoebe sighs. "Come on."

Samantha's still puttering around, putting a tray of vegetables and a pitcher of cucumber water out for everyone to share.

"Oh, Phoebe," Samantha chuckles as she places even more snacks on the coffee table. "Let your father have his fun, it's so rare that he gets one over on anyone."

"I don't think I could pull off a mohawk," Damien cuts in, doing his best to keep things light. "I'd probably go bald before trying something like that."

Louis releases Damien's hand, in silence. He looks mildly amused, clearly not upset with the joke, but not quite sure how to react. It's possible the Millers just aren't used to this kind of thing. When was the last time Phoebe said she had someone over to meet her parents again?

But before he can open his mouth and dig himself any deeper, a high-pitched squeal slices through the tension and saves the day.

"Auntie Phoebe!"

Damien spots a little blond boy high-tailing it toward Phoebe, and she catches him in a crouching scoop, lifting him into the air.

"Hi, sweetheart!" She coos, giving him a peck on the cheek. "Sorry they're late, but we got you some goodies for Christmas. From *Paris*. Isn't that cool?"

The boy nods and Phoebe carries him over, raising her eyebrows with a grin before putting him down right in front of Damien.

"Billy, this is my... boyfriend, Damien." Phoebe's smile widens. "And Damien, this is my nephew, Billy."

Demoted to boyfriend, but it's just until she can tell her family. Best to not let 'husband' slip out so casually like this.

"Hey, bud!"

He crouches down, sticking out his hand. Billy giggles and shakes it, his eyes immediately locking onto Damien's arm.

"Whoa! Cool bracelets! What are they made of?"

"You know what? I don't even really know. What I do know, is they'd probably look cooler on you than on me, wanna wear a couple for the day?"

"Oh, I don't know if..."

Samantha's interruption is cut off almost immediately by Michael stepping forward.

"It's fine mom, Tara lets him play with her jewelry all the time."

A blonde woman slips into the room from behind him, nodding her head as she sips from her coffee mug. She's got a toddler attached to her hip. Looks just like her.

"Don't worry Samantha. He loves this kind of thing."

She waves at Damien, and he smiles back at her, winking at the kid at her side as Michael steps forward.

"Hear that, champ? You can wear them, just make sure you say thank you to Uncle Damien, all right?"

"Thank you, Uncle Damien!"

"No problem, kiddo." He helps Billy slide on a couple of bangles, ruffling his hair as the boy shakes his own arm, clinking and jangling them together. "There. Now you look like you could take my job."

Samantha smiles, nodding to herself as she returns to whatever work she can find, her lip twitching ever so slightly as she backs out the room. Phoebe wasn't exaggerating. This is a woman who definitely believes 100% that she knows what's best.

Phoebe hands out the bags for gifts, making sure they all find their spots with the right people, and Her father's eyes light up as he pulls out their carefully chosen box of cigars.

"Oh!" He laughs, the joy on Phoebe's face almost palpable as she watches him. "Cubans! Thank you, Phoebe!"

"I hope I got you the right brands." She grins as she sits back down next to Damien. "I haven't had a look at a box of cigars in years."

Louis looks like he's going to chime in, but it's that moment when Samantha glides back into the room, glancing down at the box as she sits next to her husband.

"Oh, Phoebe," She sighs. "That was very thoughtful of you, but your father promised he was going to start cutting back. Cancer is a serious thing, you know."

Louis's frowns, but he says nothing.

In fact, the entire room goes completely silent, every other member of the Miller family glancing between each other for some clue to what to do next. Then, when the tension had hung for just long enough to feel like it was choking him, Samantha bursts into laughter.

"I'm just *teasing*, everyone! You all should know better than to think I'd say something like that! It's a *lovely* gift, Phoebe. Thoughtful as always."

Damien puts an arm around Phoebe, looking over at her to find a mix of relief and confusion on her face. Everyone seems to be having a similar reaction, a few tentative chuckles trickling into the room as they all smile awkwardly.

"Oh," Phoebe mutters. "Thanks, yeah, I just remembered dad liked them..."

Damien looks over at Samantha, her face still turned up in a warm looking smile. There's a little bit of something else though, something he can't quite place. He just wishes she'd stop looking straight at the two of them.

"Oh, Pheebs I just remembered! Tara and I managed to catch your appearance on the Midnight Hour."

God bless Michael, coming in clutch.

"You were incredible!" Tara gushes. "So articulate! And you handled that ambush really well."

"Oh, thank you," Phoebe grins, sitting up straighter. "I don't think he meant it to be an ambush exactly, but I wasn't going to let him steamroll me."

"Mom, dad, did you guys see it?" Michael asks. "I have it on tape if you want a copy."

"Of course, Michael, do you think I'd miss my daughter's public television debut?" She tilts her head, looking straight over at Phoebe. "It was wonderful, dear, you answered every question with dignity and poise. I wish they hadn't brought up that other disgusting article, though. To think, all the things that man wrote about you–"

"And how was Paris?" Michael asks, hopping to the rescue again as he pours each of them some water.

"Oh, well, it was amazing," Phoebe gushes. "We went to the Louvre, Notre Dame, and we got to walk the Seine... Ooh, and there were these wonderful boutiques and bakeries. I think we ate pastries every single day."

Her mother looks her up and down and as Phoebe tells her story, pushing the plate of vegetables a bit closer toward her. Something about her face when she does it puts Damien on edge, but she's so busy rearranging everything that it's possible he's imagining things.

"I'm going to go and check on the quiche, but make sure you eat some vegetables, I made more than enough for everyone!"

Her voice is a little pinched as she walks out of the room, and Michael stands up to follow her.

"I'll be right back. Gonna go help mom."

As he leaves, everyone goes silent again, glancing around awkwardly while Phoebe quietly munches on a carrot.

"You should try some of the cheese too, your mother got it at a farmer's market in Jersey," her father announces, pointing to another plate. "It's, oh dear... goat brie, I think."

Phoebe nods, forcing a smile.

"It looks good."

Damien's considering marching right into the kitchen and having a chat with Samantha, almost certain at this point there's something going on, but Phoebe must have sensed his intention because she puts a firm hand on his leg. In the meantime, Michael's wife makes her way over and takes a seat in the armchair across from them.

"Sorry, I didn't get the chance to properly introduce myself. I'm Damien."

"Tara, It really is lovely to meet you." She turns. "And Phoebe, I have to say, that engagement ring is gorgeous. I've heard The Enquirer ended up getting some blurry shots, but I can't imagine they do it any justice." She pauses, suddenly looking a little embarrassed. "Not that Michael or I have any interest in that trash, it's just what a lot of people are talking about these days."

He's a little worried the talk of more tabloids might set Phoebe off, but she only smiles, looking much calmer now that her mother's out of the room.

"Oh, don't worry about it, we're both well aware of how often we've been showing up in that rag, so we're used to it by now. And thank you! It was Damien's grandmother's ring."

"So, Damien, how did you propose?"

Tara looks extremely excited, absolutely living for the tale of their little engagement, but Damien can't help but notice even Louis seems a little interested, his eyes darting up every once in a while as he pretends to read his newspaper. But before she can begin they all hear Samantha call for him from the other room, and he excuses himself, patting Phoebe on the shoulder as he passes by.

The moment he's gone, Phoebe's face scrunches up in a clear attempt not to show how upset she is.

"I'm so sorry about that," Tara whispers. "Things aren't usually this uncomfortable, Phoebe can tell you. I have no idea what's wrong."

"I'm pretty sure I know," Damien sighs.

Phoebe sniffles as she holds back her tears.

"I'm sorry, it's me, I– mom must think I was ignoring her all those times she called, and she's trying her best she just–"

Tara shakes her head and moves to sit next to her, plopping her toddler down to play with Billy who's still enthralled with Damien's bracelets.

"Hey, you don't have to apologize," Tara whispers. "I don't think it's you, you haven't done anything wrong."

"It's just... every time she looks at me like that, I feel like I'm 10 years old again."

It hurts to watch her ache like this, to know that no matter what she does or how many expensive gifts she brings home from Paris, that her mom will find something to hold against her. Right now it's him, or maybe that she didn't call back right away, or maybe even that she hesitated before agreeing to brunch. It's starting to feel like the buzzing pleasantries are straining under the weight of all of the things Samantha Miller would rather not be happening in her life.

"Michael and I were actually surprised when she said you were coming, because she had just told us you were in Paris... I don't think you could have torn me out of that city for anything."

"We almost didn't come," Phoebe sighs. "But I wanted to. I wanted mom to see how happy I am, that I'm doing well. I just want her to stop worrying about me so much. I feel so terrible when she worries."

Phoebe lets out a deep, shuddering breath, and Damien recognizes the little ritual she does when she needs to calm herself down.

"Sorry you two, I'm gonna go and fix my makeup before brunch. I'll be back in a minute."

She gives Damien's fingers a squeeze before she stands to leave, and Damien slumps down onto the floor, ready to roughhouse with Billy.

"So, you never answered my question." Tara slips down next to him, picking up her younger son and pulling him onto her lap. "How did you propose?"

Damien grins. If there's one thing that'll take his mind off of this brunch atrocity, it'll be telling his favorite story in the world.

Landslide

PHOEBE

Phoebe dabs away the tears with a tissue, staring into the mirror with her makeup bag open beside her. She carefully places concealer on the blotchiest parts of her skin, blending it out with her finger as she keeps up her slow, steady breathing.

All they have to do is get through brunch, and then they can go back to Damien's place and relax. Just a few more hours of enduring her mother's disappointed stares and they can leave. She can cry in the car if she needs to; when it's over they won't have to worry about things for another year.

"You can do this," she whispers, angrily thrusting a finger out at her reflection, trying a slightly sterner approach to her usual self-talk. "You've fought for your job, your relationship, you laid Chris out on the goddamn floor... Hell, you went on TV and *mopped* the floor with the guy running the goddamn show. You can handle another few hours with your own mother. Tell her what you came here to tell her and she'll see how happy you are. She'll realize how wrong she's been. And even if she doesn't, you *will* get through this brunch."

Phoebe packs up her makeup bag and tucks it back into her purse, checking her teeth for lipstick before heading back out into the house. As she passes through the hallway, she notices the kitchen door ajar, a mix of Michael and her mothers' voices slipping out, both soft, but fuming.

"Michael, will you please get off of my back? Just pass me that serving tray."

"You're making her feel like shit, mom."

"I'm not, I've been nothing but polite this whole morning!"

"You are," Michael insists. *"I don't think you're doing it on purpose, but you're—"*

"Stop being so dramatic, Michael" Samantha groans. *"Phoebe's always been sensitive, you know that. I'm just looking out for her! If she's happy, then I'm happy, but I'm not completely sure about this new turn her life has taken."*

Phoebe can feel the panic begin to rise inside her. She shouldn't be hearing this. It's private; she can't be eavesdropping on her mother.

"Look, mom, like I said, I don't think you're doing this on purpose, but have you ever thought she might be so sensitive... for a reason?"

There's a long moment of silence before her mother responds, her voice sickly sweet.

"Michael, please, you know I only want what's best for the both of you, I always have. The only reason I'm so particular about Phoebe's life is because... well, look at her! She's not stable like you, she's struggling out there on her own and she needs my help."

The sound of the fridge door shutting makes Phoebe jump. There's a long silence and she clings to the wall, her heart slamming against the base of her throat. She feels like she could throw up.

"The promotion and being on TV is all very impressive, but what's she going to do in ten years when none of that matters anymore? And what about him? They got engaged so quickly, what if something goes wrong between them? What if they're not ready? I'm just concerned, Michael, You understand, don't you?"

She can hear footsteps from the other end of the hall, and she quickly darts back into the bathroom. She can't imagine how mortifying it would be to be caught eavesdropping on her own family. She'd never hear the end of it.

But she was right, at least. Her mom *does* want what's best for her. And could she be right? Of course she and Damien love each other, but they both had their doubts back in Paris. Maybe it was too fast. Maybe they should have put a little bit more time into planning things. Maybe she should have asked her mother for advice.

Phoebe stares at herself in the mirror.

"Fuck, Phoebe, you might owe her an apology..."

She opens the bathroom door, planning to slip into the kitchen without a fuss, and maybe tell her mom she's sorry for not calling. Sorry for not keeping her up to date, but she almost jumps out of her skin when she finds her father waiting in the hall.

"Your mother said she'll be done soon, and she'd like someone to help prep. Would you mind giving her a hand with that, Phoebe?"

She nods without a word, and he gives her a quick pat on the head along with his warmest smile.

"That's my girl. She'll be so happy to have some one-on-one time with you; she's been talking about how much she's missed you all week."

Phoebe says nothing, only giving him a demure smile as she heads into the kitchen. Of course her mom wants what's best for her. It's her mom, she's always been in her corner. Sure, she's a little abrasive from time to time, a bit pushy, but it's only because she's had to fix Phoebe's mistakes so many times in the past.

She slips into the kitchen silently, immediately noticing that Michael's no longer present. Her mom probably got him to see her side of things, that's the way stuff goes after all. She's always been very convincing.

"Phoebe! Come in, come in! You can help me plate the rest of this food."

She smiles politely, taking her spot beside her mother and gets to work. Her dad was right, she's just excited to see her. Phoebe can feel the guilt begin to bubble up. Why did she avoid calling for so long? Why did she make her mother worry again?

"I'm glad we're getting a chance to chat, just us girls."

"Yeah, me too, mom. It's been a while, hasn't it?"

"Far too long, I'd say."

There's none of that venom she expected in her mothers voice. None of that cool icy judgment. She really must have been imagining things back in the living room.

"So, Phoebe, tell me a little bit about Damien. He seems very interesting, and so polite! How did you two meet?"

She can feel her body tingle at the mention of him, unable to hide her smile.

"Well, it's kind of what I told you on the phone. He was the subject of my latest story, and we sort of... fell into each other's lives. We didn't actually get along very well at the start, but after a week or two we realized how well we got along." Phoebe glances down at the table for a second, her cheeks flushing red. "I'll... spare you the details, but we ended up clicking really well."

Her mother nods, passing some fruit and little pastries along the table for Phoebe to plate.

"I should hope so! I'm guessing that's why you got engaged so quickly? Because of how well the two of you ended up clicking? I have to admit Phoebe, I was a little surprised when you told me. It all seemed like it came out of nowhere. I mean, from my perspective he's a stranger, and suddenly my little girl's engaged! You understand, don't you?"

She nods. It makes perfect sense, there's no way her mom could know what she knows about Damien, but that's why she's here. To show her how much he's done for her. How good they are for each other.

"Yeah, I'm sorry mom, I know I should have kept you in the loop a little better. Everything all happened so fast, though, and with all the pressure from my deadlines, the press, the tour... I sort of let a few things slip. I promise, I'm not going to let that happen again."

Her mother puts her hand on top of Phoebe's.

"I know you won't, dear. You've always been so thoughtful. I think that's why I was so shocked to begin with. It's not that I don't like him, obviously I want you to be happy more than anything, but you can see where I could get the idea that his... influence might have been what was keeping you from contacting me. I had no idea what was happening with you for weeks! Honestly, just ask your father, I was beside myself."

She taps the table, nodding with a smile before Phoebe can respond.

"So, maybe we can have another little chat about Damien after we eat. I just want to make sure he's good enough for you, Phoebe. I'm a little bit wary about men like him." Phoebe frowns, the whiplash stunning her for a moment. "But now it's time to bring out the food! Can't let everyone starve out there because of our little chat, can we? Come along now!"

Once everyone's gathered together and they've brought the rest of the food to the table, Louis opens up a bottle of Prosecco and pours them each a glass. Phoebe keeps her hands folded in her lap, politely waiting for everyone to be served before she begins, suddenly a little self-conscious as she feels Damien's hand brush over hers.

More than anything, she's glad that he's on his best behavior. It would be mortifying if he pulled one of his stunts in front of her parents. Although, honestly, he rarely does anything but lighten the mood, and she imagines he'd probably be able to charm even her dad with some of his hijinks.

She looks over to him, and he smiles back.

He hasn't said anything snarky, or even brought up any of her mother's... less than charitable comments he's overheard on the phone in the past. At least she seems to have gotten over what was bothering her. But... What even was her issue to begin with? That Phoebe hadn't called her? She was an adult, after all. She didn't need to check in with her mother every week. She didn't need to ask for permission to make big changes.

Phoebe glances over at her across the table, her mother smiling angelically as she takes her seat, remembering for the first time in a while just how... *bad* some of those calls had been.

Samantha starts to uncover food. Pancakes, waffles, different kinds of potatoes, parfaits... it all looks beautiful, but Phoebe's already finding her appetite fading.

"What do you want? Those waffles look great, how 'bout we start there?"

Damien takes Phoebe's plate, ready to grab her whatever she needs. He's trying so fucking hard. How could her mother think anything bad about this man?

"Sure, I'll have a couple."

She forces a smile as Damien loads up her plate with waffles, fruit, and potatoes, watching out of the corner of her eye while her mother stares at them with a concerned expression on her face.

Samantha was a cheerleader all through high school. She was popular, she was pretty, and according to *her* she had the entire football team chasing after her at one point or another. Even when Phoebe stopped being a little girl her mother was still always happy to plan her meals.

"So, Damien," She smiles across the table. "What do you plan on doing after this whole rock and roll phase?"

Phoebe feels her hand clamp down on his leg before she's even aware she's doing it, but Damien only chuckles, smiling right back at her mother.

"I'm not sure what you mean, Samantha." He takes a sip of his drink and dabs his mouth with a napkin. "It's not so much a phase as it is a career. We just got out of the studio with our second album, and I'm not planning to stop anytime soon."

Her mother's smile sours a little, and she looks down at the table for a moment before continuing.

"Yes, well... It's not exactly long-term, is it? I mean, how many people in your field actually make it for more than a few years? Every other week we're hearing about some washed up celebrity getting arrested for public indecency, or getting found strung out in a motel room. Not that I'm saying *you'll* end up that way, of course, it just doesn't sound very stable, does it?"

Damien raises a brow, but he's keeping it cool, and no one else seems willing to step in as silence blankets the table. Michael looks the least comfortable, shaking his head ever so slightly to himself as he cuts into his waffles, but he doesn't do any more than that.

Phoebe finds herself stuck between a mix of confusion and mild panic. Damien's been wonderful so far, but he doesn't like to be challenged, especially not when it comes to his art. He's never wanted to be seen as fleeting, always worrying about the longevity of his music, and now her mother's digging into that. And, *why* is she doing that? What has he done to make her feel this way? She doesn't even know him.

"Oh, but I want to be clear, I'm not doubting your passion, not at all! You're clearly very talented, people are talking about your music all over the place, but... you've only been doing this, what, a year?"

"A lot longer than that," Damien smiles politely. "We started playing dive bars, spent sleepless nights rehearsing and writing... There's a lot of work that goes into making music. You have to have heard of the Rolling Stones? Or the Beatles? Nobody thought they could make it long-term either. Not at the start. And hell, there's hundreds of bands less famous than them who still make a totally decent living. It doesn't have to be all or nothing."

"Well," She laughs, "I can't imagine you're comparing yourself to The Beatles."

Phoebe feels herself sit up a little straighter, looking around the table to see if anyone else is as uncomfortable as she is, but there's zero indication they're planning to say something, and Damien only squeezes her hand.

"You're right," Damien replies. "We're not. We're our own thing. Something new."

Damien leans back in his chair, crossing his arms over his chest and tilting his head as he stares right back at her, that smile still locked onto his lips.

"Would you mind if I ask you a question, Samantha? I think it's only fair."

Her eyes flash.

"Of course, I'm an open book."

"Great. I'd love to know what you don't like about me."

For a moment, Phoebe's almost certain her heart's stopped, but her mother barely even flinches.

"Oh sweetie, I don't dislike you, I don't even know you."

Damien nods, his own face like a stone statue.

"That's true, you don't, and yet somehow I can't help but notice every single thing you've said to me has been... let's say tinged with at least a *little* bit of criticism. I'm just curious where it's coming from, that's all."

Everyone else at the table shifts uncomfortably in their seats, and Phoebe can tell her father's weighing when to get involved.

"Damien, sweetie, It's nothing against you. But you've been in the papers quite a lot, and a majority of the coverage is, let's say, less than charitable. I'm sure you're a passionate artist, and a *wonderful* person, but I'm not quite sure you're right for my little girl."

"Mom!"

Phoebe's shocked to hear not only her own voice, but Michael's as well, glancing over to see just how distressed he looks at their mother's behavior.

And finally, for the first time since they'd arrived, Damien looks like he's losing his cool. He leans forward in his seat, the smile fading from his face completely.

"Samantha? I have been nothing but respectful toward you in your home, and I really don't understand why you're treating me like this, but that's fine. We both agree you don't know me, and while I wouldn't mind proving to you that I'm worthy of your daughter, you know what? I've been listening to you all day, and the way you've been talking to Phoebe? The way you've been throwing little barbs her way, subtle little manipulative jabs at her job, her figure, about every inch of her you can get your *fucking* claws into...? That's where I draw the line."

Her mother looks absolutely scandalized, but Damien isn't done, a completely different kind of smile overtaking his face.

"Oh, I get it. You need control. You need to be in charge of every aspect of her goddamn life, and you *hate* that you might be losing that, don't you? You can't stand to see her happy if it's not because of you—"

"Watch your tone in my house, son."

Her father finally stood up, and it wasn't for her.

Of course it wasn't.

Phoebe's mother slams her hand down on the table, spitting her words back across at him.

"You want to know why I don't *like you*, Damien? It's because everyone like you is a drug addict, a womanizer, and a freak. You're going to be a washed up, unemployed musician reliving your glory days by the time you're 30, and my girl is *far* too good to be associated with you."

Her eyes sharpen as she continues, completely giving up the pretense of any sort of decorum.

"You got my daughter caught up in this whirlwind romance, swept her off her feet and kept her from seeing who you really are, just so you could propose to her far away from her family, away from the people who could have warned her away from you. When she finally called, my daughter hadn't talked to me in weeks, and the first thing I hear from her is that the two of you are engaged? I dare you to tell me you've thought this through, that you actually know what's best for her; that you know better than I do."

Damien lets out a hollow laugh.

"Fucking spare me. Who do you think was there to support her through her work, through almost losing her job? I was. Who's shared every single goddamn thought they've had with her, day after day, since almost the moment we met? Me again. And who loves every word she puts down on paper? That's fucking me, Samantha, while you couldn't even be bothered to do anything but suggest she swap careers and become a fucking *secretary*. So don't pretend that you actually care."

Her mother looks disgusted, even scandalized, as she turns back to Phoebe.

"Listen how he's talking to your mother, Phoebe. Are you going to stand for this? After we did our best to guide you through life, you're not going to let this nobody talk to us like that!"

Her mother's eyes are wide, her neck straining as she tries her best to stay in control. Phoebe sets her knife and fork down, her lack of emotion surprising even herself. All the venom that's been building up inside her sits ready on the very tip of her tongue, tears streaming down her face as she finds that somehow she's feeling almost nothing at all.

"Mom, I know you think you've always been there for me. Fuck, up until now, I thought you were too. But it's not true. You never supported a single thing I wanted to do, never encouraged me to pursue anything I was excited for, anything I wanted to try. Every single time you were *there for me*, it was with an alternative. A *suggestion*. Something else for me to try instead of what I wanted to, or some other way to live my life."

Her mother looks furious, like she's ready to burst and scream out about how ungrateful Phoebe is, and how unfair she's being. But she won't let her. Today, Samantha Miller is going to listen for once.

"But now that things are different, now that I have this great job and wonderful friends, now that I'm more in love than I've ever been in my life, your first thought, your first *fucking thought,* is to turn me right around, to convince me to throw it all away. And why? Because you weren't a part of it, mom. That's why you're doing this, because you didn't choose any of these things for me. You were only ever there for your version of my life, you were there to make sure I turned out exactly like you wanted. You were fucking there for *you*."

"Phoebe! That's– That's enough!"

Her father looks beyond shocked, jumping to her mom's defense because it's the only thing he knows how to do. She had hoped that there was a chance someone would be on her side, but...

"You know what? No, it's not fucking enough." She turns to her father, standing as she tears her purse up off the floor. "My whole life, while mom was doing *all that shit* to me? Manipulating me into being her pathetic little puppet? *You* sat by and watched it happen. If you cared, you'd have done something. But I guess that would mean you'd have to have noticed me at all."

And then there's silence, just her own heavy breathing as she stands there, half-expecting some sort of retort, but it doesn't come. So that's it, there's no coming back from this, not with everyone so wrapped around her mother's fucking finger.

"Nothing I do is ever going to make either of you happy, not as long as I'm the one deciding what to do, and I'm sick of trying to prove that I can live my own fucking life! No matter how good the career, no matter how wonderful the man, it'll never be enough." She shakes her head. "Why do you think we got married in secret, halfway across the fucking world?"

Phoebe lets out a shaking, raggedy breath, her whole body shuddering as the rush of adrenaline finally leaves her body. When they walk out that door she's probably never speaking to her family again.

"Damien? Let's go home."

He doesn't hesitate for a moment, standing with a nod to Michael, and another to Tara.

"Honestly, it was lovely to meet you two."

"Phoebe, I–" Michael stutters, quiet at first but raising his voice as he stands. "Phoebe, wait!"

But they're already halfway gone, snatching their coats from the closet and scooping up their shoes as they rush out the door.

"I hope you're happy!" Samantha calls from behind them. "I hope you're happy because you're *never* coming back here, not without one hell of an apology! You ruined everything, the whole New Year!"

Phoebe takes a deep breath and draws herself up to her full height as she stands on the concrete staircase, turning to face her mother with shoes in her hand, her feet freezing in the winter breeze.

"We could have started over, mom. All you had to do was accept him. You didn't even have to fucking like him, you just had to accept he's the person I chose. You just had to respect this one single fucking choice that I've made. But you couldn't even do that. I hope you figure out what the hell is wrong with you, and then maybe someday you can talk to me like I'm a real fucking person."

Her chin quivers, but she refuses to back down, holding her mother's gaze.

"When that happens, when you're ready to step up and be a real mom, you can give me a call."

And then she hears the door slam shut.

And then they're down the stairs and across the driveway.

And then they're finally alone.

It's Too Late

PHOEBE

Except they're not quite alone.

"Phoebe!" Michael's voice slices through the air, making her jump.

She turns, and there he is rushing toward them, in front of her in an instant and hugging her tight.

"You've been holding that in for a long time, huh?"

She can't help herself, can't hold it all together anymore and so she just weeps, pressing her hand against her brother's chest as he holds her.

"It's okay, Pheebs. You did good. It's what they needed to hear. Fuck, it's what I needed to hear."

Even as everything crashes down around her, even after she tore their family apart, it's good to know at least a single person from that whole damn house is on her side.

"I feel like I ruined everything."

"*Mom* ruined it," Michael insists. "She's been spreading kerosene all over everything our whole lives, you just lit the match."

She sniffles, wiping away her tears.

"Hey, is that bar we used to go to still open? The one we'd hit whenever we needed to have some time away from them?"

Phoebe's eyes flash in recognition.

"The Anchor? I think so, yeah. Why?"

Michael grins.

"Because I figure we could all use a fucking drink. Tara's packing up right now to take the kids home, how about I meet you two over there in an hour, what do you say?"

Phoebe lets out a shaky laugh.

"That sounds great."

He turns around, heading back up to the house as she and Damien make their way to their car, but he stops right in front of the doorway, calling back to her a final time.

"Hey, Pheebs? I just want you to know, no matter what else happens in your life, you'll *always* have your big brother."

The Anchor is just like she remembered it, filled to the brim with bikers and all manner of random guys in flannel, nursing their hangovers at the bar. It's a total dive, and the only reason Phoebe liked coming here when she was a teenager is they never ID'd, but that's morphed over time into a nostalgic fondness for this piece of shit.

"Here, got you a G&T. Shit, you still drink those, right? I forgot to ask."

Michael sets down a small tray, sliding into the booth across from them.

The drink is a little sad looking, the smell of cheap gin that's burned into her memories wafting up into the air.

"Don't worry, that's another thing that hasn't changed."

"Great, I was a little worried there for a second." He hands Damien a whiskey, raising his own glass to the air. "To Phoebe. Let's say... for living out the dream of telling your fucked up parents what's what."

"Amen," Damien replies, clinking his glass with Mike's. "To Phoebe."

She smiles sadly as she follows suit, all three of them taking to their drinks in silence. She would have loved to have launched right into lighter conversation, fun reminiscing, maybe a little bit of catching up, but a question's been nagging at her since they left. He was there after the fallout, after all. Did her mom have any regrets? Did she cry? Was there any remorse?

"Hey, so um... did mom say anything?" Phoebe asks, setting her glass on the table. "After we left, I mean."

"She was in the living room bawling her eyes out when I came back in, like she didn't spend half of brunch insulting you two." Michael scoffs. "It's bullshit,

Pheebs, she's being absolutely ridiculous."

"But... did she say anything?"

He sighs.

"Well, she said you ruined New Year's. Dad's pissed too, said he doesn't want you calling or coming around anymore until you've apologized to mom."

She figured as much, feeling the tears start to well up again. She said she was sick of crying about this, that her mom's bullshit wasn't worth the energy, but emotions have a funny way of ignoring any semblance of logic.

"Fine. That's fine. I don't want anything from them anyway. Not anymore."

Michael reaches across the table, holding his hand open for her.

"Hey, I just want you to know I'm here for you. I know I wasn't always there the way I should have been over the years, and I'm sorry. I guess I just sort of assumed things were okay, that you and mom had worked things out, even though to some extent I knew how she was treating you."

She doesn't begrudge her brother, or resent him for her mom's behavior. He just had the benefit of being the good kid of the two.

"It's okay, Mike. As far as they were concerned you were doing everything right. How could you have known how bad it was if I never realized myself? Besides, I doubt they even thought for a second you'd end up out here with us instead of back there with them. I'll always be grateful for that."

"No, Pheebs, I– it's not okay. At the very least I knew she would try to push you down whatever path she saw you on. That's what she does to people, tries to force them to fit into her perfect little version of the world. Sure, I got lucky that the place I ended up aligned with her vision, but that doesn't mean I didn't know. Hell, even though I'm happy with the way my life turned out, I didn't even wanna be a doctor to begin with."

"You didn't?"

"Not at first, no. Actually I…" A grin spreads across his face. "I really wanted to drive race cars for a while."

"Oh, shit! For real?" Damien asks, leaning forward onto the table.

Phoebe chuckles, memories of his room covered wall-to-wall with posters of cars and drivers flooding her mind. He didn't just *want* to drive them, he was obsessed.

"Yeah, but mom shut that down quick enough. She only let me keep all my stuff when I promised I'd work toward a 'real career,' something with a future."

"Well, maybe she did at least one good thing," Phoebe chuckles. "I've heard it's really fucking dangerous."

"Yeah, but that's the fun of it, Pheebs! That's why it's so exciting!" Michael sighs, tapping at their table with a bit of nervous energy. "But you're right, if I have to give her credit for one thing it's that she got me into my field. I wouldn't have met Tara, or had either of my kids if I went into racing. Hell, I might not even be here, at least not with my head intact.

He takes a sip of his drink, clearly struggling with his thoughts.

"It didn't matter how right she was, though, because I always resented her a little for pushing me into this whole doctor thing. It was the way she did it, like something so important was riding on me following this exact path. Like she was living her own ideal life through me."

Phoebe's not sure if her mom *had* any hopes and dreams outside of having a family, but it's certainly a possibility. Maybe she was more bitter about the whole thing than she ever let on. Or maybe she just had extreme expectations, and let all of her happiness hinge on them being met. Either way, failure to measure up had to have become personal.

She stares into her drink, ruminating on just how she could have gone so long without seeing her mom for what she was. The quiet manipulation through fake smiles and affirmation, the constant check-ins and passive-aggressive praise. She can't believe she didn't get more angry when her mom proposed secretarial school, like her job was just a fucking hobby.

"You know, I'm pretty sure Tara might be the one getting out of this the happiest. She's never felt like she really belonged in that house, but she always came along anyway. I think Mom would have blown a gasket if I ever showed up alone; she'd assume there was something wrong with our marriage, probably offer to set me up with someone an hour into the visit."

Damien looks completely perplexed, knocking back the rest of his drink and slamming his glass down on the table.

"Wait, what? Don't get me wrong, I don't think you could surprise me if you told me she had a grudge with Jesus himself, but what's her problem with Tara? She just seemed... I don't know, nice?"

"Actually, mom's always thought that Tara wasn't a good match for me,". Mike chuckles, shaking his head. "Just Imagine, thinking that gorgeous woman isn't good enough for an eyesore like me."

"Whoah whoah," Damien waves his hands aggressively. "First off, you're not an eyesore. You've got this whole Bo Brady thing going on. Second–"

Michael looks confused.

"Bo Brady?" He perks up. "Like, from Days of Our Lives?"

Phoebe chuckles, a look of surprise on her face as she turns to Damien.

"Don't tell me you watch Days of Our Lives. *You?*"

"Listen, sometimes there's nothing on in a hotel room, but... You know what, I don't have to sit here and take this slander! The show's a lot of fun, and the storylines aren't even that bad. Those middle-aged housewives are on to something with this shit–"

He holds out a hand, as if he's conducting himself.

"But I'm getting off topic. The point is... well, I've forgotten the point, but none of that matters. Your kids are great, you've got a sister who loves you, and you've got a wife who's got great taste in music. That's all that matters."

"Well, she'll be ecstatic that you said that," Michael laughs. "Tara gets all dolled up for these things, only to have mom make these passive-aggressive comments about her appearance. It's always such little things, you know? Like 'black is more flattering!' And it's always flattering, not slimming, but that's what she means. She's always so careful with her words, so you can never confront her directly about it, but Tara knew what she meant."

He sighs, looking a little sadder all of a sudden.

"That's what I can't get past. I'm a coward, I've let my mother talk to my wife like that for years– and then there's dad, who... well, he just fucking sits there and watches."

"Yeah, what's with that?" Damien asks. "He didn't seem as messed up as Samantha at first, like he might have been an okay guy, but then–"

Michael rubs his eyes and groans.

"I don't know, I think he's afraid of rocking the boat. Maybe cowardice is hereditary."

Phoebe had no idea Michael felt like this, that he'd been struggling in his own way this entire time. The two of them had been pretty close for a long time, and he always seemed so in control of his life, so happy. Now though, it feels like a whole other side of her brother is coming into the light. It's a little bit of extra comfort to know that someone else was going through it too, that he, with a life as perfect as he had, could still struggle. But it's a small comfort. She wishes none of it had happened to either of them, at all.

"Why is she like this?" Damien asks, just sort of throwing it out there, like one of them might somehow have the answer. "Doesn't she know her life just gets easier the less she cares about perfection, not worse?"

"I mean, as far as I remember, she's always been this way," Michael mutters. "Our grandma was almost exactly the same. Jesus, Pheebs remember what it was like when the two of them were in a room together?"

Phoebe rolls her eyes way back into her skull.

"God, you'd have to torture me to dredge up those memories."

"Yeah, you know what? I think I'd rather jump into fuckin' traffic," Damien grumbles.

The siblings cackle in unison, and Phoebe thinks she can finally feel just a little bit of that weight being lifted off of her shoulders. The grief of cutting off her parents will remain, probably years down the line, but there's only so much you can grieve for what could have been. She's always been a good daughter, always tried her best to make her parents proud, and It's not her fault that they couldn't accept her for what she was, no matter what form that took.

"So, Mike, we're obviously on the outs with the Millers for the foreseeable future, but what about you?" Damien takes a moment, raising his hand to get the server's attention and indicating another round for the table. "I imagine it's a bit harder to cut ties with your kids involved."

"Yeah, it's gonna be a bit of a fight with the two of them, but I'm pretty sure Tara's gonna agree that we need to take an indefinite hiatus for a while. I'm sure mom'll call me and tear me a new one, but family shouldn't treat you like that; she needs to learn it's unacceptable." He finishes his beer, shaking his head as his smile returns. "Okay guys, mom doesn't deserve any more of our time, so change of subject: how the fuck did this all happen so fast between the two of you?"

Damien and Phoebe exchange a knowing look. Even after so many people asking, neither of them really has an answer to the question that doesn't sound like it's right out of a Hallmark card. They both dove into the deep end, completely unsure what they'd find there, and lucked into something beautiful.

"I know it doesn't sound as exciting as It could, but it just kind of happened," she replies, taking Damien's hand. "I didn't expect it at all, I don't think either of us did. If things hadn't worked out, and we'd moved on after the story like it was just another job, I'd be back all alone in that tiny apartment in Williamsburg–" She stops herself, knocking on the table. "Well, I mean I guess I *am* technically still living there."

"Yeah, we really should figure that out," Damien laughs.

"Wait wait wait, you guys haven't moved in together yet? You took everything else at light-speed and *that's* the thing you take your time on?"

Michael leans back, grinning from ear to ear.

"Makes me kinda wanna be young again, you know? Seeing you guys like this."

"Mike, really?" Phoebe laughs. "You're 35, you're not on death's fucking door."

He stares off into the distance, nodding to himself in thought for a minute or two before laying everything out.

"So when I drove Tara back to our place, we got to talking, and we'd like to help you two out. The problem is we couldn't figure out how to do that, and you know how awkward it can be when you're offering help completely unsolicited. But since you're not moved in together yet, do you think that…"

"I'd have to break my lease this week," Phoebe replies. "And hire movers. It's gonna cost me, but–"

"I'll pay for it."

The words leave both men's lips at the same time, and she snorts.

She's making good money along with her promotion, but it'd be foolish to turn down free movers.

Damien's eyes light up, his hand shooting out to the center of the table.

"Rock paper scissors for it?"

Michael considers the idea for a moment, before countering with one of his own.

"How about a team up instead? You pay to break her lease and I'll pay for the moving truck. And as long as you know some people, we can all help move her into your place. And Pheebs, I know you like to do things your own way, but you're not lifting a finger."

Phoebe frowns, letting out a long sigh and agreeing with a curt little nod.

Actually, she wasn't planning on it, but she's happy to let them think she's only begrudgingly accepting the offer. Maybe Phoebe in her teens would have been offended, but after the couch kept sliding down the stairs when she moved into her current place, she vowed never to suffer through the indignity of asking neighbors for help ever again.

"Great, it's settled then. You two good to do this next week?"

"Sure," she laughs. "I guess I'm telling my landlord I'm finally out of there!"

Phoebe slips Damien a pen from her purse and he scribbles the address down on a napkin, sliding it toward Michael.

"SoHo." Michael whistles. "Fancy schmancy."

"Bought the place a couple years ago. Pheebs already has an office and her own writing space."

Damien looks a little too proud of himself, but he's probably earned it.

"Right on, man. That's how you win 'em over!"

The three of them finish their drinks over gentle laughter and blessedly frivolous conversation. Getting to know her brother on this level is freeing. Turns out he's actually really cool– well, he's always been cool, but after he stood up for her today, he's gotten even cooler.

As the afternoon winds into the evening, Damien finally puts some cash down on the table as they stand, and Michael gives Phoebe a big hug.

"I'll set up the moving truck for next week. But until then, you call me if you need anything, okay? We can have dinner, coffee, whatever you want. And remember: if mom calls, please do yourself a favor and don't answer."

It's good advice, but she won't call. Phoebe's certain of that.

"Thanks Mike, really. And thanks for sticking up for me today."

"Always and forever, Pheebs." Michael pats her on the back before turning and offering his hand. "It really was a pleasure to meet you, Damien. I'd tell you to be good to her, but It's pretty clear you've already got that part down.

"Hey, I just do the best I can." Damien grins, shooting a wink at her. "That sort of thing comes easy when you're crazy in love."

Start Me Up

DAMIEN

It's been a week since the big New Year's debacle, and while their lives have definitely been less dramatic, they haven't really slowed down at all. Phoebe's parents haven't called, but neither of them really expected that. Another thing they didn't expect was the card they received, addressed to the both of them and signed by her father. It simply said "congratulations," no apology and no explanation, but maybe it's a first step toward some sort of reconciliation.

Phoebe, to her credit, didn't seem to care very much, but she also didn't just throw it away, tucking it inside of a book for now. She said before any real steps can be taken, she needs a real apology, and not just from him.

Good for her.

On the flipside, Michael's been a real ray of sunshine in her life, making good on his word and taking steps to be much more involved than he had been in the past few years. Just a day or two ago they went out for dinner with him and his whole little family, and most of the past week's been spent coordinating the move with him over the phone. It's not a rare occasion to walk into the living room and find her curled up in a chair, laughing or smiling with the phone cradled against her neck.

Damien's glad she's got some actual family in her corner now.

"You know what? I think I may have overestimated our collective skills. Maybe I should have hired movers and not just a van after all."

Michael groans as they set down the last massive box of Phoebe's stuff into the moving van.

"Hey, I understand, one look at these muscles and I'd think things were handled too." She flexes, her little grin twisting into a grimace. Her muscles are probably aching just as much as the rest of them. "But look, I only dropped one thing the whole morning!"

"Two things," Damien corrects her. "The couch on my foot, and don't forget the box of books."

"Hey I apologized for the first one, and it was a group effort so it doesn't count! And the box... I mean, it felt like it weighed about a thousand pounds."

Michael chuckles, glancing over at Damien.

"Might not have been the smartest move, giving her more space to store her books. She hoards those things like a dragon. When she was a kid, she'd come home with ten of them from the library. Always forgetting to return them for months. I think something like a quarter of her allowance went to fines some weeks."

"Alright alright, I'm going to head back in for one more sweep and make sure we're not forgetting anything. You two feel free to talk about any and all of my secrets while I'm gone. After that stuff with mom I've lost all my shame, I'm basically invincible."

Damien digs his cigarettes out of his pocket as Phoebe makes her way inside, leaning against the van as he pops one into his mouth.

"Can I bum one?"

Michael's eyes were on the cig the second he pulled it out of the pack; he didn't know her brother smoked.

"Man, aren't you a doctor?"

"Yeah, sure am, which is why I get to eat greasy burgers and smoke cigarettes whenever I want. With a job as stressful as mine, you earn the right to a little reward now and then." He makes a come hither motion with his fingers. "Fork one over, rock star."

Damien smirks and passes Mike a cigarette, leaning in and lighting it himself. The doctor takes a long drag, so absorbed in the sensation that when he leans back he smacks his head against the metal of the van with a dull thunk. He snorts, not acknowledging the event with more than a little shake of his head as they smoke in silence, watching people walk by. A few of them slow down, doing a double take as they whisper to each other, and Damien waves at them with a pleasant smile.

"Does that ever get old?" Michael asks after a particularly long drag.

"The fans? Nah. I love 'em. The fuckin' paparazzi though?"

The press has definitely ramped up their coverage since the release of the album, and it's only gotten more obvious since their return. Being in Paris was a blessing for how much distance it put between them and their good friends working at the media rags. The album itself is getting a lot of attention, and the band is getting a lot of requests for interviews in turn. Luckily, Troy is a picky man, and he's been putting pretty much every single request through a rigorous vetting process.

He's been calling it *Sullivan's Gauntlet*.

"So how's Phoebe handling all of it?"

Damien blows out some smoke rings, watching as they get obliterated in the cold wind.

"It's an adjustment, for sure, but she's dealing. Luckily she's had a lot of practice. I don't think anything hit her harder than when Chris published that garbage about us."

"Yeah, that's actually where mom got the theory that she's clinging to right now. She's saying the whole thing between you two is fake. It's honestly almost impossible to talk to her these days, she can't let it go."

"You've talked to her?" Damien asks, his stomach twisting.

Michael nods.

"She's got no intention of speaking to Phoebe, not until she gets, and I quote 'the apology she deserves.'"

He put so much sarcastic emphasis on those final words Damien was worried Michael was going to throw up right on the sidewalk.

"Samantha's gonna be the one to pay the price. She'll figure that out sooner or later."

"Yeah, that's what I told her," Michael sighs. "She won't budge, but it's still early days. I don't think that woman can go too long without people to boss around in her life, but I suppose we'll see."

Damien stares up at a window, catching Phoebe and Janis looking down at them. She blows him a kiss, and even through the comedically dirty glass, he can tell they're both glowing.

1987 is starting with a bang, and Samantha Miller's made the choice to get left behind in the dust.

The two women disappear from the window with a wave, and Michael takes the one last drag on his cigarette before snuffing it out with his shoe.

"Alright, unless something goes terribly wrong, it looks like it's time. I'm gonna go start up the truck, you wanna grab the girls?"

"On my way," Damien grins. "Wanna take bets on if I feel a little nostalgic when I get up there? My money's on me just feeling relieved that I won't have to repair any of the cabinets."

Michael shakes his head, climbing into the van.

"No bet. You couldn't bribe me to take odds that bad."

Damien hits the stairs running, taking things two at a time all the way up to Phoebe's floor. When he reaches the door he's huffing and puffing, far more exhausted than he expected from such a short run. He lurches over, hands on his thighs as the nausea hits him like a truck.

"New year's resolution... I'm quitting smoking this year. Holy shit."

"Oh yeah? How long until you think you give up on that?"

When the urge to vomit finally passes, he looks up to see Janis standing in the door, with Phoebe behind her, a big grin on her face.

"Ah, still no faith in me, huh Kaneko?"

"You gotta prove yourself, Bell." She turns and heads back into the apartment. "I'll believe it when I see it."

Phoebe moves into the doorway, wrapping him up in her arms as Janis pretends to gag in the background. Michael can wait a little longer.

"We're basically done, so don't worry." She says with a sigh, "We've sort of been reminiscing as we do this final sweep. I really didn't think I'd feel a whole lot about this place, but here we are."

She takes his hand, leading him through each room as she muses on the little details of her life.

"Oh, you'll like this one. This is where the call came in that I got the job at Titanium. Janis actually had to be a reference for me. Pretended to be some bigshot at Time Magazine. In retrospect, I think Brian saw right through it, but hey, I got it so who cares."

Janis' voice carries through from the bathroom, somehow crystal clear even over the sound of the running sink.

"Just remember, you still owe me! I expect to be repaid in full, entirely in Revolver merch! Just think, we can trace your entire relationship straight back to me."

Phoebe snorts, rolling her eyes as she walks him around a little more, finally ending up in her bedroom.

"Well, I guess that's it. I'm gonna miss this shitty little apartment. There's something so special about never knowing if you're gonna find coffee or cockroaches in your cups."

Damien nods.

"You know what, me too. This place really is completely unique..." He lets his words hang in the air for far too long, Phoebe stone faced as she stares back at him, just waiting for the joke to drop. "I mean, is there anywhere else we've been in for more than a couple hours, but still haven't fucked in?"

She shakes her head, but he can see the smile tugging at her lips, and so he's content to call that mission accomplished.

"You know, it's always surprising how much It hurts to leave the things we've outgrown. Whether it's an apartment, or a person..."

Tears glisten in Phoebe's eyes and Damien takes her hand.

"You don't have to do anything on your own anymore, babydoll."

Phoebe flicks away a tear with her finger and breathes, slow and steady, just as Janis walks into the room.

"Hey, just remember now you're gonna be closer to me! So if this guy ever gets on your nerves, feel free to ditch him and head right over. You don't even need to call."

"You know what, Kaneko? That's actually really sweet. I hate to admit it, but you're a better person than me. It's a five dollar entry fee every time you ring the doorbell at my place. Don't worry, I charge everyone in the band the same rate."

Janis gives him the finger, but she's not even trying to hide her smile.

"Five bucks? That's nothing. You won't be able to get rid of me that easy."

Damien turns back to Phoebe, an exciting buzz taking him over. This is it, after today, she'll be fully moved in, and then they get to start the rest of their lives together. He wants to tell her how excited he is, tell her how much it all means to him, but he can see by the look in her eyes that she already knows.

"We're all packed up downstairs. You ready to take the first few steps into your new life?"

Phoebe giggles.

"Damien, I've been ready since Paris."

He beams, running a tender hand through her hair.

"Then let's get the hell outta here, Mrs. Bell."

The Rest of My Life

DAMIEN

Holy fuck.

Damien's been sweating his ass off for an hour hauling shit off of the truck and all the way up the stairs. Why did he choose an apartment with so many fucking steps? Either way, hours into the process, with the sun starting to dip below the horizon, he thinks they can confidently say moving Phoebe out was a lot easier than moving her in.

"Hey, Troy! Are you gonna help move the last of this shit inside, or are you gonna sit on that couch drinking beers with Shaun all night?" Damien barks as he and Johnny begin to haul the final pile of the boxes.

Troy and Shaun raise their beer bottles from their comfy spots on the sofa, making no indication they're planning to move.

"Hey, I'm 27 and my back isn't what it used to be!" Shaun calls. "So imagine how Troy feels. Besides, I earned my break after moving all those goddamn boxes of books!"

"Yeah!" Troy agrees, barely paying attention as he savors a cigar in between sips of his beer.

"Troy's closer to 227 than 27, so I kind of get it," Ophelia mutters.

She's been moving the 'light' stuff, mostly boxes of Phoebe's clothes and jewelry, but she hasn't called it quits yet.

"Nah, the old man may have a spine like dust, but there's no way he's a day older than 60," Erin cackles.

Troy casts her a dirty look as she scrunches up her nose at him.

"Moving's hard on the hands," Shaun adds, wiggling his fingers. "I gotta protect these magic babies. They're insured, you know!"

"The sad thing is, I almost believe you," Damien replies as he and Johnny hoist one of the last remaining boxes through the door to Phoebe's office.

"You're gonna need to get her some more shelves, man," Michael laughs from down on the floor. He's been in here for at least an hour, unpacking and organizing box after box of books.

"Or just build her a library," Johnny replies as he glances around at the three bookshelves already lining the walls. "She reads all of these?"

"Some of 'em," Phoebe announces from the doorway, a few beers tucked in her arms. "Some I just got so that I can look a lot smarter than I am."

She hands them each a beer, popping the cap on her own as she surveys the room.

"Looks like we've still got some work ahead of us, but that's the last of the boxes I think we can call it for now, right? Pizza's on its way."

"You're the best, Pheebs!" Johnny chirps, biting down on his bottle cap and ripping it off with his teeth as Phoebe stares dumbfounded at the display.

"Oh wow I... I thought Damien was joking about that."

"I'm telling Erin," Damien coos, taunting Johnny as he takes a few exaggerated steps toward the door.

"Don't you dare!"

"But Johnny, I thought there weren't any secrets between the two of you, don't you think I should–"

Johnny rushes out of the room, calling out to her in the distance.

"Erin, sweetie, no matter what anyone tells you I wasn't doing anything! Damien's a liar!"

Michael groans as he gets to his feet, grabbing his own beer off Phoebe's desk, along with the bottle opener.

"So, you staying for pizza?" She asks.

"Wouldn't miss it. I've got the van until tomorrow, figured it'd be better to be safe than sorry, right? I've just gotta call Tara and tell her I'll be home a little later than I expected."

"Phone's in the kitchen, dude, so feel free."

"Thanks. I'll be back in a bit."

Michael pats Phoebe on the shoulder as he heads out the door, leaving the two of them alone for the first time all day. Phoebe's dressed casually, comfortably swimming in one of his big plaid shirts that she's tied up at the front, exposing just the tiniest bit of her belly, her jeans sitting high up on her waist.

"So, was this actually the last box?"

He can already tell it's going to be a struggle to keep his hands off of her, but for the sake of her brother and their friends, he's got to try.

"Yep, that's the one, at least as long as Phi kept her end of the bargain. It looks like you're officially moved into Château Bell."

She looks around, taking everything in for what has to be the tenth time that day. Maybe it still doesn't quite feel real to her.

"It's a *big* upgrade from Château Miller, let me tell you, but I'm worried it might be a bit *too* clean in here. Where are my coffee-cup cockroaches supposed to live?"

Damien can't stop smiling. He hasn't been this giddy since their wedding day, and that was *after* the nerves subsided. Part of him still can't believe they've done it, that she's here now. Looking back on things, he used to be so freaked out about shedding that bachelor lifestyle, but as he wracks his brain he can't think of the last time it crossed his mind.

"You know, I've lived in this place for a couple years now, but this might be the first time it's really felt like home," he murmurs.

The past few days have been incredible, bouncing back and forth between her place and his as they prepared. They've already fallen into a routine, a warm little cycle of their private life, and Damien can already feel his chaotic existence begin to soften. Things are slowing down, or maybe it's just the first time in a while he's taken the time to really appreciate the days as they come.

But it's not just them.

Johnny and Erin are planning to get married in the spring, and Phoebe is already wrapped up in helping to plan the wedding. For Damien's part, he lobbied Troy and Liam to put in a word with Allan and make sure they're getting a bit more of a break than any of them initially planned for. He was a little nervous about it for a bit, but with the record being the smash-hit that it is, Allan didn't have any real reason to turn them down.

On the other hand, Shaun, Ophelia, and Janis seem to just be taking things as they go. When Damien asked if there were any wedding bells in their collective future, Ophelia only put on a knowing smile. Whether or not things end up going that way, Damien's certain he's never seen a set of people more prepared to make good use of a vacation, and he's sure they've already cooked up some solid plans for their newly freed up schedules.

The muffled ringing from the kitchen is what finally pulls him from his thoughts, he and Phoebe heading for the door at the same time.

"I got it!" Michael calls out, stopping them in their tracks. "Pheebs, Damien? You want me to grab you another beer while I'm in here?"

"Yes, please! And thank you!"

She turns to him, the big grin on her face infectious as she runs her hand up his chest.

"So, you wanna help me unpack tomorrow? I got a lot of books and clothes to hang up."

"Tomorrow? What, you think we're gonna be too tired tonight? What do you take me for, these muscles aren't just for show."

"Mmm, I'm not so sure about that, Mr. Bell." She takes a step forward, and then another, pushing him closer and closer to the wall until he's backed right up against it. "I think we might be a little too busy tonight."

"Wow, you've been here less than a few hours and you already think you're in charge, do you? We'll have to see if we can do anything about that attitude you've been building up, and I think I know just the–"

"Sorry to interrupt, and I'm gonna pretend I didn't hear any of that, for all of our sakes."

Michael's voice cuts straight through their building tension as the two of them struggle to keep from laughing, Phoebe burying her face in his shoulder as her brother makes his way in.

"Hey, Michael, my man. What's up?"

Phoebe's brother looks a little bemused, but also excited, smiling with his entire face. In fact, he looks exactly like Johnny always does when he wants to blurt something out but isn't sure quite what to say.

"Uh, someone from the Recording Academy of the United States just called to congratulate me— well, *you*–"

Phoebe stands up straight, stepping away from him and frowning at her brother, struggling to parse exactly what he's saying.

"The...?"

Damien cuts her off, the adrenaline flooding through him far too strong for him to keep calm.

"The recording academy? Like, *The* Recording Academy?"

He feels dizzy, struggling to keep from freaking out. Is Michael saying what he thinks he is? Is this some sort of prank? Where the fuck is Shaun, this has to be one of his–

"Guys, I think... I think Revolver just got nominated for a Grammy."

Dream On

The rest of the party was full of congratulations, expletives, and a *lot* more booze, but it wasn't until after the nomination that the reality of the situation started to really sink in. The following weeks were full of reporters hounding each and every band member for interviews. So much so that Troy, somewhat reluctantly, was forced to agree. What followed was more of everything: photoshoots, TV appearances, wardrobe fittings, and all of the shit that goes into preparing for one of the most important nights in the industry.

Now, even after weeks of prep, Phoebe still can't quite believe any of it is really happening. The red carpet, the flashbulbs, the photographers shouting at them to keep posing for the perfect shot. Even Revolver's album debut in Paris was nothing like this. All of her time today up until an hour before the show was devoted to preparation: getting her hair and makeup done, doing one last fitting for her gown, and then standing in the hot LA sun for hours while Damien and the band talked to reporters. It was a little panic-inducing to begin with, but they managed to get through it together.

Funnily enough, it was nice to finally be doing something in the rock-star-world where he was just as unprepared as she was.

That said, while they began the day together, it wasn't long before some photographers called for a bandmate-only mini-shoot, and she took the opportunity to take a bit of a break, leaving him to fend for himself with a playful little wave. Now, in the wake of the ceremony, and after all the awards had been given out, he's ping-ponging between his bandmates, trying his best not to get caught by any reporters or executives alone.

In true Phoebe fashion, she prefers to be a fly on the wall in these sorts of situations, and before long she found herself lingering near the bar, only mildly bewildered to be watching Mötley Crüe take turns doing shots and hitting on anything that breathes.

Phoebe smooths down her long black dress as she sips at her wine. Tonight was their first public appearance as a married couple, at least officially, and while a few people were still asking them if it was all for show, that narrative has definitely died down to its final smoldering embers.

"Well," the sound of a small thunk hitting the bar behind her grabs Phoebe's attention, and she turns to find her husband, looking slick in his black tuxedo, and fiddling with his brand new toy. "It turns out even if you're willing to tip a guy $200, you still can't get the words *World's Biggest Cock* engraved onto a Grammy. At least not at the show itself. I think I know a guy who can get the work done." He huffs and waves at the bartender. "Such bullshit, man."

They were all so excited to be there that they didn't even really consider the fact that they could win, which made the moment they heard their names ring out through the hall particularly surreal. Damien was the first on his feet, of course, kissing Phoebe and dragging her right up onto the stage along with them. They talked a lot in the afterglow of the moment, and it turns out neither of them remember his speech at all, hoping the fact that they weren't thrown out means he didn't say anything *too* inappropriate.

"Only you could think of doing something so... unique, my love," Phoebe chuckles as she winds her arm around his waist. "And I think you may need to get Guinness involved if you want your dick-title to be official."

Damien pouts, putting on his best puppy-dog face.

"Can't they just take my word for it? Am I not a paragon of virtue and honestly? What happened to trust!?" Suddenly, his eyes light up with a puckish glee. "Or maybe all they need is someone to back me up. How about an immensely trustworthy woman who has first-hand experience? Whaddaya say, Pheebs, think you can do your husband a solid?"

"I think at this point, if we're checking the balance sheet on who owes who favors, you're going to end up pretty disappointed," she laughs. "But who knows, maybe in a couple months of dinner-dates and you doing my share of the chores, I might be ready to talk to a complete stranger about the exact measurements of my husband's cock."

He rests his chin on the heel of his hand as the bartender slides a whiskey to him from across the bar.

"I don't think I'll ever get tired of hearing you say that."

"What, that I'm not arguing with a stranger about your dick, or—"

He might have gotten a little less rough around the edges since she met him, but that shit-eating grin is never going to change.

"No, you dork, *husband!*" He pulls her in close, planting a kiss on her cheek. "It's quickly becoming my favorite thing to leave your lips."

"Damien!"

Johnny barrels toward him, looking a little disheveled as he pushes his way through the crowd, his tie long since abandoned this far into the night.

"Dude, INXS just walked in. You *have* to come with me!"

"Why?" Damien laughs.

"Because I'm shyyyy," Johnny whines. "I need my social-wingman!"

Johnny's spent most of the evening on the dance floor with Erin, drunkenly giving random people the thumbs up as he practically drips with excitement. He may be three sheets to the wind, but he's having the time of his life whether he's going to remember it or not.

Damien pats Johnny on the shoulder.

"Okay, well, I'm a lot less drunk than you, which I think means I'm committing some sort of a crime of negligence if I let you go out there alone, so I guess we're doing this."

It was definitely a bit of a surprise. Even after both Liam and Troy gave him full permission to let loose, Damien's been keeping things pretty low key. For a minute there she was worried something might have been wrong, but when she asked him what was up he only smiled and said he wanted to remember every second of the night. It really was one of his greatest hopes, to be recognized not just by their fans, but his peers as well. And there they were, doing exactly that.

"Stay where Erin can see you both!" Phoebe calls out to them as Johnny pulls Damien away by his sleeve.

They're swallowed up by the crowd, all waves of suits and gowns, and once again she's on her own.

"Phoebe?"

Or so she hoped, at least.

Phoebe finds herself straightening without thinking, that familiar rush of dread trickling down her neck. Chris is clutching a pint of beer, that sickening smile that's permanently burned into her brain spread across his face. She takes a step back, ready to disappear into the crowd, but he puts a hand up, chuckling softly.

"Relax, okay? I'm not here to embarrass you or anything. I don't want a fight."

"Then what *are* you doing here?"

He looks... surprisingly good. His hair is meticulously combed, his suit is pristine, and there's a real brightness to his face. She doesn't quite know how to feel about it, happy that he might be finally getting his shit together, but a little bit annoyed he didn't show up in some shitty jeans and a wrinkled button-up. What's the name for finding joy in someone else's pain again?

"I'm still a reporter, Phoebe." His smirk barely shifts at all as he sips his drink, still confident even after everything that's happened. "And reporters go where the action is."

A bead of sweat trickles down her back and all she wants to do is run, but her feet feel like they're cemented to the floor.

"Okay, so go and report then. There's no reason to bother with me."

"Come on, Pheebs, don't be like this."

"Be like what?" She hisses, trying her best to keep quiet enough not to make a scene. "You've been hell-bent on trying to fuck up not just my relationship, but my whole goddamn career. Nothing's changed since the last time we had a little *chat,* so tell me what you want."

She can feel the anger inside her building, that fucking article of his rattling around in her head. Without lifting a finger, without even being there, he almost managed to completely humiliate her, live, in front of the entire country. It's something she'll never forget.

Chris sighs, a mousy brown curl falling into his face. He cut whatever was left of his ties with Titanium after Phoebe's promotion, although she didn't hear about it until weeks later. Brian told her that he said he wanted to take some time off for some more freelancing. To flex his creative muscles. Since then, he's been extremely prolific, bouncing between writing somewhat shady articles for the Enquirer and frustratingly legitimate pieces on some new up-and-comers.

Unfortunately, from what she can tell, there's been a lot more of the first type than the second. Sometimes the money's better in the roach pit.

"Okay, Phoebe, look, I– I wanna bury the hatchet." He extends his hand, and she can already feel the bile creeping up into her throat. "I can admit when I've lost. You beat me, Miller. You survived everything I threw at you, and when I couldn't make a dent in your amor, you didn't take the bait when I put out that—"

"Review of the new album? Yeah, I thought it seemed a bit much."

Chris chuckles, running a hand through his hair.

"So you read it?"

"I heard about it," she replies. "I try to curate what I read these days. It's important not to fill your head with trash."

Chris sighs.

"Look, Phoebe. You beat me, alright? I'm not coming after you anymore. For the record, I haven't been for a while now. That review wasn't meant for you, it was just work. I just wanted you to know that when it comes to this little feud between the two of us? I'm done."

His words hang heavy in the air between them, neither one making a move.

"Are you going to apologize?" She asks.

Chris snorts.

"For what, that exposé? For writing the truth? You beat the hell out of me, Miller. You threatened me. Your boyfriend even—"

"*Husband*," she corrects him.

"Yeah, sure. But that's not how it was back then, was it? A lot's changed is all I'm saying, and I'd like it if we could both just move on."

Phoebe swallows her rage, along with the rest of her wine, carefully setting the glass down on the bar. If things keep going like this, she may just take another swing at him, and this time she wouldn't feel a sliver of guilt about it. But that's the problem. He's right, a lot has changed. This time there are real stakes.

"That article wasn't the truth." She steps toward him, keeping her voice down. "You played dirty, Chris, and you know it. That's the difference between us. You run with sensationalist bullshit to sell copy, I write the truth."

She has no secrets anymore, but so much more to protect.

"But you know what? That's fine. You can live your life any way you want to, as long as you stay out of ours, but if you want to move past all this, if you really want to *bury the hatchet*, I want an apology. Now."

He tilts his head, his smile faltering just a little.

"You first."

Even if she hates to admit it, she embarrassed herself after that show when she unloaded on him the way she did. Even if he deserved everything he got, she's regretted it every day since.

"Alright, fair enough. I'm sorry I hit you. I still think you fucking deserved it, but... I'm sorry it happened the way it did."

Chris chuckles, shaking his head.

"You're lucky I didn't call the cops."

She hates that he's right, but he is. It's the one thing she never really figured out. Sure, maybe the evidence would have been hard to put together, but even the investigation could have done real damage to the tour.

"Your turn, Chris. Apologize."

"I'm—"

"Meyers, what did I say would happen to you if you even so much as took a breath around my wife again?"

Damien saunters up beside her, like he's materialized straight out of the crowd, and she readies herself to hold him back if need be.

But Chris doesn't scowl, or spit insults, or run.

He just nods.

"Damien, hey. Congratulations on the win."

"Thanks so much. What are you doing talking to my girl?"

"Nothing man, just a friendly conversation between colleagues. We were about to finish up anyway."

Maybe he really does just want to get past all of this.

"Hey, that's great, so how about you scurry off to whatever rock you crawled out from."

Chris sips his drink, his wry smile not faltering in the slightest.

"You know, you'll always be an asshole, Bell, no amount of accolades are going to change that."

Damien looks like he's about to shoot back at him with another barb, but Chris cuts him off.

"But you earned that award, you all did. Maybe if you manage to do it another couple times I'll finally have to admit I was wrong about you guys." He finishes his drink, walking confidently past Damien to slide his glass onto the counter. "Well, I should get going, but Phoebe? For what it's worth, I am sorry how deep we got under each other's skin."

And then he's gone, melted away in a crowd of black, white, and shimmering glamor.

Phoebe lets out the breath she's been holding since Damien arrived. She'll probably never not hate him, but at least it seems like he's got better things to do than coming after them anymore.

"How the fuck did he get in here?" Damien growls.

"Let him go." She plucks the whiskey from his hand and takes the last sip. "Tonight's about celebrating the good stuff."

Life gets a lot easier when you don't have to worry about people like Chris Meyers. If being thrust into the public eye has taught her anything, it's that everybody has an opinion, something to add to the noise, but that doesn't mean you have to listen to every last bit of it. She's content living her semi-quiet life, happy to focus on the little things like writing fiction on the side and listening to Damien play the piano on a lazy afternoon. That's the stuff people don't get to see, nor would she want them to.

The media frenzy around the two of them has basically died down for now. When they finally announced it to the public, the marriage that made headlines one week was old news the next. And everything kept moving so quickly up until this very minute that she'd barely had the chance to look back on things and reflect.

"You know what's funny? I just realized what we missed out on, even with our perfect little private ceremony: our first dance."

As the words leave her lips, music blares on the dance floor, and the unmistakable first couple bars of *I've Had the Time of My Life* ring out through the room. They both groan in unison, but then Damien extends his hand.

"You know what? You're right." He laughs. "And what are we if not painfully fucking cheesy?"

She takes his hand and the two of them glide out onto the dance floor. As they cut their way across the room she catches glimpses of so many of their friends: Johnny and Erin swaying back and forth as they stick to the edge of a sea of sweaty bodies, Ophelia bouncing between Shaun and Janis as they all dance completely out of sync with the music. Liam's at a payphone in the corner as Troy sits all alone at a table to himself, looking more content than she's ever seen him, puffing on his cigar.

Phoebe finds herself resting her head against Damien's chest, swaying slowly, surrounded by his warmth, and their love as she listens to the steady beat of his heart.

"This is all because of you, you know."

She looks up at him, her chest tight with emotion.

"Damien, no, this is your night, you're the ones who–"

"I'm not talking about the album," Damien whispers. "I'm talking about everything else. All of it."

He tucks a strand of hair behind her ear.

"No matter what happens in our lives, no matter what amazing things happen to us next, It's always gonna be you, babydoll."

In a sea of chaos and confusion, she found her home in him,

Found out what love was meant to feel like all along.

And there, his hand pressed firmly into hers,

In that crowd of vinyl, gold, and lights,

They dance, and dance again.

THE END

Thank You

The Revolver Duet was three years in the making, and coming to the end of it has been really fucking hard.

I've gotten to know these characters so well, and saying goodbye to them and sending them out into the world is terrifying, because there are so many pieces of myself and people I love so dearly woven into them.

I would not have been able to write this book without the help of so many people, who provided support, love, guidance, and a swift kick in the ass when I needed it. Being an author is hard, and some days, it really sucks, but these people have always got my back.

To my husband and my editor. You also teach me so much about writing every single day. It is a gift to be married to you and work with you on something creative. I know you love these characters as much as I do and seeing how hard you work is inspiring. Thank you for believing in me, believing in my books, and walking me through this extremely scary process. I love you to the moon and back.

To my parents. You have always encouraged me to venture off the beaten path and do my own thing. Specifically, I'd like to thank my dad, who would drive me to school while blasting '80s tunes. I think I learned the lyrics to every song on *Born in the USA* before I learned my multiplication tables. I know this duet is too smutty for you guys, but know that the love of music you both instilled into me is one of the reasons why I wrote this.

To my best friend, K. I don't tell a lot of people that I know IRL what I write about, but you supported me without judgment, and that means everything. I love you, babe 🩶

To the Sugar Club. Thank you for being a safe place for me to fall when things felt chaotic, terrifying, and when I felt like quitting. And thank you for being such a talented bunch of motherfuckers. I wake up every day striving to be as brilliant as y'all.

To my ARC readers. Thank you for taking a shot on an indie author, it really means the world to me. Seeing that people were even interested in ARC reading this, as well as Babydoll had me extremely emotional.

To my Street Team. Thank you for all of your support, for sharing and hyping me up even on days when I wanted to crawl into a hole and disappear.

About the Author

Thea Lawrence is a Canadian indie author and graduate school burnout. Originally from the west coast, she now lives in Ottawa, Ontario with her partner of ten years.

After spending nearly a decade in academia studying Criminology, Thea decided to branch out into the world of indie publishing. This is her third book.

Thea's hobbies include: lifting weights, drinking coffee like it's going to pay the bills, napping to avoid her problems, watching Chopped the same way people would watch a football game, and indulging in cult documentaries with her partner.

You can find Thea on her website: thealawrenceromanceauthor.com or on her socials below.

instagram.com/thealawrenceauthor

threads.net/@thealawrenceauthor

tiktok.com/@thealawrenceauthor

Also by Thea Lawrence

CURRENTLY PUBLISHED:

Babydoll: A Rockstar Romance

Dollhouse: A Rockstar Romance

Heathens: A Vampire Mafia Romance

UPCOMING WORKS:

Swipe Right: A Forbidden Romance (Emerald Bay, Book 1)

Ravenous: A Dark Phantom of the Opera Reimagining

Nightingale: A Paranormal Why Choose